"You expect me to bed with you?"

Jenny asked, realizing the elegant stranger regarded her as merely a tavern whore.

Kit laughed softly in the darkness. "Nay, I prefer a more romantic term—I intend to make love to you, Jenny."

Though the touch of his hands sent her blood pounding, Jenny pulled away. "You lied to me!" she spat. "For your three gold sovereigns you said you'd bought my company only for talk. Do you think me too simple to see through your ploy?"

He laughed again. "I know only that you're a maddeningly beautiful woman who's set me on fire. Come, Jenny, I'm hot for you. Can you not feel it?"

She fought him off. "I'm no half-witted country lass. My father was a nobleman!"

"Ah, then I was mistaken, mistress." He gave her a mocking bow. "Go now, and sleep well in your cold bed, for the comforting knowledge of your noble ancestry will surely keep you warm."

"Aye, good night and good riddance!" Jenny replied . . . but her body still cried out for Kit Ashford's hard masculine desire.

Also by Patricia Phillips from Jove

ANISE
CAPTIVE FLAME
LOVE'S DEFIANT PRISONER
MY SOUL WITH THINE
ROYAL CAPTIVE

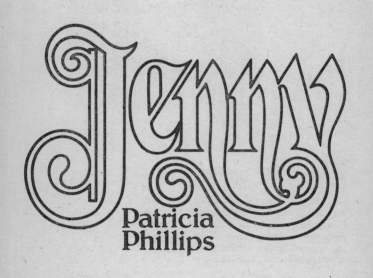

Jenny

Patricia Phillips

A JOVE BOOK

First Jove edition published May 1981

First printing

Printed in the United States of America

Jove books are published by Jove Publications, Inc.,
200 Madison Avenue, New York, NY 10016

Chapter 1

The Surrey hamlet of Addston slumbered in the soft light of a perfect spring dawn. The sun rose in a cloudless blue sky, gilding the thatched roofs of the squat cottages along the narrow village street and sparking diamond-bright flashes from the mullioned windows of the sprawling black and white timbered inn at the brow of the hill.

Jenny Dunn pushed open the rickety back door of the Rose and Crown. A soft breeze, filled with the salt tang of the Channel, stirred the new green foliage on the lofty chestnut tree overshadowing the west wall. Today was her eighteenth birthday! The thought filled her with pleasure. Before this year was out she would have fulfilled the servitude imposed upon her. She had agreed to work without wages until her mother's funeral expenses were paid, and once the debt was settled she would be free to leave Addston.

Life at Tom Dunn's shabby old inn did not suit the gently reared Jenny, who dreamed of traveling to London, a journey begun long months ago when she and her mother were turned out of the only home she had ever known, made vagrants by the spiteful sister of her mother's late employer.

Though Master Knyvett had treated his housekeeper, Nan Dunn, and her daughter more like family than servants, his sister had sent them packing within hours of the funeral. Jenny and her mother had intended to walk the thirty miles north to London to seek charity from Nan Dunn's younger brother Will, who owned a haberdashery in the warren of dark streets leading off Cornhill. When her mother collapsed a mile beyond Addston, Jenny had swallowed her pride and begged aid from her mother's older brother, Tom Dunn, and his wife Rachel, who in the past had shown little charity to Nan and her bastard daughter.

In return for board and lodging Jenny had agreed to serve in the inn's taproom. And though she hated the tipsy customers' pawing hands, their bawdy sallies and suggestive remarks, she endured them for her mother's sake. When Nan

1

Dunn died just a few weeks after their arrival. Jenny's aunt had curtly informed her that she must continue to work without wages until the funeral debt was paid. And London, that fabulous city of gilded coaches, and lords and ladies dressed in silks and ribbons imported from France, seemed ten lifetimes away.

"Here, Jen, where are you?" Babs' coarse voice sounded from the oak-beamed taproom.

For the moment Jenny chose to ignore the barmaid's impatient summons. It was too fine a morning to hasten to the public taproom, which, despite vigorous scrubbing, always smelled vaguely of vomit and spilled ale.

Jenny checked her appearance in the diamond-paned window. She smoothed her billowing chestnut hair into a gleaming chignon, securing it at the nape of her slender neck with a couple of bone bodkins. It would not do for Aunt Rachel to see her hair unbound; such a style would surely be taken as a revelation of inherited wantonness. Being the bastard daughter of a Cavalier who had fled for his life after the defeat of the Royalist armies in 1645 had made Jenny suspect in her aunt's eyes. Now, in this year of 1664, Oliver Cromwell's joyless tyranny had been over for six years. Despite this fact, Rachel Dunn's ironclad Puritan ideas of right and wrong had changed not a whit. A person conceived in sin stood in moral jeopardy. Jenny's fine, aristocratic bones and grace of movement might be kept decently covered with rough brown homespun, but her dark-lashed gray eyes, her creamy skin touched with a natural blush over the high cheekbones, and her even white teeth were Devil's snares according to Rachel.

Jenny experienced a pang of guilt when she heard the barmaid calling her name a second time. From an upper window Rachel Dunn shrilly berated a stableboy for spilling water as his heavy pail sloshed a flood across the cobbled inn yard. No one and nothing could ever please Aunt Rachel. If she could, Rachel Dunn would even stop the birds' frivolous songs! While England was being swept up in a wave of licentiousness, and yeomen and gentlemen alike aped the example of Charles II, the Merry Monarch, whose tastes ran to pretty women and the pursuit of pleasure, Rachel Dunn stood as a pillar of righteousness. The tide of change flowed on, leaving her stranded on a sandbank of joyless piety. The return of Christmas merrymaking, of May Day revels and beloved amusements like wrestling and bearbaiting, forbidden during Cromwell's time, were greeted rapturously by a populace who had smarted at the enforced sobriety of the previous decade. Aunt Rachel merely bemoaned such iniquities as an indication of the country's decadent slide into hell precipitated by the return of a wicked Stuart king.

With a sigh of resignation, Jenny went indoors to begin her morning's work.

Blackbirds trilled sweetly beyond the open mullioned windows as she wiped the scarred wooden tables. The Rose and Crown's dingy, low-ceilinged taproom was revealed with unflattering clarity in the bright spring sunshine. Chipped wainscotting, magnificent in the days of the great Elizabeth one hundred years before, gaped to reveal the uneven plaster wall. The plank floor, sprinkled with a mixture of rushes and sawdust, held the remains of last night's revel. Every fortnight the rushes were changed and the floorboards scrubbed. It was a thankless task, for within a couple of nights the covering was glued back in place by a fresh overlay of filth.

As she worked Jenny's mind soared beyond her sordid surroundings. She envisioned the teeming magnificence of London and the lavish entertainments of the King and his court. Though the greatest distance Jenny had ever traveled had been that single five-mile flight to Addston from Dutton's Green, in her imagination she walked on London's winding streets. Her vivid pictures were formed from listening to travelers' gossip and from reading the tattered broadsheets that found their way to the Rose and Crown many months after being issued.

The King's deprivations and hair-raising adventures during his long exile lent a certain reckless glamour to his person. His devastating reputation with the ladies did nothing to detract from that colorful image. Jenny found even the tales of Charles Stuart's wickedness fascinating. Sometimes she imagined she was beautiful Lady Castlemaine, the King's favorite mistress, dressed in a sumptuous jeweled creation, turning all heads at Drury Lane Theatre . . .

"You've wiped that spot a dozen times. What ails you this morning?"

Jenny gasped in surprise as her uncle's voice rumbled behind her. Tom Dunn's corpulent girth mounded his snagged leather apron to form a rest for his hairy forearms. As always when he fixed his small, hard brown eyes on her and pulled his fleshy lips sideways in an ugly leer, Jenny felt as if she was suffocating. His probing gaze stripped her naked.

"I must hurry," she excused herself, trying to sidestep his bulky frame.

"There's no need to be so hasty."

"Babs rants like a fishwife if I'm late cleaning up."

"Let her rant."

While he spoke, Tom Dunn cleverly maneuvered her against the wall. His groping hand slid swiftly over the dark wood paneling, coming to rest just inches from Jenny's shoulder. Growing bolder, he placed his large sweating hand on her neck, gripping the soft flesh until Jenny gasped in pain.

He licked his lips. "I know you're not as innocent as you pretends. Like mother, like daughter, I always says. Our Nan couldn't keep her legs together when that pretty gallant rode by—likely you're the same. Coming on sweet as cream, avoiding me, while some rich bastard's already been plumbing the well. Marry, if I'm not right . . ."

"No!" Jenny warned as he bent his sweating face to hers, so close she could see large pockmarks on his greasy face.

Tom Dunn gripped Jenny with both hands and brought her jarringly against his paunch, crushing her breath from her body. He smiled slyly, his loose red lips flecked with spittle. "You don't really think I took you in for the good of our Nan's health, do you? If you do, you're slower witted than I thought. No, Jenny, love, I wanted a taste of the sweetness between your legs."

Struggling against his overwhelming weight, Jenny freed her hand and gave him a resounding slap across his flushed face. Tom Dunn recoiled, nursing his stinging cheek, and his eyes were round with shock. Not waiting for further speech, Jenny thrust open the taproom door and ran down the narrow passage to the comparative safety of the gloomy oak-beamed kitchen, where Babs' comforting bulk was visible at the stone sink.

"What's up, Ducks? Seen a ghost?" Babs asked cheerfully as she beheld Jenny's wild-eyed expression.

"No, it's nothing," Jenny mumbled, tying a striped calico apron around her slender waist. Surreptitiously she smoothed her hair and modestly tugged her brown bodice into place.

"Come on! Did the old lecher grab you?" sandy-haired Babs asked shrewdly. Then, noticing tears glittering in Jenny's large gray eyes, her tone softened. "Aw, come on, never mind him. Randy as a billy goat, he is, and who can blame him with that dried-up stick of a wife. He don't mean no harm. A little pinch, a little feel, it keeps him quiet. You'll soon learn."

"I don't want to learn," Jenny cried angrily. "If he ever touches me again, I'll . . ."

"You'll what?" Babs' protruding blue eyes hardened. She leaned closer, her blowsy face growing harsh. "You'll go along with whatever he wants if you wants to stay here. And don't go putting on no ladylike airs—you're a little barstard, same as me. If your old man walked across this here room you wouldn't know him from Adam. Don't take no chances with your place. There's too many girls looking for work, and most of them don't mind putting out a little on the side, not when it gets them what they wants!"

Blinking back tears, Jenny stared at Babs, knowing she spoke the truth, yet hating it.

Throughout the day and evening, as Jenny carried trays of food to the customers, she reminded herself of Babs' warning. Of a Friday night the taproom was always thronged with brawny farmhands demanding mutton pasties, pickled onions, slabs of coarse rye bread and pungent cheese to be washed down by foaming tankards of ale. With ale selling for a penny per quart, even the stoutest of them could get drunk for tuppence.

It was twenty-five miles to London. Jenny had no money nor any means of transport other than her own two feet. And though she was a young, inexperienced country girl, she was not naive about the dangers to a woman walking the roads alone. However much she hated the sly comments and the ever-groping hands of these ignorant plowmen, Jenny realized that if she were wise she would stay at the Rose and Crown long enough to accumulate enough money to buy her fare to London. At least here she was clothed and fed. Her attic room was too cramped and too poorly furnished to be offered to travelers except in the direst emergency, yet Aunt Rachel frequently extolled its virtues, lauding it as though Jenny occupied the royal suite. During these balmy late spring nights the upper floors of the inn came pungently alive with the stale odor of fried foods and beer. And though the smell collected in the airless warmth beneath the eaves, Jenny had no desire to change her attic room. There was a bolt on the door, making it a safe refuge from her lustful uncle or the inn's drunken patrons.

It was almost closing time. The dark-beamed taproom, illuminated by three sputtering candles, was a shambles of snoring patrons, spilled beer, and discarded food scraps.

"Come here, sweetheart," cried a brawny farmer as Jenny passed him with a tray of food. He locked his arm about her waist, upsetting her platter of cheese and pickled onions.

Jenny tried to smile as she retrieved the wedges of crumbly cheese and the slippery, bouncing onions from the scarred tabletop. Tonight, despite her protests, the farmer ignored all pleas to set her free. Instead, he grasped her skirts and pulled her onto his lap.

"You're never too busy for this," he cried, and he grabbed her face in his huge rough hands and pressed his mouth to hers.

The unwanted touch of his slack, beery mouth made Jenny retch. Eyes flashing, she jabbed him sharply in the paunch with her elbow. "Let me go!" she cried angrily, struggling to break his confining embrace.

Once he had recovered from his surprise, the red-faced farmer laughed good-naturedly. "You be a spirited little piece," he said in admiration.

Several of the other customers laughed in amusement at her resistance, while they offered appropriate suggestions for taming the captive.

"Stop it!" Jenny shrieked, shuddering in revulsion as his sweating hands slid upward to cup her breasts. The man fumbled with her bodice strings. Twisting, turning, Jenny thumped wildly at him, but he was too intent on his lecherous pursuit to heed her blows. Jenny seized a half-empty ale flagon from the table and, lifting it in both hands, smashed it as hard as she could against the farmer's thick head. Shock widened his eyes a moment as he stared speechlessly at her before toppling from his chair with a resounding thud.

Leaping away, Jenny refastened her bodice with trembling fingers, fighting her desire to vomit as she recalled the loathsome touch of his exploring hands.

"What's up! You fool girl, what've you done? This is Ned Porter—one of me best customers."

Huffing as he tried to pull Ned Porter's bulk upright, Tom

Dunn yelled at Jenny to get out of his sight, his anger shared by several patrons who came to his assistance.

Jenny picked up her trailing skirts and fled to the safety of her room. All night she waited for her aunt and uncle to vent their wrath on her, but it was not until morning that Jenny was reprimanded for her behavior.

"Pull that trick again, my girl, and you'll be looking for new lodgings," her uncle threatened, his blue-shadowed jaw thrust forward pugnaciously. "And don't think I forgot about yesterday morning, neither," he added in an undertone, glancing behind him to make sure they were not being overheard.

"I'm here to wait on tables. I'm not a whore! And I won't have them handling me," Jenny spat angrily, as she defiantly met his gaze. "Nor you," she added after a moment's consideration. "And if you try anything again, I'll tell Aunt Rachel!"

Tom Dunn's brown eyes hardened, and he grabbed her arm. "You keeps your mouth shut, you hear, you ungrateful little tart. Nothing what goes on between us's got anything to do with Rachel."

"Leave me alone then, or I swear I'll tell her."

Triumphantly, Jenny pulled free of his grasp and walked, head high, into the taproom. When her uncle failed to pursue her, Jenny knew she had won a minor battle. The dire punishment she had expected in payment for last night's behavior must have been lessened by Aunt Rachel's knowledge of the provocation behind her crime. Rachel Dunn did not easily tolerate licentiousness.

Chapter 2

Fragrant pink and white hawthorn blossoms walled the country lanes; the woods were carpeted with a lilac mist of bluebells. So warm was this first week of June that many of the inn's customers chose to sup beneath the shade of a chestnut tree ablaze with hundreds of white blossoms.

The evening air was sweet with the scent of hay and honeysuckle when a party of finely dressed gentlemen on blooded horses rode up to the inn.

"Bring forth the ale, wench, and look lively," thundered a man's resonant voice, his ringing tones carrying inside the gloomy taproom.

Jenny darted to the window to see who ordered service in such an imperious manner.

"Coo, look at them! They're court gallants if ever I sees 'em." Babs leaned over Jenny's shoulder for a closer look at the customers. "Well, go on, get on wiv it. They're more important than this lot."

Ignoring the loud protests from the few regulars sitting inside the gloomy taproom, Jenny raced outside to attend the five courtiers who sprawled indolently on the rustic benches beneath the spreading branches of the lofty chestnut tree. She smoothed her blue-striped apron as she went, arriving breathless and more than a little apprehensive, for she had never directly addressed a member of the nobility.

"What will you have, good sirs?" she asked, curtsying

"Whatever you have to offer, sweetest," one of the men drawled, reaching out indolently to flick Jenny's chestnut curls. "God's death, you're a comely chit to be serving in such a broken-down hovel!"

"Nay, Harry, leave the wench alone. Have you not enough conquests to your name? All England rings with tales of the sexual prowess of the best dressed scoundrel in the fleet. Buckingham himself could envy your success."

Blushing, Jenny turned to look at the speaker with the rich baritone voice. She caught her breath in surprise as she gazed

8

fully on his handsome face, and her heart raced frantically when he returned her smile, his deep blue eyes meeting hers.

"Pay not the slightest attention to Sir Harry, he's been far too long at sea. Now, pray tell me, sweet, what do they call you?"

"Jenny, sir."

"And I am Kit. Bring us gallons of your best ale, Jenny. We've acquired a mighty thirst riding up from the Channel. And whatever food you have to offer, for, by God, our weary bones refuse to go a step further. Tell the landlord we'll pay handsomely—today his Majesty's captains are rolling in sovereigns."

The men guffawed loudly at the remark, finding a jest where Jenny did not.

"We only serve mutton pasties and bread and cheese," she apologized.

"Splendid. And, wench, wouldst thou bring me a bowl of clean water and some clean linen strips? I thought not to enter the wars on home ground, yet when we rested behind a hedgerow, some bastard gypsy tried to steal my horse. I trow he'll not forget me in a hurry, for I nearly clove his face in two. He caught me on the forearm with his knife."

Jenny glanced at his arm, where bright red blood still oozed from a two-inch slash in his fine velvet sleeve. She hurried inside to get the basin.

As she assembled the gallants' meal, her mind seethed with romantic visions of the dashing stranger in the red-plumed hat. He was dressed magnificently: his dark blue coat of rich velvet was embroidered with gold thread; his delicate lawn shirt was lavishly trimmed with French lace. His muscular legs were encased in enormous bucket-topped boots of jacked leather, with silver rowel spurs at his heels. Yet, splendid though his expensive finery was, it was the man's handsome face that attracted her most. His fair skin was bronzed by the sun. There were crinkles about his large blue eyes that Jenny supposed came from gazing over an expanse of sun-dappled ocean—he was a seafaring man, of that she was convinced. His straight nose was aristocratic, his sensuous mouth inviting. A delicious thrill of excitement ran through her as she imagined being kissed by him. Sighing with pleasure, Jenny paused a moment to watch him laughing and talking with the others, her view somewhat impaired by the dingy window-pane. With his mane of dark gold curls spilling from under a wide-brimmed black hat, he was a swashbuckling vision to set her heart aflutter.

Jenny had hoped the stranger would prevail upon her to dress his wound, but he laughingly dismissed her offer, saying it was a mere scratch. One of his companions deftly bound the strip of linen about his forearm. Rebuttoning his torn shirt sleeve, Kit returned to the more serious business of quenching his thirst with a foaming flagon of dark ale.

The gallants drank until dusk. A group of locals surrounded the strangers, plying them with questions about their adventures at sea. The wide-eyed countrymen were eager to hear the latest news about the rascally Dutch, who were forever firing on good honest Englishmen, continuing the undeclared war between the two great seafaring nations for supremacy over vital trade routes.

Between chores, Jenny tried to eavesdrop on the men's stirring conversation. How she wished she could stay outside to admire Kit, but she must divide her time between the half-deserted taproom and the side yard.

"Get outside and wait on the gentry," Tom Dunn snapped, when he found Jenny inside the taproom mopping up puddles of spilled ale by the feeble light of a guttering candle. "They've been asking special fer you."

Jenny hastened into the warm twilight, wondering if Kit was the man doing the asking. To her disappointment he appeared not to notice her as she moved about refilling tankards and replenishing empty platters. While she worked, Jenny watched him covertly from under lowered lashes, admiring the broad square set of his shoulders and the air of arrogant confidence he bore. As she passed the table where he sprawled, his long, black-booted legs spread before him, she gasped in surprise as Kit's hot fingers closed about her wrist.

"Caught you, sweetheart," he said, his voice husky with laughter. "I thought that beer-bellied landlord would never send you outside. Come, sit beside me. God's death—Harry was right! You're the comeliest little baggage to delight my eyes since I was a lad in petticoats."

"Oh, sir, much as I'd like to stay, I must serve in the taproom," Jenny protested reluctantly. Out of the corner of her eye she noticed Tom Dunn's bulky figure as he watched her from the inn door.

"Nay, stay here with me. Will this purchase your time?"

Jenny stiffened as he pressed three gold sovereigns into her hand.

"I'm not for sale."

Kit's generous mouth curved in a smile as he doffed his black hat, exposing long golden locks that glinted in the fading rays of sunlight. "I didn't mean to insult you, Mistress Jenny. The gold was to purchase your time for talk only. Forgive me. My manners have deserted me, so long have I been at sea."

Jenny hesitated, desperately wanting to stay with him, yet feeling that if she accepted his money she was somehow branding herself as immoral. "I'll have to ask the landlord, sir," she ventured, seeing Tom Dunn gesture from the shadowed doorway.

"Aye, well, go ask him, and look lively, sweetheart. Time's awasting."

Swallowing nervously, Jenny approached her uncle. He grabbed her hand and pried open her fingers to reveal the sovereigns gleaming against her palm. "The gentleman wants to hire my companionship," she explained, adding sharply as Tom Dunn's suggestive leer widened, "he wants to talk to me."

" 'Tis a new approach, and him fresh off the decks too. He's a rum one for a king's captain, and no mistake. All right, girl, Babs'll take care of the others. It'll do her good to shift her fat arse; she grows lazy as a sow."

When Jenny dropped the sovereigns in her apron pocket, her uncle extended his hairy fist.

"They're mine!" she exploded indignantly.

"That's what you think. Hand 'em over, you stubborn little bitch, I handle the money round here. Now, get out there and talk pretty to his lordship—but mind, if he wants a little more, you don't do nothing unless he's willing to pay for it. Understood?"

Jenny glared at him, but she nodded.

"Ah, so mine host was agreeable to my suggestion. No doubt he kept a share of the gold for his pains," Kit said in amusement as Jenny sat beside him on the rustic bench.

"A share! He took the lot."

Kit grinned. "Worry not, sweetheart, there's much more where that came from. Why, sweeting, someday, when my cross-eyed old whoremaster of an uncle goes to his just reward, I stand to inherit an Irish title and a fortune to go with it. What do you think of that?''

Jenny smiled up at him. '' 'Tis a fine future, sir, but you might have a long wait. I've learned the wicked seldom merit a swift departure to the afterlife, but live on, the more to plague us.''

''Ah, Jenny, you're witty as well as beautiful.''

The pleasure of studying his face at such close quarters made Jenny giddy. Half-moon laugh lines framed his sensual mouth; his finely drawn eyebrows were bleached pale by the sun. So attracted was she to this man that Jenny experienced a curious melting sensation in her limbs whenever he smiled at her.

''What do you wish to talk about, sir?'' she asked a trifle breathlessly as she gazed into his eyes, losing herself in their brilliant blue depth.

''Don't you wish to hear about my hair-raising adventures at sea?''

''Yes, but first I'd rather hear about London. That's if you're familiar with the city.''

''Every seething, blessed inch,'' he said, softly tracing the length of her fingers on the table. ''What do you wish to know?''

''Tell me about Cornhill—my uncle owns a shop there. 'Tis where I was headed before I came to work here.''

''Cornhill's a fine shopping region, much patronized by the Court. 'Tis but a stone's throw from the Exchange, where lords and ladies dally overlong about their purchases of French velvets and Hungary Water, the better to ogle each other. What's your uncle's name? Perhaps I know him.''

''Will Dunn. He owns a haberdashery. He sometimes serves King Charles' courtiers,'' Jenny added with pride, beginning to feel at ease. It was far easier to talk to this dashing man than she had imagined. The curious reaction produced in her blood by his nearness would normally have made a tongue-tied simpleton of her, yet Kit imparted such a comforting feeling of safety that Jenny felt as if she had known him all her life.

''Ah, then he'd best lock you in his back room, for when that breed of dissolute courtiers spy a pretty wench like you, they'll spirit you away.'' Kit laughed at her expression of surprise. His hand, half obscured by the fine French lace at his cuff inched with tantalizing passage along Jenny's arm, making her skin prickle as she thrilled to his touch.

"Oh, sir, surely you mock me," she protested.

"Nay, for you're the loveliest creature I've seen in many a day. But in truth, I've little time for the foppish courtiers at Whitehall. I'm a man of the sea. His Majesty is an old friend of mine. We shared the impoverished years of his exile, living by our wits, skipping from France to Holland and back again. He too loves the ocean, but Charles must make time to indulge his love, for, unlike me, he's unable to take to his ship and sail away."

While the warm dusk deepened to black, star-sprinkled velvet, Kit briefly recounted his life. Jenny hung on his every word, wanting to know as much about him as possible. Kit's family, unflagging supporters of the monarchy, had forfeited their vast Devonshire estates after the Civil War, and were reduced to penury. A modest house was all that remained; it had been restored to Kit by his friend, King Charles the Second, in appreciation for the Ashford family's loyal service to his father's cause. The Irish branch of the Ashford family had not taken a public stand during the Civil War. Their seeming faintheartedness, however, earned its own reward, for they managed to live amicably with Cromwell's appointed officials, thereby retaining their land and possessions. And though their political fence-sitting had not endeared the Ashfords of County Wicklow to their restored monarch, neither had it alienated them from him, Charles being of a singularly forgiving nature. Their estates were the vast Irish inheritance Kit had mentioned half jestingly, for he had been named his uncle's heir.

The reedy strains of a pipe, clashing cymbals, and the scrape of a fiddle announced the arrival of a band of itinerant musicians who had wandered into the crowded inn yard in hope of earning board and lodgings.

Jenny clapped her hands at the unexpected pleasure as a ragged-skirted girl, who could be little more than ten, danced to the primitive accompaniment. When her dance was finished, the girl made the rounds of the inn's patrons, holding a frayed cap to collect contributions.

Kit gave the girl a couple of silver coins and bade her dance again.

Jenny's feet tapped beneath the table at the lively rhythm as the musicians improvised by using an upturned barrel for a drum. Even Aunt Rachel and Babs paused in the doorway to watch the performance, though Rachel Dunn's disapproval of such wickedness was plain to see on her withered features.

The gypsy girl's purple-striped gown whirled out in a widening circle to reveal dirty brown legs as she leaped and spun for her audience, her dark, foreign face somber and aloof, her back arrow-straight in arrogant disregard for the stamping, clapping yokels who cheered her dance. At last the rhythm rushed toward its noisy finale as she swooped, in a flurry of tattered skirts, to the churned-up earth beneath the chestnut tree, dropping her head to her chest until her meager body was cloaked in an untidy mane of raven hair.

No one made a sound. Then a sudden wave of clapping and cheering erupted, and a rain of coins landed about the girl's soiled skirts. When she had gathered up the money, the little dancer obediently carried it to her master, a burly man in a patched orange doublet. The man quickly counted the take, withholding all but a single coin, which he gave the girl to purchase a mug of ale to quench her thirst.

"Even the gypsy wench was given a coin for her pains. 'Twas a more generous wage than you received, fair Jenny. That fat slug of a landlord treats you worse than a ragged gypsy brat! A pox on his miserly soul! I'll have a word with him."

"Nay, please," Jenny protested quickly, seizing his arm, afraid too much ale had turned him reckless. If he accused Tom Dunn of unfairly withholding her wages, she would be seeking new lodgings come morning.

Still muttering about the injustice of her treatment, Kit resumed his seat. "What do you owe mine host, that you have such regard for his feelings?" he asked suspiciously.

"He's my uncle. And he gave my mother shelter while she was dying in return for my labors. If you take him to task he'll likely turn me out to fend for myself."

Kit turned to look at Jenny, finding her lovely face shadowed. The weak glimmer of candlelight spilling through the inn's windows fell on her soft red mouth, making it so achingly desirable that he shuddered at the bolt of emotion charging his blood. "Ah, sweet, you know I wouldn't willingly bring you misfortune," he said huskily, his hand gentle on her silky hair. "Have you no other place to go?"

"Nowhere besides the shop in Cornhill. Once I've settled

the debt I owe my aunt and uncle, I'll be more than glad to see the last of the Rose and Crown. Being a tavern wench is not to my liking.''

Foreseeing an increase in ale consumption now that the musicians were entertaining his customers, Tom Dunn sent the ostler and stableboy with lanterns to light the yard, thus prolonging the evening hours. The lanterns swung from the spreading lower branches of the chestnut tree, where they cast a warm yellow glow over the inn yard and its merry patrons. Several men and women were dancing clumsily to the music as the musicians struck up the old English dance ''Cuckolds Awry.'' The gypsy wench darted among them, laughing, skipping, but refusing to be captured as a partner.

''Come dance with me, Jenny,'' Kit invited, his voice low.

Jenny's soft gray eyes lit with pleasure, and her heart beat wildly at the prospect of being in his arms. Though she had never been schooled in dancing—Master Knyvett's Puritan upbringing forbidding such license—Jenny possessed an innate sense of rhythm. Unbeknown to her mother's employer, she had often danced in the meadow, singing a song as accompaniment to her steps. When Kit's arm stole around her back, Jenny's heartbeat increased to a deafening crescendo as she thrilled to his embrace, to the touch of his hand, burning like fire against her flesh. Here, in the shadows, it was difficult to see his expression, yet instinctively Jenny knew Kit was about to kiss her. Mentally preparing herself for the pleasure of his kiss, she tilted her mouth upward to make his task easier. His lips came down on hers as his arms tightened, imprisoning her against the heat of his body. Her breasts tingled with a new sensation as Jenny pressed into the unyielding strength of his chest, flashes of heat piercing her flesh with exquisite torture.

''Ah, sweetheart, you've made me fall in love with you,'' he whispered breathlessly, when at last he released her, ''though we've known each other merely for the span of a twilight.''

Jenny stared into Kit's shadowed face, so close his hot breath fanned the tendrils of hair that curled across her brow. ''But we cannot love,'' she protested hoarsely, her voice failing as she desperately tried to control the delirious feeling of joy that swept through her body. ''I don't even know you, or where you are bound, or . . .''

He placed his lean finger against her lips, silencing her voice. ''I'm Kit Ashford, a gentleman from the West Coun-

try, and I command his Majesty's ship *The Royal Prospect*.
There, sweet, what more would you know of me?''

"Everything there is to know," she breathed boldly, her
hand stealing to his face. She longed to stroke his sun-
bronzed cheek, to know the feel of his flesh beneath her
fingers.

Kissing her hand, Kit imprisoned the sweetness of her
touch against his face. For a few moments he fought his
mounting passion, compounded by her nearness and the effect
of many tankards of strong ale. "Come, let us dance," he
said abruptly, breaking the spell.

Due to Kit's mild intoxication their dance was a bungling
interpretation, yet he managed to steer Jenny through the
steps of a coranto. The musicians, recognizing the quality of
their latest patron, modified their raucous efforts to a more
suitable rhythm in anticipation of a generous reward for their
thoughtfulness. Jenny barely noticed her feet moving, so
aware was she of the pressure of Kit's arm about her waist
and of his hand in hers. The music played on. They danced
through the deep, elongated shadows cast by the building.
Allowing the sweet summer air to caress her burning face,
and lulled by the magic of the captain's strong embrace,
Jenny lost all sense of time and place. As they whirled yet
again Jenny glanced up, for a strident cry of rage was ringing
out—Aunt Rachel was bearing down on her, a wooden poss
stick held aloft.

"What have we here! Get you back inside! Dancing with
the customers—how dare you?''

Jenny broke away from Kit's arms and ran indoors as the
crowd laughed and the gray-clad angel of wrath pursued her.

"Now, Rachel, the gentleman paid well for her company,"
Tom Dunn protested, coming to Jenny's defense as he planted
his solid bulk firmly in Rachel's path. "I gave her permission. 'Twill do no harm."

His gruff voice drifted inside the dim back corridor where
Jenny awaited her punishment. A burst of laughter from the
gentlemen in the yard came to her ears; uncomfortably, she
wondered if their amusement was caused by her undignified
exit.

"I'll not have her cavorting about like a brazen huzzy!"
Rachel Dunn insisted. "I only took in your Nan because you
persuaded me they were decent women. You should be

ashamed, allowing the girl to accept money! Do you seek to make a whore out of her?''

"Nay, the money's all here, wife.''

Rachel did not suggest he return the gold, which glinted in the lantern glow. "Courtiers with their loose morals!'' she spat in contempt. "If I were able, I'd ban them from the inn. Honest, God-fearing folks shouldn't have to associate with the iniquitous.''

"Now, wife, sinners they may be, but their gold's good as the next man's—and usually far more plentiful,'' Tom added as he patted his wife's arm in an effort to calm her temper. "The girl's still young. She meant no harm.''

Jenny couldn't hear her aunt's reply as she moved away from the kitchen window. When Rachel Dunn suddenly appeared in the darkened corridor, Jenny was relieved to see she had discarded her weapon.

"From now on, girl, dancing with the customers is forbidden. Would you have people think we keep a loose house?'' Then, her sharp tone softening, Rachel said with a hint of kindness, "You'll be tired, it's been a long day. Get upstairs. Babs can clear the tables.''

Jenny blinked in surprise at her aunt's unexpected consideration. She whispered her thanks. Rachel Dunn bustled away, her starched skirts crackling against the dark oak paneling. Jenny stood in the drafty corridor, wondering if she should go outside to explain matters to Kit. He must surely think her addled to have fled so hastily, yet he did not know Aunt Rachel's violent temper.

"Jenny?''

Thrilling as she recognized his voice, she answered, "Here I am.''

Kit came from the stableyard, his rowel spurs and sword clanking as he walked through the darkness. His broad-shouldered figure filled the narrow passage.

"Ah, sweet, I thought I'd lost you,'' he whispered, sweeping a trembling Jenny into his arms. He pressed his hot, tender mouth to hers; he kissed the tip of her nose, her eyelids, her brow.

"I'm sorry I ran away,'' she said, fighting the weakening surge of emotion his kisses produced. "Aunt Rachel's like the angel of wrath when she's roused.''

"You're safe in my arms, Jenny, so you've nothing more

to fear,'' Kit assured softly. Then, drawing her toward the narrow oak stairs he urged impatiently, ''Come, let us not waste a moment longer.''

''Where are you taking me?''

''To my room, for we've decided to spend the night. There are but two good rooms, so I must share one with Harry Warner—but he's understanding. He'll stay outside till I give him a signal.''

From a long, beautiful dream of romantic love, Jenny awakened to cold reality. Pain throbbed in a wave from her chest to her throat as she realized this glamourous stranger regarded her merely as a tavern whore! ''You expect me to bed with you?'' she asked, her voice sharpening.

Kit laughed softly in the darkness. ''Nay, I far prefer a more romantic term—I intend to make love to you, Jenny, for 'tis what your lovely body's designed for.'' He accompanied his words with a sweeping caress across her firm, rounded hips.

Though the touch of his hands set her blood afire, Jenny bristled with indignation at his suggestion. ''You lied to me!'' she spat, pulling away, trying to separate their bodies from the heated pressure that made it too hard to think.

''Lied? Nay, sweetheart, I told you I love you, and I do indeed. I meant every word—every kiss.''

''For your three gold sovereigns you said you'd bought my company merely for talk. Do you think me some simple chit without the wit to see through your falsehoods?'' she demanded angrily.

He laughed again, lazily drawing her back into his embrace. Burrowing his hot face in the sweetness of her neck, he said, ''I know only that you're a maddeningly beautiful woman who's set me on fire. Come, Jenny, do not deny me now. Long have I dreamed of a woman like you. Don't say no, sweeting.'' Expertly he backed her against the paneling. ''God's blood, you little witch, you'd try the patience of a saint with your modesty. I'm hot for you. Can you not feel it? I am like to explode with need.''

Struggling against the overwhelming masculinity of him, against the demanding pressure of his hard body, Jenny fought Kit off. ''I'm no half-witted country lass without the sense she was born with! My father was a nobleman,'' she added proudly as she kicked out at him when he tried to entrap her with his long legs.

Leaning back against the opposite wall, his breathing shallow, Kit gave an ugly, derisive laugh. "A nobleman indeed! Well, pretty one, 'twas on the wrong side of the blanket, or you'd not be serving ale in a broken-down wreck like the Rose and Crown."

Panting in anger, Jenny swung at him. But he grabbed her wrists and deflected the blow.

"Do you want your gold back, milord?"

"Nay, for you talked to me, and 'twas the bargain I struck. Your warmth, your eager response to my kisses, deluded me into thinking you wanted far more from me. I was mistaken. I apologize for the mistake. Go now, mistress, sleep well in your cold bed, for the comforting knowledge of your noble ancestry will surely keep you warm." He spun on his heel, his silver spurs clanking against the wainscotting. "Goodnight and goodbye."

"Aye, and good riddance," she spat, fighting tears of humiliation.

At the foot of the oak stairs, Kit Ashford paused and, sweeping off his plumed hat, he made her a mocking bow. But his scorn was lost on Jenny, for it was too dark for her to see his actions.

"Farewell, mistress. And sleep well," he added, his voice drifting disembodied from the gloom.

Jenny leaned against the wall, shuddering, fighting terrible disappointment as she attempted to quiet her pounding heart, which seemed as if it would leap through her homespun bodice. Her blood was still on fire for his touch, for his kisses; oh, how she wanted Kit Ashford's love. When he had lied in his suave courtier's manner, professing love for her, like a fool she had believed him. Yet, like all noblemen, he wanted only a romp with a tavern wench. On the morrow the handsome captain of his Majesty's ship *The Royal Prospect* would ride forth to London and forget her in much the same manner as the Cavalier who had seduced her mother beside Addston Wood all those years ago. When his passion was slaked, the man who had sired her rode away, leaving Nan to bear the burden of shame when she gave birth to an illegitimate child. All her life Jenny had been cautioned against repeating her mother's mistake; until tonight, she had not been tempted to sin. The awesome depth of her passion for Kit Ashford had nearly been her undoing.

The night noises of the shabby inn drifted disturbingly to

Jenny's room: myriad snores, a woman's smothered laughter—which suggested that perhaps Babs had not declined the gentlemen's favors—the rattle of pewter tankards being swilled beneath the creaking pump, followed by heavy, oppressive silence. Jenny tossed and turned on her narrow, lumpy bed, sweating in the close atmosphere. The small diamond-paned window stood open to the breeze, yet the overhanging thatched eaves blocked the flow of air. From the shadows Kit Ashford's handsome face mocked her. The taste of his hot, sweet mouth and the sound of his husky voice tormented her until she drew her knees to her stomach in an effort to dispel the numb ache of an emotion she did not understand.

After several more hours' tossing, Jenny could endure the stifling room no longer; she decided to go outdoors for a breath of cool air. Wrapping a thin brown cloak about her flimsy night-dress, she tiptoed barefoot to the door. The darkened corridor was deserted. On each moon-splashed landing Jenny paused to listen for approaching footsteps, trying to tread lightly so as not to set the warped floorboards creaking.

The full moon had risen high, silvering the inn yard with liquid radiance. The chestnut tree cast a giant black shadow across the ground, its fading flower candles rekindled by moonlight. In this unearthly light even the Rose and Crown's scarred timbers took on a mysterious beauty never revealed by daylight. Jenny breathed deep of the warm air, sweet with the scent of honeysuckle and dew-wet grass. How lovely everything was! Yet the magical surroundings made her even more aware of a strange yearning that throbbed insistently through her veins. Chilled at her disturbing emotions, Jenny drew her brown fustian cloak tighter about her body and went to sit on the rustic bench beneath the chestnut tree.

As her eyes grew more accustomed to the light, she realized she was not alone; a second figure stood outlined against the stone wall bordering the highway. A man's broad shadow spilled blackly across the road, the shape leaping erratically as he moved his booted leg from the low wall and turned, alerted to her presence. Even at this distance Jenny recognized Kit.

"Who's there?" he said sharply.

At first Jenny did not answer, undecided whether she should slip back to her room, or stay and identify herself.

With swift strides he approached, then he stopped abruptly.

"You!" he growled, immediately on guard.

"It was too hot in my room. But I'm just going back" she announced stiffly as she rose and wrapped her cloak tighter to mask the soft curves of her body, readily discernible in her flimsy night-dress.

"Nay, do not flee from me, Jenny," Kit said, his voice softening. "Let me apologize for my drunken behavior. The cool air's good for clearing one's head."

"I accept your apology, sir. Goodnight."

Jenny had reached the dense shadow cast by the overhanging eaves before she felt his light touch on her shoulder.

"Please, don't be so heartless, mistress. Stay awhile and talk to me. You can see I'm cruelly cast out of my quarters while Harry sports with the buxom barmaid. Have pity."

Jenny hesitated: she knew she should not stay, but his husky voice tinged with amusement was so seductive that she couldn't help herself. "A few minutes, no longer," she agreed.

"Come, let us sit beneath the chestnut tree."

Kit proffered his hand and Jenny took it, allowing him to lead her through the shadowed inn yard. How like a dream this was, sitting beside him in the fragrant moonlight, her hand clasped in his. No longer did she feel like Jenny Dunn, a lowly serving wench from the Rose and Crown; with the handsome sea captain beside her, Jenny was transformed into a lovely court lady clad in silks and satins. Perhaps she had fallen asleep after all, and at this moment was lying on her pallet beneath the eaves, dreaming a wondrous, stirring dream.

Kit smiled at her, his tender expression sending her wits awry. Trying to stifle the rapid beating of the pulse in her throat, Jenny said, "I shouldn't be here, sir. If my aunt caught me . . ."

"Sir!" he reproved sharply. "What happened to Kit?"

"Kit," she corrected, her mouth twitching in a smile.

"That's better." Though his voice sounded stern, his hand remained gentle as he stroked her flushed cheek. "Forgive me for what I said to you earlier. How could I insult you so? Though, in truth, my words were not meant as an insult. You're so lovely you make me forget myself. You are quite the most beautiful woman I've seen since I left these shores."

"No doubt you say those things to every likely female you meet."

He grinned, tracing his fingers along her browline and down the high bridge of her small nose. "For shame! Would you doubt my sincerity?"

"In matters of the heart—of course."

Now he chuckled and moved closer to her on the bench. "You're right, I fear, sweetheart. From the time he's in his teens, a man tries to charm all susceptible women. But he does not fall in love with them."

"Nay, yet he tries to convince them that he has."

"Mistress, you're far too wise for me." With a sigh, Kit stopped his tantalizing caress. "Were I to tell you how fiercely my heart pounds at your nearness, no doubt you would accuse me of lying."

"You'll have to test me on the matter, sir—Kit."

Jenny watched his lips curve. His face was dark in the moonlight, shadowed with a series of angles and planes that turned him mysterious and alluring. She was also growing aware of the heady perfume exuding from his garments—mingled musk, rose, and oil of cloves blended with his masculine scent. Even the night breeze carried his unmistakable essence, arousing her until she yearned to be pressed against the hot strength of his body. Jenny's cheeks flushed as she remembered how it had felt when he molded his hips to hers, the iron hard pressure of his urgent need driving against her, demanding that she yield. The disturbing memory shooting unbidden through her mind put Jenny on guard; she withdrew from the close proximity of his intoxicating presence.

"When I told you I was falling in love with you, it was no lie."

Jenny caught her breath at Kit's unexpected statement, finding her strange reaction to his nearness increased by his words.

"Court gallants are notorious for the ease in which they fall in and out of love," she reminded him, her voice shaking. Though she tried to retain her grasp on reality, the warm weight of his arm about her waist only complicated matters.

"And who told you such nonsense?"

" 'Tis common knowledge." Jenny's voice sounded alarmingly weak. She jumped to her feet. "I must go indoors; I've tarried outside far too long."

Kit glanced up at the window of his room, which remained shut. "Harry would never forgive me if I disturbed him now.

What say you to taking a turn around the inn with me? 'Tis light as day with this great full moon.''

Swallowing, Jenny considered the foolishness of the idea. Her common sense was numbed by his closeness, making her too bemused to decline his offer. "Once about the inn yard, then I really must go indoors, whether you swear undying love or nay, Master Kit."

"Now how did you know I was going to do that?" he asked with a throaty chuckle.

Smiling, Jenny allowed him to take her hand. They walked about the perimeter of the inn yard as if they stepped a measured dance, slowly, sedately, with no exchange of words. Just as they reached the shadowed hawthorn hedge where the fallen petals drifted like snow at their feet, Kit turned and swept her, unprotesting, into his arms.

"I jest not, mistress, when I say I love you. 'Tis not every pretty face who elicits such a vow," he whispered ardently. "I love you, Jenny, madness though it be. Tell me, sweetheart, do you care even a little for me?"

While her mind clamored against the words, her emotions spoke for her as Jenny whispered in reply, "Oh yes, Kit, I love you too!"

The tense lines on his face dissolved at her breathless vow, and he smiled tenderly. "Ah, Jenny, how I've longed to hear you say those words. A pox on my foolish tongue! I've stewed in anger these hours past, upbraiding myself for spoiling, in my drunken haste, what promised such sweet delight."

His mouth came down on hers hot, fragrant, taking her breath, her life, in the ecstasy of his kiss. Stumbling, Jenny melted into his embrace, so that Kit had to tighten his arms to prevent her falling. Tingling joy possessed her limbs, carrying her to giddy heights as she yielded against him, molding her soft flesh to his hard-hewn length of muscle and heat.

"Oh, Jenny, Jenny," he murmured into her chestnut hair, his hot lips sweeping over her brow, moving down her cheek until they came to rest in the scented hollow of her neck. "Love me, Jenny, love me," he breathed passionately.

"Haven't I already sworn my love to you?"

"Not just with your heart—love me now with your body," urged Kit. "I need you so, Jenny. My blood's on fire for you."

As if from a great distance, Jenny heard his husky, ardent

words. She should run indoors now, while she was still able, but in her heart Jenny knew it was already far too late. All her mother's warnings of disgrace and all her own natural reservations were swept away by a hot engulfing tide of passion. Her depth of emotion for this man would not allow them to part unquenched. Passion and love throbbed in her veins like primitive drumbeats until Jenny relinquished herself wholly to his will. With eager, trembling hands she stroked his smooth cheek, tracing the hot slash of his lips in his shadowed face where the moon silvered a divine halo about his golden hair.

"Kit, I love you truly. 'Tis madness, I know, for we've barely met, yet I feel as if I've always known you. I can't understand this power. But it will not be denied."

"Say you want me too."

"Yes, yes—I want you. I ache from wanting you, my love."

He welded her tight against his hard body, his gold coat buttons bruising her flesh. Jenny was suddenly aware of the thrusting pressure of his manhood hard against her thighs, where her thin clothing provided a feeble barrier. She imagined she could feel the heat of his blood surging in his veins as Kit trembled with passion.

He drew her to a mossy hollow between the twin portals of hawthorn hedge where a wicket gate hung crazily on a single hinge. Sweeping her cloak from her shoulders, he spread it out to make a bed for them. Together they sank to the ground, the fragrance of crushed grass sweet in their nostrils.

The act, to which Kit would soon initiate her, brought pain and suffering: wasn't that what she had been taught? Yet lying here in his strong arms, pressed against his throbbing strength, Jenny could think of nothing beyond the joy of possessing and being possessed by this man who set her blood on fire.

Kit swiftly discarded his coat. He took Jenny's small hands and, turning them palm uppermost, he kissed them. Allowing his lips to drift along her arm until he reached her soft neck, he buried his face there, whispering sweet love words.

Jenny sank her hands into his hair and directed his head downwards, pressing his face against her tingling breasts. He kissed those firm swellings through her thin night-dress. Impatiently he untied the neck of the garment, parting the gathered fabric, eager for the sight of her breasts. Jenny

quivered beneath his hot-eyed gaze; no man had ever seen her
naked to the waist.

"You are perfect," he whispered ardently, cupping her
smooth breasts. At first his hands gently molded the rounded
contours, gradually increasing the pressure as he correctly
gauged her shuddering response.

Jenny felt as if she were dissolving as she writhed beneath
his expert touch. Kit's mouth fastened over her nipple, which
rose to meet his lips. Fire sped from the contact. Each kiss,
each flick of his tongue, was like a fresh stab of fire, searing
through her body. Boldly now, Jenny followed his urging as
Kit laid her hand against his muscular thigh where the straining pressure of desire stretched the blue velvet taut. His hot
throbbing flesh expanded beneath her caress! Never before
had she uncovered the mystery of a man's arousal, and Jenny
shuddered in mingled awe and delight at the discovery.

"Be not afraid of me, Jenny," Kit soothed, noting her
startled reaction, keeping his hands gentle as he valiantly held
his passion in check. "I'll try not to hurt you."

His soothing voice inspired confidence to match the delight
of his touch. Aroused trembling, Jenny slid her hands inside
the open neck of his lace-trimmed shirt, sweeping the hard
breadth of his chest where wiry curls matted in a golden
expanse. Admiringly she caressed his smooth, hard shoulders, marveling at the muscular strength and beauty of his
body. And she would have continued her exploration had Kit
not urgently pressed her back on the mossy carpet beneath the
hedge, sprinkled with fading Mayblossoms.

"Jenny, I must have you," he whispered hoarsely. "You
are driving me to distraction."

She smiled up at him, finding his handsome face shadowed
by moonlight.

"Love me, Kit, dearest, but please be patient," she murmured, her hands tangling in his hair.

Yet when she felt his hands gently exploring the heated
core of her passion, opening her, positioning her limbs, Jenny
forgot her plea for patience. Their mouths seared together.
She shuddered as if possessed of the ague, the affliction
increasing as he placed her hand around the blazing strength
of his manhood. Kit too shuddered in ecstasy before he
hastily stayed her hand; he wanted to prolong their pleasure.
He kissed her eyelids, her nose, her mouth as he guided the

searing velvet tip of his organ against her resisting flesh; then he thrust. A sudden stab of pain made Jenny cry out, but Kit covered her mouth with his own, absorbing her cries, which soon changed to whimpers of delight as he slowly slid home within the hot sheath of her body.

Shuddering, crying, no longer aware of her surroundings, Jenny gripped Kit's square shoulders in her small hands, digging in her nails as she felt the delight of the searing length of flesh expanding inside her, filling her with flame. Rhythmically he moved, sweeping her upward, attuning his passion to her own. She strained for him, anxious to take him even deeper inside her; Kit responded eagerly until she sobbed with pleasure. No longer able to withstand the muscular contractions of her passion, he groaned aloud as he dashed her from that pinnacle of ecstacy, tumbling her down into roaring blackness as he carried her to a magic place Jenny did not know existed.

Gradually Jenny came back to her surroundings, growing aware of the chill night air wafting across her face, and of Kit's warm strength covering her nakedness. Languidly she stroked his smooth neck, burying her hands in his hair answering his lips as they sought hers.

"Never before have I felt like this," he breathed, smiling at her, so small beneath him, her lovely face silvered with moonlight. "I've waited a lifetime to find you, Jenny. Dear God, I can't bear the thought of parting. Say you'll come with me, sweeting, that you'll stay with me forever. Promise."

Jenny smiled at Kit's fevered words, thrilled to hear him speak so, yet understanding there might never be anything more than this between them. Somehow, with her awakened passion, had come awakened knowledge of the difference in their stations. He was a gentleman, a captain in the King's fleet: she was a bastard tavern wench, working for her keep.

"Nay, Kit, you've no place for me in your life," she whispered, fighting the tears that dimmed her vision. "This is all there'll be for us. I don't expect you to make vows you cannot keep."

"Nay, I'll come back for you, I swear it. We were born for each other, Jenny, of that I'm convinced. Nothing can keep us apart. I'd take you with me tomorrow, but I must meet with the King. But later, once my orders are secure, I'll return. Perchance I need not set sail for several months. Say you'll wait for me, promise me that much."

"I'll wait forever for you, Kit," she vowed as tears spilled down her cheeks.

With an exclamation of dismay, he caught her tears, salty against his mouth, and kissed them away. "Don't weep, I make no idle vow. You are mine forever. I sought to purchase you with three gold sovereigns, but you've bought me with naught beside the sweetness of your love."

She smiled wanly as she pulled his mouth to hers. "Ah, but you lied so prettily, sir, when you said you merely wished to talk."

"Oh, Jenny, sweet, how I wish this night would last forever," Kit breathed fervently against her ear.

They kissed and touched until, as she had known they would, her caresses fired him to renewed desire. No longer abashed at the awesome discovery of his arousal, Jenny eagerly sought the heat of his passion, shuddering in delight at the touch of his searing flesh. She eagerly directed his hot hands and mouth to her breasts. Now, when he entered her, she knew what to expect, knew what joy he would create. Eagerly she welcomed him, opening wide to receive the utmost heat of his thrust, and once again Kit swept her to that other plane where they shared untold rapture in the moonlit summer night.

Chapter 3

For three weeks Jenny lived in a world of contentment. No longer was the dingy, candlelit taproom, with its crude, raucous customers, repellent; she had a glorious secret to sustain her. Hope glimmered bright down the corridor of her future. Soon Kit would return to claim her, bearing her away to his home in Devon. Like a miser hoarding gold, Jenny hoarded her precious memories of Kit's love. Only when she was alone in her stuffy attic room did she dwell in detail on their shared delight; when she relived his ardent caresses, Jenny tingled from head to toe, aching for his swift return.

Babs roared with coarse laughter when she revealed her expectation, condemning Jenny's dreams as sheer moonstruck fantasy.

"You're a daft one, all right, Jenny Dunn. You should know by now them sort never come back. You should've got something to show for your troubles, like me." Babs patted the concealed pocket beneath her full blue skirts, where two coins nestled against her fleshy hips.

"We're so much in love; I know he'll come back when he's able," Jenny said. She no longer minded Babs' crudeness, though in the beginning she had resented the fat barmaid's knowledge of her lover.

"Lord 'Enery Warner, mine was. A grand gentleman if ever I sees one. Fought at Edgehill and Naseby, 'e did, right at the old King's side. Saved 'im a time or two as well."

Jenny hastily bit back the correction that sprang to her lips. It would be unkind to remind Babs that her "gentleman" had merely been a "sir."

"Didn't your bloke 'ave a title?" Babs asked, clanking the dented pewter tankards together on the dusty shelf.

"No. He's a captain in the King's fleet. Captain Kit Ashford," Jenny repeated dreamily.

"Coo, iggerent you are. Kit's short for Christopher. Don't you know nothin'?"

"I like Kit better."

Jenny watched Babs roll toward the kitchen to fetch platters of victuals to provide the hungry plowmen's noon meal; her ample hips swayed rhythmically beneath her blue homespun skirts. Though Jenny had intended to keep her lover's existence a secret, the observant barmaid had seen her kissing Kit goodbye the morning he departed for London. At least the amoral Babs had not castigated her for falling so desperately in love, or for yielding her virginity to a stranger—a kindness she would be spared if sour Aunt Rachel ever had an inkling of her fall from grace. Fortunately, because she valued Jenny's silence about her own activities, Babs would not disclose what had taken place on that warm June night when the company of lace-bedecked gallants stayed at the Rose and Crown.

Jenny's dream world came to an abrupt end one sultry July evening when the taproom and the inn's side yard were bursting with thirsty customers. Long denied by edict of Cromwell's parliament, this year the week-long Addston Fair was being held in the broad meadows beyond Ned Porter's farm. Villagers from miles around flocked to the fair to trade and to gawk at the varied entertainments. The blood sports, banned by the Commonwealth not out of pity for the animals involved but because they provided pleasure, were the most eagerly anticipated. The primitive bear pit, where great shaggy beasts threw off an assortment of mangy hounds, was the foremost attraction: the cockpit, where the impoverished yokels laid penny bets, came a close second in popularity. Because the Rose and Crown was the nearest inn to the fairground, many fairgoers trudged the extra mile for its good, strong ale, indignantly refusing to pay the elevated price charged by the itinerant stallholders, and complaining the brew they offered was either sour or so watered down it had not the strength of dishwater.

At first Jenny had hoped she too would be allowed to visit the fair, but her aunt and uncle had informed her that they would go to the fair and she would stay behind. Since Babs had worked for them the longest, it was to be she, not Jenny, who would be honored by a half day's holiday to sample the fair's noisy delights.

Tonight the summer heat had left the inn's patrons with an unquenchable thirst. Jenny bustled back and forth, with brimming tankards strung on her fingers like massive rings. Just as she was returning to replenish the tankards of a party of drovers beneath the chestnut tree, Jenny heard a snatch of conversation that stilled her heart. Blanching, she sagged against a scarred table as she heard a man say:

". . . There's *The Royal Prospect* with a bloody great 'ole tore in 'er side, listing like a drunken sailor. Bloody shame, it was, all them 'ands flailing about like drownin' rats while them Dutch bastards picked 'em orf like bloody Christmas geese."

Her hands frozen to the brimming tankards Babs had thrust upon her, Jenny turned to find the speaker was a bowlegged little man in a fusty gray doublet with darned red hose wrinkled about his scrawny ankles.

"*The Royal Prospect*," she croaked in horror, "did you say *The Royal Prospect* is sunk?"

The little man turned in surprise, his expression changing to one of sympathy when he beheld her stricken face. "Aye, wench. Did ye 'ave a sweetheart aboard her?"

Dumbly, Jenny nodded, not trusting herself with words; the tankards had tipped sideways and were pouring a steady trickle on the floorboards.

" 'Tis a pity, but there it is; that's the fate of a seafaring man. Most hands was lost at sea, but your lad might've swum to safety. Never can tell about a jack tar."

"Most hands," she repeated numbly. "The officers—the captain too?"

"Them too. Shot to pieces with the others. Them Dutch bastards tried to say they was pirating. Never 'eard such nonsense! Everyone knows England's ruled the seas since the days of good Queen Bess."

"Are you a seaman?" Jenny whispered, leaning heavily on the scarred table, needing its strength to support her. She righted the spilling tankards and fixed her large gray eyes on the man, beseeching him for more news.

"Nay, wench, I'm no seafaring man. Just a poor dockhand come in for the fair. The sinking is the talk of London. I 'eard it from a couple of sailors, but on good authority, mind, seeing as they served on the vessel that rescued the few poor sods who survived."

Woodenly Jenny thanked the man and stumbled outside with the ale. The heavy air, rumbling with thunder, took her breath, making her gasp as she fought to hold on to consciousness. She leaned against the blistered inn wall, taking advantage of the narrow wedge of shade beside the open door.

A wave of misery pounded through her limbs, robbing her of strength. Kit was lost at sea! That was why she had not heard from him! Though Babs suggested it had never been his intention to return, Jenny knew he must have been detained. After his meeting with King Charles he must have been reassigned to duty. And now her beloved was dead! Never again would he take her in his arms and press his mouth to hers, firing her with delicious rapture. Kit was dead! Dead! There was no use in hoping he was one of the rescued crew members. Had the captain himself been saved, it would surely have been part of the tale going the rounds of the alehouses. Yet try as she might, Jenny could not accept his death. In the breadth of an evening she had found ecstatic love; now she had only its memory to sustain her during the endless nights to come.

The sultry days dragged by. Faint hope, sparked by the realization that Kit might have been rescued, dwindled to naught as Jenny asked first one and then another of the inn's customers about the sinking of *The Royal Prospect*. They all told the same story. One man assured her the captain had been fished lifeless from the water.

Babs puzzled over Jenny's relentless pursuit of details about the sinking until, remembering Kit Ashford was a sea captain, she realized *The Royal Prospect* must have been his ship. Babs finally got Jenny to talk about him, and her own bulbous eyes filled with swift tears of sympathy for the other girl's loss. Jenny took comfort from Babs' solid bulk as she laid her head on her shoulder and wept as if her heart would break.

On the morning of the long anticipated visit to Addston Fair, Babs sang as she scrubbed and wiped.

"I'll bring you something to cheer you up, Jen," she promised, feeling sorry for the other girl who must stay behind, and who was grieving so deeply. "What'll you 'ave? 'Ow about some gingerbread? Or a ribbon?"

Jenny smiled wanly at Babs, touched by her unexpected generosity. "You needn't buy me anything, Babs. I don't mind staying behind."

"I'll bring a ribbon for your hair," Babs decided, continuing as if she had not heard Jenny's protest. " 'Ow about cherry red, or blue?"

"Blue. And can you please bring me some more thread?

I've no money now, but I'll repay the debt when I'm able.''

'' 'Sall right, I knows yer honest.'' Babs grinned as she hung up the dishcloth and untied the apron from about her thick waist. ''Always sewing away, ain't yer. Tell the old skinflint to buy you a new skirt instead of making you sew patch on top of patch. That's what you should do.''

Though Jenny agreed with Babs, she did not seriously consider the idea. A new skirt would be produced for a price; the cost was more than she chose to pay.

At twelve sharp Babs was ready, dressed in her best bodice of green watered taffeta, laced, busked, and boned until she could scarcely breathe; her ample breasts fought for space. Her red linen skirt, though frayed and spotted, boasted a moderate train. The barmaid wore a wide-brimmed crushed-straw hat, its curling white feather spearing a cascade of purple ribbons that brushed her fleshy shoulders. Swathing such excess poundage, the garish color combination of her best attire was an astounding sight.

Jenny squeezed Babs' hand and told her how grand she looked, knowing it was the kind thing to say as she watched the other woman strutting about, proud as a peacock in her brilliant finery.

When she joined Babs, clad in her own best gown of decorous gray homespun, Rachel Dunn was aghast. Repeatedly circling Babs as if she were a sideshow exhibit, she muttered about her employee's unseemly attire. ''You're bright as a . . .''

''Now, mistress, don't spoil me day,'' Babs cautioned, her eyes turning steely. ''I've had enough years of dressing like a sparrer. Old Noll be dead now, there's no one to gainsay bright colors these days, thank the Lord. This is me best and I'll . . .'' She stopped speaking as a bellow of pain sounded from the cellar where the kegs of ale were stored.

''Merciful heaven, 'tis Tom!''

Rachel scurried to the top of the stair, clutching her starched gray skirts about her as she peered into the gloomy cellar. ''What ails you, husband?''

''I've ricked me back. A keg toppled over and I tried to salvage it.''

Rachel gasped. ''And the ale—is it spilled?'' she demanded, mentally totting up the loss of a keg of best brew.

''Nay, I saved the ale, wife, but in so doing I nearly cracked my spine.''

Sweating and red-faced, Tom Dunn emerged slowly from the cellar, brushing cobwebs from his clothing as he came up through the hatch.

"Lie down a spell," Rachel suggested. "Maybe you'll soon be mended."

Clutching his lower back and grimacing fiercely, Tom shook his head. "Nay, wife, you and the girl go ahead. I'd find no pleasure in the fair. The pain's like to cripple me. I think I'll lie down the rest of the day—if I can climb the stair." Groaning loudly with every step, Tom Dunn moved slowly toward the staircase, liberally massaging his lower spine as he went. Rachel clucked along at his side, berating him for his foolishness in going down to the cellar within a few minutes of their departure on so cherished an outing.

Once her husband was comfortably settled in his bed, Rachel reluctantly left him, coming downstairs to join the impatient barmaid. "Mayhap we should stay behind," she said thoughtfully, "with poor Tom a-groaning in his bed. Besides, 'tis not seemly to be enjoying ourselves at sinful entertainment. Bound for hellfire, that's what this country be, now the rule of the ungodly holds sway. No, to save our miserable souls, 'tis far better we stay home." At Babs' noisy howls of protest, Rachel finally relented. "Very well, we'll go, but we must be home long before dusk. And I'll be watching for any unseemliness, my girl," she warned Babs, her face grim.

Turning to her niece, Rachel set her thin lips in an unrelenting line as she gripped Jenny's slender wrist, her bony fingers biting in. "Jenny, you're to manage everything by yourself. No calling for Griffiths or young Billy to help. No batting your eyelashes, or smiling at them like a wanton. I've seen you wheedling for help with the chores from the mindless fools. Chores are good for a body. Work takes the devil from you, and with a mother like yours, you've got a goodly dose . . ."

"My mother's dead. I'll thank you not to speak ill of her! Didn't you punish her enough while she lived?" Jenny cried, unable to stand by meekly and accept such slander.

Rachel drew in her breath in shock, angrily facing her young niece, whose flashing gray eyes and heightened color betrayed her temper. "Don't you come over all insolent with me, my girl! Now Nan's gone there's nothing to hold you here. And let me tell you—" Rachel drew close, her lined face tight as a shriveled apple. "If you don't put out a deal more work, it's out on the road you go! I expect twice as much as you give me. Your Uncle Tom's too soft with you. You've got a week to show improvement, or it's out with you, Nan's girl or no. And you won't get as much as a groat from me. Likely you'll be howling down the road with a flea in your ear!"

Without waiting for Jenny's retort, Rachel swished about and, gripping Babs' fleshy arm, she propelled her through the doorway. Babs winked at Jenny as she waved goodbye, ignoring her mistress's hostility.

Jenny watched them go, fighting the anger that speeded her heart and brought blood burning to her face. Twice as much work! She did more now than should be expected from a body. A double output would be impossible. There were rooms to clean, beds to change, chamberpots to empty; they even pushed her into the kitchen to help the scullion when things were slow. Only in the evenings, when the men jammed the taproom, did her uncle insist on her presence, for he knew Jenny's decorative appearance was a major asset to the inn.

The warm afternoon passed pleasantly with only a handful of customers to attend to. The long-awaited wrestling matches at the fair must have kept the spectators on the fairground drinking inferior ale.

As Jenny was sweeping the corridor, she caught her brown skirt on a splinter and tore a jagged rent in the threadbare material. She saw that the customers' tankards were full and that they had sufficient food before she went upstairs to fetch a needle and thread.

It was dark and cool on the upper floor, the rooms shaded by the heavy-leaved chestnut. The immense tree, its network of branches tapping against the timbered walls in the summer breeze, created the illusion of living in a tree house, for it shielded the inn yard from sight. Jenny paused beside the window, lifting her heavy hair from her neck to cool her skin, enjoying the luxury of solitude. She held her sewing materials in her hand, yet still she hesitated, reluctant to exchange this blissful privacy for the beery haze of the public room.

"What you doin' up 'ere?"

With an exclamation of surprise, Jenny spun about to find her uncle in the doorway, his frayed shirttail dangling loose over the top of his breeches.

"I thought you were lying down."

"I was." He stepped across the threshold and closed the door behind him.

Fear pierced her flesh as Jenny stared at him. A menacing expression lurked about Tom Dunn's heavy face, warning her to beware.

He stepped toward her, his brown eyes hard as he allowed his speculative glance to dwell on her rounded figure, lovingly molded by the thin homespun gown. The sight of the bright billow of her unbound hair excited him. When he noted the unfastened eyelets at the top of her low-cut bodice, his pulse raced.

"My skirt ripped. I came to get a needle and thread to mend it."

"Too bad that, ain't it." Tom Dunn stood in the middle of the room, grinning meaningfully at her neatly made bed. His bulk seemed to fill the small room, menacing and repellent.

"I have to go downstairs. They'll be calling for me."

Ignoring her protest, he grabbed Jenny's hand. "I heard what Rachel said to you—her voice'd wake the dead. Don't listen to her. It's me wot runs this inn, not her, and if you works like you've been doing, I won't worry none about it, Jenny, love."

Staring up at him, Jenny swallowed nervously. "I work hard," she said.

"I know, too hard for a pretty little thing like you. Pretty wenches have no need to work hard, leastways not while they're standing upright." His fleshy red lips curved to reveal crooked, stained teeth as he grinned at his thoughts.

"No," Jenny warned, wrenching her arm from his grasp.

"No? No what? 'Tis a funny thing to say, that is."

"Don't touch me . . . ever!" Eyes flashing, Jenny spat the warning. To her alarm she discovered that he effectively blocked her passage to the door and the escape it offered.

"Touch you? Why, lass, you know I've hurt me back. How could I touch you? Ask our Rachel what terrible pain I'm in. I could hardly drag meself upstairs. Nay, wench, you've got it all wrong." As he spoke, Tom Dunn slid his stubby fingers inside the straining waistband of his soiled breeches.

"You lied! You never hurt your back," Jenny cried, eyes dilating in fear as she guessed his purpose. "You intended this all along."

"Oo, clever little thing, ain't yer?"

"Don't touch me! I told you before if you ever lay a finger on me, I'll tell Rachel."

Her uncle grabbed her and pulled her against his body. "Oh, no, you won't, you little tart. I knew you was no innocent first time I laid eyes on yer. Pretending like that, simpering all white as milk and sweet as honey—I heard you outside with that fancy gentleman wot come by last month. Him with 'is sovereigns for talk. That's rich, that is! Talk—'tis the funniest name I ever heard gived to it and no mistake. Like mother, like daughter, you be. Just like I says."

Appalled by his knowledge, Jenny stared at him, her gray eyes dark with fear. "I don't know what you mean," she managed at last, her mouth going dry.

"I'll show you what I mean, just to set your mind at ease." He unbuttoned the straining top button on his breeches, revealing a corpulent girth generously matted with dark hair.

Struggling against him, Jenny tried to break his grip, but Tom Dunn imprisoned her wrists in one huge hand as easily as if she had been a moth. Outstretching his brawny arm, he held her away while he fumbled with his clothing, clumsy in his excitement. Unable to strike him with her hands, Jenny kicked him, but her uncle was far too aroused to be deterred by her feeble efforts.

"Now, now, you be a good little wench," he admonished with a leer. "I've got a nice big surprise for you, something better than that lace-trimmed bastard could produce, I'll be bound." So saying, he quickly exposed his turgid flesh.

Jenny gagged, shuddering in disgust at the sight. Advancing a step, he pushed her, toppling her backwards to the bed beneath the eaves. She cried out in shock and pain as she hit her head on the sloping ceiling. Jenny tried to push him away, but her uncle's heavy arms and legs were everywhere. Squirming to the edge of the bed, with a massive effort she levered their combined weight onto the floor, where they landed with a resounding bump. Tom Dunn laughed as he fell with a sickening thud on top of her, crushing out her breath. Her resistance both excited and amused him.

"You can't fight me off, Jenny, so what's the good of trying?"

Stunned, Jenny lay still, staring up at him, her heart pounding with fear and revulsion. She grew aware of the rapidly darkening room. The sun had gone behind the clouds, and in the distance an ominous roll of thunder sounded. Laughing at her helplessness, Tom Dunn writhed above her soft curves, delighting in the feel of her body beneath his.

"I've waited a long time for this," he whispered, his lips wet with spittle. Fumbling with her bodice, he pulled at the lacings. "Come on, let's 'ave a look at your titties. You owe your poor old uncle a feel. 'Tain't right to keep such . . ."

Working her hands free, Jenny thumped him hard on top of his head.

"That won't get you naught but trouble," he threatened, as, with his free hand, he pushed up her skirts and greedily fondled her silky thigh.

The thunder rolled closer, reverberating in the room; the first stirrings of wind pattered a hail of chestnut leaves against the pane.

Tom Dunn negotiated her bodice ties, his sweating hands greedily mauling her tender flesh until Jenny gasped in pain. In the semi-darkness she touched something on the floor beneath the window; with quickening heartbeat Jenny's fingers closed around the icy metal of her sewing scissors.

"A pox on it," growled Tom Dunn, glancing at the threatening sky. "Come on—bloody rain'll be starting soon. Then our Rachel'll be coming 'ome. Stop mucking about, you bitch!" Jenny lay still, unresisting. "That's better. I knew you'd like it once we got started."

Jenny jerked her head away in revulsion as her uncle's slack, wet mouth closed over hers. She hated the taste of his lips, the horrible intimacy of his fleshy body grinding hard as if he would thrust her through the floorboards. Tightening her grip on the scissors, she raised her arm, the weapon poised above his shadowed bulk.

"Come on, open your legs," he panted. "Make it easier for me."

Mustering all her strength, Jenny plunged the scissors through his gray homespun shirt. Yelping in pain, Tom Dunn shuddered beneath the impact, shocked by the sting of steel penetrating his flesh. He rose long enough for Jenny to roll free. In one agile movement, she sprang upright and crouched in the corner.

He reared back, scrabbling wildly for the weapon. With a shudder of fear, he yanked the scissors free, releasing a gush of crimson that trickled to the floorboards. Jenny realized her efforts had been in vain. Though the scissor wound was

painful, it had not killed him, nor had it even effectively
stayed him from his purpose. Her aim should have been
between his shoulder blades . . .

"You'll pay for this! By God, you see if you don't. I'll
tear your bloody legs apart!" he threatened, clutching his
wounded shoulder as he stared at her in disbelief, his sweating face suffused with hatred.

Tom Dunn lunged for her and Jenny darted away. He trod
heavily on her skirts; the thin fabric ripped and she was free
again. Pushing the bed toward him, Jenny effectively halted
his advance, sending him toppling, cursing and fuming, to the
floor. He upset the chamberpot; he tangled his feet in the
trailing bedclothes; but a moment later he was up again. Next
Jenny seized the water pitcher and hurled it at him. The white
pottery shattered against his skull. Dazed, her uncle wavered,
and once again Jenny rammed the bed against his legs, buck-
ling his knees. This time Tom Dunn smashed his head against
the slate washstand as he fell. He did not rise.

Gagging as bile rose bitter in her throat, Jenny's only
thought was to escape from this room. She approached her
uncle's sprawled body, expecting him to make a grab for her
as she reached the door. He did not move. By now her heart
was thumping so loudly that she barely heard the rolling
thunder and the patter of rain against the open windowpane.
An awesome thought possessed her as she looked at Tom
Dunn's still body: what if she had killed him?

The light was dim in the darkened room, yet as she turned
his ashen face toward her, Jenny could not mistake the gaping
horror of his eyes. Tom Dunn was dead! Appalled by her
discovery, Jenny drew back, trying to still the fit of trembling
that seized her limbs. The summer storm would drive Babs
and Rachel back to the inn sooner than expected; they could
be approaching the door this very minute! No one would
believe her uncle had tried to rape her. And certainly not
when Rachel told her story about her husband's painful back
injury. The fact that his breeches gaped open, that he was
here in her bedroom, would most likely be explained away,
leaving Jenny to take the full measure of punishment for
killing a man.

The realization of her probable fate once her crime was
discovered spurred Jenny to immediate action. Leaping over
the body, she wrenched open the door. Because Tom Dunn
lay across the threshold, she could barely open the door wide

enough to squeeze through. Forcing herself to remain calm, Jenny raced around the bends in the staircase, ears cocked for the sounds of the returning women. From the taproom could be heard the strains of a rollicking country round as she sped along the narrow passage leading to the stables.

A few minutes later Jenny stood outside in the unearthly stormlight, fledgling raindrops pattered cold against her face. She ran across the road and crouched behind the hawthorn hedge, where she attempted to formulate a plan of escape. Though she had no money, nor any place to go, she had killed a man and must get away, or else face death or imprisonment for her crime. No one would believe her pleas of self-defense, for Tom Dunn was a respected local citizen. When Rachel found the bloodied scissors beside her husband's body, she would immediately name Jenny as the culprit. Such a hue and cry would be raised that hysteria would possess the villagers, who would thirst for her blood.

Running feet sounded close at hand. Jenny peered through a gap in the hedge to see Babs and Rachel, skirts held high, racing toward the inn, desperate to reach cover before the storm erupted in full fury. Within a few minutes of their entering the inn, her crime would be discovered. Jenny's stomach lurched at the realization that the constables would soon be combing the countryside in search of the fugitive. She had to find somewhere to hide!

Once the running women were safely past the gap in the hedge, Jenny darted back on the highway. Hoping the constables would first search the London road, she headed in the opposite direction from Addston village. Splashing heedlessly through rapidly forming puddles, her torn skirt trailing sodden behind her, Jenny fought for breath as she tried to put a margin of safety between herself and the Rose and Crown.

For the next hour she darted in and out of hedgerows until she finally abandoned the highway and set out across open country in an effort to avoid groups of drenched villagers straggling home from the fair. Brambles snatched at her clothing. Jenny tore a strip of tattered fabric from her skirt, shortening it until it barely reached her calves; dirty, ragged, she looked like a beggar maid as the pelting rain plastered her clothing to her skin. Twice she turned her ankles on the rough ground, falling sickeningly to the wet grass as a fiery pain shot up her throbbing leg. Jenny limped on until she could go no further. Fifty feet ahead lay a copse of trees, and she sought the shelter of its gnarled branches as the rain pelted with renewed fury.

Two trees twisted together to form a cavern, and Jenny thankfully scrambled inside the protective hollow, wrapping her sodden skirts about her legs. The bulbous growths on the old trunks made a knobbly bed, but she was so utterly exhausted that she curled up contented as a babe. No sounds of pursuit followed her here. And Jenny slept, thankful for these few minutes of blissful rest.

Chapter 4

When Jenny first opened her eyes she did not know where she was; then, as her memory returned with sickening clarity, she jerked awake, startled to find she had slept with total disregard for her safety. It was night. The rain had stopped, but the wind still whipped the trees, cascading cold showers on her head. Shivering, Jenny looked about in the inky darkness, trying to get her bearings. She chose what she assumed to be a southerly direction and set out over the squelching fields toward the road.

As she rounded the thick black bulk of the hawthorn hedge, Jenny leaped back in alarm. Torches flared along the road leading to the Rose and Crown. The search party must be drawing near!

Heart hammering with fear, she retraced her steps, ignoring her painful ankle as she plowed through rank, weed-choked ditches and across boggy pastures. A huge white shape loomed before her and Jenny squealed in alarm, only to discover her captor was a cow placidly munching the lush meadow grass growing along the bank of a ditch. Jenny stifled an impulse for hysterical laughter as she clutched her arms about her chill body, rocking back and forth before she gained her wits sufficiently to resume her journey.

Ahead lay a field dotted with more large, dark shapes. When she drew closer Jenny found not cattle, but a wagon encampment. Her first inclination was to shy away from all habitation: rising voices and flickering torches, gleaming orange in the night, rapidly changed her mind. Leaping forward, she crushed through the hedge dividing the fields, battling brambles that raked her skin and tore her hair. Jenny scrambled out of an icy ditch on the other side and ran barefoot over the grass; her shoes had fallen off in the water and she dared not go back for them.

The first wagon loomed ahead. Empty shafts lay on the ground; the unharnessed horse grazed nearby. Ever mindful of the bobbing lights of pursuit visible beyond the hedge,

Jenny climbed the wagon steps. Praying no one slept inside, she crawled forward into the dark, odorous interior. The smell was unpleasant, but this was no time for delicacy; she burrowed into a bed of rags and drew a quilt over her body.

Even as she lay still, Jenny heard men's voices close at hand; at the thought of discovery, her breath caught in her throat. To her surprise, as she strained to catch what was being said, Jenny found that the speakers were conversing in a foreign tongue. For what seemed like hours she crouched there in the fetid darkness, knowing if she could remain hidden until the search party had gone, she had a chance to escape. Suddenly the wagon was filled with a flood of light. Heart pounding in fear, she held her breath, not knowing how much the lantern revealed. When she heard a man's gasp of surprise, Jenny knew she had been caught.

"Why you here?" he demanded in a guttural voice, but he sounded no alarm.

Blinded by the glaring light, Jenny could see nothing as she raised up to beg, "Please, don't give me away."

"You the one they want. You kill a man . . ."

"I didn't mean to. He was trying to . . . it was in self-defense," she gasped tearfully.

The man set the lantern on the wagon step. Jenny could distinguish his slender form, but his features remained a dark blur. From his accent she guessed him to be a foreigner. He moved the lantern, and light glinted on dazzling gold earrings above a lavishly embroidered purple shirt; it was then Jenny realized she had strayed into a gypsy camp.

"You are murderess."

"I didn't mean to kill him. It was an accident. He hit his head."

The gypsy nodded. He leaned inside the wagon, staring at her. Jenny wrinkled her nose at the stench of him, his odor was not of horses, but of something infinitely more unpleasant.

"You want to stay?" he asked at last.

Jenny's face lit with relief. "Stay! Yes, please . . . just till morning."

"Not till morning . . . always. You please me, little *gorgio* girl."

As she understood his meaning, Jenny recoiled from the dark-skinned hand he stretched toward her "No, not like that," she protested, drawing back.

"Like that only way you stay," he said, his voice turning unpleasant. "No use for *gorgio* women. You *mokadi*—taboo."

With pounding heart, Jenny scrambled backward, vainly trying to elude his embrace as the gypsy vaulted inside the wagon. He lunged for her. They wrestled for a moment, thrashing about in the tumbled quilts. Though he was slender, the gypsy was wiry and strong: Jenny was unable to vanquish him. Exhausted, she lay still and the gypsy, thinking she would now be receptive to his advances, rocked back on his heels, his dark lips curving in a smile of possession as he surveyed his prize.

"That better. You be sensible now . . . no fight."

Seizing her opportunity, Jenny leaped for the yawning opening to freedom, her action taking the gypsy by surprise. Landing on the ground, she bounced up, stumbling away from the wagon as the agile gypsy leaped after her. The grazing horse stood nearby, and she wondered if she could escape on horseback, but when the animal shied away from her, Jenny discarded the idea. As she rounded the side of the wagon she discovered they were on the fringe of a large campground, for a dozen separate campfires glowed in the night. She could seek aid from the other gypsies, yet they might turn her over to the constables. And if their intentions matched those of her erstwhile rescuer, they would do far more to her than that!

Jenny screamed in fear as a bulky form loomed out of the darkness. The rancid smell she associated with the gypsy was stronger here, the shaggy bulk moving toward her suggesting animal instead of man. A huge creature, its eyes gleaming red in the darkness, reared up on hind legs, great arms outstretched as if it would crush her against its body. Jenny screamed again and fell back. To her horror, rapid grunts and snorts directly behind her betrayed the presence of a second creature, which lumbered toward her on all fours. This animal too reared upward, swinging massive paws treacherously close to her face; deadly curved claws gleamed against its dark fur. For a hideous moment the wild beasts stood etched against the feeble lantern glow.

Sinking to her knees on the boggy ground as the grunting beasts closed in, Jenny was too terrified to move. She could not run, nor could she defend herself against these massive beasts with the gleaming eyes.

"Gregor! Boris!"

From a great distance Jenny heard the gypsy shouting. A moment later he was dragging her upright while the two bears, grunting and snuffling in disappointment, lumbered away. Only then did she see the collars round their thick necks and massive chains tethering them to iron stakes on the ground.

"Come, little *gorgio*, they'll not hurt you. Bears are gentle creatures."

Women's excited voices sounded close at hand. The thunder of running feet echoed over the meadow as the other gypsies were alerted by her screams. A few minutes later Jenny found herself surrounded by a menacing band of strangely attired people; both men and women wore jangling beads and bracelets, and their long raven hair fluttered unbound about their shoulders. Against the garish background of lantern light, their lean, dark faces, their hawklike noses and glittering black eyes, presented a frightening picture.

"She's mine," the gypsy man announced, guarding her from the others. In the background the bears grunted and snorted, woofing like dogs as they thumped each other about rolling in the grass.

Frightened by this sea of hostile faces, Jenny beseeched the gypsies for help. Though she doubted they would understand her, she knew she must try to reach them. "Please, help me," she pleaded, looking from one dark face to another, finding no more sympathy in the women's faces than in the men's. Suddenly the watching group parted like a field of wind-borne grain to allow a tall, scrawny woman in a flowing crimson gown to reach the front of the crowd.

Jenny gazed up at the newcomer, somewhat repelled by the menacing appearance of this gypsy woman. Fully as tall as any man, the gaunt woman stared down at her with inscrutable black eyes; about her wizened face fluttered disheveled gray locks, so wildly disarrayed they appeared never to have known a brush.

No one else spoke; even the gypsy man who claimed Jenny as his own said nothing while he awaited the decision of this old woman.

"Are you the one they're looking for?" the gypsy woman asked, extending a clawlike hand to assist Jenny from the ground.

"Yes. Oh, please, protect me from them. I never meant to kill . . ."

''Sometimes killing's necessary. We don't hold that against you.''

They stared at each other. Jenny's frightened eyes held the fathomless black depths of the gypsy woman's gaze. As if coming to a decision, the woman jerked her head toward the assembly. ''She stays,'' she said simply. ''Not with you, Petrov—with me.''

The gypsy man stepped back, disappointment flooding his dark face, but he did not question the decision.

Hardly able to believe her good fortune, Jenny clasped the proffered hand, allowing herself to be pulled upright.

''I'm Rosa,'' the gypsy said.

The others stood respectfully silent as Rosa took Jenny's arm and marched her through the center of camp toward her own wagon.

''Are you the gypsy queen?'' Jenny asked curiously as Rosa ushered her inside a red-painted wooden wagon decorated with lavish flower design.

Rosa laughed harshly at the idea, shaking her tangled locks. ''Nay. I lead these people, wench, but there's little of royalty about me.''

Jenny discovered Rosa's wagon was infinitely cleaner than that of the bear trainer. As she remembered her narrow escape from him and his fearsome beasts, she shuddered anew.

Rosa tossed her a scarlet skirt with a yellow frill; a low-necked black bodice followed. ''Here, take these; your rags are soaked. Besides, in these you'll not look so much like a *gorgio*.''

That night Jenny slept in the gypsy's wagon, exhaustion robbing her of all fear and caution. The following day, when she learned Jenny was an experienced seamstress, Rosa gave her a black silk shawl to finish embroidering with yellow roses. The task was meant to keep her safely confined, for the gypsy warned that the local constables were still nosing about the fair, convinced their fugitive had sought shelter in its anonymity.

On Sunday the gypsies broke camp. Separating into family groups, the largest band, led by Rosa, headed north; the others went south and east. The gypsies intended to circle through Surrey and Sussex before converging on London at the annual St. Margaret's Fair. The age-old fair, formerly held each September at Southwark beyond the Thames, had been revived by King Charles II. There every rogue and cutpurse, every drab and pickpocket headed, eager to avail themselves of the easy pickings to be had at the teeming, brawling riot of bear baiting, cockfighting, freak shows, and dawn to dusk carousing. Londoners, attired in their holiday finery, would flock to the fair by the thousands to partake of all the well-loved pleasures too long denied by a dismal, abstemious regime.

"Now you can come out," Rosa announced cheerfully one cool morning when the dew-wet grass sparkled diamond-bright in the sun.

Though she was grateful for the gypsy's gruff kindness in sheltering her, Jenny was more than glad to be free of her prison. Too many hours alone gave her time to grieve for Kit, time also to agonize over her probable fate if she was apprehended by the village constable.

Jenny jumped from the wagon and landed in a lush, daisy-splashed meadow beside a winding stream. "Where are we now?" she asked curiously, glancing about at the rolling pastureland gilded with buttercups. Purple loosestrife and clumps of pink marsh orchid fringed the sluggish stream, threading color like a giant necklace among the rank grass and weeds.

"Farnham, but I doubt that means much to you. It's a poor pigsty of a place, but you can begin to earn your keep here. The constables won't come this far in search of you."

To Jenny's dismay, she found she was shunned by the other gypsies, who treated her as an outcast. Only Petrov, the odorous bear trainer, paid the slightest attention to her. She was uncomfortably aware of his soulful black gaze following her every movement. Nevertheless, mindful of Rosa's stern edict that the *gorgio* be left alone, he made no attempt to speak to her.

Now that she was clear of Addston and its neighboring parishes, Jenny no longer needed the gypsies' protection. She planned to slip away from the sleeping camp, yet after further thought, she decided it would be far wiser to travel to London under the vagabonds' patronage; once there, it would be a simple matter to go in search of her uncle's shop.

To earn her keep, Jenny was instructed to sell gypsy charms and lucky tokens. Rosa cleverly disguised her fair complexion with a herb dye, then gave Jenny a black linen coif to cover her bright hair.

As Rosa said, Farnham was a poor village. The local fair

was a shabby event, hardly worthy of its name. Too poor to possess a bear pit, the Farnham villagers had to be content with the spectacle of Boris and Gregor, tawdry yellow ruffs about their thick necks, dancing clumsily to Petrov's squealing violin. Inside a patched, sun-faded tent, Rosa told the fortunes of local wenches while other members of the gypsy band juggled balls or somersaulted about the chalky ground, eyes craftily alert for goods left untended. When three local musicians played on shawms and sackbut for the crowd's entertainment, several of the gypsy women executed abandoned Slavic dances, leaping and spinning high in the air. Their menfolk passed a battered hat to collect the meager contributions from the awestruck crowd.

Though pickings for the first day of the Farnham Fair had been lean, come nightfall fat chickens stewed in many a gypsy stewpot. Jenny did not ask from whence they came, suspecting that while their owners were visiting the fair, nimble dark hands had wrung the fowls' necks. It was a gypsy custom to travel with a cage of chickens of assorted plumage; if a villager found stray feathers similar to those of his stolen birds, such evidence did not condemn them. Masters at acting the role of injured party, members of the gypsy band would hotly deny all accusations, swift to point out they owned fowls of the self-same color.

On the second day of their stay in Farnham, Rosa appointed a young, attractive gypsy girl named Marta to instruct Jenny in the fine art of picking pockets.

"You'll starve at it!" the sloe-eyed Marta remarked scornfully as they walked back to camp for their noonday meal.

"I'm sorry," Jenny apologized, declining to reveal she had no intention of mastering the art.

Marta snorted disdainfully at Jenny's seeming stupidity. She quickened her pace, anxious to be shut of this hampering novice.

Unused to going barefoot as she was, however hard Jenny tried to keep pace with Marta her tender feet caused her to lag behind. Numerous cuts and bruises made walking difficult, though the springy turf was a soothing balm after the flinty chalk fairground.

"Hopeless," Marta announced gleefully as Rosa came to meet them.

The old gypsy woman sighed. "I was afraid of that. Can you sing, or dance, or ride bareback?"

Jenny shook her head. "There's nothing I can do well enough for money."

"Give her back to her own kind," Marta advised sagely, swinging inside her battered, green painted wagon after first kissing the carved hawthorn symbol above the door. This crudely finished good luck token surmounted each window and door of the gypsy vardo. Poking her dark head through the doorway, Marta said, "Better yet, sell her to the Southwark stews. That's something she can do well enough for money." With this the gypsy girl disappeared in a flurry of yellow frilled skirts.

She was a country girl, but Jenny had read enough London broadsheets to know that a stew was a brothel, the reopening of which, after years of Puritan suppression, had been lauded by rich and poor alike. "You won't do that—will you?" she ventured, aghast at the idea.

"Come inside the wagon. We must talk," was all Rosa said.

It was murky and cool with the flowered curtain drawn across the opening to shut out the sun. Rosa sat at the table, chin in hand, staring at Jenny, who was seated opposite.

"Being a whore's not as bad as starving," reminded Rosa. When Jenny gasped, she grinned, displaying a gap in her blackened front teeth. "Come, I have a joke with you. Go back to selling charms, it will be safer. You'll land us all in the stocks with your bungling. Here, wear this, 'twill bring you good fortune." Rosa draped a small, exquisitely carved fish on a silk cord about Jenny's slender neck. "Fir for luck, *gorgio*. This lingam will protect you."

Touched by Rosa's generosity, Jenny smiled her thanks.

Rosa took Jenny's hand, gazing thoughtfully at the lines crisscrossing her palm. Suddenly Rosa's hooded eyes narrowed menacingly; leaning closer, she studied the series of lines foretelling Jenny's destiny.

"What is it? What do you see?" Jenny demanded, looking down at her palm but seeing nothing more than the grime of a morning's toil.

"Nothing!" Rosa snapped, thrusting her hand aside as she stood up. "You don't really think I have the gift to see your future, do you? Such nonsense is a trick to fool the *gorgios*."

With that the incident was dismissed. Yet to her discomfort, Jenny found the old gypsy woman regarding her with hooded gaze, a forbidding expression crossing her gaunt face.

From that moment on a definite change in Rosa's attitude became apparent, suggesting that perhaps she attached far more significance to palm reading than she professed. Not once, despite repeated questioning, could Rosa be induced to reveal what fate she had seen.

Much against her better judgment, Marta took Jenny with her to the fair the following afternoon. She was annoyed at being hampered by the *gorgio's* presence. When men became tipsy they grew careless with their wealth; Marta had no desire to share her bounty with a despised *gorgio*.

Jenny wove her way among the noisy, jostling throng, carrying a neck tray of small carved wooden fish, horns, and sachets of herbs. At the end of an hour she still had nothing to show for her pains, despite the fact that she had plucked up sufficient courage to cry her wares.

Marta beckoned to her from the shadows of a mutton pie stall. "Work in the crowd watching Micah's monkeys. I'll follow," the gypsy girl commanded. " 'Tis usually easy pickings when the fools are gaping at the act."

Jenny mingled with the staring crowd gathered about a portable wooden stage where six bright-eyed monkeys, dressed in miniature green suits, danced and shook ribboned tambourines. Next the monkeys walked a tightrope, their small, red-feathered hats teetering askew, much to the audience's delight.

From under the shade of a canvas awning slung before a knifegrinder's stall, Jenny watched the gaudy scene with pleasure. How welcome it was to see splashes of bright color among the sober blacks and grays of serviceable homespun garments. So severe had been the restrictions of dress imposed upon Englishmen during Cromwell's time that once released from bondage the people had gone wild with frivolity. Even these sober, hard-working yoemen had grown their hair long and taken to wearing ribbons in accordance with the current fashion. Women had lowered their necklines, edging the boat-necked openings with scraps of ribbon and lace. And though this humble crowd displayed not the froth of finery to be found at the King's court, where men decked themselves as gay as maypoles with ribbons and lace, the stolid farmers had made concessions to the new order. Gaudy knots of ribbons were sewn to the shoulders of brown fustian coats; wildflowers and feathers adorned their hats. A stall selling blue loveknots had done a roaring trade. Before the day was out every sweetheart wanted a token of their beloved's devotion.

Reluctantly Jenny rejoined the press of sweating spectators, knowing she must make an effort to sell her wares. A young man, leaning against a tree, attracted her attention. His fashionable spring-green velvet coat, lavishly laced with silver, stood out in this crowd of countrymen. As Jenny drew closer to him, she was disappointed, for her expectations promised far more than he could deliver. Under closer scrutiny the man seemed not to be a gentleman at all: frayed coat cuffs, tarnished silver, and the general soil of his lavish, lace-decked shirt betrayed a more humble background.

As the crowd surged away from the monkey act, Jenny was pushed toward the man with the green coat. A blowsy farmwife, carrying a wicker basket of pungent pickled neat's tongues, spun her off balance so that she fell hard against him. Jenny's profuse apologies were cut short by his iron grip clamped about her wrist.

"Got you, you little thief," the man snarled.

Jenny gasped, her gray eyes widening with fear. She looked into his face, surprised to find the man's skin as swarthy as any gypsy's. His green eyes held hers, startlingly pale in his dark face; his relentless expression bored unmercifully into her brain. "No, sir, I swear, you are mistaken," she cried, desperately casting about for someone to come to her aid. Jenny caught Micah's eye, but the monkey trainer deliberately turned away, pretending not to see her danger. Marta was nowhere to be seen.

"Mistaken, you scurvy wench, how so?" The man in the stylish coat demanded fiercely, his wide, thick-lipped mouth set hard in his gypsy brown face. Beginning at his mouth was a fresh scar bisecting his left cheek before it disappeared beneath the wide brim of his black, green-feathered hat.

"I was pushed. You must have seen the woman . . ."

"Lying won't get you out of it."

" 'Tis no lie! I'm not a thief!" Jenny wracked her brain, trying to find a solution to her predicament; she could only think of one. Sighing, she gazed soulfully at her captor, practicing the only wiles she knew. He was young and, despite his disfigurement, still handsome in a coarse, earthy way; perchance, like others of his sex, he could be wooed with smiles and the promise of more to follow. Once he released her she would be off, fleeing between the ramshackle stalls she had come to know so well.

"Please believe me, I wasn't trying to steal your purse."

"Ha, that's what they all say!"

The man pulled her closer until the soft material of his fine velvet coat brushed the down on Jenny's arm. Giving him her sweetest smile, she allowed her body to press against his, inviting, but not wanton.

"Do I look like a thief?" she asked, smiling sweetly, though her heart raced with fear. "Please, kind sir, don't call the constables."

The young man snorted with disdain. "You're a piss poor liar, wench, but a comely one at that," he added, his expression still unyielding. "Tell me, what does a gypsy wench with gray eyes?"

Jenny's mouth parted in surprise while her mind reeled to supply an answer to his unexpected question. The man gripped her shoulders and twisted her about, marching her out of the crowd.

"You little gypsy whore," he growled, giving her a shake, "methinks a taste of the stocks wouldn't come amiss. 'Twould teach you a good lesson. Come to think of it, you're not even a gypsy, are you?"

Appalled by his threat, Jenny stared at him, swiftly weighing the advisability of lashing out at her captor and hoping to flee into the crowd instead of making an effort to woo him to her cause. She could not risk apprehension by the local constable; it was too soon after Tom Dunn's death for that.

Suddenly the man in the leaf-green coat let out a splutter of laughter. "Come, give Manuel a kiss, little *gorgio* bitch," he rasped. "Have no fear, I'll not turn you in."

Now that he had dropped his cultured tones, Jenny was even more baffled. The man flashed her an engaging grin, displaying dazzling white teeth in the frame of his wine-dark lips. That word he had used—*gorgio*—was what the gypsies used to indicate she was not one of them. Was this stranger a gypsy too?

"Who are you? Are you one of Rosa's people?" Jenny demanded indignantly, her anger rising at the thought he had frightened her so badly out of a perverted sense of humor.

"Has she not told you about Manuel?"

"No, she has not."

He was laughing openly now and his dark hand stole to her neck, stroking the soft skin as he grinned down at her. "Ah, but she has told me much about you. How you are such a beautiful little *gorgio* orphan, the very image of her poor, long-lost Josie. 'Twas the only reason she took you in. We're not in the habit of extending charity to runaway *gorgio* wenches."

"Who's Josie?"

"My half sister. Two years ago she was taken by the constable for stealing eggs. Deported to the colonies they told us, yet in truth she probably warms some fat advocate's bed. Rosa's my mother."

"Your mother!"

"Aye, even the likes of me must have a mother."

"Why did you try to frighten me?" Jenny demanded angrily.

"Try! I succeeded, did I not?"

He was laughing again, and Jenny wrenched her arms free of his bruising grasp. "Aye, mayhap you did, but I don't find it amusing."

"Come, no anger, surely I deserve a kiss for saving you from the law."

"You'll get no kiss from me!"

"Then I'll have to steal one, for kiss I shall have."

Jenny gasped as he grabbed her about the waist and she leaned away from him, trying to evade his mouth, amazed by the strength of his arms. Kicking out at his shins and pummeling his broad back, Jenny fought him, but Manuel laughingly subdued her defense. His hot mouth came down hard on hers, stifling her breath, cruel in the extraction of his due.

So swiftly released was she that Jenny stumbled and fell to her knees on the chalky ground. Bristling with anger, she glared up at him; she throbbed with fierce emotion. His mouth had been brutally demanding, but there had been a spark of fire in his kiss that might have kindled a response had she allowed it to.

"You're none too clean," he complained, flicking dust from his finery.

Indignant, Jenny scrambled to her feet and struck at him with clenched fists. "Not clean! I'm cleaner than the majority of your people!"

Manuel laughed again at her angry words as, with a flurry of red skirts, Jenny swished away from him and darted inside Rosa's tent.

The gypsy was seated at a makeshift table, an opaque glass ball before her. As the tent flap lifted, allowing a shaft of sunlight to pierce the gloom, Rosa began a whining sales pitch, irregardless of the identity of the person. She knew her customer was a woman by the swish of her skirts.

"Come, pretty mistress, let old Rosa tell your fortune. Know what riches lie in store, what lovers . . ." Rosa glanced up and her practiced whine stopped as she beheld Jenny. "God's blood, *gorgio*, what are you doing here? Get out!" Waving her scrawny arm toward the tent flap, she screeched, "Get back to work!" Then, as the flap lifted once more and two giggling, rosy-cheeked wenches entered, Rosa's voice turned wheedling. She waved her customers to the rickety bench beside the table. "Come, pretty ones, let Rosa foretell your destiny." Glaring at Jenny over the girl's heads, she motioned for her to leave.

Jenny tried to regain her composure as she stood in the shadow of a ramshackle booth. Now that the danger of apprehension was past, her heart raced suffocatingly, choking the breath in her throat. Oh, she would make Manuel pay for his teasing arrogance . . .

"Come, let's go back to camp. There's nothing for you here. I could've told you Rosa would scream at you. She doesn't like to be disturbed at so serious a business."

Gasping at the unexpected voice, Jenny spun about to find Manuel waiting for her in the dim, refuse-filled alley between the stalls. He held out her tray of charms, having retrieved them from the dirt.

"I'm not coming with you!"

"I can carry you like a sack of grain. An undignified exit, but a speedy one."

Jenny fought the anger that speeded her heart until it virtually leaped from her body, visibly fluttering the thin fabric of her tight black bodice. Manuel saw it too, or perhaps it was not her fluttering heart he studied with such intensity.

"You give me little choice."

Keeping her distance, Jenny hobbled beside him through the noisy fairground, wincing at each thrust from pointed sticks and rocks.

"Where are your shoes?" Manuel demanded, noting her gasps of pain.

"My shoes fell off in a ditch over a week ago."

They said no more.

Old men, women, and children were left behind to guard the gypsy camp during the day; great smiles of joy wreathed those dark faces as Manuel strode among them. Tears glittered in many a black eye as he conversed fluently with them in their Romany tongue.

Manuel's welcome was like one afforded royalty, Jenny thought, as she waited for the greetings to end. King Charles himself could expect no more. The gypsy received his people's homage with graciousness, yet he still bore that overwhelming air of arrogance that had set them at odds. Jenny shifted her weight from one foot to the other, becoming conscious of the blood trickling from her cuts.

"Ready?" Manuel asked at last, pushing up his hat brim to wipe his sweating brow.

"Certainly, Your Majesty, I was waiting for you to finish receiving your subjects."

Manuel's dark face tightened at her sarcasm, but he said nothing, ushering her inside Rosa's wagon. Jenny sank thankfully on her narrow bed, slung hammock fashion from the wooden sides of the gypsy caravan. She was hungry, dusty, and humiliated; her feet stung and her belly gnawed.

"Rita's cooking rabbit stew. I'll get you some," he offered, his voice softening as he saw her weariness.

When he returned Manuel carried two wooden bowls brimful of succulent stew. He set one before Jenny on the rickety table at the rear of the wagon. The delicious rabbit stew was fragrant with a dozen mysterious spices whose flavors were unknown to her. While they ate, Manuel watched her, his unblinking green gaze disconcerting.

"Why do you stare at me so?" Jenny demanded at last, unable to remain silent any longer.

"You don't look like Josie—at least, I don't feel brotherly toward you," he replied with a grin.

"Well, as I don't feel like your sister, we should both be happy."

His thick lips twitched in amusement at her scorn, but Manuel let her remark pass. "Rosa means well, but you need shoes. And you should be dressed as a *gorgio*. Not in a hundred years would any discerning man mistake you for a gypsy wench."

Surprised by his statement, Jenny managed a tentative smile. "I'd be grateful for a pair of shoes. My feet hurt so much I can hardly walk."

"Wait here then and I'll bring some to you."

Jenny expected to have to wait some time for her shoes; she was surprised when Manuel appeared a few minutes later carrying a bulging saddle bag over his broad shoulder. Without ceremony he dumped the bag's contents on Rosa's bed, dropping a heap of brightly colored silk and satin on the embroidered counterpane.

"Oh, how lovely!" Jenny gasped in delight, caressing the jewel-bright fabrics. There was a full gold satin skirt and an embroidered lavender silk bodice. The tissue-fine lawn chemise was trimmed with wide galloon lace. Beneath the mound of fabric she found a pair of narrow, square-toed shoes of smooth brown leather, topped by a lavender silk rosette. As she lovingly held the dress against her body, Jenny discovered worn spots on the skirt hem, a stain at the bodice armholes, and a frayed patch at the chemise neckline.

Noting her disappointment, Manuel shrugged. " 'Tis the best I have to offer, my fine lady—take it or leave it."

"I'll take it," Jenny decided at once, thrilled to have such finery, even though it was secondhand. "Where did the clothes come from?"

"A woman should never ask such a question."

"Why not?"

"She might learn something she doesn't wish to know."

"Don't answer then, it's all the same to me."

Manuel grinned as she turned her back on him. "I assure you, the lady divested herself of the garments willingly . . ."

Jenny rounded on him, her cheeks flushed. "I don't want to hear any more."

Unabashed, Manuel continued, "For my great services, surely it was the least she owed."

"You actually stole some poor wench's clothes?"

"She never missed them, for when I left she was sleeping like the dead."

Jenny looked at him, wondering if he spoke in jest. By the knowledgeable expression playing about his wide-lipped sensual mouth, by the way his gaze lingered overlong on the display of flesh poking above her bodice, Jenny was assured of an answer to her question. Some squire's unsuspecting daughter had been blinded by Manuel's dark gypsy charm, paying with her gown for her foolishness. As he held her gaze, Manuel's green eyes suddenly changed expression; a shock wave passed through Jenny's body. It was not difficult to see why some nameless wench had parted so readily with her favors, for he possessed an intriguing, earthy attraction to match his roguish manner.

"You're despicable," Jenny snapped, guarding against any softening of her decision to dislike him.

"Never once did she call me that."

"Well, if I'm to wear such finery, first I must wash. Sister or no, I'll thank you to let me alone while I dress." For a moment Jenny thought he was going to refuse, for his eyes darkened and his facial muscles tautened beneath his smooth brown skin.

"Certainly, my lady." Bowing to her in mocking fashion, Manuel swept his broad-brimmed hat from his head to reveal an unfashionable short mop of springy black curls, gleaming bright as a blackbird's wing in the sunlight. He backed from the wagon. "I'll visit my subjects," he said sarcastically. Then he spun about and strode toward the group gathered around the central campfire.

When Jenny had washed her face and hands in the pewter basin, shivering at the chill of fresh drawn spring water, she stripped off her gaudy gypsy finery. Sighing with pleasure, she donned the full-sleeved chemise. The thin fabric was almost transparent, revealing her nipples as the lace-trimmed bodice hugged her full breasts like a second skin. The gold skirt fitted perfectly at the waist; the short-sleeved lavender bodice, lavishly embroidered with yellow and white silk roses, was too snug. Jenny slackened the lacing to accommodate her more generous figure, trying to inch the frilled chemise higher to conceal a little more of her flesh, which bulged provocatively above the lace-trimmed neckline.

An unexpected sound drew her attention, and she saw Manuel swinging agilely into the wagon. "Ready?" he asked, his face lighting with a smile of approval at her vastly improved appearance.

"Would it make any difference if I wasn't?"

"No—oh, come, enough battling. There's no need to hotly defend your modesty. Besides, you look not like a trembling virgin to me. I'll warrant at least one man's uncovered your secrets. Am I right?"

"Seeing as you're such an expert, why bother to ask?" she snapped, trying to straighten her hair, which hung to her waist in hopeless snarls and tangles.

"Here." Manuel handed Jenny an engraved silver-handled

brush. Lounging against the wall, he watched with satisfaction while she brushed her billowing chestnut tresses, an unfathomable expression crossing his dark face. "A suggestion, my lady," he said when she was finished. Stepping forward, Manuel deftly flicked curls toward Jenny's face and onto her brow. He coiled a twist of bright hair over her shoulder.

"What are you doing?"

"There, now you rival La Belle Castlemaine for beauty," Manuel explained softly, his eyes bright. "Nay, do not disarrange my handiwork," he protested suddenly when Jenny would have destroyed his arrangement. " 'Tis all the latest fashion. The curls even have names: on the brow, favorites; against the cheek, confidants; over the shoulder, heartbreakers."

"And how are you privy to such feminine fashion?"

"Ah, you underestimate my charms, mistress. Once we reach London town, I assure you, Manuel has no need to settle for dockside drabs. There are many ribboned bitches in Whitehall itself whose tails wag merrily at the sight of . . ."

"Manuel! Manuel!" A woman's shrieks of joy startled them. Marta scrambled inside the wagon, her flashing black eyes brimming with tears of delight. At the unexpected sight of Jenny dressed in such finery, Marta paused, her full mouth tightening with anger.

"Marta! 'Tis too long since I've seen you," Manuel cried in surprise, seizing Marta's shapely body and crushing it against his own in a breathtaking embrace.

"What's she doing here?" Marta demanded, her eyes turning hostile.

"Here? Why, 'tis where she lives, sweeting," Manuel replied as he spun Marta about. Feasting his eyes on her neat waist and full breasts, he seized her once more, sinking his hands in her streaming raven hair as he pressed her full mouth beneath his, devouring her soft red lips.

Jenny quickly turned from their embrace, overcome with pain at the sight of such unbridled passion, finding it more than she could bear. All the cherished memories of her lover flooded back, until she bit her lips to contain her grief. Seeing Manuel kiss the gypsy girl so warmly brought a stabbing reminder of the delight of Kit's mouth and his strong, protective arms. Never again would she know his touch. A lump rose in her throat, borne by the swift, throbbing tide of heartache. Blindly Jenny stared at the gaudy, poppy-embroidered curtain covering the back window of the wagon; the blood-red flowers blurred together to form a puddle, much as dear Kit's blood must have done on that fateful day aboard *The Royal Prospect* . . .

"She's gone."

From a great distance Jenny heard Manuel's voice, the faint lilt of an unknown accent marking his words. He touched her shoulder, spinning her about. Through a mist of gray his features swam into focus. Impatiently she dashed her hand across her face; forcing her lips to remain steady, Jenny rapped, "Good. I expected you to drag the wench to bed," in continuance of the prickly manner of their relationship.

"Enough!" Manuel's voice turned harsh as he angrily seized her wrists. Noting the tears trembling on her thick dark lashes, the quiver of her full pink mouth, his voice softened as he asked, "Why do you weep?"

"I was feeling sorry for myself. You needn't concern yourself about me."

Manuel puzzled over the source of her sudden grief. Then, as enlightenment dawned, he said, "Were I half the conceited dolt you suppose me to be, I'd swear you wept because I kissed Marta instead of you. Yet he who has the right to your kisses is gone—am I right?"

Jenny nodded, not trusting herself with words, amazed by the depth of his intuition.

"And you love him dearly?" Manuel received another nod in answer to his question. "He left you—no, not that." Hastily he changed course as her head wagged negatively. "Is he dead?"

"Aye, lost at sea. I knew him such a short time." Jenny hung her head, feeling suddenly small and vulnerable, disarmed by grief.

"Sometimes lack of time serves to heighten emotion," Manuel observed softly. " 'Tis not a new affliction, Jenny, for such partings are older than time itself. Remember the sweetness of his love if you wish, but do not torture yourself with his memory."

Sage advice. Jenny raised her head, looking Manuel full in the face. "Thank you for your kindness," she whispered. "I did not mean to be shrewish."

"Come, we must get back to the fair," Manuel said gruff-

ly. "Rosa will be beside herself with rage. I've a performance to give and here the sun already hangs low in the
sky."

Jenny blinked in surprise as he rapidly divested himself of
his green velvet coat and lace-trimmed shirt. Now Manuel
stood before her, naked to the waist, unexpectedly revealing
bulging muscles rippling beneath an unblemished skin the
color of light ale.

"A per—performance," Jenny faltered, averting her gaze
from his broad shoulders, from his brawny chest with its
sparse pelt of tightly curled black hair.

"Didn't you know? I'm a strong man, world renowned for
my great feats of strength," Manuel boasted with a laugh,
striking an attitude as he flexed his muscles for her benefit.
"This afternoon you can go round with the hat to earn your
keep."

He helped her from the wagon. Delaying her a moment
between the shafts, his green eyes squinting against the bright
sunlight, Manuel said, "You're the loveliest *gorgio* bitch I've
ever laid eyes on. Work hard, and I promise to *buy* your next
gown."

Drawing in her breath in surprise at the intense expression
lighting his eyes, Jenny retreated a pace, overwhelmed by his
powerful masculinity. Noting her reaction, Manuel threw back
his head and his laughter pealed out.

"Fear not, virtuous one, the stars that guide our futures
have ordained Marta to be my woman. In order to bring
prosperity to our tribe, I must lead it and she is the one I must
marry." Then leaning toward her, his dark face shadowed,
his hot breath stirring the hair on her brow, Manuel whispered, "God's love, how much I wish the stars were wrong.
But then, Rosa would never sanction me planting a *gorgio*."
And with this, Manuel grabbed Jenny's hand and raced her
toward the noisy fairground.

Begging for consideration, Jenny stumbled about in the
brown leather shoes, her feet turning over in the ruts as she
discovered the unknown wench's feet were several inches
longer than her own.

"What is it now?" Manuel stopped, frowning impatiently.
"Can you still not walk?"

"The shoes are too big," Jenny protested, dropping thankfully on the grass.

Cursing over the unexpected delay, Manuel ripped clumps of dried grass from the meadow and stuffed them into the toes of the shoes. "Here, try those."

Walking carefully in her grass-stuffed shoes, Jenny maintained a sedate, ladylike pace as they crossed the meadow.

"I'll go on ahead," Manuel suggested, pausing a moment. "All you need do is look pretty, little *gorgio*—it should be the easiest day's work you've done in your life."

With that, he left her, running fleet-footed over the uneven ground until he disappeared between the ramshackle wooden booths. As he ran Manuel snatched a hot mutton pasty from a pie stall where the stout goodwife had momentarily stooped to adjust her shoe.

Jenny watched him, her emotions jangling as she discovered she was disturbed, repelled, and attracted all at the same time by this gypsy strongman who had so confidently revealed his own preordained destiny as savior of his tribe.

During the long summer days, Jenny traveled with Rosa's gypsy band as they meandered along leafy Surrey lanes, halting at fairs that grew successively poorer. Eventually the villages all began to look alike. Jenny was frequently tempted to run away from her gypsy protectors as they neared London, yet their presence gave her that needed sense of security. There were far too many vagrants abroad for comfort, all seemingly headed for the teeming metropolis where they expected to take advantage of untold riches that merely awaited their arrival. Wisely Jenny kept all plans for flight to herself; she knew not what Rosa intended for her future, but she suspected the old gypsy would be furious to learn she had been used.

By now income had virtually dried up. It was time for the gypsies to resort to more devious methods to stay alive. Because she was *gorgio*, Jenny was chosen for the important role of "poisoning the pig," a colorful expression that meant exactly what it said. A fat porker, housed in a pen next to a ramshackle farmhouse beside the stream encirling the camp, was to be the hapless victim.

Jenny's conscience made her hesitate to practice such deception; not until her gnawing pangs of hunger grew acute did she abandon her principles. On the pretext of pausing while on a country walk, Jenny asked the farmer's wife for a cup of water from her well. Readily ingratiating herself with the talkative goodwife, on her return through the farmyard Jenny fed the sow a compressed sponge dipped in lard. The animal greedily gobbled the delicacy. Once inside her body the offering would swell, blocking the sow's intestines and killing her.

To make sure the family would not eat the dead sow themselves, Rosa, going from door to door selling clothes pegs, foretold a terrible ailment destined to kill the farmer's prize sow. The farmwife, who had expected naught but good tidings from her doorstep fortune telling, angrily shooed Rosa away with a broom. Undaunted, Rosa returned the following night, offering to cart away the dead animal before the contagious disease spread to the farmer's cows and chickens. Thus the dead sow was triumphantly borne back to the camp, where for several days the gypsies feasted off succulent roast pork.

"You're going to be one of us yet," Rosa commended Jenny as she handed her a bowl of stew. "No one guessed you were anything other than a lady on a country walk. If one of *us* had gone near the pig, the farmer would have set his dogs on us."

After thanking Rosa for the unexpected words of praise, Jenny retired to the shade of the wagon to eat her supper. She still felt unwelcome beside the family fire, for the gypsies often conversed in their own tongue, deliberately excluding their *gorgio* guest from all discussions. Tonight, as she dozed in the warm, firelit dusk, Jenny understood snatches of conversation spoken in Romany English patois.

"She'll never be one of us—she's *gorgio*!" Marta reminded her aunt with a scowl, turning to glare at Jenny where she leaned against the wagon wheel. "Sometimes I think you forget she's not your Josie!"

Rosa raised dark, hooded eyes, a warning frown crossing her face, but she did not reprimand Marta. As the niece of the family's matriarch, Marta was allowed privileged speech denied others; the fact that she was Manuel's ordained bride was a further point in her favor.

"I forget nothing. She provided food, how would you quarrel with that?"

"There's no quarrel with it. I'm grateful for the food," Marta mumbled, growing shamefaced before Rosa's penetrating gaze.

"Then shut your mouth and let me do the thinking."

Rita watched her daughter slink away to the back of the wagon. "She's jealous, Rosa, 'tis nothing more."

"Jealous! Of the *gorgio*?"

"She thinks Manuel and she . . . well, you know." Rita swallowed, unprepared for the anger rippling over her sister's haggard face.

"Never! Manuel is to lead you one day. A *gorgio* woman will never be at his side! He alone is capable of bringing a turn in our fortunes!"

"Perhaps not at his side, Rosa, you misunderstand. I meant only that he . . ."

"I know what you meant." Rosa stared broodingly into the campfire, her black eyes fathomless as the flames danced a garish pattern across her face. Her sister leaned forward to catch her words as Rosa spoke her thoughts aloud. "Journeys by sea and land . . . fortune and ill fortune . . . I saw it clear. Danger for more than one man if he falls under her spell. There's the sign of royalty in her palm. Likely she'll form a close attachment with a man of high birth—mayhap a king . . ."

"A king!" Rita's bronzed face tightened. "Manuel's ordained by the fates to rule as our king."

"I told you!" hissed Marta, who had rejoined them at the fire. "A thousand curses on the *gorgio*!"

"Ssh!" her mother cautioned warily, "the *chovihani* still speaks."

"Sickness and death will strike many of our people," Rosa droned on, her face hard as granite. "Yet Manuel will live to lead you into the sun."

Her sister and her niece waited breathlessly for Rosa's further revelations, but when she stood, shaking her tangled locks as if awakening from sleep, they both knew she would reveal no more tonight.

Numb with surprise at what she had overheard, Jenny drew farther into the shadows, hoping the gypsies had forgotten her presence. Some of the exchange had been lost to her, but she was alarmed by the flaring hatred she had seen on Marta's face. Though Manuel's sexual interest in her came as no surprise, the revelation of her own hallowed destiny did. A king! Surely Rosa was mistaken, for how would she attract a king's attention? Unless Marta's suspicions were founded after all! Had the omnipotent fates linked her destiny with that of the chosen king of this gypsy band?

Chapter 5

The milling throng surrounding the county courthouse cheered and hooted as Jem Skeffles, heavily manacled, was taken to the cart that was to transport him back to prison. The raffish, dark-eyed highwayman was garishly bedecked for the occasion in soiled finery. His green petticoat breeches sported yards of purple ribboned loops in bright contrast to his white velvet coat, spotted with blood, the sleeve rent in two by a bailiff's sword thrust. On his head the highwayman wore a battered beaver hat, which was sadly the worse for wear after a dousing by a summer thunderstorm on his way to trial in the morning.

"Go to hell with a smile on your lips," Manuel exhorted, waving his own black plumed hat in farewell to his condemned acquaintance.

Jenny shuddered at his suggestion; the nearby spectators laughed.

"Come, 'tis growing late," she reminded, trying to stand her ground as the crowd eagerly surged forward, anxious to catch a final glimpse of the straw-filled cart bearing away the notorious highwayman.

"Aye, 'tis time to start back," Manuel agreed reluctantly. " 'Tis a pity Jemmy's not hanging today. A hanging's a fine sight. All the wenches sport with the condemned—they throw him nosegays. It's a rousing sendoff to hell. And Jemmy deserves no less. No greater thief have I known—as a little lad he could steal the bibles from Cromwell's Ironsides, so nimblefingered was he. Faith, but he's had a grand life, that boyo. 'Tis a shame we won't be able to stay to see the hanging."

"Well, I'm not sorry, his trial was bad enough," Jenny remarked as she recalled the painted prostitutes who had called out witty quips in answer to the prosecutor's questions. Such a teaming uproar of a trial it had been, with peddlers bawling their wares and bold streetwalkers arranging future

63

assignations; the event was more like a sideshow than the execution of his Majesty's justice.

Several fine, gilded coaches, carrying splendidly dressed gentry, blocked the narrow roads leading to the courthouse. Inside the elaborate conveyances richly gowned court ladies fanned themselves languidly in the afternoon heat. Their delighted laughter greeted the bawdy sallies Jem Skeffles flung in their direction before he finally disappeared around a bend in the road.

The exit of the star attraction signaled an end to the merriment. Pie sellers, women bearing wicker baskets of pickled herrings, cockles, and prawns, ale sellers, prostitutes, and pickpockets flowed together in a motley tide, dispersing now that the excitement was over.

Raucous cries of "Buy my fine pies" deafened them as Manuel and Jenny extricated themselves from the odorous press of people, still in a holiday mood. Manuel lingered on the fringe of the crowd, alternately ogling the handsome women and plying his light-fingered skill.

Jenny stared enviously at the fine gentry inside their coaches, awed by the beautifully dressed women in patches and paint lolling against Spanish leather seats, all come down from London for a sight of the notorious highwayman. Jem Skeffles had selflessly given of himself on many an occasion in exchange for a lady's valuables; this amorous bent served merely to inflate an already colorful reputation.

For so important an event Jenny had worn her second-hand finery: Manuel his silver-laced leaf-green velvet suit. Though she wasn't sure if the gypsy expected to give assistance to his condemned friend, Jenny's apprehension had been great when they set out to the trial. As she left the campground Marta glared at her, hatred blazing like coals in her dark eyes, jealous that her beloved should have chosen the *gorgio* woman to accompany him to the spectacle. To Jenny's relief, she discovered that Manuel merely wished to lend moral support at his friend's trial; the evidence compiled against the highwayman was overwhelming, assuring him of a hasty dispatch at Tyburn.

Stopping the closest pie seller, Manuel purchased four pasties, using money still warm from its owner's pocket. The mutton was gristly and the gravy had congealed unpalatably inside rock-hard pastry, suggesting that the pies may not even have been fresh yesterday. But they were both so ravenously hungry they eagerly devoured the inferior fare, washing it down with a flagon of warm, flat ale.

Jenny noticed a splendid gentleman in a black, full-bottomed wig ogling her, his wide mouth curving in a definite smile of invitation when he caught her eye. She would have returned his smile but Manuel seized her arm and yanked her about, marching her purposely toward the crossroads.

"Why did you do that? You spent enough time ogling the ladies! Besides, he was a very handsome gentleman," Jenny protested heatedly, wrenching free of his grasp. "Can I not at least return a smile?"

" 'Tis different for me. Besides, I would not want to have to murder yon rich bastard!" Manuel growled, his face dark with anger. "See this!" With shaking hand he pointed to the angry scar beginning to fade on his cheek. "I've tangled with the gentry before—the bastard who marked me for life was such as he. A gypsy's life's worth no more than horse dung to them." Manuel spat on the ground in contempt. "I'll meet yon bastard again someday and by God he'll pay for this." Absently he stroked the puckered scar. "Life may have improved for us now that old sobersides Cromwell's laid to rest, but 'tis not secure enough to engage such as he and hope to live through it," he added, scowling at the gilded coach with its scented, lace-bedecked occupant.

"You need not engage him. He merely smiled at me."

"Aye, smiled—and what next? He'd have you tilted arse up in his fine coach in no time, you lack-wit. His kind are all alike."

"I hate it when you act as if you own me."

"You're under my protection. Would you want me to withdraw it and allow Rita and Marta to decide your fate?" Manuel challenged, seizing her wrist and spinning her about. "You'd be selling flesh in short order if they had their way. 'Tis only through Rosa's good graces you stay—and mine."

Flinching slightly beneath the fire of temper blazing in his eyes, Jenny made no further protest.

As they walked along the flinty road, the sun raised waves of heat from the roadway puddles. The grass verges were ablaze with scarlet corn poppies and white flowery heads of yarrow, while purple clumps of "love in idleness" peeped shyly from the moss beneath the trees. Birds sang overhead; bees and butterflies flitted from flower to flower. Above them the blue July sky was cloudless. A warm breeze, heavy with the cloying fragrance of limes, wafted over the hedgerows.

Presently they rested, basking in the scented warmth. The languid breeze stirred the fine curling hair on Jenny's brow and danced fretwork patterns across her closed eyelids as alder branches whispered overhead.

"Christ! I'm on fire with these damned nettles."

Manuel's bellow of distress shattered Jenny's feeling of contentment. Sitting up, she turned to see him hopping barefoot out of the tall bracken. He was such an amusing sight that she had to stifle laughter as she helpfully suggested, "Here's a clump of dock leaves."

With a grunt of thanks Manuel snatched handfuls of the wide green leaves, laying their cooling balm on top of the stinging patches of nettle rash. He wrapped more burdock leaves about his ankles. Gradually the fire cooled and he paddled his feet in the shallows of the lapping stream. His stolen boots, though of fine black leather, pinched; when he took them off to rest his feet, Manuel had stumbled into a clump of stinging nettles hidden among the knee-high bracken edging the wood.

"How far is it back to camp? Shouldn't we be going?" Jenny asked, reluctant to leave the sun-dappled peace of this meandering stream.

"No more than two miles," Manuel replied, swishing his feet in the cooling water. "We've plenty of time left."

Jenny wished she could take off her clothes and bathe in the stream. The cool, soothing water felt heavenly against her hot blistered feet. A thicket of willow and alder screened them from the road, but Manuel's presence forbade such indulgence. They had spied the inviting stream from the lane, and a break in the hedge afforded them entry to this spacious estate where they now trespassed, recklessly gambling against seizure by an irate gamekeeper. Beyond the beech wood could be seen the twisted rose brick chimneys of the spacious country house to which this land belonged.

"I wish we could go closer and see the fine house," Jenny said wistfully, straining to glimpse its gables through the swaying trees. "It's like a palace! Whoever lives there must be immensely rich to own all this land."

"Aye, rich indeed," Manuel agreed, his dark face turning solemn. "What's it like to live in a house?"

"I've never lived anwhere nearly as grand as that, but it's vastly different from life on the road."

"Do you prefer it?"

"Of course! I'm not born a gypsy like you. I like a roof over my head. And I like a bed with clean covers. I want to wash with soap and know where my next meal's coming from . . ."

"Then why do you stay with us?" he snarled, scowling as her ready answer tumbled forth to displease him.

"Because I've no one in the world beside some distant relatives in London. Besides, you forget, I'm wanted for murder in Addston. Your life's become my life, whether I want it or no."

"Someday I'll have a proper roof over my head. No leaking *vardo* for me! This wandering's no good when a man grows old."

"Isn't it your destiny to lead the gypsies?" Jenny asked in surprise, recalling their conversation on the day they met.

"Destiny! Do you call performing like a dray horse for a crowd of addlepated yokels, or foraging the countryside for anything portable, destiny?"

At least Manuel's scornful retort helped explain his frequent absences from camp. Several times a week he rode to an unknown destination, only catching up to the ramshackle gypsy caravan when they had set up camp in the next town. The horses, sheep, and assorted goods Manuel brought back with him must have been stolen. Jenny could only guess his connection with Jem Skeffles, the condemned highwayman. No wonder the gypsies must constantly be on the move! Though a fair might last two weeks, they usually spent no more than three days at the same place. Knowing there were many secrets these dark-skinned vagabonds did not wish to share with their *gorgio* companion, Jenny had never questioned Rosa about her son's secret forays.

"I thought you enjoyed being a gypsy, Manuel."

"This life was thrust on me as a child. I'd no choice in the matter. That doesn't mean I like it," Manuel snapped, drying his feet with a handful of grass. "Besides, I'm not full gypsy—my father was an Irish farmer from County Wicklow. Turned off his land by a fat, pompous bastard called Lord Ross, he turned tinker to keep body and soul together. As soon as I was old enough to understand, I vowed to reclaim the land." Manuel's eyes narrowed menacingly as he dwelled on the burning fire of his long-harbored resentment. "The first day I set foot on our land his fine Lordship's arrogant nephew had me clapped in jail—God, how much I hate him. 'Tis many years now, but I won't forget the debt he owes me. Ten acres my father had—chickens, cows—the gentry wanted to build a kennel for their bloody hunting hounds. For that my inheritance was stolen! Someday I'll get it back, though it take a lifetime to accomplish. I've vowed before God to have satisfaction, whether it be with the old lord or the young.''

Jenny stared at his dark face suffused by hatred, surprised by his vehemence, surprised also to discover he did not enjoy his reckless, vagabond way of life. '' 'Tis where you get your green eyes then, from your Irish father.''

''Aye, and the brogue I carry is his. Can ye not hear it in my speech?''

''There's a lilt there, but not knowing it for Irish, I was none the wiser. Why did your father take up with the gypsies? They have such scorn for *gorgios*—I of all people should know that.''

Manuel's face softened slightly in sympathy. He laid his hand on her arm as he said, ''I'm sorry they've not been kind to you, Jenny, but you must try to understand why. They distrust that which they don't know. We steal not from each other, nor do we cheat one of our own—'tis a different story where *gorgios* are concerned. That's how they see you—as one of the enemy.''

''You're the first one who's put it in words.''

''That's how they regarded my father when he first took up with the gypsies. His name was Patrick Brandon. He had no education, but he was so sharp that he picked up their gypsy tongue the better to woo the prettiest of old Bias Krasko's three daughters. He won their admiration. And because of some of their primitive religious practices, on further examination he became an object of good fortune for the tribe.''

Manuel gave Jenny a knowing grin, but he did not elaborate further.

''She was the prettiest?'' Jenny asked, hardly able to conceal her surprise.

''Rosa was his second wife. Nation was my mother. She died birthing me the year before Cromwell's men drove us from the commonland and set us on our wanderings. After Nation died, my father took Rosa to wife. She has raised me as her own. Polygamous marriage amongst my people's not unknown,'' he added. ''At least my father waited until Nation was dead to take Rosa to wife.''

A sudden squawking of birds alerted them to danger. From the wood came a rapid beating of wings as a flock of cooing wood pigeons emerged, disturbed from their nesting. Warily Jenny and Manuel waited, poised for flight. Nothing more menacing than a fox appeared; standing a moment on the fringe of the trees, bewildered at the unexpected sight of humans, he turned and plunged back into the bracken.

Grinning at her, Manuel edged closer, relieved to find no gamekeeper bearing down on them. "There are many strange customs surviving amongst the Romany. Though they accept the Christian God and take Saint Sarah for their patron saint, they also revere a lingam as a source of good fortune." He reached for the small gilded fish swinging on a cord around Jenny's neck.

"A lingam? That is what Rosa called this charm."

" 'Tis an old phallic symbol. The fish, the horn, the haw-thorn symbols fastened above our doors and windows to keep out the evil one, all are phallic symbols from an ancient time. You did not know what this innocent little fish symbolized did you, *gorgio*?"

Jenny dropped her gaze from his, seeing something in his eyes she had not seen before, something that heightened her discomfort.

"This is the symbol of the greatest force of nature. A man's organ is a source of well-being and good fortune to the gypsy people. The more generously endowed he is, the more fortune will smile upon him and his people. It is a belief Rosa's tribe have held since antiquity. Because of certain God-given gifts, I have been selected to restore our sagging fortunes. Though I would choose otherwise, for my people's sake it is the course I must follow."

Such confidences paved the way for Jenny to disclose the details of her crime, for no longer did any barrier exist between them now that Manuel had revealed the very intimate aspects of his selection as savior of his tribe. Jenny told him the whole story of Tom Dunn's lechery; there was no reaction of shock or surprise on Manuel's solemn face as he listened intently to her tearful account. He was the first among the gypsy band to hear any but the constable's version of her crime.

When Jenny was finished there was a silence between them. Manuel stared up at the cloudless blue sky, not meeting her eyes when he asked in a strained voice, "And what about him—your lover?"

The subject was a painful one, but she forced her voice to remain steady as she said, "He was a sea captain on his way to London to meet with the King."

Manuel was definitely impressed, but he could not keep the trace of aggression from his voice, as he said, "I knew he must have been a rich man. Meeting with the King—I had no idea he was of so great an importance."

"He shared King Charles' exile after Worcester. He was a gentleman from the West country."

"After we crossed the water from Ireland, we made our home in Cornwall. Surrounded by sea, rocky, free—it's a land apart. Perhaps I'll take you there someday."

Smiling at his suggestion, Jenny shook her head. "No, Manuel, already your betrothed hates me for sharing these hours with you, let alone wandering the length and breadth of the country at your side. Will you and she soon be wed?"

He shrugged his broad shoulders. Delving in his pocket, Manuel produced a silver snuffbox, acquired a few hours before. He took a generous pinch of the white powder, then began to sneeze convulsively until tears ran down his cheeks.

Jenny laughed at his predicament, until she too found tears in her eyes. Whether they were solely tears of humor or more from pain over rekindled memories of Kit, she did not know. Whatever had caused her heightened emotion, Jenny grew wary of her own treacherously vulnerable state. Her unease increased as Manuel rolled toward her. He plucked a plumy stalk of sweet grass, trailing it over her face as he smiled down at her where she lay bathed in sunlight.

"Someday I suppose I'll marry Marta," he said thoughtfully. "But not this year. I've not enough money set aside. If the London fences are good to me, when the fair is done, I'll have several bags of silver for my pains. Before I die, Jenny, I'm going to live as a gentleman. 'Tis a solemn promise I made long ago as a ragged, barefoot brat, when they rode by on their fine horses and forced me off the road. Every time I brush with their world, it only reinforces my vow to join it." His face darkened as he gazed far beyond her head into the cloudless blue distance, focusing on some faraway point unseen by others. "May they all rot in hell," he growled, his mouth tightening, "including the bastard who cleaved my cheek in two. The gentry are all tarred with the same brush.

They even look alike. That bastard who slit me with his sword had a look on him of Lord Ross's arrogant swine of a nephew, and, had my sense not told me otherwise, I'd have sworn they were the same. God rot him, for what he did to me! How bitter it is to be denied revenge. It would have given me the greatest of pleasure to have slit his aristocratic nostrils in the gypsy fashion—his lily-handed leman would have none of him then! Nay, Jenny, I'm no gypsy at heart. Leading the gypsy tribe to glory is Rosa's dream, not mine.''

''Does she know how you feel?''

Manuel hooted in derisive laughter. ''Do you think me mad? Of course she doesn't know. Besides, she's *chovihani*—a witch. I don't want my liver turned to stone or my eyes to pebbles. No, you alone, little *gorgio*, share my terrible secret.''

As he gazed down at her the intense expression in his green eyes sent a ripple of sensual anticipation through Jenny's body. Alarmed by the unexpected reaction, she sat up, glancing at the cloudless blue sky. ''Shouldn't we start back?'' she suggested, making an effort to still the flutter in her throat as he continued to look at her. By sharing such confidences the invisible barrier she had maintained between them had fallen; Jenny did not welcome the change. Before this afternoon she had successfully turned aside all of Manuel's romantic overtures, knowing her own abysmal loneliness would not allow her to remain aloof in the face of tenderness. Though Kit was dead, his shadowy presence was with her always, reminding her of the depth of their brief, ill-starred love. Jenny's feelings for another man could never attain such depth, yet it was hard to resign herself to a loveless existence within the shadowy memories of the past.

''Go back, what's your haste? We've plenty of time yet,'' Manuel dismissed, moving closer. His strong brown hand sought hers. The touch of his hot fingers released a mounting wave of excitement that surged through her body. For the first time Jenny really looked at him, forgetting he was a gypsy, forgetting he was Rosa's son, remembering only that he was a man. The discovery shocked her. His wide-set green eyes framed by a heavy fringe of black lashes held hers, speaking such forbidden things, though Manuel's full, wine-dark lips never moved. His sun-bronzed skin was stretched taut over prominent cheekbones; his strong nose had a flattened area on the bridge. Suddenly Jenny realized she wanted to touch his hair, his mouth . . . "Manuel," she breathed, conscious of the blood roaring in her ears.

"Don't tell me we must return," he cautioned, his voice muffled and strained.

"We should, 'tis growing late," Jenny ventured as she tried not to meet his eyes, tried not to see what naked emotion blazed there. Manuel was so close that his silver coat buttons chilled her arm, making her shiver at the unexpected contact.

"You are very beautiful, Jenny," he breathed huskily. "And to me you are also *mokadi*, little *gorgio* bitch."

While he spoke Manuel ran his blunt fingers through the bright billow of her hair, smiling in admiration at its sun-steeped color.

Jenny looked up at him, finding his intriguing face shadowed as he leaned over her, his back to the sun. He had called her *mokadi*—the word Petrov had used that first night—taboo. Yet something about Manuel's taut, bronzed face told her he did not fear the consequences of breaking the unwritten commandment of his people. She should warn him to go no further. Even now, as his fingers wandered to her brow, she should protest the intimacy. But Jenny did not want him to stop. A hot primitive instinct shot from his muscular body to her own, arousing with invisible force. She had willingly surrendered her virginity to Kit, whom she had loved with all her heart; her body alone clamored for this Irish gypsy with his strange, foreign ways.

"*Gorgio* women have never kept you celibate before," she reminded, her red mouth curving in a smile, "*mokadi* or not."

"Ah, how well you know me." Manuel laughed, his confidence growing when she did not repel his advances. This moment was what he had worked toward since the first day he had laid eyes on her. "But with them I never felt the way I feel about you," he added huskily.

Jenny satisfied her curiosity about the texture of his skin, shivering at the hot smooth contact beneath her fingertips. "And how do you feel about me?"

"I love you."

His words, spoken with such passion, startled her. Jenny had expected Manuel to confess desire for her, but never to reveal love. "Love!" she repeated, her voice breaking on the word, as a haunting picture of Kit's handsome face flitted through her mind and was gone.

"Question me not," Manuel commanded, his face intense. "Forget all loves you have known before. Manuel does not tempt the evil one for a chance passion. What I feel for you in my soul surpasses everything I've ever felt before."

Taken back by his unexpected declaration, Jenny gazed into Manuel's dark-lashed eyes where black flecks marred the green iris. As he moved his head and the sun flushed his face with gold, the tawny gleam of a wild creature's stare glinted hypnotically in the green.

"How can you have such intense feelings for me?" she asked. "Never once have I . . ."

"Encouraged me," he supplied, his dark lips curving to reveal the flash of even white teeth. "What I feel in my heart is old as time itself. Now, little *gorgio* bitch, you talk too much and the hour grows late."

"What would you have me do instead?"

But Manuel did not treat her to an answer. His dark hands skimmed her sun-kissed cheeks and trailed across her warm, trembling mouth. For a moment Jenny panicked as his face loomed closer, but Manuel pressed her back on the lush carpet of grass. When his mouth engulfed hers with a tide of heat, Jenny thought she would faint, so overpowering was the sensation before memories of the man to whom she had given her heart flooded back to dim the fire. Manuel cupped her breast in his square hand, feeling the warm flesh through her embroidered lilac bodice; as he molded the pliant globe, sliding his thumb back and forth over her nipple until it stiffened beneath his touch, Jenny passed from memory to reality. At this moment her body ached beneath Manuel's expert manipulations. Kit was gone forever, but she still lived. And though she had vowed to remain loyal to her dead lover's memory, it was hard to exist on memories, however ecstatic they might be. The burning arousal of passion Kit had so expertly kindled on that moonlit night refused to obey such ideals.

"I think I'll die from the wonder of this," Manuel whispered against her ear, trailing his hot lips over her skin. "You feel just the way I dreamed you would."

He rapidly unlaced the top eyelets of her gown. Slipping his trembling hands inside her chemise, he eased her full breasts over the lace-edged fabric. He shuddered as he gently drew on her pink nipples, making them stand stiffly to attention. Manuel bent his head and teased her with his hot tongue, flicking her hard nipple with quicksilver movements.

No longer able to fight the building tension in her blood, Jenny imprisoned his head against her breast, delighting in the touch of his mouth. Manuel trembled against her, his muscles steel hard, quivering. Soon he moved his mouth in a passage of fire from her breasts, over her chest, to her throat; when he finally reached her mouth, Jenny was beside herself with passion. The hot fragrance of his lips covered hers, no longer tender, but hard and demanding. Manuel pried her lips apart, stabbing his tongue inside her mouth. Abandoning herself completely to a mounting surge of desire, Jenny responded to the novel arousal, sinking her own tongue deep within the furnace of his mouth.

After a few moments Manuel pulled away from her and swiftly divested himself of his velvet coat and lace-frilled shirt. Though she had often seen him stripped to the waist when he performed feats of strength for the wide-eyed fairgoers, never before had Jenny fairly assessed him as a man. He had always been just Manuel—the gypsy's son. Eyes narrowed, she allowed her gaze to roam over his bulging arms, the deep, heavily-muscled chest with its sparse pelt of coal black hair. So well developed, so smoothly fleshed, was Manuel's beautiful torso that it appeared to have been sculpted from marble the color of golden ale.

"I find you very beautiful," she breathed, her voice throbbing from somewhere deep within her chest.

He grinned with pleasure at her praise as he pressed his naked chest against hers. "Your body's far more appealing," he whispered, thrilling at the arousing pressure of her full breasts.

Jenny rolled his dark nipple between her finger and thumb, pleased when she heard his gasp of delight as the fire shot to his loins. Manuel pressed against her, his weight driving her deeper into the pliant earth as he imprisoned her with his superior strength. Jenny gasped at the delicious torture of ironhard muscle and bone conquering her own yielding softness.

"God's blood, how much I want you, *gorgio*," he rasped painfully.

They kissed deeply, then drew apart. Manuel smiled as her gaze wandered to the bursting pressure beneath his leaf green breeches. Taking her hand, he guided it to his swollen manhood, pleased by her shudder of delight as she explored the hard strength of his throbbing flesh. Fumbling, shaking with increased desire, he helped her to expose the secrets of his body.

Manuel's breathing grew shallower as he pushed Jenny's skirts to her thighs, stroking her silky flesh, exploring higher until he encountered the fiery center of her passion.

Jenny writhed beneath his hand. When at last Manuel knelt astride her thighs, his searing flesh demanding entrance, she sobbed deep in her throat. He plunged inside her like a bolt of flame. Writhing, Jenny dug her nails into his back, thrilling to the burning sensation consuming her belly. Suddenly Manuel moved too rapidly, sweeping her onward, no longer allowing her to bask in the delicious heat of mutual arousal. Jenny lost control of her passion and she plunged down, down, into warm, liquid blackness.

They lay still, their bodies entwined. Blackbirds trilled in the alder trees. Manuel suddenly withdrew from the pleasure of their embrace, leaving Jenny lonely and bereft. Grief replaced her joy as she futilely reached out for comfort as a name came to her bruised lips—and it wasn't "Manuel."

"You are mine," the gypsy vowed intently, his stern expression baffling as he studied her lovely face. "Nothing, or no one, can separate us now—except death."

Sadness and loss brought tears hovering near the surface as she looked at him etched dark against the golden sun. Manuel's earnest declaration should have thrilled her, but instead Jenny shuddered, for the fierce emotion suffusing his arresting face bore no resemblance to love!

Chapter 6

From atop a mound of earth amid the confusion of the Southwark fairground, Jenny had her first glimpse of London. For as long as she could remember she had dreamed about visiting this famed city. Beyond the wide silver ribbon of the Thames huddled a vast jumble of aged timbered buildings tottering along narrow, winding streets, their overhanging upper stories nudging gables over the cobblestones. A forest of church steeples thrust toward the clouds with great St. Paul's Cathedral, perched atop Ludgate Hill, dominating the skyline.

"Here, Jenny, the water's ice cold."

Berta offered her a brimming pitcher of water. Recently Jenny had made friends with the ragged little gypsy dancer who had entertained the Rose and Crown's patrons on the night she'd met Kit.

"Thank you, Berta. How did you know I was thirsty?"

Berta shrugged, her face wreathed in smiles at the knowledge that she had pleased her much admired friend. Her narrow, berry-brown face grew solemn as she studied the panoramic view that compeltely absorbed Jenny's attention. "Will you leave now?" she asked quietly.

Jenny swallowed in surprise at Berta's unexpected question. "As soon as I'm able," she confided after first glancing about to make sure they could not be overheard.

"Don't worry, I won't tell anyone." Berta clasped Jenny's hand in friendship; they stood, hands locked, until Berta abruptly turned away, a flood of emotion forcing her to leave her *gorgio* friend.

Jenny watched the small gypsy girl racing over the rutted ground, her thin figure rapidly disappearing in the crowd milling around the gaudily painted gypsy wagons. Berta was an orphan from a tribe whose welfare came under Rosa's jurisdiction. And though at first the dark-eyed girl's presence had awakened painful memories of Kit, Jenny soon warmed to her offer of friendship. It was good to have an ally in the camp. Since Manuel had openly taken her into his wagon, Jenny was shunned by the others. Toward their future king the gypsies' attitude had remained unchanged; the *gorgio* woman alone bore the brunt of their disapproval.

The scrubby fairground came awake long before first light. Bellowing voices mingled with the grunts and neighs of protesting animals serenaded Jenny as she jumped from Manuel's scarlet-painted *vardo*. The dew-wet grass felt cold against her bare feet.

"So, you're awake at last, you lazy sow!" Manuel reached for her and spun her against him, his warm body dispelling the early morning chill, which brought gooseflesh to her arms.

"Lazy! It's barely light," Jenny protested indignantly as she accepted his ardent kiss. This morning he was in a good humor, so she allowed herself to relax within the circle of his strong arms. Manuel's vagaries of mood made for a volcanic existence.

"The sun's almost up. Get your bread and ale and follow me. We must work the horses."

The six, high-spirited animals had been stolen from a horse trader who had ended his days moldering within a Surrey thicket. Manuel had coaxed the horses into performing a simple dance routine, winning their confidence with the utmost patience; only in his dealings with humans did he give rein to his vicious temper.

At first Jenny had been afraid of the horses, for although she was a country girl, she had never been closer to the snorting, flashing-eyed monsters than the door of the Rose and Crown's stable. When Manuel suggested she ride the lead animal while it performed to music, she was appalled. Gradually Jenny mastered her fear, until she was able to perch atop a pink-fringed saddlecloth while the bay mare pranced, tossing her proud head in time to Micah's shrill pipe; behind her, clinging to their horse's manes, rode Micah's chattering monkey troupe. The routine was elementary, but since the fair opened on the morrow, it was the best they could manage at such short notice.

"Rest!" Manuel shouted. He reached up and swept Jenny from the horse's back. As she came into his arms he crushed her against his broad chest, stifling her breath with a savage kiss of passion. "I've been away from you far too long," he breathed harshly, his green eyes holding hers, desire blazing undiminished in their depths.

Manuel slid his hand over the warm prominence of Jenny's breast, kindling a responsive fire within her blood. She shuddered at the unexpected reaction, swallowing the ache of unquenched passion that constricted her throat; then, as she smiled up at him, she became uncomfortably aware of Marta standing in the shadows. "Not here," Jenny cautioned hastily, watching Marta's blazing countenance over his broad shoulder. And she struggled for release from Manuel's demanding embrace.

A rough voice yelled for aid, the summons echoing from amidst a jumble of stacked poles and canvas. Abruptly Manuel released her and stepped back.

"Later tonight there'll be no prying eyes," he said, his harsh words both a threat and a promise.

Jenny's heart thudded unevenly as she watched him running to assist the others. She could not name the emotion Manuel aroused within her, but she doubted it was love. When she thought about him, she did not dissolve into liquid pleasure; at times she even came close to hating him for his vicious temper and the streak of brutality flickering beneath the surface of his complex personality. Yet again, when Manuel stirred her blood, as he had done a few moments ago, Jenny toyed with the idea of staying with him instead of going in search of her relatives in Cornhill.

" 'Tis a pity Micah doesn't own trained dogs," Marta drawled spitefully, as she strolled to Jenny's side.

Warily, Jenny eyed the other girl, conscious of the hostility rippling between them. "Why do you say that?"

"Then you could have headed the troupe as chief bitch!"

Stung by the insult, Jenny raised her hand to strike Marta's bronzed face; just in time she saw the gleam of steel in the gypsy woman's hand. Surprised by her unexpected strength, Jenny viciously twisted Marta's wrist, forcing her to loosen her grip. The dagger fell harmlessly at their feet.

Faces inches apart, all the burning hatred she felt for her rival apparent in her tawny features, Marta spat viciously, "Leave him alone, *gorgio*. He's mine! You can't alter the fates."

"Then take him! He's free to go. I don't lead him by a chain like one of Petrov's bears."

Marta could find no immediate response to Jenny's challenge. Their gazes locked, Marta muttered a string of Romany curses. Aloud she said, "You've been warned, so, if you fancy a watery bed, *gorgio* bitch, disregard my words. I'll warrant such a resting place will be far colder than the bed you share with him."

Jenny released Marta's slender wrist, conscious of her own pounding heart as she battled to control her temper. "I'm not the only one who's been warned."

They glared angrily at each other, then Marta stooped to retrieve her dagger from the grass. Without a backward glance she walked toward Rosa's wagon.

While the tents and wooden stalls were noisily assembled, droves of flotsam and jetsam from the nearby dockside dives greeted Rosa's band like long-lost relations. One-legged seamen with patches over their eyes and scabrous thieves and beggars, who appeared to have emerged from the very sewers of London, exchanged comradely greetings and shared cups of ale with the gypsies. Out of respect for Manuel, none of the men approached Jenny, yet her skin crawled beneath their lecherous scrutiny. Proud of his beautiful mistress, Manuel presented her to his underworld contacts: One-eyed Bill, Cross-eyed Jack, Loopy, Scam, and Gyves were important enough to merit formal introductions. Their stench made her retch as the vile odor from so many louse-ridden, unwashed bodies tainted the air.

To Jenny's great relief the rabble finally departed as the sinking sun heralded the beginning of their workday. Soon eager customers from London town would be ferried across the shimmering river to partake of the ribald entertainments of Southwalk beyond the Thames. By dark, thieves and cutthroats, pimps and panderers, took to the dismal streets to ply their dishonest trade; at sunrise they melted into the shadows, slinking like so many rats to their fetid haunts to await the blessed anonymity of night.

"Mistress, be thou aware of the error of thy ways?"

Jenny turned to see who was addressing her and was surprised to find not a ragged habitué of London's underworld, but a clean, if somewhat shabby, parson. The man wore a wide-brimmed black hat and a knee-length coat of shiny bombazine; in his hand he carried a dog-eared bible.

"Are you speaking to me?"

"Aye, for beside the Almighty thou art the only one to

hear.'' The pasty-faced man smiled, his thin lips parting to reveal discolored, uneven teeth. ''Come with me, mistress, 'tis no place for a gently reared wench. These sinners turned their backs on redemption long years ago. They are already doomed. But thou art different. There is still time. Come, take this chance for salvation. My wife will offer thee succor. Follow me, mistress.''

To her surprise, Jenny discovered she was on the verge of taking the persuasive minister at his word. These past hours spent in the company of such subhuman creatures, the like of which she had never dreamed existed, had destroyed her temptation to stay with Manuel. In the companionship of those coarse men, an unpleasant change came over him: no longer was he tender or compassionate toward her as he slid easily into their crude ways, waxing surprisingly fluent in London street jargon.

''Be gone, you sobersided hypocrite! We've no use for the likes of you!''

The sheer anger throbbing in Manuel's voice as he rounded the back of the red *vardo* sent a chill through Jenny's body.

''Ah, so you're with Manuel.'' The minister shook his head in disappointment. ''I should have known.''

''Aye, and if you don't want your throat slit, you'd best keep walking.'' Manuel grabbed the parson's bony shoulder in a steel-hard grip, moving him several feet across the rutted ground. ''Go save sinners elsewhere, parson, for, by God, if ever I find you talking to my woman again, you'll meet your maker far sooner than you dreamed possible.''

Jenny gasped in alarm, staying Manuel's arm as he shook the minister till his broad-brimmed hat fell over his eyes. '' 'Tis all right, Manuel, he does not offend me. Let him alone.''

''He offends me mightily,'' Manuel growled in anger. But he released the man.

The minister straightened his hat and smiled reproachfully at Jenny. ''Mistress, the House of the Crossed Keys beside St. Savior's is where I can be found should you change your mind. My wife will make you welcome. God be with you.''

Manuel advanced to strike the minister, but he neatly sidestepped between the wagons and was gone. ''Bastard!'' Manuel spat, allowing Jenny to detain him, though he longed to follow the fawning creature and beat him to a pulp.

''He means no harm,'' Jenny said, wary of the blazing

light in Manuel's eyes. "Preaching is what he is fitted for, and saving souls his lifework."

"Well, by Christ, he can save souls elsewhere. I've told the pasty-faced bastard as much two years running. Whether he offend you, or nay, if he comes back, I'll spit him. He professes to be saving children, going about asking them if they're mistreated—I'll have no more of it! I ran him off the fairground last year. If he wants to rescue starving waifs, the London streets can provide him with more than enough. I've a mind that he comes to spy. Probably sent by the bailiffs to see if we've stolen goods . . ."

"I feel he's sincere, misguided perhaps, but sincere."

For a long time Jenny lay awake in the darkness thinking about the pale-faced minister with his Christian mission. He would aid her in her flight from the gypsies. Yet she knew, if she disappeared tonight, Manuel would head directly for the House of the Crossed Keys, where he would swiftly silence the man's ministry. Give the incident time to fade from his mind, Jenny thought resignedly, stretching beneath the warm blanket in a state of drowsy semi-consciousness. Once the fair opened and the crowds choked the fairground, it would be a simple matter to slip away to the refuge beside St. Savior's church.

Frenzied activity heralded the opening day of the Southwark Fair on this warm September day in the fourth year of his Majesty's restoration, 1664. Amid great pomp, the Lord Mayor himself opened the annual event. The words of his lengthy speech were blown away on the breeze, yet the sight of the scarlet-and-gold-gowned aldermen, of the richly clothed townspeople, was reward enough for Jenny.

Manuel indulged her by allowing her to watch the ceremony, but once the fair had officially opened Jenny was swept away to prepare for their act, for he was anxious to earn all he could before the aleshops and the painted prostitutes relieved the Londoners of their gold.

After the first performance, Jenny rested in the shade of a canvas awning stretched between Manuel's and Rosa's wagon.

Nowadays the old gypsy woman spoke infrequently to Jenny, silence expressing her extreme disapproval of her son's involvement with the *gorgio*. Despite her new-found hostility, however, Rosa liked the pretty girl too much to choose the harsh solution suggested by her sister Rita.

"The performance was well done," Rosa complimented

gruffly. She was loath to offer praise, yet she knew how much courage it had taken for Jenny to master her fear of horses. The compliment given, Rosa swept toward the striped tent, where she hoped to swindle as many Londoners as possible before nightfall. A complete fortune telling ranged from one to ten pence, the charges shrewdly adjusted according to the customer's means.

Gray eyes closed against the sun's glare, Jenny tried to calm her jangled nerves. Performing for an audience astride the prancing mare had been an ordeal. The noisy fairground had spun dizzily into a blurred kaleidoscope of color and at every turn she had expected to fall to her death beneath the thudding hooves.

A rising murmur of admiration from the crowd sounded in the background as Manuel lifted bales and barrels to demonstrate his strength; for his spectacular finale he would lift a wagon, shouldering it for a full minute. Manuel's voice drifted to her on the breeze, his Irish brogue more pronounced as he bantered with the audience, softening them up for this extraordinary feat. Suddenly, above the sporadic laughter, above Manuel's showman's patter, came another sound: a high, anguished wail of pain echoed from the wagons to Jenny's right.

Leaping to her feet, Jenny darted toward the source of those inhuman cries. A crowd had already gathered about the wagons; the men shook their heads, the women wrung their hands, but no one attempted to relieve the suffering.

"What is it? What's happened?" Jenny demanded breathlessly as she joined the hovering crowd.

"A little wench is trapped yonder," a man explained, jabbing his forefinger toward a cloth merchant's loaded wagons.

Great bolts of linen, barrels of trimmings, and tall cones of thread had been stacked aboard the wagons, which groaned beneath the weight. The front vehicle, burdened beyond endurance, had cast a nearside wheel. And there, jutting from under the splintered wood, was a thin brown leg wrapped about in tattered purple cloth.

"Berta!"

Jenny flew to the wrecked wagon. Futilely she pushed against its unyielding bulk. In desperation she spun about to face the semi-circle of able-bodied men who stood helplessly by, shaking their heads over the tragedy. "Help me!" she beseeched them. "Help lift the wagon off her! She'll die if we don't free her from the weight!"

A couple of men stepped forward, but after lifting half-heartedly, they turned away. "Nay, mistress, 'tis no good. She be dead already. See, the wench doesn't move."

"She's likely unconscious with pain, you fools!"

Jenny crouched beside Berta and smoothed back her straggling black hair, which was plastered to her skin with sweat. The pulse in Berta's neck still beat strong beneath her fingers.

" 'Tis no use, mistress, we must hitch the horses to pull her free. There's no need for haste, we can do naught but bury the wench." The burly speaker helped Jenny to her feet. " 'Tis no cause for grief—she's but a gypsy brat."

Eyes blazing, Jenny slapped the man's ruddy face. Then spinning about, she ran as fast as she could to where Manuel was preparing for his grand finale, his audience already primed for the superhuman feat.

"Manuel! Manuel! Come quick! Berta's trapped beneath a wagon."

Manuel turned, displeased that Jenny should interrupt his performance at so crucial a point; however, one glance at her stricken face told him this was no idle request. He leaped forward, following her lead as she wove recklessly through the jostling crowd. They veered away from the central alley between the booths, heading for the jumbled outer fringe of stalls. A crowd of spectators, sensing a pressing tragedy, straggled behind them, gesticulating wildly to passersby as they encouraged others to follow and share the excitement.

Someone had already gone to fetch the dray horses tethered some distance away.

Manuel lost no time in assessing the situation. He shouldered the crumbling wagon, grunting and groaning as he heaved; his muscles bulged; his sinews strained like great knotted cords beneath his tawny skin until the loaded cart finally shifted, creaking as it raised. The awestruck onlookers gaped open-mouthed, amazed by his strength. Several men leaped to his assistance. Between them the wagon bed was soon lifted high to release a shattered barrel whose bowed iron staves had protected the upper portion of Berta's thin body.

"Oh, Berta, thank God, you're safe," Jenny cried tearfully as she crouched beside the girl and slowly drew her from her prison. The barrel's splintered wood had slashed Berta's flesh.

Crooning softly to her, Jenny held the battered girl against her breast, tears of relief welling in her large gray eyes. When she saw who held her, Berta's purple lips moved in a murmur of thanks.

"Give her to me," Rosa commanded, coming from no-where to claim the injured gypsy girl.

Jenny relinquished the small purple-clad form to Rosa, and she rocked back on her heels as she tried to regain her composure.

Manuel was resting thankfully against the lopsided wagon, taking great gulps of air, his face red, his body drenched with sweat. Fairgoers crowded around him, offering congratula-tions over his miraculous rescue and he grinned at them, proud of his achievement.

When the men finally arrived with the dray horses they stared goggle-eyed at the overturned wagon, unable to believe the animals were no longer needed; they were so impressed they fought for the honor of purchasing pints of ale to quench the hero's thirst. Not one to refuse his just rewards, Manuel was only too pleased to allow them to lead him to the ale sellers' tent.

The following day Berta limped about the fairground, her right leg swollen and bruised, her thin body so lacerated she looked as if she had been in a battle.

"Thank you, Jenny," the gypsy girl said, giving her friend a shimmering, gap-toothed smile. "They told me it was you who brought Manuel."

"I'm sorry I couldn't have helped you sooner."

"I shouted, but no one would do anything," Berta con-fided bitterly as, wincing in pain, she eased herself to the ground. "Rosa says she'll rebind my leg when she's done for the day."

"What were you doing beneath the wagon?"

"Blount made me dance so long I was tired. I fell asleep," Berta explained ruefully, massaging her swollen leg. "But I'll not dance again at this year's fair."

Even though Rosa lavished her expert attention on Berta's injury, the girl's prediction became fact. Only after repeated applications of a magic herb poultice was the swelling suffi-ciently reduced to allow a splint to be applied. Petrov, the bear trainer, whittled a miniature crutch for her. While the majority of the gypsies were thankful that Berta's life had been spared, Blount, her surly master, burned with ill-concealed rage at having his livelihood wrenched from him during the opening days of the great Southwark Fair; without his fleet-footed dancer, he knew he had little hope of earning his keep.

Jenny had never liked Blount, whom she still thought of as "the man in the orange doublet"; indeed, the filthy, sad tawny garment looked as if it had not been off his body in years. He was a cruel, beetle-browed, shifty-eyed man, perfectly at home with the worst of Southwark's criminals. It was no surprise therefore when Jenny came upon him deep in conversation with some of the more unsavory of those slum denizens. The stallholders customarily rested during the noon-day lull and Jenny had gone to fetch a cup of water and Manuel's shirt before the afternoon performance. When she heard Blount's voice outside the *vardo*, she paused to learn what treachery he was about. An involuntary shudder ran through her body as she recognized his companion's distinctive rasping voice: Scam was the very foulest of Southwark's thieves.

"Twenty quid! It's robbery!" Scam cried indignantly.

"Nay, she's young. Never been plumbed. 'Tis a bargain, you ungrateful sod," protested Blount.

"If it's such a bargain why's she still for sale?" Scam asked suspiciously. In the ensuing silence he hawked and spat on the ground.

"Because this bargain was saved for you, Scam, old friend," Blount said at last. "Friends deserve special consideration. The scrawny bitch is no use to me like this. And I have to eat."

Jenny gasped in horror as the subject of their discussion became sickeningly apparent: Berta was the goods for which they bargained! Unable to dance and earn her master's keep, the child was to be disposed of in a more lucrative fashion. The thought of Scam, with his pock-marked face and rotting teeth, his scabrous, filthy body, touching Berta in that most intimate of ways made Jenny's flesh crawl.

"Naw, she's not worth twenty quid. Her tits are like hazelnuts . . ."

"Look, you leprous bastard, I could get twenty-five easy from one of those lace-decked Whitehall gallants. They fancy a bit of young gypsy meat . . ."

"Then get it! Keep your battered bag of bones. I doubt one of 'em would even look at her the state she's in."

Scam growled to his companions to accompany him as he

turned to leave. Jenny flattened herself against the red *vardo*, hoping the shadows would conceal her bright yellow skirts from view.

"Nay, Scam, old friend, wait—what say you to eighteen guineas?"

"Fifteen and a little dip in the well just to make sure it's worthwhile," Scam offered, his grating voice tinged with laughter.

"Fifteen it is . . . but no free samples."

The two swore fluently at each other for a few minutes, then a bellow of coarse laughter announced the sealing of their bargain.

Jenny closed her eyes, trying to shut out the leacherous expression on Scam's battered face. Poor Berta! To have perished beneath the cloth merchant's wagon would have been preferable to a lifetime of sexual servitude to that most loathsome of creatures.

"When do I get her?" Scam asked eagerly.

"Tomorrow. Got to break it to her gently—the wench's no mor'n ten. Satisfy your itch at Bessie Dragtail's tonight."

"Tomorrow then."

"Aye, tomorrow—*after* you've given me the cash."

With muttered curses the men went their separate ways.

Jenny stood in the shadows, aware of her pounding heart. She had to rescue Berta from so terrible a fate! There must be a way . . .

"Jenny! Jenny! Where are you?"

It was Manuel. The closer they had come to London, the greater his vigilance had been; this past week he had hardly allowed her out of his sight.

"Here." Quickly Jenny stepped from the shadows. Perhaps Manuel would help her save Berta, for she knew he liked the child. Why else had he come so readily to her rescue?

But later that evening, to Jenny's great disappointment and surprise, Manuel shrugged indifferently when she revealed her knowledge of the hideous bargain.

"If Blount sells her to Scam at least she'll be fed."

"But Scam's so hideous!"

"Christ, anyone would think it was you he was intending to ride! The little wench can endure it. Anyone who's lived with Blount for five years must be used to rough treatment."

"But Blount didn't . . . did he?" Jenny asked, appalled at the thought. "She was just a little girl."

"It's not my affair what he did or did not do to her. Stop worrying your pretty head—you'll get wrinkles." With that the subject was dismissed. Manuel stooped to kiss her brow. "Stay close to the *vardo*," he warned gravely. " 'Tis not safe to wander abroad in the dark. I'll be back around midnight."

Manuel picked up his plumed hat and, slipping on his coat, jumped down into the gathering dusk.

The pulses in her temples throbbed painfully as Jenny desperately tried to formulate a plan to aid Berta. Manuel had been her only hope; the other gypsies would not even do her the courtesy of hearing her out if she tried to appeal to them for help. If only she could hide Berta until the fair was over; more than likely by then Scam would have lost interest in his purchase.

A solution to Berta's predicament suddenly occurred to her: she could send the gypsy girl to the parson at the House of the Crossed Keys! If Berta slipped away in the dark, her absence might not be noticed until morning, giving the minister's wife ample time to take her to safety. A chilling thought crossed Jenny's mind: what if the man had merely assumed his divine occupation the easier to obtain females for slavery in the city's brothels? The idea made her quail. But at least with the minister Berta had a chance for salvation; with Scam the course of her miserable future was clearly charted.

The September night was damp; white fog swirled eerily from the river, eddying in a dense shroud between the painted wagons. Jenny shivered inside the dark blanket she used as a cloak. This weather was perfect, for under cover of fog it would be easy to walk unseen to Berta's *vardo*.

With pounding heart Jenny safely negotiated the brief journey. Beyond the fairground echoed a steady hum of laughter, mingled with raucous voices and snatches of tinny music drifting from Southwark's infamous taverns and brothels. Here, on the fringe of the campground, all was quiet; most of the gypsies appeared to be taking advantage of the area's novel entertainment.

"Berta," Jenny called hoarsely, afraid to raise her voice in case she was overheard. She waited a few minutes for a reply, shivering in the dank atmosphere.

"Who is it?"

" 'Tis Jenny."

Scuffling sounded inside the *vardo* and Berta stuck her head through the opening. "What do you want?" she whispered, warily glancing about for her master.

"Blount's probably with the others at an alehouse," Jenny assured her as she moved closer to the *vardo* when a muffled cough sounded nearby. "Can you walk?"

"Aye, well enough with the crutch. Why?"

"Hurry, Berta, get your wrap, we haven't much time."

For the few minutes it took Berta to clamber from the wagon, Jenny grew stiff with tension. At last she helped the small dark-swathed figure to jump to the wet grass.

"Where are we going?" Berta asked.

Placing her fingers on her lips, Jenny cautioned her to silence. They headed toward the river. Dark shapes loomed out of the fog as people walked along the towpath, and the distant lap of oars came from the water.

Jenny slid her arm comfortingly about Berta's bony shoulders as she said, "Berta, you're to go on a journey. Can you be brave?"

"What?" The gypsy girl's dark eyes widened, the whites gleaming a moment in the murk. "A journey to where? Oh, Jenny, you're taking me with you!"

Jenny quailed at the excitement in the girl's voice. Returning Berta's eager handclasp, she shook her head. "No, Berta, I'm sorry, but I can't come with you. You must go alone."

"Why?" Berta was crestfallen.

"Blount has sold you to Scam."

Berta's indrawn breath whistled in the darkness. "Are you sure?"

"Yes. That's why you must leave tonight."

"But I don't know anyone," Berta protested, her voice quavering close to tears. "How will I live?"

"Hush," Jenny soothed, hugging her close. "I intend to help you. St. Savior's—do you know where it is?"

"St. Savior's? Aye, 'tis near the bridge."

"On this side?"

"About a hundred yards from the foot. Why ask you? A gypsy's never welcome inside a church—they fear we come to steal the poorboxes."

"Is the House of Crossed Keys close by?"

"There's a tumbledown inn of that name. Why?"

"You may have seen the wandering preacher who was

anxious to save my soul—'tis to him I send you. Here, three shillings are all I have," Jenny said, reaching inside her skirt pocket to withdraw the silver coins. "Tell him: 'Manuel's woman sent you.' He'll remember me."

"You can't stay here," Berta protested, her voice cracking. "When they find out you helped me they'll beat you . . . or worse. Oh, no, Jenny, you must come too."

"If I leave with you tonight Manuel will know where to find us. That's why you must go alone. Get away from Southwark as soon as you're able. The minister's wife will help you. Go now, before they return. 'Twill be a difficult enough journey with your lame leg. See, the fog's starting to lift. You'll better find your way, but you can be seen more clearly."

They clasped each other in tearful farewell, Berta's bony frame bird-frail against Jenny's body. Fresh tears of pity pricked her eyelids when she reviewed the gypsy girl's plight.

"Godspeed, Berta," Jenny whispered, kissing the child's forehead.

"Thank you, Jenny."

Berta gave a faltering wave before she turned and hobbled away, rapidly disappearing in the fog. Jenny murmured a fervent prayer of assistance for the child, still not wholly convinced she was sending her to safety.

It was well after sunrise when an uproar began in the gypsy camp. Being lazy and well into his cups after a night's carousing, Blount had not risen until fairgoers began to trickle inside the fairground; only then did he discover his bird had flown. A search for Berta was organized, but no sign of her could be found.

"Ask her what *she* knows. Lately the *gorgio*'s been acting like her sister," Blount snarled, his ugly face livid with rage.

Manuel turned in surprise toward Jenny, who was standing on the fringe of the group. Once her friendship with Berta was brought to their attention Jenny had known it was merely just a matter of time before she became the gypsies' prime suspect.

"What can she know? Watch your tongue, Blount, before I cut it out," Manuel threatened, his face darkening. "Why so concerned about the wench, anyway? Yesterday you barely cared if she lived."

Blount colored slightly. "Nay, Manuel, I've grown attached to the little wench. She's been with me for years. I don't want anything to happen to her.''

''Why would she run away in that pitiful condition?'' Manuel asked next, voicing a question many of the others had considered but had not the courage to ask. ''Did you beat her?''

''Not that.''

''What then?''

''Well,'' Blount swallowed, uncomfortable with his thoughts. ''She being crippled and not able to dance . . . I . . . I . . .''

''You sold her to Scam. Right?''

All eyes swiveled from Blount to Manuel and back again.

''To Scam . . . why . . . I . . .''

''There's no use lying to me.''

''That scabrous bastard told you! I should've known!'' Blount spat, his face purple with anger. ''I'll string his cod round his neck for this . . .''

''Are you so ashamed of the bargain it must be kept secret?'' Rosa asked as she thrust her way through the on-lookers, still clad in her scarlet working costume, ajingle with bangles. ''You broke your word to me. When Berta was given to you, you promised to raise her as your own. Would you sell your own child?''

''Aye, and his mother too,'' Manuel spat. ''Scam didn't tell me, Blount. You should know him better than that.''

''Then how?'' Suspicious, Blount turned toward Jenny, recalling that he had seen her yesterday walking in the vicinity of the wagons. ''She done it! She listened and she squealed,'' he bellowed, leaping toward her.

Manuel caught Blount as he moved. With a great heave he sent the other man sprawling in the dirt, where Blount rolled over and over, his orange doublet gathering a patina of dust.

''I don't know where Berta is, nor do I care. Tell Scam she's gone and repay him whatever he gave you. I'll have no trouble here.'' Manuel turned away, leaving Blount to pick himself up out of the dust.

Jenny shrank from the hostility reflected in the gypsies' faces: they spared no sympathy for Blount, she could readily see that, yet at the mere suggestion that she was at fault they were ready to vent their anger on her.

Rosa and Manuel stood apart from the others, heads bent in conversation; that Jenny was the subject of their discussion was obvious as Manuel angrily flung away from his step-mother, his face set.

"Come, we've a performance to give. Afterwards you can tell me the truth," he threatened, yanking Jenny about.

And the blazing emotion in his eyes made her quail at the prospect of that discussion.

Chapter 7

"Don't lie to me," Manuel growled, clenching his fist.

Jenny stared at him, afraid of the menacing glitter in his eyes as shadows from the wavering lantern played across his dark face, transforming him into a stranger. Light evening rain pattered softly against the roof; that, and Manuel's harsh breathing, were the only sounds beside her thudding heart. It had been a mistake to feign innocence in Berta's disappearance; she saw it now, but it was far too late to act upon the knowledge.

"'Twas not a lie," she whispered huskily. "I know not where Berta is at this moment."

"Aye, but you've a damned good idea. You know where she was sent."

"Manuel, I didn't think you cared what happened to her, not after last night when . . ."

"Care—I don't care! All I care about is your interference in gypsy matters!"

"She's so young. I had to help her. But 'twas not done to anger you."

Manuel leaped forward and caught her a glancing blow on the side of the head. The force of his unexpected action sent Jenny reeling against the iron stove, where she bruised her hip.

"I knew it! Though I defended you to the others, I knew all along!" he growled, standing over her, his nostrils flaring. "This was between Rosa and Blount. I lose face by having my woman interfere. You had no right, do you hear, no right!" Again Manuel raised his fist to strike her and, her temper erupting, Jenny lashed out at him.

"None of it was done to anger you! 'Twas merely to save Berta. And though you beat me, I'm not sorry I helped her! She's ten years old! I'll not have her a slave to a creature like Scam!"

Goaded beyond endurance, Manuel grabbed Jenny and flung

92

her viciously on the bed, setting it creaking and swaying.

"Don't you ever speak to me like that again," he growled, his face dark with anger.

He grabbed her by the shoulders and dragged her upright. Struggling and kicking, scratching like a wildcat, Jenny raked her nails down his face as she fought him off. Manuel struck her again, then he flung her away, banging her shoulder into the wall.

"It's true and I'm not sorry!" Defiantly Jenny met his glare, wary of his doubled fists, and of the blazing anger that heaved his chest. "Berta loved me. It was the least I could do for her," she added when Manuel did not advance on her.

"You bitch! I should beat you black and blue for that."

"Aye, and you've the strength for it, but I still won't be sorry for what I did for Berta," she challenged, fighting tears of fear and anger.

He lunged at her, falling across her body and trapping her on the bed. Pummeling his broad back, Jenny twisted and turned in an effort to evade his punishing blows. Suddenly, while they struggled together, Manuel's heated emotion switched course; now, instead of hatred, passion flamed his blood. To have her shapely body writhing beneath him and not claim her was too much torment to endure. Fierce emotion whipped him to a frenzy: where a woman was concerned it was but a short step to desire. And Jenny was the most desirable woman he had ever known.

"Jenny! Jenny, stop!" Manuel ordered harshly, grasping her flailing wrists in an iron grip. "Enough!"

Panting, her vision dimmed by tears, Jenny lay still. Her full breasts heaved from her exertion and her smooth white limbs trembled with anger. The pain from the blows Manuel had given her gradually crept in as she lay there, fighting for breath, the dull ache of bruised flesh making itself felt in many places.

"I was not the one who struck the first blow."

Manuel's breath quickened at the feel of her beneath him; the fact that her hard-won submission was from exhaustion, rather than desire, mattered not. "Forgive me," he pleaded gruffly, "please forgive me. You shouldn't have crossed me. You usurp Rosa's authority by your actions—but I won't betray you. Oh, Jenny, I never meant to hurt you."

A rustle and a click outside the door took Manuel's attention. In one bound he wrenched open the painted door and peered outside into the fine rain. Satisfied they were still alone, he banged the door closed.

"Are you sure no one was there?" Jenny asked suspiciously, for she too had heard the sound. She chilled at the thought someone was eavesdropping on their conversation. Manuel's chastisement of her was no secret—his angry voice must have carried throughout the campground—but her confession had been meant for his ears alone.

"Nay, no one," he assured, kneeling beside her. Manuel lifted her heavy hair from her face, saddened to see a bruise coloring her cheek. "God, I'm insane to mark you thus. Say you forgive me," he whispered, consumed by remorse.

Jenny swallowed, knowing his words were sincere, but the pain of his anger still throbbed dully in her limbs, preventing her acceptance of his apology.

"Speak to me—nay, don't turn away," Manuel pleaded urgently, taking her face in his hands and turning her toward him. Gazing down at her in the yellow lantern light, he whispered, "I'd forsake them all for you, *gorgio*." Manuel gently cradled her head against his broad shoulder as he breathed, "I love you, Jenny. You matter more to me than any gypsy."

For a few minutes longer Manuel stroked her face, his fingers gentle in their passage down her neck, trailing soft over her bare shoulder. Still Jenny refused to respond. Anger and hurt throbbed a tide of emotion through her body. Unlike his, her frenzy was not as readily converted to lust. Alternating between hatred and the treacherous acknowledgment of that other feeling she knew so well, Jenny would not meet Manuel's gaze.

"Jenny, forget what happened tonight," he pleaded, his green eyes luminous in the lantern light. "I'll defend you with my life against them all."

"And how am I to be defended against your fists?" she demanded, burning with resentment.

Manuel hung his dark head in shame. "I could kill myself for losing my temper with you. My angel—my life—love me. Bring my body alive. Come, I'll make you forget all the pain. You know I can."

She finally met his gaze; remorse glittered wetly in his green eyes, and that other familiar expression, the forerunner of Manuel's burning passion, hovered there as well. A kindling response flickered in Jenny's loins as she looked at his

beautiful body, recalling the driving pleasure Manuel sometimes gave her. This Irish gypsy was an enigma, a misfit in
both worlds. Only with her had he revealed that streak of
tenderness buried beneath the hatred.

"Do you promise never to strike me again?"

"I swear. Whether a thousand gypsies die because of it, or
nay," Manuel vowed gruffly, clasping her hand and pressing
it to his mouth. "I'll swear to anything if only you'll truly
love me. Love me of your own free will," he urged, his
breath hot against her fingers.

His impassioned words surprised her. Manuel demanded;
he took; he did not plead for favors. Obsessed by fierce
masculine pride, he had naturally assumed she derived im-
measurable pleasure from the welding of their bodies, but he
had never asked. To even suggest he needed her cooperation
during the act was a direct blow to his own virility.

"You really do love me?" she whispered, reaching for his
dark face.

"Aye, more fool me. I care not what Rosa says, nor about
the wise prophecy of ten thousand of my ancestors, nor even
how many gypsies disapprove my actions—I know only that I
want you more than any man should want a woman. The fact
you are a little *gorgio* bitch matters not a whit."

His full mouth upturned in a wry grin, Manuel stroked the
back of his hand over the warm prominence of her breast,
softly outlining the contours of her body as his hand traveled
downward. He lifted Jenny's crumpled skirts from her smooth
white legs, thrusting the fabric higher to reveal her firm
thighs.

"You're no longer angry with me over Berta?" Jenny
whispered, catching at his springy black curls, staying his
actions.

"Not angry. But hot. And needing you desperately, *gorgio*."

Manuel buried his face in the depression between her thighs,
his breath curling hot and tantalizing to the core of her being.
Jenny shuddered at the awakening emotion she could no
longer deny. A trail of fire burned through her belly to her
breasts, following the passage of his kisses. They stared
unspeaking at each other in the faltering lantern light as naked
passion rippled between them; no longer was there a need for
pleas. Manuel pressed Jenny into the coverlet, his weight of
muscle and sinew imprisoning her there while he rejoiced in
the unbridled straining of her thighs against his.

"Yes, Manuel—make me forget," Jenny urged hoarsely, not revealing that which she sought to forget in the dark tide of passion.

"You'll not even recall your own name, *gorgio*," he promised eagerly, showering her with ardent kisses.

Jenny writhed beneath him, anxious to lose herself in that heated release: for the time it took her to return from passion's sweet oblivion, she was free of painful memories of the past.

Manuel uncovered her full white breasts, shuddering as he always did when the arousing sight spilled from its embroidered silk prison. Her breasts, with their erect pink summits, thrust toward him, an invitation he could no longer ignore. Fiery delight speared Jenny's body as he drew on her nipple, his tongue, his lips, exerting enough pressure to give pleasure without pain. They kissed open-mouthed, eager to absorb the lifegiving ardor of desire. Throbbing, trembling, Manuel divested himself of his shirt, hastily ripping open the buttons on his breeches, too eager, too desperate, for care. He shuddered from head to toe as Jenny encircled his burning flesh with her small hands, fondling him carefully lest she move too hastily and destroy his pleasure.

Outside there came another clink, then a scrape and a scratch against the window. Manuel dismissed the sound as wind-driven branches on the *vardo* roof. Too engrossed was he in bringing this beautiful creature to the pinnacle of desire to spare more than a passing thought for the outside world.

"Oh, Jenny, I'll never let them take you from me, never," he vowed, his green eyes moist with emotion.

From a great distance Jenny heard his fervent vow, heard the emotion vibrating through the words, but his movements pushed her too close to losing control to heed his extravagant promises. Slowly he moved back and forth across her flesh, taunting, tantalizing, his strong hands cupping her breasts, crushing the pliant flesh.

Grasping his hair, Jenny pulled Manuel's mouth to hers, anxious to silence his words, to stop all but the flow of passion. Manuel's lips opened to hers as his tongue joined hers, striving for an unattainable goal. It was at that point he entered her in a searing, blazing bolt of strength. Jenny cried out in surprise and delight, twisting upon that impalement, driving him deeper, deeper. All the heat, the passion, throbbing through his body, she jealously took for her own. Passion carried her beyond the sordid surroundings of the Southwark fairground, beyond the gypsy *vardo* with its painted roof, until Jenny stepped free in the black night. She needed Manuel's driving emotion in this ultimate expression of desire, for afterward, when he was spent, there was no warm loving, no lull of drowsiness strong enough to exclude those painful memories of he who had first taught her how to love.

By ten o'clock the next morning the rain had stopped. The sodden fairground was a quagmire. People squelched between the stalls and sideshows, their shoes caked with mud. Despite the unfavorable conditions, hordes of Londoners still came to enjoy the freak shows and the bear baiting, with all the noisy clamor of an hysterical populace in the mad pursuit of pleasure. When the sun peeped wanly from behind banks of cloud, a rousing cheer greeted its appearance. Soon cloaks were cast aside to reveal gaudy holiday finery, the crowd's humor brightening accordingly.

Manuel had not worked the horses this morning, too occupied was he with two foreign seamen who had kept him busy examining the contents of numerous chests and barrels.

"Eager to begin?" he inquired with a grin, noting Jenny's dark scowl over his prolonged business activities.

"Though I'm no bareback rider, 'twould certainly be preferable to being jostled off my feet by the crowds."

"Faith now, I'm disappointed in you, *gorgio*. Passion usually improves your disposition," he added in an undertone, with a trace of his old banter.

Jenny smiled back. It was encouraging to discover a remnant of Manuel's more cheerful personality. He had become so deeply involved in numerous ventures outside the law that the hazards of his occupation, coupled with the rough element with whom he must deal, had wrought an unpleasant change in his character.

"It did. You wouldn't have wanted to know me otherwise."

Now Manuel laughed out loud, his humor returning by leaps and bounds. "Bitch! Come here . . . come now, no one's looking—and even if they are, who gives a damn." Sweeping her against him, Manuel disposed of her protests with a kiss. "I shall have you a gown with silver trimmings come nightfall," he promised huskily, tracing his tongue over her lips. "What am I to get for a reward?"

"It should be I who am to be rewarded for deigning to wear your stolen finery."

"Who says it's stolen? Have you no faith in me?"

"None whatsoever."

He kissed her again, sweeping her in his arms and lifting her a foot clear of the ground. "Will you do me a favor, sweetheart?"

"That depends."

"Take a packet to a chandler's in Maypole Alley. I'd carry it myself, but I must wait for word from their skipper. There's no one else I trust with this bargain."

Jenny accepted the small packet wrapped in oilskin; it looked like a seaman's pouch. "Is the alley close by?" she asked, placing the packet inside her bodice, where the crackling surface scratched her breasts.

The oilskin's hiding place was an immediate source of interest to Manuel, whose speech faltered as his mind strayed to more appealing subjects. "Christ, you torment me! Would that I were snug inside that packet this very moment," he breathed harshly, pulling her close. Then, forcing his wandering senses back to business, he added, " 'Tis off the borough High Street, directly across from the prison. You can't miss it. Take them with you."

From the shadows stepped two stalwart gypsy youths clad in homespun breeches and gaily colored shirts; Manuel often used them as messengers, for they were mute and could not read or write. However hard an enemy might try to extract information, neither Brac, nor Dom, could betray him.

"There's no need to hurry. I'll be busy till noon," Manuel said, stooping to kiss Jenny's mouth in parting. "Talk not to wandering gallants," he added, his face hardening. "They'll have their hands up your skirts before you can blink an eye. And I'm too busy to have to slit some rich bastard's throat."

Concealing a smile at his stern warning, Jenny nodded. Manuel's suggestion that she need not hasten back told her he did not want her privy to his business arrangements. Brac and Dom were such able messengers that there was little need for her to accompany them to Maypole Alley. Now, at last, when she had the opportunity to leave the campground, slipping unnoticed into the city was not going to be as easy as she had anticipated. Manuel had no intention of letting her out of his sight alone. Last night, when he struck her, she had loathed him; yet when he caressed her, making her treacherous body respond passionately to his touch, the loathing tamed to become something else. That other strong emotion was all that made her falter in her resolve to put as much distance as possible between herself and the gypsy campground.

Jenny walked along the alley between the cooked meat stalls, the primrose yellow sunlight warm on her face. Twice she glanced back to see if she was still being followed; the two swarthy gypsy bodyguards walked half a pace behind her.

"Jenny! Jenny, where are you going?"

Marta's shrill question brought her no pleasure. Mystified that her rival was attempting friendship, Jenny stopped. "On an errand for Manuel," she replied shortly, unable to force a smile; the memory of Marta's blazing hatred was still too fresh for that social nicety.

"Into Southwark?"

"Yes."

"Let me come with you. I must fetch supplies for Rosa. We'll keep each other company."

"They're with me."

On cue Brac and Dom stepped forward, extricating themselves from the press of people. Because Marta was the *chovihani*'s niece she was afforded certain courtesies; the two youths bowed solemnly to her.

Attracted by the flurry of movement a bewigged gentleman in rose-colored velvet paused in his leisurely saunter between the stalls, his eyes lighting with pleasure when he beheld Jenny. The sunlight set her chestnut hair alight and washed her smooth skin with liquid gold.

"I'll come too," Marta decided, a sickly sweet smile on her red lips. "We must try to be friends, Jenny. Though it's taken time, I finally concede defeat. I'll join you in a moment," Marta added, as the richly dressed courtier stepped forward.

"Mistress, you are the loveliest of creatures," he breathed, ogling Jenny openly from his superior height, his eyes straying to the deep valley between her breasts. Her gypsy bodyguards closed in and the gallant stepped back a pace.

"Forgive me, sir, but I'm about an important erand. My brothers are most impatient to be gone," Jenny said sweetly as she sidestepped her admirer.

The swarthy youths each clasped one of her arms and propelled her forward. The total shock on the courtier's face made Jenny smile. The man was left gaping after her in disbelief until he was eventually jostled off balance by a blousy fishwife, screaming her wars.

Marta stood deep in conversation with someone in the shadow of a clump of alders on the river bank. As Jenny passed the man raised his head, and she chilled when she recognized Cross-Eyed Jack, one of Southwark's well-known underworld figures.

Jenny hastened her steps, intending to give Marta the slip, but as soon as Cross-Eyed Jack turned onto the London road, Marta raced over the grass to join her. Though Marta had professed a truce, Jenny was extremely wary of her uncharacteristic behavior; never would Marta willingly concede defeat until one, or both of them, moldered beneath the sod!

"It's this way," Marta said breathlessly, falling into step beside her.

The rutted farm lane they traveled was fringed with dusty ox-eyed daisies and meadowsweet, the tangled hawthorn hedges ablaze with honeysuckle and woody nightshade. But they soon left the pleasant countryside behind as the dirt lane became a narrow city street. As they advanced over the slimy cobblestones, the air grew fetid. Decaying buildings huddled close, shutting out the light. And the dilapidated lathe and plaster tenements creaked and groaned, threatening to topple in the rising wind. A few grand establishments remained, their square-bowed, mullioned windows overhanging the narrow street. An odorous central kennel, down which all manner of filth flowed, ran the length of Southwark High Street; here swift-flowing rainwater formed minor waterfalls as it cascaded over offal and other refuse on its race to the Thames. People were everywhere; walking shoulder to shoulder along the street, huddling in doorways, hanging from the windows in various stages of undress, the citizens of Southwark greeted this fine September morn in a babble of noise. A multitude of tongues wagged in accents and dialects so foreign, Jenny might have crossed the Channel instead of the fairground.

"Where are you bound?" Marta shouted above the noise. While she spoke she cast about the crowded street for a likely victim, automatically flexing her fingers in preparation for work.

"Maypole Alley."

Marta smiled and nodded while she expertly relieved a passing shopkeeper of his watch. "'Tis down the street a pace."

Jenny scanned the jumbled forest of creaking wooden signs protruding above the shop doorways, searching for a chandler's shop. Halfway down the street was a peeling board where the name Wm. Wick. Esq. Chandler was lettered in faded blue paint.

"I'll wait here for you." Marta suggested while she studied the passersby with unusual interest.

With Brac and Dom still in tow, Jenny precariously picked her way over the mounds of refuse, heading for the chandler's. An unpleasant mixture of smells swirled around her, boiling cabbage, unwashed bodies, rain-wet wool, and the freshly awakened stench of sewage from the steaming cobbles thickened the air. Once too often her attention strayed, and she found herself spun against a building by a fat woman carrying baskets of lavender on her monstrous hips. Instead of apologizing for her clumsiness, the gray-haired harridan screamed a torrent of abuse, threatening Jenny with her grimy fist until the two gypsy youths stepped forward to defend her.

Maypole Alley was even filthier than Southwark's High Street. A huge dead cat, its face contorted in a death grin, barred the entrance to the alley. Jenny recoiled from the sight. Fastidiously lifting her skirts, she stepped over the rotting carcass, averting her face from its horror while she held her breath against its foul perfume.

Outside the chandler's she took the oilskin packet from her bodice, ignoring a loitering apprentice's hooted comment as she stepped inside the dark shop. The package delivered, Jenny paused in the shop doorway, her heart thumping as she looked about for her bodyguards, hoping, by some immense stroke of fortune, they had relaxed their vigil. To her disappointment the two mutes emerged from either side of the door. With a sigh of resignation, Jenny stepped back into the slimy alley. She could try to outrun them, yet she was totally unfamiliar with the layout of Southwark's streets, whereas the gypsies knew the district well. Wistfully she thought about the blessed sanctuary awaiting her at the House of the Crossed Keys. Perhaps tomorrow she would find a chance to give Manuel the slip. When they were apart his arousing body became a paltry fetter to hold her captive . . .

"There you are! Come, we should be starting back," Marta urged sharply.

The gypsy woman carried no packages. And Jenny's suspicion mounted as she recalled the reason Marta had given for accompanying her. What had been her real purpose behind this journey?

Brac prevented Jenny from being knocked into the fetid kennel by a baker pushing through the crowded street bearing great double panniers of loaves. For once the reassurance of her bodyguard's presence was welcome. Whatever devious reason was behind Marta's sudden friendship, no danger would befall her while she was in Brac and Dom's company, for the mutes remained loyal to Manuel.

"Oh, Jenny, take heed," Marta cried a few minutes later, her voice shrill with alarm. She made much of pulling Jenny out of the way of a lumbering coal wagon. Sweeping her into her arms, Marta cried, "You must be more careful. Manuel would never forgive me if I let you come to harm."

Jenny righted herself, suspicion gnawing at her peace of mind. There had been no actual cause for concern, or surely one of the mutes would have come to her rescue. Marta's false, smiling countenance, her undue regard for her rival's safety, stank of treachery!

At the end of the street they encountered a cheering group of townsfolk gathered about a couple of yelling apprentices who scuffled in the filth. Two burly constables from Marshalsea prison were forcing their way through the crowded street, anxious to restore law and order. Marta could not resist such a heaven-sent opportunity. She skillfully plied her trade on the fringe of the crowd as they slowly skirted its ragged edge, their passage slowed in the congested thoroughfare. The surging mass of bodies suddenly swept Jenny aside as the arena shifted, plummeting her into a second group of bystanders. She collided with a corpulent shopkeeper; crushed against the man's ample girth, Jenny fought for breath, inhaling the foul odor of his sweat-soaked jerkin. Her profuse apologies died in her throat as she heard a raucous cry:

"Hold her! The wretch stole my watch!"

Two beefy hands gripped Jenny's shoulders. Fear licked through her belly as she understood the meaning behind that cry: Marta had been caught picking pockets; now she, her innocent companion, would also be condemned.

"That one!"

The crowd hastily parted to allow a man through. To Jenny's horror she discovered it was not Marta, but she, who was accused of theft! Her gray eyes dilated with shock when she identified her accuser as Cross-Eyed Jack!

"No!" she cried struggling to be free. "I stole nothing."

Triumphantly Cross-Eyed Jack stepped forward and thrust his nobbly fist inside Jenny's apron pocket. The worn fabric split and a battered watch fell to the cobbles.

"Took nothing from me, eh." He leered at her as he retrieved his watch. "This 'ere's my watch," he pronounced, thrusting the dented case under her nose.

"I never saw it before."

A hooting chorus of derision greeted her protest.

"If you ain't seed it before, why's it in yer pocket, you lying little tart?"

"I don't know," Jenny whispered, feeling suddenly weak and defenseless. Brac and Dom were staring wide-eyed at her, not fully understanding the situation, yet knowing she was in danger. And there, her scarlet gown a bright stain against the dark wooden buildings, stood Marta, her tawny face wreathed in a triumphant smile. How the watch came to be in her apron pocket was no longer a mystery: that imaginary danger of a few minutes ago had given Marta ample opportunity to plant the damning evidence, the trap arranged this morning during her furtive conversation beneath the alders.

"Out of the way! What's going on 'ere?"

Cross-Eyed Jack skipped aside as the two constables arrived, red-faced and panting. "This slut pinched me watch," he accused loudly, pointing his finger at Jenny, who was still struggling in the ham-fisted grip of an irate citizen.

"Take her in! The streets is no fit place for decent folks," Jenny's captor grumbled, giving her a vicious shake to emphasize his words.

"This the watch?"

"That's right. I found it, neat as a whistle, in her apron pocket. The lying little tart tried to say it was all a mistake."

"It was put there deliberately. And you know by whom!" Jenny cried angrily, her eyes flashing as she rapidly regained her faculties. "She did it!"

A murmur rose from the crowd as Jenny, who had finally freed her hand, pointed to Marta.

"They both be in it then," someone rumbled.

"That's right. I seed 'em walking together. A couple of gypsy whores come in from the fair."

"Lock 'em both up."

The cry was taken up and the ominous rumble burgeoned to a roar as Marta attempted to flee into the crowd; she was yanked back, kicking and screaming for justice. While the crowd's attention was focused elsewhere, Jenny made a bolt for freedom. A passing man grasped her skirts and a dozen eager hands helped haul her back, wrenching on the material until, much to the men's delight, it split to provide a glimpse of her rounded white thighs.

Aware that the situation was getting out of hand, the constables seized both women and manhandled them against the closest building before brusquely ordering the crowd to disperse.

Punching wildly at her captor, Jenny desperately struggled for freedom, but her cries for justice went unheeded.

"Naw, look 'ere, constable, I never seed this other tart," Cross-Eyed Jack began uneasily, pulling at the constable's worn wool sleeve to attract his attention. "No need to take her to jail. I could do with a bit of that. What do you say now?" he coaxed, winking at the younger man, his gaze lingering on Marta's full-blown body.

"You've got yer watch—clear off. It's a change you being on the other end of a theft, me lad, it is indeed," the older constable remarked sternly, giving Cross-Eyed Jack a shove. "Go on, clear off."

"You can't put me in jail, I'm innocent!" Jenny cried, while behind her Marta gave vent to a stream of Romany curses.

"Shut your face you," the constable ordered, punching Marta in the mouth. Turning back to Jenny, he growled, "The same goes for you. You'll have plenty of chances to squeal before you're through!"

Jenny implored Dom and Brac to aid her. When the mutes moved closer, the angry constables waylaid them about the head with their cudgels, giving vent to a torrent of oaths as the fleet-footed gypsies took to their heels amid a shower of filth hurled by the spectators.

Once more Cross-Eyed Jack attempted to save his accomplice. "What about the watch? You can 'ave it in exchange for that one," he offered, grabbing Marta's shoulder as the constable shoved her before him.

There was a pause while the bargain was considered.

"Naw, I'll 'ave 'er meself. She be worth more than that heap of rusty springs. Get yourself another doxy, Jack, me lad, this one's mine."

With that Cross-Eyed Jack was sent sprawling in the odorous kennel as the long arm of the law moved on.

Chapter 8

It was bitterly cold inside the cell; the stench was abominable. Jenny tentatively stretched her foot amid the fetid straw, hastily drawing back her leg when she encountered something slimy and foul. The jailers had taken her embroidered bodice and ripped the lace from her chemise: such luxuries fetched a good price on the streets. She was lucky, they had told her; she could have been thrown in the big room, where there was barely a free breath of air. She had been afforded privileged treatment because she caught the eye of a prison official; fortunately, the man had been called away to Kensington on business and would not return before tomorrow night, somewhat delaying his eager sampling of his latest prize. Jenny shuddered as she thought about tomorrow.

The cell contained ten women, separated from the others because of their ability to pay for such luxuries as air, food, and water. God knows what penniless wretches must endure! This bare room contained naught but flea-infested straw swimming in a lake of filth; it stank worse than most stables. A furtive rustling in the corner betrayed the presence of other guests and Jenny recoiled in horror as a large rat scuttled over her feet.

She had not seen Marta since they had been dragged inside the foul environs of Marshalsea prison. How close was Southwark fairground, yet how far in terms of aid. More than likely Brac and Dom would try to tell Manuel what had happened to her, but Jenny doubted if he would understand. Compared to this hideous place, the shelter of a gypsy *vardo* seemed like heaven.

Sometime in the night the door grated open and a figure was thrust stumbling amidst the reclining occupants of the cell. It was Marta.

"Oh, so you're here too, *gorgio*," she snarled, when Jenny spoke to her. "Christ, was there ever a woman with such ill fortune. I should have been free—'twas only you who were intended to taste Marshalsea hospitality."

"I ought to kill you for what you've done to me."

"Try it, *gorgio*." Marta laughed scornfully. "Even I have no knife tonight."

In the semi-darkness Jenny glared at the blur of Marta's body, hating her so much in that instant that she wouldn't have needed steel to sever her windpipe. Forcing herself to keep a safe distance between them, Jenny leaned against the damp wall, fighting the burning ache of fatigue that invaded her body. She must not sleep: she must stay awake to defend herself against these others, against the rats and the lice, and most of all against the lecherous subhuman jailers who waited beyond that barred door.

"What did they do to you?" Jenny mumbled when, after a few minutes, Marta slumped beside her. Though she hated the gypsy woman, a kindred thread of emotion bound them together.

"What do you think?" Marta snarled contemptuously. "Were you raised in a convent?"

Jenny shuddered, knowing a similar ordeal awaited her when the jail official returned. The thought of those filthy animal bodies, those hands, those mouths . . .

"And you?" Marta asked.

"Not yet. They're saving me."

"Lucky. At least you have a few hours to call your body your own."

One of the others crawled beside them, her bony claws fastened on Jenny's chemise as she tried to rip it from her body. They grappled a few minutes in the filth; then, to Jenny's surprise, Marta came to her rescue, swiftly raking her nails across the woman's cheek. Such a vehement stream of gypsy curses issued from Marta's lips that the other woman fell back, afraid to pursue her theft.

A light filtered over the wall, high up near the ceiling. It must be close to dawn. Jenny swallowed the lump of fear and pain in her throat as she stared at the lightening patch. Suddenly the light was extinguished. For a moment her dazed mind failed to grasp the unusual nature of this sunrise. Alerted to a sound high above her head, Jenny sat up. A scrape and a dull thud followed. Then there was silence.

"What was that?" Jenny asked, gripping Marta's arm.

"Nothing." Marta shook her off, returning to her own patch of wall. "Go to sleep, *gorgio*."

After a few minutes the bumping began again. This time,

when it reappeared on the ceiling, the light was diffused into a wider banner. Something whacked the wall inches from Jenny's face; when she reached out she encountered a thick rope. A man's hoarse voice drifted out of the darkness. Her cellmates heard the voice too and they eagerly crowded about her until Jenny thought she would suffocate in the press of their foul bodies. The other women began to sob, to call out, desperate to claim for their own this guardian angel who dangled the sweet temptation of a rope within their hellhole.

Marta called something in Romany; the voice replied in kind. "He's come," she croaked. "Manuel's come to save me!"

Jenny's stomach pitched. Oh, please God, she prayed, let it be Manuel. Aloud she called, "Manuel, is it really you?"

His gruff answer was like music to her ears.

Crouching in the black night, high above Southwark High Street, Manuel strained until his sinews mounded in great humps, until sweat ran in rivers down his neck, until he all but sweated blood in his desperate effort to release his beloved from prison. At last the bars were pushed far enough apart to afford an exit.

"Jenny, climb the rope, hurry, we haven't long," he hissed, leaning, eyes closed, against the cold masonry, his heart pounding as if it would leap from his chest.

Jenny wanted to tell him she did not know how to climb a rope, but she was too desperate to allow such obstacles to stand in her way; tonight, in the midst of this stinking cell, she was going to learn. Grim with determination, Jenny thrust Marta aside when she would have gone first. The others crowded around her as she jumped to reach the rough fiber. She strained and pulled until she thought her hands would catch fire. Jenny kicked at the other women who clung to her legs, trying to pull themselves to freedom.

"God, hurry—'tis near daybreak." Not waiting for her reply, Manuel winched the rope, summoning enough strength to haul Jenny above those reaching hands.

It seemed an eternity as she bumped against the slimy wall, and Jenny prayed as she had never prayed before. At last she was close enough to touch the bars; arms trembling and stomach cramping, she gripped the cold metal. The hole Manuel had created between the bars was so narrow that her shoulders would barely fit. In panic Jenny realized she was trapped, wedged firmly by her breasts.

Above her Manuel cursed. "By the Christ, I won't be defeated by a pair of tits," he growled, wrenching cruelly on her shoulders.

Jenny gasped with pain as the bars ground into her soft flesh. With a final mighty heave she was free. Cool, sweet air rushed around her as she crouched beside Manuel on the stone parapet, trembling so hard she was afraid she would fall to her death in the street below.

"Hurry, climb down," Manuel urged, nearly pushing her from the ledge. "We can't both stay here. There's not room."

A second rope dangled against the outside wall and Jenny grabbed it. The drag on her aching arms as her body swung free almost pulled them from their sockets. Voices below urged her to hurry. Soon eager hands reached up to catch her, and Jenny collapsed tearfully against strong male bodies as she relinquished her hold on the rope.

Marta was already emerging through the grating; agile as a monkey, she had taken but a few minutes to negotiate the journey. In a matter of moments she stood below in the filthy Southwark street.

Manuel joined them. He seized Jenny, welding her against his body in a deathlike embrace.

"Oh, sweetheart," he whispered brokenly, burying his face in her tumbled hair.

So overjoyed was she to be free, so thankful that Manuel had risked his all to effect her escape, that Jenny forgot the pain of the blows this man had dealt her; tonight she remembered only the warmth of his regard for her and his God-given strength that had bought her freedom.

"Oh, Manuel," she whispered, hugging him close. "I've never loved you more than I do at this moment."

Her sincere words totally disarmed him. Tears dripped from his eyes and ran into Jenny's chestnut hair; then, remembering they were not alone, Manuel mastered his weakness. Gripping Jenny's arms, he propelled her forward ordering his companions to follow. Brac and Dom, shouldering a stout coil of rope, brought up the rear.

The sky beyond the Thames was already stained pink as they hastened down the narrow, dark street.

"Near five o'clock on a fine, dry morning," echoed the watch as he lumbered between the houses, anxious to finish his shift and go home to bed.

They flattened themselves against the buildings, hardly

daring to breathe until the watch was out of sight; when his squat figure blended into the black shadowed alleys, and only then, did Manuel resume their flight. Gradually, as sufficient distance was put between themselves and Marshalsea Prison, Manuel picked up the pace. To the chorus of church bells heralding the five o'clock dawn, they ran inside the fairground, weaving around tents and piled goods, darting between booths, anxious to reach the safety of the gypsy encampment.

Before long the details of Jenny and Marta's arrest were all over the camp. After the noon meal Rosa held an official inquiry into the matter. Though he had been summoned, Cross-Eyed Jack failed to attend the meeting, having gone underground to avoid gypsy justice. Marta, still stoically maintaining her innocence in the affair, was the only conspirator available for questioning.

Each story was patiently heard, including the recounting of Cross-Eyed Jack's excited message that had sent Manuel racing to the jail, beside himself with rage at his beloved's capture. Yet, consumed with rage though he had been, Manuel was wise enough not to antagonize the jailers. He learned the location of Jenny's cell, but was denied a visit until he produced something of value in exchange for that privilege. Manuel had no intention of returning by daylight; he had all the information he needed to set her free.

"Why should Cross-Eyed Jack seek help in rescuing you if he was part of the conspiracy to imprison you?" Rosa puzzled, her hooded eyes inscrutable.

"Perhaps because Marta was arrested by mistake," Jenny offered lamely. The need to face this gypsy tribunal as if she were on trial was an added torment to bear.

Manuel stood, his face dark with anger. "Do you swear you didn't take the watch?"

"Yes."

"Yet it was found in your apron pocket."

"Yes."

Nostrils dilated, Manuel rounded on Marta; giving vent to a bellow of anger, he seized her slender arm and swung her about. "You planted it there!"

"No, Manuel, I swear. Why believe her—a *gorgio*. I'm your own betrothed. I swear on my soul I'm telling the truth. It's she who lies!" Marta cried, her large black eyes filling with tears.

"Enough!" Rosa stepped forward and extricated her niece from Manuel's grasp. "If Marta swears it's so, then, it's so. Have you taken leave of your senses?"

With flashing eyes, Manuel stepped back. He thumped the steps of Rosa's wagon in frustration as he shouted, "Me? I would ask you the same question?"

"The hour grows late and I'm satisfied with the story. We know not Cross-Eyed Jack's part in it. Mayhap he had a grand plan that went awry. All that's important is that Marta and the *gorgio* are free. We must turn our energy to concealing them from the authorities."

Anger flashed dark color across Manuel's face, but he did not challenge Rosa's decision. "The *chovihani* has spoken—let it rest," he said gruffly, flinging away from the group.

In the warm darkness, freshly bathed, her multitude of bruises dressed with goose grease salve, Jenny lay in Manuel's *vardo*.

Had he not rescued her, tonight she would have been lying beside some hateful creature who would extract full payment for his charity in sparing her from the rigors of Marshalsea's communal cell. Jenny shuddered so hard at the loathsome thought that the bed creaked.

She finally grew drowsy in the dark silence, only to be disturbed a few minutes later by a woman's muffled sobs.

Jenny peered through the *vardo* window to see who was crying. A pale sickle moon glimmered in the black sky. Here, on the fringe of the campground, she and Manuel enjoyed a position of relative privacy, for no one strayed without invitation into Manuel's territory. The bodyguards, Dom and Brac, crouched beside the dying campfire, their long black shadows spilling over the grass. Neither of the mutes had stirred from their post, so whoever came close must be known to them.

Two dark figures appeared around the shafts of the *vardo*. By the breadth of his shoulders Jenny knew the man was Manuel, and the woman he dragged after him must be Marta, for though he was unstinting in his distribution of favors to *gorgios*, Manuel paid court to no other gypsy girl save she.

"Please believe me," Marta sobbed, her voice heavy with grief. "Ah, Manuel, I love you so . . ."

"Shut up!" he growled, shoving her aside.

Jenny's heart raced. At first she had thought perhaps they kept a moonlit tryst, but his anger told her otherwise.

"You're bewitched!" Marta spat as she grabbed Manuel's

white Holland cloth sleeve. "Look at me! Have you forgotten I'm to be your wife? God knows, I even wondered if you'd free me once you'd taken her."

"And had I known your vile treachery you could have rotted in Marshalsea jail!"

"What must I do to prove my innocence?"

"You cannot prove it because it's nonexistent."

Suddenly tiring of meek subservience, Marta's temper bubbled forth; she grabbed Manuel's black hair and wrenched his head about. "Kiss me, damn you! Or have you squandered them all on her?"

"Aye, I'll kiss you, you lying whore."

Marta screamed in pain as Manuel struck her. Knocked off balance, she scrambled through the grass, trying to get to her feet, but Manuel yanked her back by her flying locks. He shook her, ranting all the while, his rage gaining momentum. "I should rip you limb from limb for doing that to her! If she'd died—or if some filthy scum of a turnkey had had the measure of her, you'd have felt my anger then." Boiling with rage, Manuel slammed Marta's head against the wooden chicken coop setting the hens squawking in indignant protest.

Unable to endure more, though Marta had given her sufficient grounds for hatred, Jenny scrambled from her bed to go to the gypsy woman's aid. The damp grass was slippery underfoot as she jumped from the *vardo* into the pale moonlight.

Manuel dragged Marta upright after he had repeatedly cuffed her to the ground.

"Stop, Manuel! Enough! You'll kill her," Jenny cried, running at him and trying to pull him away.

Dazed, Manuel turned around, his ill temper making him unreasonable. "Get back where you belong," he growled at her, shaking Jenny off. "This is gypsy business."

"No, though she's given me much cause for hate, you mustn't kill her. Don't have that on your soul, Manuel."

"Think you I've never killed before?" he rasped scornfully, his fists netted in Marta's streaming hair. "Think you this one miserable whore would make a difference to my soul?"

"For my sake then—let her live. If you hit her again you'll kill her," Jenny cried, as she tried to pull Marta's inert body away from him. "See—she's unconscious."

Manuel looked down at the woman they were pulling this way and that like a huge rag doll. Suddenly, as if all the fight

had left him, he let Marta go; she fell heavily on the ground
and lay still.

When Manuel turned back to Jenny, the smell of strong
spirits wafted on his breath. "You're an angel," he muttered
gruffly, his steps wavering in the moonlight, "an angel,
gorgio. Any self-respecting gypsy would've begged me to
beat her to a pulp for what she did."

"Aye, an angel, Manuel," Jenny repeated, dropping to her
knees beside Marta's inert body. The gypsy girl's long black
hair straggled sticky across her brow; her face was a mass of
blood. Fear gripped her as Jenny wondered if Marta was
dead. But no, there was still a faint pulse fluttering in her
neck.

"She's all right," Manuel muttered defensively. Dazed by
the events, he leaned against the *vardo* and rubbed his face,
trying to gather his wits.

"Take her to Rosa."

"No."

"Take her now! If you don't get help she'll die. When you
cracked her head against the coop . . ."

"Christ! Be quiet! You women are all alike." Flinging
himself from the side of the *vardo*, Manuel scooped Marta
from the grass in one easy movement before throwing her
over his shoulder like a sack of flour.

When Rosa met them, her stony expression did not change.
"So, you've had your justice, Manuel," was all she said as
she looked at Marta's still form.

"Not nearly enough justice," he growled. "Were it not for
this *gorgio* angel, Marta'd be dead." His brows drew together as he added gruffly, "She tried me too much. She
deserved no less."

"Lay her inside."

Jenny met the old gypsy's eyes, finding sorrow and hatred
blazing there. "Will Marta live?"

"Have you forgotten the prophecy? She's to be Manuel's
bride. For that she must live, *gorgio*."

Jenny shuddered at the depth of hostility in Rosa's voice,
yet surely her intervention to save Marta from Manuel's rage
had met with her approval.

Manuel was already stumbling away, muttering to himself,
his anger not entirely dissipated. When Jenny turned to join
him, Rosa grabbed her shoulder, her bony hands biting into
the flesh.

"Once I thought I could love you like my Josie—I was wrong," Rosa hissed. "You're *gorgio*, and you always will be. To your misfortune there are many unpleasant things I've learned about Manuel that I didn't wish to know, painful, condemning things—all brought about by his insane regard for you."

As Jenny held Rosa's hooded gaze, she was surprised by the knowledge in those piercing black eyes. And she knew, just as surely as if she had been told, that the eavesdropper on the night she had admitted her guilt in freeing Berta had been Rosa. During that rainy night of passion Manuel had bared the innermost secrets of his soul; his confession had condemned her.

The first words Manuel spoke to Jenny the following day filled her with alarm.

"Stay inside the *vardo* whilst I'm away. You mustn't wander abroad. It's too dangerous!"

"How long must I be imprisoned?" Jenny demanded indignantly, yet more than a little afraid of his foul humor. Since last night Manuel had treated her to sullen silence, saying not a word while he donned his shabby finery in preparation for going into London.

"I'll be gone most of the day and I can't have you exposed to danger. The prison officials might be looking for you. Besides, who knows what other tricks Marta's hatched."

"Marta's hardly in a position to hatch tricks. You nearly killed her!"

Manuel gripped Jenny's arm, his fingers bruising the flesh. "Don't ever judge my actions!" he snarled menacingly. "Here you'll stay if I have to tie you up—yes, that's just what I'll do."

"No," Jenny cried in alarm as Manuel whipped a length of cord from beneath the table. Seizing her slender wrists in one hand, he pinned her in the corner while he swiftly looped the cord. Though she struggled with all her might, he soon bound her wrists behind her back.

"If you don't want your ankles tied too, keep your mouth shut."

When she hurled abuse at him, Manuel tied a linen cloth about her face, knotting it behind her head; that done, he looped the free end of Jenny's bonds about the leg of the cast iron stove. Relenting a moment, he hesitated, his hand gentle on her bright, silky hair.

" 'Tis for your own safety," he said gruffly. "Believe me when I say that. If I'm not back from Turnmill Street by dark, Brac will bring you food." He took his black plumed hat from the wooden peg. "If all goes well, there'll likely be enough silver out of this to outfit you from head to toe in satin and lace."

Above her gag, Jenny's gray eyes were wide with distress. She struggled ineffectually against the restraint, but the ropes held.

Manuel pulled some loose threads from his leaf green coat, which had become much the worse for wear. "Remember, it's for your own sake, sweetheart," he said, before he jumped down the steps.

For how long she sat on the floor, tethered like an animal, Jenny did not know. Faint laughter and the hum of fairgoers' conversation penetrated the silence within the gypsy *vardo*. A beam of hazy golden sunshine slanted warmly across her face as she moved to a more comfortable position against the chill iron stove. Jenny was furious with herself for not putting up more resistance, yet she realized it probably would have done little good: had she fought Manuel too strongly, he would merely have beaten her into submission before tying her up.

She dozed in the warm sun until she was alerted to the presence of someone on the *vardo's* creaking steps. When she glanced up she saw Rosa silhouetted against the light.

"What's this?" Rosa muttered in disbelief. "Does he tether you like a beast?"

Jenny fixed Rosa with her wide gray eyes, silently beseeching her for help. Through the wad of linen she mumbled a plea as best she could, appealing to Rosa's charity.

"He'll not be back for hours." So saying, Rosa swiftly slit Jenny's bonds with the small jeweled dagger hanging at her waist; the gag followed.

"Oh, Rosa, I'm so grateful to you," Jenny gasped, absurdly close to tears as she struggled to her feet. "He said it was for my own safety, but I . . ."

"Manuel's mind's been turned by your beauty. I've heard tell of it before."

"He's afraid for my safety."

Rosa's mouth curled in scorn. "You're safe with me. Come, you must be hungry."

The plate of bubbling fricassee of mutton, carrots, and onions that Rosa set before her made Jenny's mouth water. While she ate, Jenny became aware of moaning inside Rosa's *vardo*.

"Marta," Rosa supplied, anticipating her question. "My sister tends her."

"How is she?"

Rosa shrugged. "She'll never be beautiful again, but she'll live." With that the old gypsy disappeared inside her *vardo*. When she returned to find Jenny had finished her meal, Rosa handed her a leather bucket. "Here, fetch me some fresh water, *gorgio*. There's a conduit by the lane—'tis far easier than drawing it from the river."

Feeling it was the least she could do to repay Rosa for her unexpected kindness, Jenny set off to fill the bucket. It was only as she threaded her way between the noisy citizens, wholly absorbed in the exotic delights of the sideshows, that she came to an astounding conclusion: she was alone and unwatched! It would be a simple matter to mingle with the crowd and pass unnoticed from the fairgrounds. Once free of the camp, she would make her way to sanctuary at the House of the Crossed Keys! Reeling with excitement at her discovery, Jenny stopped beside a stall, trying to calm her racing heart as she made sure she had overlooked nothing: Manuel was gone for the day, the mutes were nowhere in sight, Rosa was attending Marta . . .

"Good morrow, mistress."

Jenny was startled by the unexpected voice, a ring of familiarity present in the wheedling tone. Looking up, she recoiled in horror, for she stared into the unlovely face of Cross-Eyed Jack!

"You!"

The criminal smiled a gap-toothed smile. "This is my chance to redeem myself. Gypsy vengeance is never pleasant."

His strange statement struck fear through Jenny's heart; without waiting for an explanation, she dived between a couple of large goodwives bearing wicker baskets of cockles. She had no idea what Cross-Eyed Jack meant, nor did she intend to stay to find out. Not knowing where she ran, Jenny darted this way and that until she halted for breath between an ale stand and an apothecary's stall. It was gloomy in the shadowed recess, providing a perfect hiding place from her pursuer. Jenny tentatively poked her head around the ram-shackle wooden boards at the back of the stall; then she screamed in alarm as something black was dropped over her head.

"Got you, my pretty."

Kicking, fighting her abductor like a frenzied wildcat, Jenny found herself totally disabled in the heavy folds of a smothering cloak. A sharp blow to her stomach robbed her of breath; a second blow to the head rendered her unconscious.

"Get 'er in the sack."

From a great distance Jenny heard the hoarse voice, loud then soft, penetrating the waves of pain in her head.

"What's in it for us?"

"Rosa'll make it good. We've got her word," Cross-Eyed Jack assured his accomplices. "And don't cross her neither. She knows all the tricks. Took her less than a day to get me, though blind me if I didn't think I was hid so good me own mother wouldn't find me.

Jenny banged about, trying to free herself, releasing the odor of dank earth from the sack muffling her face.

"Cosh 'er, she won't be no trouble then."

Those were the last words Jenny remembered before she was engulfed by a wave of fire-sparked black.

Chapter 9

When she opened her eyes all Jenny saw was a red blur; her vision gradually cleared to reveal tawdry scarlet bed hangings. The pain in her head throbbed so fiercely that it was agony to move. After making a supreme effort to recall how she came to be in this strange bed, she remembered being pursued over the fairground by Cross-Eyed Jack. Rough voices grated in her ears and the suffocating earthy smell of the sack was still in her nostrils—beyond that she recalled nothing.

Jenny propped herself on her elbow and parted the bed hangings. The room beyond this murky red island had a poverty-stricken air. A dingy banner of light filtered through the small window to reveal filthy, warped floorboards and crumbling plaster walls. Beside this sagging, scarred bed, the room's only furniture was a broken chair and a used chamberpot placed conspicuously in the corner.

Splinters from the dirty floor speared Jenny's bare feet as she staggered to the window. Unresisting, the dingy latticed pane creaked open to reveal a sea of rooftops; multileveled gables and twisted, soot-grimed chimney pots partially blocked her view of the Thames shimmering in the distance. She glimpsed London Bridge's crowded throughfare spanning that wide ribbon, and the stretch of skyline beyond the river appeared so familiar that Jenny was convinced she was still in Southwark.

"Feeling better?"

She spun about at the unexpected question to find a blousy, middle-aged woman in a soiled orange silk negligee that failed to cover her pendulous breasts; the gray-haired stranger was slovenly and unclean.

"Where am I?" Jenny demanded.

"In my house, pretty one. I'm Annie Strength-in-the-Lord Wooten. That be the pious name my father saddled me with— damn his soul—him being a bible-quoting Puritan. Everyone calls me Annie."

"Why am I here? Are you a friend of Cross-Eyed Jack?"

Annie beamed a toothless smile. "You might call me a friend—that's when the dirty sod remembers to pay his bill."

Annie advanced inside the room and stopped a few feet away to critically study Jenny's appearance.

"You didn't answer my question," Jenny persisted, growing uncomfortable beneath the woman's intense scrutiny.

"How old you be?"

"Eighteen."

"Hm, not bad preserved. You should fetch a pretty penny. Most of my drag-tailed bitches are worn out long before they're that age."

The statement, so casually made, revealed the hideous truth of Jenny's surroundings. Disgust and fear washed over her in a nauseous wave as she realized that the solution Marta had proposed, and Rosa had resisted for so long, had finally come about—she had been sold to a brothel!

"No!" Jenny cried, recoiling in horror as Annie reached out to squeeze her breasts, expertly judging their firmness.

Her good humor flown, Annie gripped Jenny's arm, annoyed at being shaken off. "That'll do, you. I don't want no trouble."

"I won't stay here. When Manuel learns . . ."

"You'll stay here because you ain't got no choice."

"I won't! Let me go!" Jenny fought off Annie's restraining bulk as the madam tried to subdue her protests with a few well-placed slaps. As they struggled there was the sound of tearing cloth. Annie cursed as the front of her soiled finery gave way, allowing her pendulous breasts to swing free; in retaliation she seized the neckline of Jenny's chemise and ripped it apart. Desperately Jenny defended herself, punching and scratching until Annie seized her by the hair and slammed her hard against the wall. The blow momentarily knocked the wind from her, and Jenny slithered to the floor.

"That's enough out of you!" Annie pronounced vehemently, attempting to hold her torn negligee together in a curious effort to preserve her modesty. "You'll be sorry for that, my fine one."

The door slammed closed; a bolt shot home. Jenny ran to the window to investigate her chances for escape, but the pane was too small for her to squeeze through. She beat loudly on the door, shouting to attract attention. As the time passed and the hopelessness of her predicament grew only too clear, she came close to hysteria. At last she was rewarded by the sound of heavy steps thumping toward the door.

Thrust backward as the door swung open, Jenny stumbled against the sagging bed. The man who walked inside the room was an ugly, barrel-chested creature with huge arms swinging loose at this sides; dressed in baggy seaman's breeches, his yellow torso gleamed naked above the waist. He glared at her, his cruel, slanting black eyes nearly buried in rolls of greasy, pockmarked flesh lying between a shiny bald pate and a flattened pug nose.

''Don't touch me!''

The man said not a word. Before Jenny could defend herself, she was sent spinning into the wall from the force of a mighty blow. The agony dealt by his immense fist was more acute than any she had suffered at Manuel's hands. Too stunned to speak, Jenny fell in a heap on the protesting mattress. Now she found her voice, but her piteous wails seemed only to spur the man to greater brutality. Seizing her by the hair, he dragged Jenny to the floor, where he kicked her, repeating the action each time she tried to scramble to her feet.

Just when Jenny was convinced she was going to die, a second voice echoed from a vast distance.

''Back! Would you kill her? Get out!'' As if she addressed a disobedient cur, Annie ordered the man from the room. Like an animal, he shambled away, dragging his great feet in their soft hide shoes.

''Now, do you still feel like fighting?'' Annie demanded, pulling Jenny onto the bed. The madam scowled in displeasure when she saw disfiguring purple bruises spreading across Jenny's face.

''No,'' Jenny whispered at length through painfully swollen lips, ''no more.''

''That's better. Well, at least you'll eat here, and that's luckier than some wench's has it. I don't expect much work from you—a dozen men a night's all I ever ask.'' Poking the swollen patches on her body until Jenny screamed in agony, Annie shrewdly ascertained the extent of her injuries. ''The mindless fool!'' she spat in disgust as she pitched a tattered coverlet across the bed. ''I can't use you for at least a week. I told him to be careful, but I never can rely on him. You're not even fit for a drunk in this state. We'll have to see how you look by weekend. And think yourself lucky you're getting a rest—it'll probably be the last you'll get.'' With that, Annie pattered from the room in her down-at-the-heel velvet slippers.

Jenny never knew how long she lay in that third-story room at Annie Strength-in-the-Lord Wooten's house of ill fame; days and nights blurred into a nightmare of pain. When she finally felt well enough to take note of her surroundings, Jenny regretted the improvement, for now she must face the full realization of her hideous future. The hurt from her bruises pained her not as much as the hopelessness of her situation.

Several times during the following week Jenny attempted to escape, only to be returned by the walking mountain of flesh employed by Annie to mete out justice to disobedient whores. All hope of rescue gradually dwindled. In the beginning Jenny had expected Manuel to appear and spirit her away, but when the days passed and there was still no sign of him, she decided he was not coming: he must have accepted whatever lie Rosa had told him to explain her disappearance.

The blazing orange sun hung low in a hazy golden sky. It had been such a beautiful September day; Jenny ached to wander the Surrey countryside. Though she was imprisoned within the odorous warren of this slum, her mind wandered free to the country lanes of her memory, where the hedgerows were loaded with ripe brambles and crimson-streaked honeysuckle, and migrating swallows swooped over the fresh harvested fields on their journey south. Stunned by loneliness and self-pity, she had wept again and again as she stared through the narrow window at the depressing vista beyond. Apart from her abortive forays down the rickety staircase, she had never left her prison. The sun straddled the neighboring roof, flooding the tawdry room with russet light, laying bare its appalling poverty. The hateful reminder made her shudder.

When the door opened unexpectedly, Jenny spun about in surprise, only to recoil from the two figures who stepped inside the room. And she knew this was the day she had long dreaded: Annie had brought her first customer.

The young, fair-haired man was barely old enough to grow the golden mustache he had lovingly coaxed above his soft upper lip in faithful imitation of the fashion set by King Charles. He was finely dressed in a sapphire-blue satin coat and breeches, and his full shirtsleeves fell in cascades of lace over his slender white hands. He was young, rich, and exceedingly drunk.

"Oops, my fine lord, careful there," cautioned Annie, grabbing his sleeve when the young man lurched in the doorway. "Here she is—the most beautiful wench you've seen in your life! I don't offer her to many, but seeing as yourself's such a fine gentleman . . ." Annie winked broadly and the young man uttered a hiccuping laugh at her statement.

"Shplendid piece of flesh by the looks of her," he approved as he moved forward, stepping too high off the floor, as if he walked a rolling deck. "She must be virgin . . . very partial to virgins . . ."

"Why of course she's virgin!" Annie cried indignantly.

And the young nobleman was far too befuddled to find fault with her statement.

"You behave yourself," Annie reminded Jenny in an undertone. "This one's going to be easy. And stay out of the light," she snarled as an afterthought, critically viewing the fading black and yellow patches on Jenny's face. With a parting nod, Annie slammed the door, leaving them alone.

Jenny stared dully at her customer. Curiously, all her will to fight had flown. Nothing that had taken place inside this room seemed real any more, not even her pain.

"What's your name?" the young lordling asked, leaning against the open window as if he felt the need for air.

"Jenny."

"Thash pretty."

They stared at each other. The man inclined his head toward the bed. Without protest Jenny crossed the bare floor and slithered beneath the bedcover. It took him a few minutes to reach her because at first he walked into the wall; then, laughing at his own foolishness, he carefully retraced his steps. He steadied himself against the wormy post at the foot of the bed, smiling as he said, "Ah, there you are, wench—wash the matter with your face?"

Jenny gasped in surprise; he was drunk, but not that drunk. Was he going to refuse her now? She prayed he would not, because the blame for such failure would be laid to her surly attitude. In punishment Annie would unleash the "creature" to inflict more pain on her poor, weak body . . . To her horror, but discovering she was quite unable to stop, Jenny crawled along the bed toward the man, virtually begging him to use her in order to avoid another beating.

"Oh, please, kind sir, don't leave, they'll beat me again," she pleaded, her eyes filling with tears.

"They've bruised you! I'll have none of it! I paid well for unmarked goods. This is out . . . ra . . . geus . . ."

"What's your name, fine sir? For in truth you are a most handsome gentleman." Was that her voice speaking the professional whine of the fairground?

"Talbot March," he said, surprised by her question.

"Come then, Talbot March, and see what fine goods you've purchased," Jenny coaxed winningly. "You'll not be disappointed. You have my word on it." His eyes closed and he swayed precariously beside the bed. If he succumbed to the vast quantity of liquor he had imbibed, she might be spared the indignity of bartering her body in exchange for freedom from pain.

The man smiled eagerly as he said, "I may look soft as a girl, but underneath . . . I'm . . . I'm . . ."

"Lusty as a sea captain," Jenny supplied, wincing in pain at her own poorly chosen comparison.

"Exactly! 'pon my word, you're a clever wench," said Talbot March.

Jenny moved aside as he fell heavily across the bed, his black plumed hat sliding down over his eyes. Laughing, he sailed the hat across the room, where it landed scant inches from the chamberpot.

"Handsome indeed," Jenny whispered, forcing herself to stroke his fair hair, which curled soft as a girl's about his shoulders.

Talbot March reached for her and pulled her on top of him. He kissed her mouth with slack, moist lips. " 'Odd's blood! If only I weren't so damned, infernal drunk," he muttered, flopping back on the bed in frustration.

"Being drunk won't matter. I'll help you," Jenny offered, desperate to keep him here just a little longer.

"Will you, by God? You're a good wench . . . a good wen . . ." He belched, then giggled stupidly at his bad manners. "Should've come here first, Jenny, seen you in the light."

When his hands molded her breasts, Jenny forced herself not to recoil from his touch. Unfortunately, rather than succumbing to drink, Talbot March appeared to be rallying. He raised up on his elbow and began to hiccup; with an oath of disgust he sprawled spread-eagled on the bed.

"Hiccups don't prevent . . ."

"They did it on purpose," he moaned, not listening to her. "They planned it all. 'Now, let's take him to a whorehouse', they said . . ."

"Come, Talbot, I'll help you," Jenny coaxed as he began to get off the bed. Though she hated to do it, she reached for his shoulders and pulled his slender, unresisting form toward her. "You'll have the last laugh on your friends, you'll see," she promised with a smile.

Her words encouraged him. Rallying once more, Talbot March rolled on top of her. Jenny fingered the soft fall of lace at his shirt neck while they looked at each other, unspeaking, unmoving.

At last he asked, "Would you be my woman?"

Jenny nodded and smiled, wondering uneasily if he was going to talk himself sober. It no longer mattered. For how long this man had purchased her services she did not know, but he was probably as pleasant a customer as she could expect to meet in a Southwark stew.

"Damn me, but I'll do it!" he exclaimed loudly. "The King's got a whole stable of fillies—all I want's one little wench. My father's a courtier, did you know that, Jenny?"

She smiled until her face ached while he rambled on about the injustice he endured at his father's hands. Suddenly, in mid-sentence, he welded his mouth to hers and kissed her so hard her lips bruised against her teeth.

"Do you know the King?" he asked later, as he positioned her against the lumpy pillows.

"No, I've never seen him."

Talbot began to giggle foolishly until he held his sides with mirth. "They do say his . . . his scepter matches . . . his . . . his . . . prick!"

Jenny was rapidly tiring of Talbot March. Though he still giggled and spluttered, it seemed unlikely now that he would succumb to the effects of his drinking. She waited stoically while he fumbled with his breeches, trying to negotiate the buttons. With an oath he finally ripped the garment open; then, as if the exertion had proved too much for him, he fell back on the bed.

"Take off your coat, you'll be more comfortable," Jenny suggested, her spirits soaring. Maybe he was going to pass out after all! For as long as she dared delay matters, she pretended to help him undress.

A rap sounded on the door and Jenny leaped with fear. Was his time up?

"Talbot, by all that's holy, are you not done yet?" called a man's deep voice.

"No, by Christ, I'm just coming up for air. Go to Hades, Ralph," Talbot replied with great bravado. "Pay the madam for another hour. This one's too boo . . . booful to give up."

Chuckling over his friend's words, the other man walked away.

Talbot sweated profusely as he lay back with a great sigh of relief. Jenny, lying beside him, echoed his sigh. Another hour! Thank heaven for a young man's pride.

"You won't tell them—will you?" he asked after a long silence.

"No, of course not."

Eventually Talbot March rolled Jenny to her back and he fumbled blindly with her chemise, pushing it up around her thighs. For some time he attempted to pull off his breeches before he finally fell forward with a groan. When Jenny turned his face toward her, she discovered he was sound asleep.

She had an hour's grace! Almost as soon as she realized that, Jenny began to formulate a plan of escape. New life surged through her veins, dispelling her apathy. Talbot March's companion had probably taken him at his word and paid Annie for another hour. For some time there had been no sound in the corridor. The "creature" must be safely below stairs. She would slip away unmolested in the deepening twilight.

The idea was so electrifying that Jenny trembled from head to foot. On legs that felt alarmingly weak, she stood, swaying on the bare floor. If only she had a decent gown to cover her body; this dirty, torn shift would never pass for street wear. Jenny turned to survey Talbot March, snoring peacefully in his drunken stupor, and an idea occurred to her: they were of a like height and build—she would strip the nobleman of his finery. It would be far easier to slip away unnoticed if she was dressed like one of the brothel's noble customers.

Talbot March was limply unresisting as she rolled him about while removing his expensive clothing. Jenny took everything but his drawers, so that he might retain a little dignity. With trembling fingers she negotiated the unfamiliar fastenings. Though slender, Talbot March was broader than she in the shoulders and his blue satin coat sagged a good two inches at the seam. In the pocket was a purse containing three gold sovereigns; the money would provide her with food and lodging for the next few weeks. Unfortunately, the young nobleman had not worn loose petticoat breeches, and his close-fitting lace-trimmed breeches fit so snugly over her hips that Jenny could barely fasten the buttons. Though it was the current fashion for men to wear their hair long, she decided her own abundant tresses were too obviously feminine to be convincing. Hastily braiding her hair in untidy plaits, she stuffed it inside the crown of Talbot March's black plumed hat. Now she was ready.

It was pitch dark in the odorous passage outside her room. Inching along the filthy plaster wall, Jenny froze in horror as Annie's voice drifted upstairs. The madam was stumping up the stairs, deep in conversation with a man; Jenny recognized him as a nobleman by his deep, well-modulated voice and careful speech. Annie treated the man with deference to his superior rank, for her conversation was liberally sprinkled with "my lords" and "your graces."

"She's not for sale to the usual customer, you understand, my lord," Annie was saying, as she paused in the stairwell one flight below. "A shy girl, newly come from the country."

Jenny froze as she realized it was she they discussed.

"March's a randy goat, keeping her busy all this time. I'd never have thought . . ." The man broke off abruptly as someone called his name from below.

"Three guineas, she is, your grace. And cheap at that."

"Three! You only charged March two. Has the price increased this past hour?"

"Nay, my lord, you misunderstood," Annie explained hastily. "I said three."

"I distinctly heard two . . ."

The footsteps stopped. Then a door slammed below and all was quiet.

Jenny could not believe her good fortune: Annie's greed was to be her salvation!

Racing down the stairs, she stumbled in the ungainly shoes her unconscious benefactor had bequeathed. Terrified that her clumsiness had alerted the household, Jenny paused to listen for sounds of pursuit; satisfied that no one was coming, she raced down another flight. By an immense stroke of fortune the door to the alley stood open, a pale ribbon of twilight bisecting the peeling plaster wall. Jenny ran the last few feet to freedom, her heart hammering in her chest.

Once she was in the alley she did not stop to look about, but ran as fast as her feet could carry her, discovering hidden strength as her bruised limbs responded magnificently to her command. No shouts echoed after her, nor did she hear pursuing steps.

The last vestige of this long twilight glimmered in the west as Jenny leaned against a peeling doorway, gasping for air as if she were drowning. The pain in her chest was excruciating. Around her citizens strolled about their business, oblivious to the disheveled young lordling who had just fled from Annie Strength-in-the-Lord Wooten's bawdy house as if the devil himself were in pursuit.

When she finally regained her breath, Jenny assumed a more leisurely pace in order not to draw attention to herself, for though this fine clothing was a reasonable fit, she doubted she would pass close scrutiny. The deepening dusk was a blessing in disguise. Jenny headed in the direction of the bridge, which she had seen from her window, yet the route she took through winding alleys and narrow byways seemed to lead away from her goal instead of toward it. These fetid dockside dives and the crumbling tenements of the poor were a frightening reminder of all she sought to escape. The smell of tar, rope, and mingled refuse in the river blew about the buildings in the salt-tinged breeze. Suddenly Jenny glimpsed sun-spangled water beyond the dark silhouette of ramshackle timbers as the orange sun slid to its death. A few minutes more and she would reach sanctuary—the House of the Crossed Keys.

The unmistakable lap of water and the cries of watermen sounded from the Thames as Jenny drew close to London Bridge. The last shred of daylight illuminated the sagging buildings lining the ancient thoroughfare. As she approached St. Savior's tall stone edifice, Jenny recoiled in dismay from the sight which greeted her: the neighboring building was gutted! Charred timbers yawned to the sky, a blackened slab of plaster bearing a symbol of Crossed Keys was all that remained of the blessed sanctuary she had sought. Berta and the minister had gone!

Jenny supposed she could return to Manuel, but that idea

was not appealing. Besides, once Rosa learned where she was, it would be only a matter of time before she was back in the Southwark stews. And this time the "creature" would be given no orders to spare her pain, for when she discovered she had been cheated, Annie would be beside herself with rage. Only one option remained: she must go to Cornhill in search of Uncle Will's shop.

Assuming an arrogant air in keeping with her fine clothing, Jenny boldly accosted a passing urchin to ask for directions. Just in time, she remembered to deepen her voice. "Can you direct me to Cornhill, lad?"

"Whereabouts in Cornhill?" the boy asked suspiciously, his dark eyes busy about her fine gilded buttons, the exquisite lace at her throat and wrists.

"Dunn's Haberdashery. I must rouse the old skinflint from his bed. I need a length of lace for my shirt." Though at first she was proud of her inventive speech, Jenny began to grow uneasy as the filthy urchin merely looked her up and down.

"What's a fine gentleman like you doing afoot?" he demanded.

Jenny had not thought about that. "My horse went lame," she explained quickly, hoping it was a convincing answer. Still the lad hesitated and she realized he was awaiting payment for his pains. All she possessed were three gold sovereigns; a sovereign was far too much to pay a street urchin for directions, yet if she would learn the information, she had no choice. "Here, lad, maybe this'll loosen your tongue." Careful not to let him see what else was in the purse, Jenny extracted one glinting coin.

The urchin's eyes rounded at the sight of gold. He bit hard on the sovereign. Satisfied it was genuine, he quickly concealed it about his ragged person. "Right, my lord," he said, his eyes brightening in his filthy face. "You keeps right on across the bridge, up Fish Street Hill, along Gracious Street, turn to your left, and you're in Cornhill. Don't know no Dunn's, but 'spect you'll find it soon enough." Then politely touching his forehead, the lad skipped away. He was soon lost in the shadows.

Success increased Jenny's confidence by leaps and bounds. It was not until she had negotiated the great bridge, thronged with people and vehicles passing to and fro, that she began to grow uneasy. While on the bridge, where the houses crowded close, shutting out the night, Jenny had felt comparatively safe; but here on the opposite bank of the Thames, where a wide expanse of star-dotted sky spread a canopy over the countless winding streets of this vast city, she grew afraid of the concealing darkness. How many thieves lay in wait in that black warren of streets, crouching in alleys, in doorways? Noblemen did not venture abroad unaccompanied in the night, even she knew that. Jenny wished Talbot March had possessed the forethought to wear a sword, though being totally unskilled in the art of swordplay, the weapon would have been poor protection.

Jenny walked briskly up Fish Street, following the stinking kennel in the middle of the street, keeping as far as she could from the shadowed doorways. As she walked, she had the impression she was being followed; another hundred yards further on and she was convinced of it. When she paused for breath at a street corner, she saw her pursuer darting into a doorway; it was the urchin who had given her directions! Her heart thumping with fear, she quickened her pace; the stealthily pursuing shadow merely adjusted his own accordingly. Finally Jenny broke into a trot, but she could not shake her pursuer, for the thud of bare feet followed ever closer. Panic seized her as she realized the lad intended to jump her, choosing his own favorite spot for relieving an idle young lord of his purse. He might even kill her!

Suddenly, like a divine messenger from heaven, there appeared a night watchman at the corner of Fenchurch Street; swathed in a dark cloak, he carried a lantern that flooded the narrow street with light.

Jenny stepped forth, almost forgetting to deepen her voice in her haste. "I'm being followed by a thief," she blurted breathlessly. "See him lurking in the shadows?"

The watchman glanced where Jenny pointed, but saw nothing: the urchin was lying low. "'Tis a dark night to be abroad alone, my lord," he wheezed, peering into her face beneath the shadowing hat brim.

"Can't you catch him?"

"He's but one of many. Where are you headed?"

"Dunn's Haberdashers in Cornhill. Do you know the shop?"

"Aye," The watchman swung his lantern in an arc over Jenny's head. "What do you want with Master Dunn at this hour? He'll be abed."

"He . . . he has a package of . . . of lace for me," Jenny

faltered. '' 'Tis most important.'' Her hesitant explanation died as she saw disbelief on the watchman's grizzled features.

"What do you really want with Master Dunn?"

"I . . . I've already told you."

"The shop be yonder. Turn to your left and come by Dunn's that way. Not a league from the Change, it be. But as for you going there alone at this hour, young sir—I'd best come with you."

The watchman's suspicion accelerated when he reached for Jenny's arm and she darted away, fleeing in the direction he had indicated. With a bellow of rage, the lumbering watchman gave chase. Through slithering heaps of refuse Jenny skidded, adeptly dodging the contents of chamberpots emptied indiscriminately from upper windows. Here and there, a flickering lantern lit the way, but for the most part the cobbled streets lay in darkness. Only the watchman's halo of light, bobbing and swaying as he raced along behind her, shed a constant gleam. Not even sure she was still on the right course, Jenny kept on running, her legs aching, her feet rubbed raw by the ill-fitting shoes. When the night watchman caught her, he would soon discover she was not whom she pretended to be. She would be accused of stealing Talbot March's clothes and locked up somewhere equally as hideous as Marshalsea Prison! This horrid realization spurred her laggard legs to greater speed.

As Jenny sped around the corner of a narrow street, she tripped over loose cobblestones and hurtled against a shuttered window, knocking the breath from her body. Stunned, she hung there, her arms draped about a metal bar, her chest heaving as if it would burst. Across the street a lantern swayed in the tainted breeze blowing around the exposed corner, full of the abominable stench of the London streets. And there above the lantern, illuminated by a flickering pool of light, Jenny saw the magic word—Dunn.

Rousing herself, she leaped forward, praying she had not imagined it. Over her head creaked a painted board bearing the words "Wm. Dunn Esq., Haberdasher."

Jenny went weak in the knees from relief. She thundered on the shop door until her knuckles ached, but no one came to investigate the commotion. Desperate, she rattled the closed shutters over the shop window. If they did not open to her soon, the watchman would round the corner and she would have to start running again; even if she was fortunate enough to give him the slip, in all likelihood she would never find her way back to this spot.

"Uncle Will, open the door. It's me, Jenny—Nan's daughter. Open the door!"

Her voice died away. No response came from Dunn's Haberdashery, but an irate householder thrust his nightcapped head from a window across the street and swore at her to be quiet. While she stood poised for flight, the wind tossing the plume on her borrowed hat, Jenny heard the rattle of a window above.

A man's balding head poked inquiringly from the casement. "Get on home, you drunken fool! Can't honest citizens get their rest?" he shouted in anger.

"Please, let me in, Uncle Will. It's Jenny."

"Jenny?"

"Your niece Jenny—Nan's daughter."

Will Dunn leaned farther into the street in order to see the speaker; he saw only a slender youth wearing a broad-brimmed black hat. "Go on with you, you rogue, go home and sleep it off," he cried in disgust, withdrawing his head and preparing to close the window.

Her stolen clothes had created an unexpected barrier. "I'm Jenny," she cried desperately. "I swear, if you'll just open the door, you'll understand."

"Lord have mercy, who are you blathering to, Will?" A second head, decked in a frilly nightcap perched atop a mop of yellow curls, poked from the window. "Who's there?" the woman demanded.

"Jenny Dunn."

"You don't look like Jenny Dunn to me."

"See." Jenny swept off her hat, allowing her hair to tumble down. She pulled open the fine sapphire-blue coat, stretching the shirt taut about her breasts as she stepped into the pool of lantern light. "See, I am a woman."

An appreciative comment came from the window across the street, but Jenny ignored the man's bawdy remark. Will Dunn craned forward until he had a clear view of the figure beneath the lantern.

"Why, Pet, love, 'tis a woman, after all, for I n'ere saw a lad with a chest like that."

"Are you really Niece Jenny?" Pet Dunn asked eagerly, leaning far out into the night in her excitement.

"Yes. Oh, please let me in. I'm being chased by a night watchman. He'll be here any minute."

The two heads were withdrawn and Jenny could hear the Dunns debating the issue. At last footsteps sounded behind the closed shop door, followed by the welcome crash of bolts and chains being drawn back.

"Oh, Uncle Will, thank God!" And weeping for joy, Jenny fell into Will Dunn's outstretched arms.

Chapter 10

The first pink flush of dawn strained the eastern sky before Jenny lay down to sleep in the luxury of a soft feather bed in the guest bedchamber overlooking Swann Alley. She still could not believe she had been welcomed so eagerly into her uncle's household. After her tragic tale had been unfolded before the sputtering blaze of a newly lit sea coal fire, both her aunt and uncle had wept over her misfortunes. Their emotional reaction to her plight gave Jenny a few pangs of guilt, for her story had not been without a little judicious editing, yet she consoled herself with the fact that her kind-hearted relatives would have been far too disturbed had she retold her odyssey in intricate detail. As she lay in the warm, murky darkness, Jenny gave fervent thanks for her deliverance. No longer need she fear Annie Strength-in-the-Lord Wooten's vengeance, for the shadow of that sordid house of ill fame had been lifted forever. She was also free of Rosa's absolute authority, of Marta's hatred, and of the thinly disguised hostility of the gypsy tribe; she was even released from the bondage of Manuel's obsessive passion. How fortunate she had never told him her uncle's name. Even with the help of his underworld contacts, it was doubtful Manuel could trace her to this dark-beamed shop. The fetters of the past fell away, leaving her giddy and lighthearted.

"What a beauty she is," blondhaired Pet commented to her husband as they admired Jenny in her new taffeta gown. "Never would I have guessed your niece to be so lovely." And she beamed in high delight as she studied Jenny from every angle. In fact, Pet's plump, dimpled face had been transfigured from the moment she beheld her niece freshly bathed, her gleaming hair brushed, and clad in a gown chosen to accentuate her charms. She virtually bubbled with good humor.

"Oh thank you, Aunt Pet, it's such a lovely gown."

Jenny's gray eyes shone bright with pleasure over this unexpected gift of fine clothing.

"Fie! 'Tis no less than you deserve. Would you have me send you abroad tired in rags?"

"But, loveday, the cost," Will interjected dolefully, his pudgy face crumpling in concern as he mentally calculated the loss to his purse.

"Tish! What care I for cost when we have such a wondrous fair creature in our midst," Pet replied as she swept across the room. "You're nothing more than a skinflint, Will Dunn—a common, dyed-in-the-wool skinflint."

"Now, Pet, such harsh words."

"Harsh they may be, but 'tis something I should have said long ago. I need gowns. We need new draperies for the parlor—and the bedding is in absolute tatters. No, there's no kinder way to put it, Will, love, though it pain my heart to have to admit such a thing about my own husband."

Jenny smiled as her aunt's and uncle's voices faded away; though she had lived here only two days, it had not taken long to discover that Pet ruled Will Dunn with an iron hand. And ever anxious to satisfy his young wife's demands, poor, harried Will was perpetually in need of money to provide the luxuries her frivolous nature demanded.

"You don't deserve such a fine dress," Doll snapped, scowling as she possessively fingered Jenny's blue taffeta gown. "It should have been mine. I've not had a new gown for nigh on a year."

From the beginning Jenny had disliked Pet's seventeen-year-old sister who was employed to serve customers in the shop. She was always referred to as "poor Doll," as if she were an object of great pity. Thin and bad-tempered, Doll was a chronic complainer, the unlovely trait readily reflected in her pinched face; her lank blond hair was tortured into spindly corkscrew ringlets that dangled on either side of her narrow, pale face; her long, scrawny neck projected from an equally scrawny body. Seemingly possessed of a perpetual cold, Doll sniffled constantly, habitually dabbing at her reddened nose with a grimy linen handkerchief.

"I couldn't wear men's clothing forever," Jenny pointed out.

Doll sniffled and hastily dabbed her nose. "How do we know you're even related to us?"

Tiring of the conversation, Jenny turned her back on Doll.

"You don't, so you'll just have to accept my word for it," she countered as she admired her reflection in the dingy mirror.

The full-skirted blue taffeta gown had a low, boat-shaped neckline that emphasized her beautiful bosom and shoulders; the snug-fitting bodice ended in a point below the waist, while deep lace flounces edged the full three-quarter-length sleeves, cascading elegantly over her hands. Aunt Pet had chosen the gown carefully, not even trusting its detailed alterations to the shop's apprentices, preferring to undertake the task herself. Beneath the gown Jenny wore a lace-trimmed chemise of fine lawn. Her feet were encased in delicate blue kid slippers. In this beautiful clothing she felt like a duchess. And not even Doll's sour presence could detract from her pleasure.

At twenty-two, Pet Dunn was young enough to be Will's daughter. In payment for her favors being wasted on such an old man, she demanded much in return. Their narrow, three-storied home above the haberdashery was as fashionably well-appointed as she could make it. Though merely a cloth merchant's daughter, Pet had always aspired to be thought a member of the lesser nobility; to this end she took great pains with her speech, dropping her cultured tones only in moments of extreme stress. Since her first angry tirade at the beginning of their marriage, Will had lived in constant fear of arousing his wife's temper. On the whole, it was a situation Pet found immensely to her satisfaction. In keeping with the image she wished to project, Pet dressed fashionably, avid for news of the latest court fads, which she promptly adapted to her own circumstance. The scope of contacts from whom she obtained her gossip was large, their friendship purchased in several ways, for Pet never allowed a false sense of morality to interfere with her ambition. Ranging from the borough watchman through local tavern wenches to a servant of Lady Castlemaine herself, Pet's network spread across the city.

When she walked inside Jenny's chamber early one morning, Pet wore her new trained negligee of chocolate-brown velvet with a ruched trimming of bright yellow satin. A lemon silk lace-edged cap perched on her fluffy blond curls.

"Good morrow, Jenny." Pet smiled to reveal small sharp teeth. "It's such a perfect autumn day, I declare, I can smell the countryside in the air!" Pet flung back the diamond-paned

bedchamber window and leaned out into the street. She called
a greeting to someone passing below before turning back to
her niece, who was propped against the goosefeather pillows
in the high tester bed.

"I know Will said you could work in the shop, but we
really don't need another assistant beside 'poor Doll.' "

Jenny swallowed uncomfortably at this unexpected information. "Can I not help in the house?" she suggested hopefully. The Dunn's serving woman was so overworked she
could barely cope with running the household, let alone feed-
ing the family and their four apprentices. A second pair of
hands would be more than welcome.

"Tish, what a suggestion!" Pet cried, scandalized at the
mere thought. She playfully tapped Jenny on the tip of her
straight nose. "A beauty like you wasted as a household
drudge—certainly not! I've much grander plans for you. What
would you say to carrying a tray of choice goods through the
streets? You can tell people where they may find an even
greater selection of ribbons and lace. The apprentices are
absolute dolts at it. But you're so pretty, Jenny, you're bound
to attract custom to the shop." Pet smiled, a calculating
gleam in her eyes. "One look at you and all the gallants in
Whitehall will be beating a path to our door."

"You've both been so kind to me, it's the least I can do,"
Jenny said, smiling at her young aunt, while she concealed
her doubts about the wisdom of the proposal. She had hardly
expected to be thrust into the streets, where she would be far
too visible for comfort. Though it was improbable that the
gypsies visited this fashionable district, the danger of being
recognized still remained.

"Poor Doll's as attractive as a wet weekend, there's no use
denying it. She's of little value to me." Pet plopped on the
edge of Jenny's bed. "Still, even so poor a wench has her
uses—was that not a fine haunch of meat we enjoyed last
night, niece?"

Jenny had no trouble in recalling the juicy beef roast they
had eaten for supper the previous evening; smothered in tasty
gravy and accompanied by fresh white bread and golden
butter, the beef had made a meal to remember. "It was
delicious."

"We have poor, drab little Doll to thank for that superb cut
of meat." Pet smothered a suggestive giggle as she considered her statement; then, mastering her humor, she continued.

"Lymon Perse is the butcher who supplies our table with meat. Poor, washed out little Doll kindly supplies Lymon with . . ." Pet paused, choosing her words with care. "Doll is Lymon's betrothed."

"Oh, I see," Jenny said lamely, suspecting Pet concealed far more than she cared to reveal.

"I'd given up hope of her making a good marriage, so 'tis as well Lymon's taken a fancy to her. And with the price of food these days, one can never afford to look a gift horse in the mouth."

"Do you wish me to take out a tray of goods today?" Jenny asked, reluctantly sliding from the warm bed to the harsh rush matting.

"You can't begin to be noticed soon enough, my love." Pet kissed her lightly on the brow before holding Jenny at arm's length to survey her fair skin, unblemished now, the legacy of bruises faded. "Absolutely lovely, and so early in the morning too! What a treasure," she breathed, almost to herself. "Wear the blue taffeta and allow me to dress your pretty hair with blue ribbons."

"Oh, will you!"

"It'll be my pleasure. I've quite a flair for hair arrangement. You know, Jenny dearest, even his Majesty has been known to walk this street. Everyone goes past here on their way to the 'Change. You never know what influential man might take a fancy to you. Therefore, my love, we must make you as enchanting as possible."

When Pet departed, leaving her to dress, Jenny uneasily reviewed their conversation. Rather than displaying choice merchandise to be purchased at the haberdashery, she had the distinct feeling she herself was to be the most important item on display.

Uncle Will appeared somewhat scandalized when he learned that his niece was to walk the street with a tray of goods, but, as Pet usually had her way in the end, Will's protests gradually subsided until he finally left Pet to her scheming.

After her first afternoon of hawking ribbons and laces to the motley street crowd, Jenny was relieved to be back inside the safety of the shop. She had been jostled against buildings by the press of people, and received many a black look from other vendors, who thought she was encroaching on their territory. Every passing man had ogled her: the better dressed, the more persistent they became; one gallant growing so bold with his hands that Jenny threatened to slap his face if he persisted in his amorous overtures. When she revealed her unpleasant experience to Pet, she was amazed by her aunt's heated reaction.

"Slap him! I've never heard such nonsense!"

"He would not be dissuaded. He was deaf to my protests!" Jenny defended herself indignantly.

Pet smiled as she slid her plump arm about Jenny's shoulders. "Noblemen's attentions are to be encouraged, Jenny. I'd no idea you were such a prudish little provincial. Smile at rich men, flirt with them, be not too particular where they place their hands—but never, never slap them."

It was with growing apprehension that Jenny ventured forth on the second day to cry her wares. "Who'll buy my fine ribbons?" she cried, following Pet's implicit instructions for attracting custom. Such a babble of noise filled the narrow cobbled street that Jenny's soft voice was quickly drowned by the other vendors' raucous shouts of "Fresh cockles," "Buy my sweet lavender," "Hot mutton pasties," and "Ale to quench the stoutest thirst." She soon abandoned her feeble street cry and contented herself with smiling at potential customers.

By noon she had emptied her tray of bright ribbons and lace. Most sales had been to well-dressed gentlemen who had purportedly purchased the trimmings for their ladies.

"Splendid! I'd no idea you'd be such a success," exclaimed Uncle Will in amazement when Jenny returned to the shop to refill her tray. "Nay, wench, sup first, I'll not have it said Will Dunn starves his employees."

Jenny smiled as her uncle tweaked her shining chestnut curls, which Pet had wound about a wired arrangement of silver-edged blue ribbons.

Jenny relished the steaming mutton pasty Will set before her. Tim, the oldest of her uncle's apprentices, brought her a fresh gooseberry tart with a generous dollop of clotted cream, and a mug of foaming ale.

Pet bustled inside the room just as Jenny finished the last flaky crumbs of gooseberry tart. "What are you doing in here?" she demanded sharply, her face betraying a telltale flash of temper.

"I sold everything. When I came back for more ribbons, Uncle Will insisted I eat."

"Sold them! Oh you're doing even better than I expected,"

Pet said, her disagreeable expression dissolving in a smile of satisfaction. "We shall up the price this afternoon, my dear. 'Twill make little difference to your custom, you mark my words." Dimples showed in Pet's plump cheeks. "Your pleasant smile and obliging attitude have already rewarded you, niece. There's a very rich man absolutely enchanted with you." Pet's breathing quickened in excitement, betraying her sheer delight over this new development.

Pet's concern over her romantic affairs seemed little more than a refined version of Annie Strength-in-the-Lord Wooten's business interest in her body. "Who is he?" Jenny asked.

"Oh, I can't tell you that. But he's very rich. An important courtier—Oh, Jenny, you're to be truly blessed," Pet cried, unable to contain her excitement any longer. She hugged her niece in a spontaneous embrace. "He's ordered more expensive merchandise from us than ever before—all because of you, my dear."

The mellow afternoon sun washed over the cobbled street, glancing diamond flashes from the mullioned windows of the overhanging upper stories as Jenny, her tray refilled with merchandise at an inflated price, began her slow passage along Swann Alley. The light on this early October day held a soft, misty quality far removed from the brazen glow of summer. Despite a growing feeling of living in a fish bowl, Jenny enjoyed these hours spent outdoors, for too often of late had she been confined to quarters. While she walked the cobbled streets, Jenny formulated a speech wherein she told her aunt she was not prepared to barter her body to a noble patron to make their shop prosperous. "Poor Doll" had snared only a master butcher; Jenny's eye-catching appearance promised to net far bigger fish.

"Wench, have you silver ribbons in your tray?" To gain her attention the man grasped her arm, halting her passage. He was richly dressed in a red and black beribboned suit, his head eclipsed by a mammoth scarlet hat swathed in fluffy pink plumes.

"Yes, good sir, more than a dozen lengths," Jenny answered quickly, forcing a smile. Since Pet had spoken to her about her admirer, every well-dressed man who exhibited an interest in her—and there were many—came under her uneasy scrutiny. "I'll take all the silver ribbons you have. 'Odd's death, but you're a comely wench to be hawking ribbons," he exclaimed as he moved closer.

Smiling up at him from beneath a fringe of thick dark lashes, and completely unaware of the coquettishness of her action, Jenny politely thanked the gentleman for his compliment. She selected a handful of shimmering silver ribbons from the tray. The nobleman smiled at her in an intimate manner, his pale eyes probing her low, boat-shaped neckline with the utmost appreciation. He paid for his purchase with several gold coins of a far higher value than the goods were worth.

"Why, sir, 'tis far too much," Jenny protested, wide-eyed as the man withdrew yet another coin to press upon her.

"Nay, one of your smiles is worth a thousand guineas," he remarked extravagantly.

His face loomed closer, his protruding blue eyes boring into her brain as if he sought to possess her mind as well as her body. "You are too kind, my lord," Jenny said quickly, stepping back.

"You are becomingly modest. Your aunt told me what a treasure you are. And now that I've spoken to you myself, I could not agree more."

This was he! Startled, Jenny looked full into the man's florid face, seamed with the legacy of dissipation. She encountered watery blue eyes, heavy-lidded and couched in generous folds of skin; a fine network of broken veins formed a tracery over the narrow bridge of his nose. Perhaps in his youth he had been handsome, but a lifetime of carousing had tarnished his appeal.

"You are exceeding kind, sir," she said, finding her tongue at last.

"I hope you'll allow me to be far kinder in the future," the man replied huskily as he bent over her, his thick plush velvet sleeve brushing her hand. "Until then, sweet wench, I bid you good day."

As the tall, well-dressed figure blended into the crowd traversing Swann Alley, Jenny breathed an immense sigh of relief. After his close scrutiny she almost felt as if she had been violated.

A veritable storm would be unleashed when she told her aunt she had no intention of going along with her schemes. A bitter smile touched Jenny's mouth as she considered the reason Pet had been so overjoyed by her appearance. Even this lovely blue gown, which she was rapidly growing to detest, had not been given out of kindness: it was a shrewd investment for the future.

Jenny paused on the street corner to watch the milling throng of people heading toward the magnificent 'Change, where any luxury under the sun could be purchased. Used only to country districts, Jenny never ceased to marvel at the multitudes of citizens to be seen any hour of the day or night. London did not need carriages and wagons to jam its narrow byways; pedestrians alone could make these narrow streets impassable. To the south, beyond the rows of shops and tenements, lay Lombard Street, one of the city's more pictur-esque districts; there bankers and wealthy merchants lived in the ornate dwellings built to house the Lombards, who had been old London's money lenders. On such a street money would be plentiful, yet despite Pet's suggestion that she ex-tend her route to this quarter, Jenny had ventured no farther than Swann Alley and its immediate environs. So far her luck had held, for she had seen none of Manuel's street acquaint-ances; were she to venture further afield, however, it might prove her undoing.

"Lambert, buy some scarlet ribbons to match my gown."

Jenny turned expectantly at the woman's high-pitched com-mand. A fine lady, resplendent in a billowing red and silver striped satin gown, was hurrying toward her. This gorgeously gowned woman was accompanied by an equally richly dressed man, whose softly handsome face was suffused by an indulgent smile.

"I have silk and satin—some edged with silver." Jenny held out her tray so they could view the merchandise. The pouting woman studied the jewel-bright ribbons a moment before selecting a love knot of cherry satin.

"Ah, even satin's no match for your lips," breathed her companion ardently, his attention riveted on his beloved's face.

"Fie, he's so like a little dog." The noblewoman laughed, a tinkling high-pitched tone, while she leaned closer to Jenny as if she would reveal a confidence. "And if the truth were known, wench, his attentions are probably just as faithless. When the next little bitch wags her tail—what ails you?" The noblewoman broke off abruptly, for Jenny was no longer listening to her.

Barely aware of her surroundings, Jenny stared fixedly

across the narrow street at a tall, broad-shouldered man dressed in an elaborate court costume of pink and purple shag silk. Something about the way he walked, the distinctive way he inclined his head, crowned by a wide-brimmed felt hat mounded with purple plumes, tugged at her memory. But it could not be! It was impossible! Her knees grew alarmingly weak and clammy sweat gathered at her brow. The cacophony of street sounds receded and swept back as Jenny wavered, pale with shock. It was as if all the blood had drained from her body in that moment of recognition. Now, as the man turned to face her, she knew beyond any doubt—the splendidly dressed courtier was Kit.

Life surged anew through Jenny's body as she became aware of her rapidly pounding heart shuddering her chest, racing to certain destruction. Kit had taken a step in her direction, but she knew he had not seen her, hidden as she was by the richly dressed couple who were viewing her wide-eyed gaping as certain evidence of lunacy. Her beloved Kit had not died in the sinking of *The Royal Prospect!* No ghost, that tall, golden-haired figure in the preposterously gaudy suit. A heady tumult of joy shot through her. The only man who would ever possess both her heart and her body stood before her, vital and alive in the warm October sunshine. What was she waiting for?

Jenny had taken an eager step forward, aching to be in his arms, longing to shower him with kisses, when she stopped, clutching her heart in sudden anguish at what she saw: a beautiful woman, clad in sweeping emerald-green velvet, a yellow straw hat heaped with green plumes set rakishly on her long black hair, emerged from a silversmith's on the opposite side of the street. Immediately Kit's attention focused on the beauty in green. The woman smiled invitingly into his handsome face as Kit slipped his arm protectively about her diminutive waist, inclining his head toward hers until the dancing purple and green plumes were wedded . . .

"Wench—have you lost your wits?" demanded Jenny's customer, his face setting in a scowl as she heeded not the coins he offered for the ribbon.

Nausea, fiercer than any she had ever experienced before, gripped her in a suffocating wave. Jenny numbly accepted the coins the man pressed into her ice-cold hands. There was nothing crueler than to have seen Kit after all these months of believing him dead, merely to witness his obvious affection for another. Having him this close at last, only to discover his heart was no longer hers, was more torment than she could endure. The familiar manner in which Kit embraced that woman, the way she leaned her head against his shoulder, spoke volumes.

With a strangled sob, Jenny blindly thrust the knot of cherry-red ribbons at the noblewoman and, mumbling an apology, she turned and plunged into the crowd. Her sudden flight caused a momentary flurry of attention along the street. The hastily flung ribbons had landed on the filthy cobbles and her indignant customers shouted for her to come back. People stared after Jenny's fleeing blue skirts, heads wagging in consternation until, the excitement over, they went back to their own business.

Jenny stumbled on, unseeing, crashing blindly into people who failed to move from the path of her sightless flight. Ribbons from her neck tray fell to the street as she rounded a corner, setting off a scuffle of activity from a group of street urchins who retrieved the valuables and nonchalantly wiped away smears of sewage onto their already filthy garments. Jenny gave no thought to the lost ribbons. Her burning purpose was to put distance between herself and him whom she had loved so dearly, whose memory she had revered with near religious devotion . . .

"Jenny! Jenny! Stop!"

At the sound of his voice, she froze, her legs refusing to heed her commands. Kit had seen her after all! A vision of that woman's full-lipped, pale and lovely face beneath the plumed straw hat danced through her mind and Jenny's limbs returned to life. She would not speak to him; she could not speak to him—the pain of her discovery was still too fresh. Already she had considered him lost forever; how little difference there was in truth. With a lovely mistress from his own class beside him, handsome Captain Ashford had little use for a lovesick tavern maid. What a fool she had been! His treachery made her feel humiliated and terribly betrayed. Oh, why had he not stayed dead? That way their love would have remained a cherished thing, unviolated by his infidelity . . .

"Jenny! Jenny!"

Faster she ran, charging down dark odorous alleys where the surface beneath her feet grew slippery with filth. Though

Jenny had explored Swann Alley's adjoining streets, she had little idea of the layout of this dark warren of byways weaving back and forth between overhanging bow-fronted houses, whose sagging gables excluded all but a thin wedge of daylight.

To her horror, when Jenny was forced to stop for breath, her body heaving in great wracking shudders, she saw Kit's fashionable purple-plumed hat bobbing not thirty feet away above a knot of gossiping goodwives.

Once again Jenny resumed her reckless flight. What matter if her lungs burst? She could not confront Kit now with all her pain apparent in her eyes. He must never know how much she had loved him. All those wondrous things he had said were nothing but lies, extravagances easily spoken by fickle courtiers. She had discovered that fact these days past, when other men had paid her lavish compliments in hopes of exchanging pretty words for a few hour's freedom with her body.

"You little fool! Are you trying to kill yourself?"

Through ears that roared like the ocean, Jenny heard Kit's angry shout as she darted recklessly before a heavy-laden farm cart. The cabbage-filled cart delayed him just long enough to allow her to escape down a fetid alley that ran at right angles from the main street. How foul was the air trapped beneath the rotting woodwork of these decaying upper stories! The noxious stench from the choked kennel took what little breath Jenny had left. Reeling drunkenly, she leaned against the wall of a nearby building, panting in a desperate effort to draw breath.

"There you are, by God . . ."

The purple plumes of Kit's hat waved beneath the crumbling woodwork of a neighboring house as he sped along the alley. Rousing herself, Jenny resumed her flight, the empty goods tray still banging about her neck. Blindly she ran on until she rounded a corner and came to a dead end: here a destitute family had erected a wall of timber across the end of the alley to form a primitive dwelling. She was trapped!

"Jenny!"

With supreme effort she tried to wrest herself free as she became imprisoned in Kit's bruising grip. All the pain of her lost love, her agony when she discovered he had betrayed her trust, came uppermost in a great sob of anguish.

"Let me go!"

"Jenny, it's me—Kit!"

"Why else do you think I ran?"

He stared at her, his jaw tensing. "I don't believe this."

"Believe it or not—it's so," she cried, trying to master the ache in her throat.

"Well, by Christ, we'll settle it elsewhere. This place stinks worse than a sewer."

"I'm not going anywhere with you!"

But Kit did not heed her protests; he grabbed Jenny about the waist and half-carried her along the dark alley. She was still fighting him when they emerged in Rose Alley, where sunlight dappled the street with gold. Only then did Kit relax his punishing grip. Swinging her about, he thrust Jenny at arm's length against the wall of a nearby house, pinning her there, his breathing ragged.

"Explain yourself, wench, for surely to God there's some reason to your behavior," he snapped, his face set.

"Me explain! Why should it be me first? You explain. You're the one who's supposed to be dead!"

"And would it please you more an' that were true?" he challenged in anger.

Jenny tried to say yes, tried to defy him to salve her pride, but she could not. "No . . . no, it would not."

Kit's face softened. "Then, Jenny, sweetheart, tell me what ails you? Why did you run from me? What do you in London? I've a million questions to be satisfied . . ."

"What happened aboard *The Royal Prospect?*" she asked, her voice thick with tears. "From all sides I heard that you went down with your ship."

"After the bastard Dutch sank us, I managed to swim to a spar of driftwood. A French vessel fished me half dead from the water."

"Why did you not let me know?"

"How was I to let you know? Talk sense, wench. Half dead, lying wounded in a foreign land . . ."

"But you're no longer in a foreign land."

"Nay, that I'm not, but 'tis only two days past I set foot in London. I thought never to lay eyes on you again. Forever have you been on my mind. That night, those precious hours we shared, sustained me through the agony, the despair. It was for you I clung to that cask, though my blood reddened the sea where I floated, for you I braved the cold water till dark, though I'd damned near given up hope of rescue. For you! Do you hear me, you idiotic wench?''

Jenny stared up at him, his face a small crystal image through her tears.

''Oh, Kit,'' she whispered brokenly, all her anger, her hurt evaporating as the warmth of his nearness thawed the chill of spurned love. The well-remembered fragrance of his clothing assailed her nostrils, the weakening memory only abetting her capitulation. The aura of virility he exuded, the magnetism of his personality combined to disarm her, until Jenny slid weakly against the wall, conceding defeat. ''Oh, Kit,'' she repeated, blinking and spilling her waiting tears.

He seized the empty wooden tray hanging around her neck and pitched it aside. ''We'll have done with that,'' he declared, ignoring her feeble protests.

It seemed an eternity between the thud of the tray on the cobbles and the touch of his mouth against hers. Kit moved through the spill of October sunshine slanting golden between the buildings; though his face was shadowed by his hat brim, within that dark pool his blue eyes blazed fiercely, reflecting an emotion that took her breath. Helplessly, as if her legs were too feeble to support her, Jenny slid another few inches against the wall. Kit's strong arms shot out to save her. Suddenly she found herself welded against his hard body, the contact kindling a fiery wave of emotion in her limbs. Blood surged hot and heavy in her veins, until she thought she could no longer endure the torment of waiting for his kiss.

''Oh, sweetheart, how much I've longed for this,'' Kit breathed huskily when their lips parted.

So intoxicating were his kisses that Jenny knew not where she was as her surging blood carried her to that secret land of dreams where too many times she had dwelt in pain and heartache. ''Dearest Kit, this is like a wonderful dream I've dreamt so often before,'' she whispered, when at last he allowed her speech, overcome with longing as he crushed her against his tremoring body. Kit's strong heartbeat thudded against her chest, and she thrilled to its rhythm.

''This is no place for lovemaking,'' he said gruffly, becoming aware of the crowded street. It was no uncommon sight to find richly dressed gallants seducing maids in the shadows; even couples consummating their heat in London's forgotten alleys was scant cause for comment. But he could not cheapen their love like that. "Come, sweetest, I know a far better place."

"But I can't go with you," Jenny protested in alarm as she remembered her purpose on the streets. "Oh, where are we?" she cried in dismay, looking around at the unfamiliar surroundings.

" 'Tis no matter where we are, you little goose. All that matters is that I've found you again."

With a tremulous smile Jenny rested her head against the heated scent of his neck, shivering in ecstasy as his strong arms came about her in a comforting embrace. "I'm supposed to be selling ribbons," she whispered.

"A pox on ribbons."

"My aunt will be furious."

"Let her rant herself into apoplexy."

"Oh, Kit, be serious."

"I am serious. Now enough protests. I'll take you to Spring Garden to gaze upon the beauteous flowers while I, my love, shall gaze upon you."

And the intensity of Kit's burning eyes sent delicious shivers of anticipation along Jenny's spine. For an instant she hesitated, as a transient spark of loyalty to her relatives came uppermost; but when he slid his strong arm about her waist, when he hugged her against his side, whispering all manner of endearments, her resistance evaporated.

"Oh, yes, we'll go to Spring Garden," she agreed in delight.

They abandoned Will Dunn's empty tray at the entrance to Rose Alley. Jenny walked through the noisy, congested streets in a trance, unable to accept this miracle. From time to time, just to reassure herself she was not dreaming, she stole secret glances at Kit's handsome face. A hot rush of pleasure surged through her veins when he smiled at her, a sensuous curve to his finely chiseled mouth, a world of promise in his deep blue eyes. Jenny listened eagerly as Kit recounted his adventures, thrilling to his rich voice. As they walked she grew aware of the envious glances of grand ladies and serving wenches alike as they beheld her handsome lover. Yet so sublimely happy was she that Jenny took no exception to those hungry, wistful glances. There was but one pretty face that caused her grief: Kit had not yet explained his relationship with the woman in the green plumed hat!

Chapter 11

They crossed the Thames by boat to Foxhall Gardens. Jenny had never been in a boat before, and her exclamations of wonder as the craft sliced through the gray water, rolling with the swell of passing crafts, highly amused Kit, who promised someday to take her on a real voyage.

The early October sun shone warm on her face as Jenny gazed at his sensuous mouth, mentally reliving the delight of his kisses. And her stomach churned in delicious anticipation of the pleasure awaiting her once they disembarked on the opposite shore. The contagious high spirits of passing boat-loads of brightly dressed Londoners bound for the famed pleasure garden greatly increased her feeling of euphoria, until Jenny was positive there could be no happier woman in all England. Even the air of this bright autumn day had a heady, intoxicating quality, she decided, breathing deep of its wine-sweet rapture. With a contented sigh she rested her head on her lover's broad shoulder, watching the widening ripples as they sliced through silver-dappled water.

Hand in hand, Jenny and Kit strolled along the broad gravel walks of Foxhall Gardens, golden in the mellow afternoon sunshine. Though it was already October, frost-free nights had extended the blooming period of many summer flowers: roses, pinks, and hollyhocks created bright islands of color against the grass; fragrant yellow and pink honeysuckle twined sinuously along the hedgerows, where flocks of speckled thrushes feasted on crimson haws. Rose beds, bordered by clipped gooseberry hedges, were gay with brightly colored blooms. As they passed, birdsong chorused from the shielding wall of limes and Lombardy poplars.

Pleasure-loving Londoners, dressed in their finery, were taking advantage of the mild afternoon; chattering, laughing groups gathered around bands of strolling players, while outside the inn a gaudily dressed bear danced for the patrons' amusement. Having little interest in the entertainments of the common man, splendidly dressed Whitehall gallants, sporting narrow mustaches in faithful imitation of their sovereign king, openly indulged in amorous dalliance with perfumed ladies of the town. It appeared as if all London had decided to stroll in Foxhall Gardens today, yet so absorbed were they in each other that Jenny and Kit might have been adrift on an empty sea.

While they walked Jenny recounted the unfortunate chain of events that had brought her to London: the kindness of the gypsy band in taking her in, she mentioned; her relationship with Manuel, she did not. It would be sacrilege to confess such sins inside this lovely garden. Perhaps, when they were old and totally secure in each other's love, she could tell Kit about her gypsy lover—but not yet.

"This aunt and uncle for whom you are working, what manner of people are they?" Kit asked suspiciously, for he liked not the loving attentions bestowed by her Addston relatives.

"They've been kind to me," she allowed, choosing her words with care. It was wise not to reveal her suspicion about Pet's intentions: given his swift temper and the constant desire to see justice served her, Kit might march to the haberdashery and give both Pet and Uncle Will a sizable piece of his mind. Jenny quailed inwardly at the thought. Though she desperately wanted to believe that from now on she would share Kit's life, the memory of that woman in green nagged at her peace of mind. Was it because of his attachment to the lovely noblewoman that Kit had not discussed their future? He had vowed to marry her, yet despite her deep love for him, Jenny wisely understood the improbability of a love match between such an important gentleman and a poor orphan wench—to become his mistress was the most she could expect.

They stopped at the timbered inn within the garden, where they supped on cold beef, egg custards, and warm cheese tarts, washed down by copious amounts of strong ale. After their meal they rested on a bench beneath a broad oak tinged russet and gold by the changing season. A trio of strolling musicians serenaded them with fiddles and harp, the delicate chords of the poignant love song selected in their honor, bringing ready tears to Jenny's eyes. When the song was over, Kit tossed a handful of coins to the musicians.

As evening approached, the purple shadows lengthened; beyond the Thames the setting sun burned a great orange disk surrounded by haloed gold cloud. In the deepening twilight, amorous couples sought secluded corners. Jenny found the spectacle of other lovers' passion painful to watch, for though he had kissed her ardently, Kit had still not attempted to make love to her.

"Let us rest awhile," he suggested at last, his handsome face taut with inner conflict. Kit led her to a bench out of the press of people. All afternoon while they had laughed light-heartedly, the news he must disclose had weighed heavy on his mind. Each passionate kiss speared his heart afresh with the mocking reminder that sorrow's parting lay but a heart-beat away.

Beside this secluded arbor a fronded willow weeped a curtain of feathery green, while a trellis of full-blown pink roses arched above the stone bench. They sat in uncomfortable silence before a splashing fountain, the constant flow of water from a marble nymph's upturned pitcher creating a tinkling background to their thoughts. As the breeze rose, fading pink rose petals rained down on them.

Kit turned to Jenny, his blue eyes troubled. Tonight her beauty moved him so deeply that emotion stabbed knife-sharp in his chest. "Jenny, sweetheart, when I left you at Addston, I promised we'd marry," he said softly, clasping her small hand in his own. "You're a good wench who deserves an honorable proposal. And though it pains me to have to tell you this, I cannot honor that vow."

Kit's words fell like stones on her ears. Jenny suspected this speech was no easier to make than to listen to. All the fond hopes she had lovingly nurtured plunged to an early death.

"You also promised me your heart," she reminded in a small voice.

"Aye, sweetheart, and you have it still."

"Then why do you speak so strangely?"

"You deserve a man who can stay beside you, who'll give you babes. Mine will always be a life of arrivals and departures. It's unfair to ask you to share it with me."

"Oh, Kit, I don't care how many departures there are, just as long as there's an equal number of arrivals," Jenny whispered, clinging to his arm, thrilling to feel his hard muscles contract beneath the velvet nap of his silk shag sleeve.

"That, sweetheart, is something I cannot promise."

"I demand no iron-bound guarantees. That's not what I want."

"What do you want?"

"You."

Moved almost to grief, Kit crushed her soft body in fierce embrace. Gruffly he said, "War's imminent. Everyone but the King urges it and I think he still hopes to negotiate with the Dutch. However many years the war lasts, wherever it takes me, I must serve his Majesty. At this moment a vessel's being outfitted—I'm its captain. Do you understand what I'm saying? I must return to sea. And I can't take you with me."

Jenny swept Kit's broad-brimmed hat from his head and dropped it on the bench. Her hands soft against his face, she turned him about. "Those things I accept. That you still love me is all that matters. Don't you see, Kit, for so long I thought you dead—but you're alive and this is the most wonderful day of my life."

Kit shuddered with emotion at her fervent declaration, and he slid his strong arms around her back, drawing her silky head into the heated hollow of his neck.

"You're sure it doesn't matter that we cannot be wed?" he whispered hoarsely against the perfumed brightness of her chestnut hair. "Do you really mean that?"

"Yes."

Kit's hot mouth fused with hers, and Jenny shuddered from head to toe at the delirious sensation sweeping through her body. Wrapped in each other's arms, they watched the splashing fountain, silver in the uncertain light; from a nearby mulberry bush came the sweet, full-throated song of a nightingale.

"Oh, sweetheart, I didn't dare hope you loved me that much," he whispered.

"I'll love you forever, Kit. From that first time I saw you I've known we were born for each other."

His hands trembled as he caressed her. As if by mutual consent, they stood, the unnatural light lending an eerie beauty to their features. He kissed her again, holding her tight as if he would never let her go. For a long time they stood unmoving, locked in each others arms, until the silence was broken by a burst of laughter and sporadic applause drifting from the nearby tavern.

"Oh, Jenny, sweetheart, I want you so," Kit breathed

raggedly, his heart pounding a deafening rhythm. "All this time I've longed for you . . ."

"Come," she said simply as she took his hand, placing her fingers against his hot lips to silence his impassioned speech.

The grass was fragrant in their nostrils as Kit pulled Jenny against him, covering her with his warm body.

"What foolish promises we make ourselves," he whispered huskily. "I even vowed the next time I took you 'twould be in a bed."

"Nay, I would not want it so. The night and the sweetness of growing things are part of our love."

Jenny's words totally disarmed him. Kit welded his mouth to hers, searing her lips with passion, making her moan with delight as she shuddered against him. The ache between her thighs swelled close to bursting, compounding the curious heaviness that possessed her limbs; each touch, each ravishing kiss, made her blood roar like a mighty ocean. Kit covered her throat with kisses, his lips spreading liquid fire; he stroked her back, his hands so arousing that she thought she would die from the delight. In that instant the vital difference between the emotion she felt for Kit and that uncommitted heat of desire she had known for Manuel became crystal clear: this all consuming passion touched her soul; the other was merely of the flesh.

As Kit kissed and caressed her in expert arousal, passion shot through her belly, consuming her with fire. She gasped in delight, pressing herself against him, rejoicing in the quick, hot surge of his manhood against her thighs. When he uncovered her full breasts, gently tracing his thumb over her erect pink nipples, his touch turned tantalizing and whisper soft, bringing hot tears to her eyes. Jenny wanted to weep, to scream, to die with pleasure.

Slowly Kit led her to the brink of climax and back until Jenny cried out, demanding release. This was not the time, nor the place, for nakedness. With trembling hands he lifted her skirts, fighting the cumbersome yards of blue taffeta that came between them. Kit laid her on her back, trailing hot, fiery kisses along her thighs, moving higher, until Jenny clutched wildly at his hair, threading her fingers in the gold to imprison the delight against her flesh. No other man possessed the skill to delay her plunge over that precipice of desire, keeping her on the brink of fulfillment, the more to savor each shuddering pang of delight. Jenny kissed him deeply, their eager tongues straining within each other's mouths. Now her hand trembled about the hot smooth strength of his throbbing flesh, and she moaned at her loss when the delight was suddenly wrenched from her. Tonight her desire for Kit went beyond the mere welding of flesh, becoming a total commitment of heart, body, and soul. A tumultuous cry was torn from her lips as he slid inside her, filling her with throbbing heat. Slowly, and with the utmost control, Kit extracted each fraction of pleasure she was capable of experiencing, until Jenny writhed delirious beneath him. Gradually, as the tempo of his strokes increased, the tumult could no longer be contained; like a bursting dam the tide of ecstasy carried them to heights never before attained. Now only vaguely aware of her own cries, of Kit's muffled voice, Jenny was swept away by a devastating sensation close to death.

Serenaded by a pair of sweet-voiced nightingales, they dozed contentedly in each other's arms, Kit's warm embrace imparting comfort in that aftermath of lovemaking when sorrow sometimes replaced her joy. Later, when Jenny woke, his arms were still wrapped protectively about her. She opened her eyes and Kit kissed her tenderly, his hot mouth vulnerable with spent passion.

"That was worth enduring hell for," he whispered hoarsely, his cheek against hers. "No other woman can compare with you."

No other woman! The huskily whispered compliment struck an icy chill through Jenny's heart. Surely he did not picture that woman in green even now while he held her in his arms, while his body was still part of hers? Gnawing jealousy over this afternoon's discovery crept in to steal her bliss. With supreme effort Jenny thrust the painful memory aside. "Nor any other man," she whispered as he withdrew from her.

The rising crescent moon sparkled silver in the black sky as they left their bower. A fresh breeze blowing off the water made Jenny shiver, and Kit gave her his silk shag doublet to ward off the chill.

"Come, sweetheart, we'll drink a cup of mulled ale to warm us," he suggested as he guided her along the path to the tavern.

With arms wrapped about each other's waists, they entered the lighted tavern, where roisterous celebrants drank beneath its blackened oak beams. They downed two cups of mulled ale in short order. Kit brought dark rye bread and a wedge of

Cheshire cheese to eat on the homeward journey. They left the noisy inn and headed toward the river steps.

Jenny was overwhelmed with sadness when she realized that once they crossed the Thames, her wonderful day would be over. Kit would return to his lodgings and he had not invited her to accompany him! Though she tried to fight against suspicion, Jenny could not help picturing that dark-haired vision impatiently awaiting his arrival, prepared to accuse him of dallying with another, for surely when Kit deserted her in Swann Alley the woman had seen the object of his mad pursuit. Kit had said they could not be wed because of his imminent return to sea, yet sea captains had wives ashore. Was that woman in green's prior claim to his affection a greater barrier to their marriage? To her knowledge Kit had never lied to her, but perhaps his sins of omission far outweighed those of commission.

Kit hailed a waiting waterman. Soon Jenny was huddled beside him as they skimmed across the Thames faster than she had dreamed possible, rapidly speeding her cherished day to its death. Mist wreathed about the boat in thick white streamers, trapping the bone-numbing chill of the river.

At the foot of Blackfriars' Stairs, Kit stopped to pay the waterman, haggling over the outrageous fare the man demanded, the charge doubled because of the late hour. While the men cursed and bargained, Jenny stared through the wisping fog at the lapping black water where a scum of flotsam bobbed against the steps. One question repeatedly curled through her brain, drowning the men's angry voices: what was Kit's relationship to that woman?

"Where are we going?" Jenny forced herself to ask as they finally walked up the steps, the fare paid.

"To my house, of course."

"You have a house in London!"

He laughed at her surprise. "Think you I sleep beneath the arches of London bridge? It's a grand townhouse in Lombard Street, hard by Sir Robert Vyner's, the city sheriff. But I must confess, 'tis only rented lodgings. The house is owned by a family friend who is currently abroad."

"And do you live there alone?" Jenny asked, intently studying his face. They paused beneath an iron lantern swinging above the door of a waterfront tavern. Did she imagine the cloud passing over his features?

"Not completely alone," he admitted gruffly.

"Who else lives with you?"

"At present, friends are staying with me. But do not worry, sweet, there's more than enough room for you."

"Me?"

"Aye, do you not intend to accompany me?" All pleasure died in his face as she shook her head.

"Much as I long to go with you, I cannot."

A baffled expression crossed Kit's handsome face as he gripped her upper arm. "Cannot? Why? Explain yourself."

Swallowing the lump that came into her throat, Jenny tried to remain calm. "First you must explain something to me, Kit. So wonderful was it to find you alive, I neglected to ask, but I should have demanded an answer long before . . . before . . ."

"An answer to what?"

"Who is she?"

"She?"

"Aye, *she*—oh, enough play acting," Jenny cried, her voice brittle as pain twisted like a blade in her heart when he pretended to misunderstand. "The woman you were with today—yon beauty with the coal-black hair!"

He stared at her, his face grim. "So that's why you ran—you saw me with Louise."

Jenny fought tears of pain and anger, her cheeks afire; she wished she need not ask the hurting question. "What is she to you?"

"Since you've already decided on an answer, why bother to ask?"

The rising wind swung the lantern, setting golden shadows dancing across Kit's face. They glared at each other. A small voice of caution screamed inside Jenny's head, but she recklessly disregarded its warning. "Seeing that you're being so evasive, my conclusion must be right!" she cried, fighting the desire to burst into tears.

"And that is?"

"She's your mistress!"

Kit gripped her upper arms, his fingers biting deep. "And believing that, you still lay with me?"

"Tell me the truth, that's all I ask. She's waiting for you now, isn't she? And she too expects your loyalty." Fighting for breath, Jenny gulped. "It's little consolation that you've deceived her also!"

Angrily Kit pulled her against him. "Stop it!" he cried,

shaking her until her chestnut hair spilled from its silver-edged ribbons. "I'll not deny Louise is living at my house . . ."

"I knew it!"

"You know nothing about it! Louise de Brand's an old friend. Her brother captained the French vessel that rescued me. They are lodging with me because they're strangers to the city. It's the least I can offer in return for the great service they performed for me!"

"*His* service I grant you—'tis only hers which causes pain."

"She's not my mistress!"

"I don't believe you! Can you deny you've lain with her?" Jenny demanded, her gray eyes flashing as she tried to extricate herself from his grasp. "Tell me true—can you deny it?"

Kit looked away and Jenny had her answer. A sob was wrenched from her throat, dying somewhere deep, robbing her of breath . . .

"There are a hundred women I've bedded! None of them matter but you. Why won't you believe me, you little fool?"

"Because, Captain Ashford, yon raven-haired beauty made you forgetful of your promise to return for me!"

"I did return!" Kit cried, slamming Jenny against the tavern wall. "You were gone. And the barmaid would tell me naught. What was I to do? Combing Cornhill is like seeking a needle in a haystack.

"Are you sure it was not because you found it sweeter between your French woman's legs?"

Anger blazed in Kit's face; when he spoke, his voice was tight. "Why should I waste my time? You've already tried and condemned me. I owe you no further explanations, Mistress Dunn."

Appalled by his terse statement, Jenny stared in horror at Kit's hard features; all the love, the tenderness, was gone as his mouth formed an unyielding seam. How much older he appeared in anger. And she had wrought the terrible change in him by her jealous accusations. Yet he had not denied lying with Louise! Pain stabbed afresh at the reminder. Whatever accusations she made had not altered the truth. How did she know he had gone in search of her? How did she know tonight was not merely a welcome change of pace to relieve the tedium of an established relationship? Women stared openly after him on the streets, revealing that hers was not the only quickened blood when Kit Ashford choose to bestow his sensual smile!

"What a fool I was to believe you'd stay faithful. Babs was right—you never had any intention of coming back."

Kit did not reply. The rumble of approaching wheels warned him to move out of the way as a horse-drawn hackney rounded the corner; the driver stopped halfway down the street to allow his passenger to alight.

"Are you coming home with me or not?" Kit demanded through clenched teeth.

"And watch you with her? Do you think me mad?"

"I've told you, Louise is merely a friend."

"There's no need to lie!"

Kit raised his hand to strike her, anger blazing in his face. "Never call me liar again, mistress," he snarled, allowing his hand to drop. "There's a hackney hell cart. Do you choose to ride home in style? For I'm done with this ridiculous conversation."

"I'll walk."

"Nay, you'll do nothing of the sort. Here, I'll pay your fare—'tis the least I can do considering how well you serviced me!"

Jenny gasped in shock at his cruel statement. "Oh, how could you!" she gasped, no longer fighting her tears.

But Kit paid no heed to her question as he hailed the approaching carriage. "Take this wench to her lodging," he commanded the driver. Turning to Jenny, he said, "Give the driver your destination, sweetest."

Pain and nausea throbbed in a hot tide through her body as Jenny stared at him, so handsome, so arrogant, in his splendid clothing. How could she ever have thought he loved her beyond all measure? How could she have believed he would return to make her his own? Swallowing the choking lump in her throat, Jenny mumbled her address to the grizzled hackney driver. Kit swung open the carriage door, offering his hand in assistance. Jenny proudly declined the courtesy. The door slammed and she heard him give an abrupt command to the hackney driver to hasten. The man pocketed the coins Kit had given him and, clicking his whip, he set the grays in motion.

Though she tried to resist the urge, Jenny could not help turning for a final glimpse of him. Kit stood motionless in the street, illuminated by a flickering pool of light as the lantern swung above the door, the plumed hat adding inches to his height, his elaborate, beribboned shag silk suit clinging to his magnificently muscled torso to accentuate his broad shoulders. How much she loved him still, she admitted miserably, choking on her grief. Trampled pride over his betrayal had roused her quick temper, spurring her to recklessly sever the bonds between them.

Kit swung about and walked away, not even waiting until the hackney rounded the corner, his stride lengthening until he was swallowed by the shadows.

Was he that impatient to return to Louise? Even tonight, after they had made love, was he that eager to go home to his Frenchwoman's arms? Jenny buried her face in her arms and sobbed as if her heart would break.

Chapter 12

Her tears mastered, Jenny spent the remainder of the bone-shaking hackney ride to Cornhill wondering how she could slip unnoticed into her uncle's house. By this late hour everyone would be asleep. The more she thought about returning to her uncle's haberdashery, the more uneasy she became. She had lost both the tray and the money in her mad flight through the streets. She must now face Uncle Will empty-handed, her crime compounded by the lateness of the hour. Nervously twisting her hands together, Jenny took a steadying breath as the hackney driver deposited her outside the corner shop.

Swann Alley lay in darkness, the only sounds being the squeaks and thuds of scavenging rats in the dungheaps. A moonbeam slanted across the cobbled street, shimmering briefly across the buildings before scudding clouds eclipsed the moon. Jenny tried to tidy her disheveled hair, numb with pain for what she had found and lost today. When she first saw Kit with that noblewoman, she should have guessed he merely sought to dally with her body. All his vows of tender devotion and eternal love had been merely a courtier's silver-tongued lies. Besides, what actual right had she to condemn him for unfaithfulness? Kit had thought her lost to him forever. And when she had believed him dead, it had taken little persuasion to break her self-imposed chastity. At the reminder of Manuel Jenny's cheeks flamed red—no, she had no right at all to condemn Kit's actions.

Skirting the blackened store front, she squared her shoulders, freshly determined to confront her uncle with the truth, rousing him from his bed to admit her if need be. The dishonesty of trying to slip unnoticed to her room would be pointless once he learned his goods were lost.

Jenny caught her breath as the shop door was flung open, shedding a pool of lantern light over the cobbles. Pet, with Will and Doll peering over her shoulders, blocked the doorway, arms akimbo, her face dark with wrath.

"By all that's holy! So at last you come dragging home!

And, my fine lady, just where do you think you've been till this hour?''

"Jenny, wench, where's the tray?'' Will asked, his soft round face creased with concern. ''Where are the goods . . . and my money?''

"Well you might ask, husband. Methinks this slut's been traipsing the streets with little concern for your goods,'' Pet concluded, reaching out to drag Jenny over the threshold.

"That's not true!'' Jenny protested indignantly, finding her voice as Will slammed the shop door. To the accompaniment of sliding bolts and rattling chains, she attempted to explain herself. ''I met someone I know. He took me to Spring Garden and we forgot the time. I . . . I did not intend to stay out so late.''

"But the money, wench? The tray? Where are they?'' Will seemed more perplexed than angry as he shuffled to Jenny's side, his gray flannel nightshirt fluttering about his spindly shanks.

"They're . . . lost,'' she mumbled penitently.

"Lost! Lost! Did you hear that, husband? The foolish wench has *lost* them! Are you a lunatic?'' Pet demanded as she grabbed her niece's flying chestnut hair and hung on, anger and temper darkening her round face. ''How could you lose a tray of goods? How could you lose our money?''

"I didn't mean to.'' Jenny used her utmost control not to slap her aunt, whose detaining hand tangled painfully in her hair. Sense told her such retaliation would sound the death knell on her continuation as a member of this household, and, however despised she felt here, Jenny needed the shelter of their home. She had nowhere else to go. Her mind strayed to that parting jibe Kit had flung at her. And the pain of the reminder began her tears afresh.

"Nay, wench, don't weep so,'' Will comforted gruffly as he patted her shoulder.

"Wouldst thou seek to comfort the wench?'' Pet shrieked in rage, ''a wicked wench who's wasted a tray of our best goods—who lost our money? And, for all we know, was out whoring the best part of the night . . .''

"Loveday, please, accuse her not of . . .''

"Why not? Because she's pretty? Well, Will Dunn, you're just as big a fool as other men, taken in by a pretty face!''

"Can I go back to bed?'' Doll interrupted with a loud sniff, ''I'm tired.''

Pet swung about to face her sister, fury reddening her face. "No, you may not go to your bed! You'll stay and hear this out! You can learn firsthand what happens when a flighty wench disobeys her betters."

Duly chastised, Doll retreated to the corner of the shop, where she perched on an upturned barrel, her habitual sniffs punctuating the remainder of the conversation.

"I'll leave Jenny's punishment to you, Loveday," Will said gruffly, clearing his throat, ill at ease at the thought of having to mete out justice to a female. To his apprentices he dispensed canings with ease; his pretty niece was a different kettle of fish. The very idea of hurting so lovely a creature, of making her cry, tore his soft heart to shreds.

"Very well, go back to your warm bed. Leave me down here to do a man's work."

"But, loveday, if you'd rather I . . ."

"Go! Waste not another moment of your precious rest." Dramatically Pet pointed her finger toward the dark stair. "Be gone, Will Dunn, and leave this unpleasant task to me. At least *I* have the stomach for it."

Looking extremely sheepish, Will mumbled a hasty good night before escaping up the stair.

"Doll, fetch the whip."

Jenny was shaken out of her stupor when she beheld a cruel black whip in Pet's raised hand. Her first inclination was to fight her aunt's chastisement, but ever mindful of her precarious position in this household, Jenny gritted her teeth, forcing herself to endure two lashes.

"Get you to bed, sister, I'll manage alone," Pet commanded, shooing Doll from the shop.

Once Doll had left, Pet flung the whip aside. "Two lashes I've given you, my girl; you deserve a dozen more. And I warrant you'd have them, if it weren't for a certain gentleman's interest in you. How dare you stay out half the night?" Pet stopped, her speech growing labored. She boiled with fury at having her plans go astray: tonight she had promised to deliver Jenny to a certain rich nobleman for his inspection; when the man arrived, she had to dismiss him with a gaggle of foolish excuses. She dared not reveal she had no idea where the wench had gone, dared not intimate that at this moment she might be writhing in an alley with some jumped-up pot boy . . .

"Never cross me again!" she cried aloud. "You've been

treated royally in this household—clothed, well fed, pampered. What more could a wench ask?''

"I'm sorry, Aunt Pet, truly I am. I never meant to anger you," Jenny apologized meekly, while she smarted inwardly with angry humiliation. Yet the physical pain of the whipping was small compared to her inner misery.

"Very well, I accept your apology," Pet conceded begrudgingly, her small mouth tight. "Don't leave the house again without my permission. Do you understand? Who is this man? Someone from Addston?''

"Yes, I knew him there," Jenny mumbled, anxious to escape from her aunt's cross-examination. "I'll try not to anger you again.''

"See that you don't. Next time I'll not spare you. You'll be lashed until you bleed," Pet shouted, her cheeks flushing dark red. "I won't have my plans destroyed by a foolish, brainless wench who hasn't . . ." She stopped, realizing she was revealing far too much. "Get to bed. Rise at first light and help Jessie lay the fires. It'll be a good punishment for you.''

"Yes, Aunt Pet. I'm sorry.''

"Sorry!" Pet muttered to herself as she stooped to retrieve the whip, listening to Jenny's retreating steps on the uncarpeted stair. "Sorry!" In anger she lashed out at a bolt of fabric, giving a few extra strokes in an effort to vent her rage. All ready, eager, hot—the fool man had been virtually foaming at the mouth. And for what? That mindless little slut was out bedding some hayseed in an alley! With a final vicious slice at the fabric, Pet flung the whip aside; then, gathering her voluminous nightgown in her hands, she marched upstairs to bed.

Jenny lay staring through the unshuttered window at the bright moon, aching, yearning for all that might have been and was not. She was not prude enough to think Kit had not taken dozens of women in foreign ports; a man as attractive as he never wanted for feminine attention. Repeatedly he had sworn he loved only she. Had he spoken the truth when he said Louise de Brand was merely an old friend?

Not long after she had counted three strikes on the parish church clock, Jenny lapsed into fitful sleep. When she jerked awake a few minutes later, she was shivering, her shift soaked with sweat. She had awakened from a nightmare wherein she saw Kit drowning, yet the pole she stretched out to save him stayed beyond his reach. On the opposite shore she beheld the lovely Frenchwoman in her fashionable green gown, beckoning to him. And though Kit bled profusely from his terrible wounds, he swam eagerly toward Louise's outstretched arms.

Pale gray light gleamed over the rooftops, heralding the dawn. Jenny wondered if she swallowed her pride and told Kit she did not care what Louise had been to him whether he would welcome her back.

There was but one way to learn the answer to her question.

The household was still abed when Jenny crept downstairs. As she stood in the darkened shop she could hear the apprentices stirring in the back room; if she unlocked the door herself, the boys would not know she had left the shop.

"Is that you, Tim?" Jenny called the oldest boy's name.

"Aye, who's there?" he answered sleepily.

"It's Jenny. I'm to unlock the doors this morning. 'Tis my punishment for staying out late. You can go back to sleep for a few minutes."

Tim grunted his assent, barely remembering to thank her before he snuggled beneath the wool blanket covering his straw-filled pallet.

With trembling hands Jenny drew back the bolts and fitted the key in the huge padlock, unlocking the main lock. The stout chain clanged against the heavy oak door with a crash loud enough to wake the dead. Her heart pounding, she waited, but no one came downstairs to investigate the noise. Swiftly she unchained and unlocked the remaining locks; then, replacing the keys on the nail beside the door, she stepped forth to freedom.

It was chilly in the early morning gloom and she wished she had remembered to bring a cloak. Though she did not know in which house, she knew Kit lodged in Lombard Street close by the Sheriff of London's house. She was confident she would find someone to direct her to his residence. As Jenny sped toward Lombard Street the watch called the hour, his gruff tones followed a few minutes later by the deafening clangor of church bells reverberating through the narrow cobbled streets to announce the beginning of a new day. Everywhere she looked doors were being unlocked and shutters taken down.

Many of the old lathe and plaster dwellings on Lombard Street were elaborately ornamented with bright colors and

gold leaf design. Jenny paused before the distinctive house of
Sir Robert Vyner, so large that it covered half an acre; she
had been provided with a description of the Sheriff of London's palatial residence by a master baker who had come out
of his kitchen for a breath of crisp morning air. But when
Jenny glanced about the deserted street for someone to direct
her to Kit's house, she saw only a ragged street urchin
picking through a pile of refuse.

"Lad, can you tell me where Captain Ashford lodges?"

The boy squinted up at her through a thatch of filthy blond
hair. "Don't know no Captain Ashford."

"You must have seen him—a sea captain with golden hair.
A fine figure of a man, newly come to the city. There's a
foreign lady and gentleman lodging with him," Jenny added
uncomfortably.

"Aw, 'im. That 'ouse there. The one with the bloody great
bird over the door."

Jenny thanked the boy and stepped briskly toward the
house he had indicated. A huge stone eagle, poised for flight,
was mounted above the red-painted door. The prevailing style
of architecture in Lombard Street being medieval, the smooth,
uncluttered lines of this modern red brick dwelling contrasted
severely with its more ornate neighbors. The row of shuttered
windows fronting the street lent an air of desertion to the
house; nor were there any sounds of activity within. Jenny
nervously lifted the heavy brass knocker, her heart pounding
and her throat going dry as she wondered if Kit would refuse
to see her. The painful humiliation of his rejection would be
like dying.

A red-liveried footman finally opened the door, disdainfully looking down his long nose at Jenny's hastily brushed
hair and crumpled gown. "What do you want?"

"I came to see Captain Ashford."

"Captain Ashford's not in residence."

When the man would have closed the door, Jenny put her
foot in his way. "Captain Ashford was at home last night,"
she challenged, looking the footman straight in the eye. "Why
is he not here this morning?"

Muttering beneath his breath at her impudence, the red-
coated footman glared at her. "Because Captain Ashford left
before dawn on urgent business."

"I don't believe you!"

"Then don't believe me, wench, but get yourself gone."

"Where did he go?" Jenny asked, feeling suddenly nauseated. Kit had said nothing about leaving this morning; he had suggested his voyage was to be sometime hence.

" 'Tis none of your affair. On urgent business is all I'm at liberty to say," the footman announced, pursing his thin lips.

"Did the French sea captain and his sister go with him?"

"I'm not at liberty to say," the footman repeated.

"But a message . . . he must have left a message . . . he . . . he wouldn't go without leaving me word," Jenny stammered, her heart beating so rapidly she thought she would faint.

"He left no message for you, you addled wench. Rich men do not concern themselves with dockside sluts," he sneered unpleasantly. "Now be gone, or I'll have you thrown in jail."

Jenny moved slightly, giving the footman room to slam the heavy door in her face. Stunned, she waited a long time on the broad steps until she finally turned aside and stumbled blindly to the street.

Where could Kit have gone? Had he taken Louise to France? Despite their bitter quarrel, surely he loved her enough not to have left without some word. The sky behind great St. Paul's turned vivid orange as Jenny walked along Lombard Street, tears spilling uncontrollably down her pale cheeks. All her doubts about Kit's fidelity were rekindled by her discovery; now she boiled with passionate rage over his deception. He had known all along he was to sail on the morning tide. Had his tender words of concern over his inability to promise marriage been part of a devious plan? If so, his deception had succeeded, for she had willingly allowed him to seduce her—nay, not merely allowed, but aided and abetted the crime! Last night's lovemaking had been naught but a bittersweet farewell. Lacking the courage to reveal his intentions, Kit Ashford had lied convincingly. Her own accusations, spawned out of jealousy, had likely proved a boon to extricate him from a difficult situation. Had she not stormed away in anger, Kit might have been hard pressed to dispose of her before dawn. French Louise would doubtless have been enraged to discover another wench invading her territory.

By the time she entered Dunn's Haberdashery, Jenny was drained of both hate and sorrow; she walked like someone dead, oblivious to her surroundings.

For the remainder of the morning she trailed about the

house like a pale ghost. Doll stopped her on the stair, her pinched face alight with rare excitement.

"See, Jenny, see what I have!" Proudly Doll held out her scrawny hand, where a gold ring, set with a single creamy pearl, gleamed in the murky light.

Though Jenny admired the expensive ring, she was so preoccupied with her own misery she gave no indication of having heard Doll's exclamation. During the past hour massed rain clouds had given way to a cold autumn deluge; she stared at the dismal gray world beyond the latticed casement, watching raindrops forming widening rivers on the glass. Across the alley the buildings wavered, a distorted wall of pied timbers.

"You're so jealous you can't even praise it!" Doll cried, snatching back her hand. "I suppose you think it should be yours. You get everything else around here."

"I'm pleased you have a fine ring," Jenny said, her voice gruff with weeping.

"I always knew you were selfish, but not to even praise my ring," Doll grumbled, giving her a vindictive shove.

Normally Jenny would have retaliated, but this morning she felt too drained to respond to Doll's spite. "I must be going," she mumbled, tearing her gaze from the spattered pane. Raindrops were an unpleasant reminder of her own barely restrained tears; she must not weep before Doll.

"Go then! It gladdens my heart to see you knocked off your pedestal. You're not the only one who has admirers. And this ring proves it!"

Jenny quickly descended the stairs, leaving Doll muttering to herself. Doll watched her go, hugging the beautiful pearl ring protectively against her body. For the hundredth time she held out her arm to admire her latest acquisition, sighing in rapture over its beauty. Making sure Jenny was safely out of sight, Doll pulled a paper from inside her bodice. There was no reason to keep the message. It had been so easy to convince the messenger she was Jenny Dunn. That selfish creature did not deserve so lovely a gift! Besides, Doll thought sadly, pretty Jenny would receive many more expensive gifts from admirers, while she had little chance of receiving anything more exotic than a beef roast or a brace of partridges.

The window squeaked as Doll pushed it open; raindrops spattered over the sill. Scowling in annoyance, Doll tore the note to shreds, which she fluttered to the wet cobbles. Then she slammed the window and ran upstairs.

One strip of parchment curled about the paving, momentarily resisting the gush of water before it whirled down the central kennel of Swann Alley. The paper lodged face uppermost against a drain, where water blurred the elegant handwriting, leaving only three words decipherable above a smudge of blue: "My dearest Jenny," it began . . .

For four days the rain did not stop. Cold, damp air penetrated the old timbered house like icy fingers; everything was wet to the touch as the uneven plaster walls weeped streams of moisture. Miraculously, Thursday dawned clear, with puffy white clouds scudding across the sparkling blue sky. During the recent deluge much filth had been washed into the Thames, so even the usual stench of the streets failed to taint the pleasant morning breeze.

It was such a golden day that it put Pet in an unusually cheerful mood. It was high time she put resentment aside and forgave her niece. Never had she thought the wench would take her disgrace so much to heart. Why, she had been like a wraith these days past. Jenny had been put to work helping the apprentices and assisting in the shop, but today her demeaning penance was at an end. Pet felt positively beneficient as she pictured the sheer delight on the poor wench's face when she told her she was forgiven. Besides, it was unwise to leave an amorous man to cool his heels too long: if her rich quarry slipped the noose, she would never forgive herself.

"Jenny, dearest, I hope you understand why I've been sharp with you of late," Pet began, smoothing the embroidered front panel of her magenta silk gown with a plump, nervous hand.

"I may not have liked it, but I understood," Jenny said, forcing a weak smile. "You had cause for anger. I behaved like a senseless loon."

"Nay, be not so harsh with yourself," Pet chided as she slipped her arm around Jenny's shoulders. "We all make mistakes. And we all expect forgiveness."

Jenny nodded her agreement and dutifully accepted Pet's damp kiss on the brow. But though she smiled sweetly, Jenny was not taken in by Pet's generous speech: her aunt must have hatched a plan that demanded her cooperation.

"Dress you in your fine blue gown—'tis all ·clean and pressed, the 'prentices saw to it yesterday. How I've hated to see you wearing that old sack.'' Pet tugged the rough linen gown Jenny had been wearing during her disgrace. ''Throw this thing out! I can't bear to see such a lovely creature dressed in rags. Soon, my love, you'll have not one splendid gown, but a whole wardrobe of gowns. You mark my word, Aunt Pet knows what she's talking about, she does indeed. We'll soon be rich—rich, I say.''

This bubbling speech further served to convince Jenny that Pet had a new scheme under way.

''Am I to go back into the street?''

''Nay, for we've had a request this morning from a rich household to view our wares. We've never done that type of trade before. And it's all possible because of you, my sweet girl. Oh, someday my Will's going to be so rich!''

It was late afternoon before Jenny set about her important errand, taking a select package of imported lace and satin ribbons to her prospective customers. Pet had given her specific directions for reaching Sir Miles Russell's mansion off Cheapside: the residence, Pet told her, was near the church of St. Mary-le-Bow, which, after St. Paul's, was London's most famous church. Traditionally, only a person born within the sound of Bow bells could claim to be a true Londoner.

The broad thoroughfare of Cheapside was even grander than Cornhill, which Jenny had thought must be the widest street in London. Cheapside was lined with tall houses, some reaching more than four stories in height. In this wealthy district there were a number of goldsmiths' shops; the glitter of their displayed merchandise, worth a king's ransom, made her gasp in awe. The tall, grand houses and Cheapside's many colorful taverns also fascinated her.

While she walked beneath the blue October sky, Jenny sought to lose herself in her surroundings, seeking a balm for the pain in her heart. This morning Pet had lavishly praised her appearance, unaware that she was little more than an empty shell. Kit's betrayal and subsequent desertion had wounded her more deeply than she had believed possible. Never before had she felt so friendless and alone. She had vowed to have naught more to do with men—they were liars and deceivers—but the heated surge of her blood at fondly remembered passion warned her that for one of her nature, such drastic measures might prove too stern a remedy. Poignant memories of Kit's love, the fire of his kiss, tormented her unbearably. Though she fought hard against the admission, Jenny knew no other man would ever make her feel that way again. When Kit Ashford had sailed on the morning tide, her heart had sailed with him.

During Pet's recital of Sir Miles Russell's wealth, complete with the inevitable reminder of Will's future prosperity should Sir Miles carry word of their goods to court, Jenny's mind had strayed to her own misery. Even the Dunns were not the loving, welcoming family she had at first supposed them to be. Pet's affection for her was based solely on her value in pandering to the King's profligate courtiers. No doubt, when presented with his wife's latest immoral scheme, Uncle Will would protest, but Jenny suspected his overwhelming desire to obtain noble patronage would effectively salve his conscience. When she refused to cooperate, doubtless she would be shown the door.

Sir Miles Russell's impressive house of buff stone stood near the end of the street, adjacent to the ancient churchyard of St. Mary-le-Bow. Straggling branches of a large plane tree overshadowed the shallow flight of steps leading up to the blue painted front door. Jenny paused to admire a group of well-dressed passersby, and she stared in awe at the splendidly appointed carriages traversing the broad thoroughfare. It was easy to see why Pet had been so anxious to obtain Sir Miles' patronage, for he dwelt among the well-to-do.

As she opened the narrow wrought-iron gate leading to the side entrance, Jenny wondered if the nobleman had a lecherous young son whom Pet intended to snare, using her tempting niece as bait.

The housekeeper answered her knock. Mrs. Kent, a tall, gaunt woman dressed in stern black bombazine, wasted little time in pleasantries, for the unexpected appearance of this pretty piece immediately put her on guard. "And what be your duties?" she demanded, motioning Jenny indoors.

"I've brought samples from Dunn's Haberdashery for the lady of the house. There are some fine lace whisks and embroidered caps . . ."

"Samples! I never heard of such a thing. Who sent you?"

"My aunt made prior arrangements with Sir Miles Russell," Jenny announced, disliking this hard, unsmiling woman who acted as if the house belonged to her.

Mrs. Kent haughtily thrust her nose in the air. "Well, if you say so," she allowed doubtfully. "Come, this way, wench, and be careful not to touch the furnishings."

Jenny followed the stiff, black-gowned figure up a flight of dark stairs, around several corners, and down a gloomy corridor. At last they stopped before closed double doors.

"Wait in here. I'll tell the master."

"It's the mistress I'm here to see," Jenny corrected, stepping inside the chill room.

"I give the orders here. And don't sit on the furniture." Mrs. Kent marched to the hearth, where a sluggish fire sulked in the grate; irritably she jabbed the sea coal with a thick brass poker before stalking from the room.

The large, gloomy room was elegantly furnished; gold-tooled leather covered the walls above waist-high wainscotting. Ovals set in the leather panels bore paintings of blue, red, and gold. From her limited knowledge of art, Jenny supposed the scenes to be biblical, yet the buxom ladies appeared to be far too scantily clad for a sacred subject.

"Are you the new girl?"

Jenny turned around to find a young manservant in the doorway, looking her up and down with an insolent gaze. "I'm Jenny Dunn. And I've brought samples of goods to show your mistress," she announced coldly.

"Come with me, Jenny Dunn, it's this way."

"Is your mistress expecting me?"

The man grinned. "No, I doubt that she is," he said, attempting to hide his mirth.

Not sure what he implied and disliking his familiar attitude, Jenny made no further attempt at conversation. The manservant led her to a ground floor room at the rear of the house overlooking a walled garden. Here sunlight splashed warmly over a brilliant red patterned Turkey carpet in the middle of the highly polished floor; two giant brass urns filled with artificial grasses flanked the door. Beside the windows a walnut gateleg table was set with a sparkling crystal decanter of dark red wine and two long-stemmed glasses.

"The master will be with you presently," the manservant announced as he made her an impudent bow.

When the man had departed Jenny felt more at ease. The package of goods she clutched beneath her arm had become crumpled and she guiltily laid the package on the table beside the wineglasses.

The deep window opened onto a narrow terrace leading to the garden. At the sight of the beckoning garden, Jenny had a sudden urge to walk on the velvet-smooth lawn gilded with autumn sunshine. A vine-clad arbor was set at an angle in the far corner, overshadowed by espaliered pear and apple trees; roses marched in stiff precision beside a walkway of chipped gray marble. In the center of the lawn was a diamond-shaped bed of massed purple and bronze flowers, their bright colors contained within a narrow border of clipped barberry. Clumps of purple Michaelmas daisies straggled untidily at the base of the shallow terrace steps, where a naked marble cupid aimed at them with drawn bow.

"So you are come at last!"

Guiltily Jenny spun from the window, knowing she should not have been prying into the nobleman's private garden. When she faced the speaker, her heart lurched: Sir Miles Russell was the well-dressed courtier who had virtually devoured her with his bulbous blue eyes on the day he purchased silver ribbons in Swann Alley. Flustered by her unpleasant discovery, Jenny curtsied to him as best she could, managing little more than a bob.

Sir Miles walked inside the room and closed the door behind him.

"I expected to show my wares to the lady of the house," Jenny remarked quietly while he poured wine from the crystal decanter.

"I'm afraid the lady of the house has been unavoidably called away. She's attending a family funeral with her sister," Sir Miles explained pleasantly, his mouth twitching in an amused smile.

"I see."

"Won't you join me in a glass of wine? No, I insist," he added sternly, when she would have declined his offer. He half filled a second glass with heavy red wine. "This, sweet wench, is tinto, fresh from Spain. The very finest. Drink."

Jenny accepted the glass, glancing away in discomfort from his penetrating gaze. "Here are some fine lace whisks," she began, unfastening the bundle of merchandise.

Not exhibiting much interest in ladies' collars, Sir Miles selected the samples of brightly colored silks and satins that Pet had included; there were also snippets of expensive velvets fresh off a merchantman only yesterday. He absently laid aside several Genoa velvets brocaded in gold.

As the potent tinto sped hotly through her veins, Jenny felt somewhat light-headed. While her patron picked through the bundle of lace and ribbons, she watched two blackbirds scrapping over a worm on the lawn. The minutes ticked by on the large ormolu clock on the mantel; from somewhere in the front of the house came the resonant boom of a clock striking five. She must start back soon, for the October night was drawing in and she had no wish to be abroad after dark.

"Have you made your selection, sir?" she asked, not sure if it was considered proper to remind a customer of the late hour.

"Oh, yes, sweet wench, my selection was made some time ago," Sir Miles said, treating her to a brilliant smile.

Jenny swallowed, sensing that he did not mean exactly what he said.

"Perhaps then, as you have already chosen, I should take your order and be gone. The hour is late and I do not wish to be out after dark."

He smiled and nodded, appearing highly amused by her speech. "You are unbelievably modest, my dear. It becomes you." Sir Miles stretched out a white beringed hand and stroked her arm. "You needn't walk, however, for I intend to send you home by coach. And I won't hear of you leaving before you've supped—that too is part of your aunt's agreement."

Jenny wanted to decline his offer of refreshment, yet in dining with Sir Miles, she made no compromise with her conscience. She supposed Pet would consider it rude to refuse his hospitality, especially after he had chosen their most expensive merchandise. "Very well, if you insist. It's most kind of you, Sir Miles," she said, choosing her words with care, for it was not her intention to offer him any encouragement.

Sir Miles summoned his servant. When the man appeared, he carried a silver tray laden with covered dishes. "Our supper, my dear," said Sir Miles, indicating the man was to set the food on the table. "I'll serve, Jack, you may go."

The servant nodded and backed away. As he was opening the door, he caught Jenny's eye and winked heavily as if at some private joke.

Sir Miles opened the French windows, admitting a flood of cool evening air. A night bird trilled sweetly from the arbor. Sir Miles drew up two tall-backed walnut chairs upholstered in purple Genoa velvet, and he politely ushered Jenny to her seat. Then he lit a triple-branched silver candelabra and brought it to the table, where the soft light shed a mellow glow over his pewter satin suit and the froth of silver-edged lace at his throat. As was the custom, Sir Miles still wore his magnificent crimson felt hat laden with silver plumes; the brim cast shadows over his face, turned almost handsome by the soft candleglow.

This was the most luxurious room Jenny had ever seen, and this nobleman the most important person she had ever met, but she was not at ease. She held her head and shoulders so stiffly that her back ached as she maintained an unyielding posture on her purple velvet chair, highly aware of an undercurrent of danger that destroyed her pleasure.

Sir Miles refilled their wine glasses before removing the silver covers from the dishes on the tray. A delectable aroma filled the room as mingled savory flavors arose from the appetizing food. The entrée was a small leg of roast lamb reposing on a bed of parsley; there was also a lamprey pie with flaky golden crust decorated with pastry vine leaves. For dessert individual codling tarts, warmly spiced with cloves and swimming in a lake of thick yellow cream, awaited them.

'' 'Tis but a small repast, for the hour's still early,'' Sir Miles apologized as he served Jenny a generous portion of lamb and a slice of steaming lamprey pie.

"Nay, sir, this is a banquet. A merchant family usually does not eat so fine.'' The plates were white porcelain, beautifully decorated with pink and blue flowers entwined on a gold embossed trellis. Jenny thought it a shame to cover such a work of art with food.

"Ah, my dear, you are far too kind,'' Sir Miles breathed, his bulbous eyes riveted on her lovely face washed golden by the candlelight.

The food was delicious, its superb flavor surpassing her expectations, but Jenny's enjoyment of the meal was marred by Sir Miles' calf-eyed attentions. At first he questioned her closely about her background; the cross-examination at an end, he then attempted to bring her to humor with tales of the antics of Whitehall's worst scoundrels. The clock struck seven, then eight, and there was still no sign of their impromptu supper coming to an end; Jenny's apprehension mounted. While he discussed Lord Rochester's latest scandalous verse, and the escapades of the most notorious young blades at King Charles' immoral court, Sir Miles poured glass after glass of wine, drinking the strong tinto as if it had been water. Jenny had consumed only two glasses of the heady red wine, but already her temples pounded. And the spiced lamprey pie did not lie gentle on her stomach.

"I thank you for your generosity, Sir Miles, you have been most kind," she said at last, pushing back her chair from the gateleg table. She began to gather the fabric samples in preparation of her departure.

"Nay, be not so hasty," he urged, his cultured voice slurring slightly. "First I have a gift for you, sweet Jenny."

"A gift!"

"Aye, your aunt tells me your life has not been an easy one. And from what you told me tonight, I must agree. Fear not, from this time forward, sweet angel, heaven will smile on you."

Jenny gulped uneasily at the nobleman's extravagant speech while she wondered how she was going to handle this latest development: when a rich courtier like Sir Miles Russell presented a wench with valuable gifts, his interest was becoming unmanageable.

"It is most kind of you, Sir Miles, but I can't accept your gift. This meal has been gift enough."

Ignoring her protest, he crossed to a small gilt table in the corner where he opened a drawer and withdrew a filmy bundle of fabric. "You are a delight," he praised, a bemused smile playing about his full mouth. "Ah, sweet Jenny, would that I had met you long years ago when the blood of youth still surged in my veins. There've been too many women, too much living . . ." he paused, his voice growing unsteady with emotion. "Here, 'tis but a poor tribute to your beauty."

He thrust a filmy blue organza scarf into her hands; inside the fabric was a perfectly formed rose of silver ribbon.

"Oh, the ribbon you purchased from me!" she exclaimed in surprise, holding the flower to the light.

"A Huguenot seamstress who produces veritable masterpieces fashioned this especially for you. But you've not looked close enough—see, my dear, there's a slight addition. 'Tis but a small token of my regard for you."

Jenny followed his perfectly manicured fingertip to discover two dewdrops set on the petals, winking rainbows of color in the candlelight.

"Brilliants! Oh, how lovely! They look exactly like dew drops."

"They're not brilliants, dear heart, they're diamonds."

"Oh, but I can't accept it," Jenny gasped, her gray eyes widening in amazement to think so influential a man sought to give her precious gems. Her understanding of what Sir Miles would expect in return for his generosity sent a chill down her spine.

"Yes, my love, you must accept them, they are only the beginning . . ."

"No."

Jenny backed away as he stepped toward her.

Sir Miles swept his hat from his head and bowed low. "My angel, you'll be the toast of London. Even Lady Castlemaine must look to her laurels when I present you as my . . ."

"I'm not *your* anything!" Jenny cried, stepping away as he eagerly pursued her. "If I gave you that impression by accepting this invitation, I'm truly sorry. Now I must leave. Already the hour is exceeding late."

Sir Miles threw back his head and bellowed with laughter. "A treasure," he said, when he finally mastered his mirth. "Right up to the last you appear so innocent. Jenny . . . Jenny, sweetheart, there are many gifts I wish to give you. This is but a paltry offering. Come, my arms ache to hold you. My lips burn to wed yours in bliss."

Hastily Jenny thrust a spool-backed chair between them as Sir Miles lunged for her. Far from repelling him, her resistance served to excite him all the more. Though he was somewhat tipsy, the wine did not impair his pursuit of her as he chased her around the room, dodging every obstacle she thrust in his way.

"Let me go!" Jenny cried when he leaned across a chair and seized her wrist.

"Enough, wench! Would you have me spend all my energy in pursuit? Come, my sweet, the game's at an end. You are fairly caught. Though, I declare, thou hast refined the chase to a fine art. I'm already panting with need of you, you temptress, and this is the first time I've touched your flesh. 'Odd's blood, but you led me a merry dance. Come, no more, sweet wench."

Without further ado, Sir Miles dragged Jenny toward him, upending a nearby spindle-legged table of ornaments and sending them crashing to the Turkey carpet. Jenny struggled desperately against his superior strength, but Sir Miles was deaf to her pleas; this too he assumed to be another act in the long drawn-out game of seduction. His rapacious mouth loomed above hers and he kissed her brutally, ardor suddenly getting the better of patience. Hating the wet touch of his lips, Jenny gagged. She managed to pull away from him and, freeing her hand, she slapped his face.

"I'm not here for your pleasure," she panted, her eyes flashing in anger.

"Eh, what's that?" he mumbled, taken aback as he blinked in amazement. Was the slap also part of her feigned resistance? Something about her angry face told him it was not.

"I'm not here to amuse you."

"Aye, and your actions have ceased to be amusing," Sir Miles snarled, his mood gradually changing as he realized Jenny's resistance was genuine. "What mean you? Your aunt assured me of your cooperation."

"She what! Oh, she had no right, no right at all!"

"And cooperate you will, you addlepated hussy. I mean to ride you, wench—here on the floor if needs be. Tonight you're mine!"

Jenny fled toward the door, but he was there before her. Sir Miles grabbed her about the waist, molding her against his body and she was repelled by the hard outline of his rising passion clamoring against her. While she struggled for freedom, he plunged his hand inside her bodice, plundering her breasts, his breathing growing harsh. Jenny kicked his legs, but so great was his arousal that her blows were no more deterrent than flea stings. Pinioning her arms behind her back, Sir Miles forced Jenny down on a velvet upholstered couch beside the open window.

"Jenny, sweet, resist me no longer," he breathed urgently. "I'm like to explode with need of you. Come, a kiss, a caress—'tis not much to ask," Sir Miles rasped as he imprisoned her beneath the weight of his body while he rained hot kisses on her neck and breasts.

Jenny twisted and turned, trying to avoid his mouth; his hot, searching hands seemed to be everywhere at once. "I know nothing of these arrangements! The bargain was struck without my consent," she cried when she managed to tear her mouth free of his smothering flesh. "I don't want you. Nor will I ever submit willingly." She thrust at his chest, using her utmost strength to keep him at arm's length.

"Then I'll take you *unwillingly*, but take you I will."

All his previous good humor had flown. It was as if in that moment of realization Sir Miles had shaken off his partial inebriation, for his steel-cold statement was made in sober rage.

Jenny screamed, hoping to bring the servants to her aid. Sir Miles flung her to the carpet, and the jarring thud as she hit the floor shook the breath from her body. Freeing his hand, Sir Miles struck her hard across the mouth to silence her screams.

"Be quiet, you little tart! This rape was your doing, not mine. Passion was to have been the dessert of the evening, but seeing that you prefer this, 'tis all the same to me." His breathing had grown labored as he pinned her down, fumbling with his clothing.

Tears of fear and rage slid from Jenny's eyes. Sensing he was momentarily off guard, she lunged at him, hitting his soft midsection as hard as she could. Startled by the unexpected pain, Sir Miles gasped, his hold on her arms slackening. With a burst of renewed strength, Jenny thrust him aside. She scrambled to her feet and fled toward the open French window, sobbing as she ran. She tripped blindly down the shallow steps, jarring her ankle as she landed with a thud on the dew-damp grass.

"Where think you to go out there, you fool wench?" Sir Miles bellowed in anger as he reeled through the French window. He stood on the terrace, peering blindly into the garden until his eyes grew accustomed to the darkness. "Ah, so there you are. Well, by God, there you can stay. Think over your obligations to me while you're at it, you ungrateful wretch. 'Odd's blood, I'll be damned if I'll soil my shoes coming to claim you. Stay where you are! By the time I return you'll be more than anxious to fulfill your bargain. I'm not so much in need of you I can't wait! There's a comely wench at the Half Moon who's not near so stinting with her favors. Mayhap I'll make use of her and save you for my serving man. Young Jack would enjoy a dip in so comely a well." And chuckling at his own suggestion, Sir Miles went back inside the room and slammed the French window.

From where she crouched on the lawn, Jenny heard him lock the window; a few minutes later the candles were extinguished, the room plunged in darkness. It was chilly in the garden and she hugged her body, shuddering from a mixture of cold and distress. If Sir Miles Russell expected her to calmly await his return, he was going to be disappointed! Jenny struggled to her feet, wincing in pain. Her ankle felt better after she massaged it, and she was able to walk to the door without difficulty.

The door was locked. And though she banged loudly, no one came to let her in: Sir Miles must have given orders to the servants to ignore her. A second door in the garden wall was padlocked; the wall itself was surmounted by iron spikes and broken glass as a deterrent to thieves.

A wave of sickness washed over her as she stood in the chilly darkness, wondering what to do. She went into the arbor, finding it warmer out of the wind, which blew dank and chill from the river. Huddled in a miserable ball, she clutched her protesting stomach while her tears erupted in a great wave of grief. Tears would not extricate her from this walled garden, but she seemed quite unable to stop. Anger gradually overcame self-pity when she remembered her seduction had been neatly arranged by loving Aunt Pet, who had assured the nobleman she would willingly go along with his suggestions. Like an unsuspecting fool she had accepted this romantic tryst as a genuine appointment to display her uncle's latest wares to the lady of the house. And though she had belatedly wondered if the nobleman's young son was Pet's intended quarry, she had walked into the trap, unaware that Sir Miles' lady was conveniently away from home.

Jenny thumped her fists against the seat in frustration. Fool! Fool! When she returned to the shop, Pet would have a taste of her anger over tonight's scheme. Whether out of cowardice, or because of her general apathy following her quarrel with Kit, Jenny had not yet presented the heated speech wherein she told Pet she had no intention of being sold in exchange for noble patronage.

Fiercely Jenny dashed trickling tears from her cheeks. Nothing had ever been the same since that nightmare day at the Rose and Crown when she had been given no time to weigh the consequences of her desperate action. Nausea churned through the pit of her stomach at the memory of her dead uncle. That stormy day, the horror of his sweaty body engulfing hers, was like a terrible nightmare!

From atop the garden wall a night bird mocked shrilly, his dark body a tiny shadow in the moonlight. A nightingale sang that night in Foxhall Gardens. The sweet, melancholy birdsong directed her sadness toward her lost lover. Would she ever see Kit again? she wondered wistfully. But what matter if she did see him? Nothing on earth could alter the treachery in his heart!

Her tears began anew as Jenny tortured herself with memories of Kit, repeating his cruel parting words as they stood in that shabby riverside street. Of all the hurts he could have inflicted, to taint her deepest love by referring to it as a "service" had been the cruelest slur of all.

"Damn you, Kit Ashford," Jenny muttered fiercely, "if you came crawling on your knees, I'd not even deign to speak to you." The statement brought comfort, even though in her heart Jenny had to admit those defiant words were a terrible lie.

Chapter 13

Jenny was alerted to a scraping, rustling noise behind the arbor, followed by a soft thud, as someone dropped over the wall from the neighboring garden. A man, dressed in black, emerged from the dense shadows.

"Go away!" she cried in alarm, moving defensively along the wooden bench.

"Mistress, have no fear," he soothed, his voice bearing the cultured accent of the rich.

"Go away, I said."

"Nay, be not afraid of me."

Though the man stood close, Jenny was unable to distinguish his features, for his lean face was overshadowed by a mass of curly black hair. His plain black suit and fashionable short cloak were of good cut. She noticed his long-fingered hands were ringless as he held them out to her in mute appeal. This stranger appeared kindly, but after tonight's experience, Jenny was taking no chances.

"I asked you to go away. I assure you, I'm no easy mark for an hour's dalliance."

The man's mobile mouth twitched to a smile. "Nor did I suppose you to be, mistress. I'm not here to take you by force, I'm here merely to offer comfort. So piteous were your sobs that I braved that hellish wall to render aid. 'Odd's fish, but 'tis not every day I scale a wall to find myself accused of such evil intentions when my heart beats solely to a song of pity."

"You're very kind. But, thank you, I'm quite recovered," she announced stiffly, betraying herself immediately by the telltale catch in her voice.

The man went down before her on bended knee, and seizing her hand, he implored, "Pray tell me what ails thee. 'Twas such a burden of grief for one so lovely. And, sweet mistress, you surely cannot accuse me of ulterior motives when until this minute I never even looked upon your face."

Jenny smiled wanly at his words. "My grief is very private

. . . there's nothing you can do to help.'' That bursting lump erupted again in her throat, forcing her to gulp. Oh, why did he not go away? If he continued with this kindness, she knew she would begin weeping afresh. His soft voice and concerned expression were more than she could bear. Tonight she ached for the comfort of loving arms, for a broad shoulder on which to rest her head; this nobleman—for she was sure he was—could readily provide those comforts. It was the price he would demand in exchange for his kindness that chilled her heart.

''You're afraid I intend to take liberties with you, disarmed as you are by grief. I swear, 'tis not my intention. I've too soft a heart to ignore a pretty maid in distress. Can you not tell what makes you weep? I'm a good and patient listener.''

To divulge the secrets of her heart had been the furthest thought from Jenny's mind, yet when this tall nobleman sat beside her on the bench, when he slid his arm about her in comforting embrace, instead of objecting to the familiarity, Jenny rested her head against his broad shoulder and all the painful reasons for her tears spilled forth. The man listened attentively, making appropriate noises of comfort while he cradled her gently against him. Jenny told him of her heartache and of her fear. When she recounted her recent misadventures with Sir Miles Russell, he swore softly.

''Did he harm you?'' the man asked gently when she was done with her story. And he dabbed away her tears with his soft cambric kerchief.

''No, beyond a few bruises,'' Jenny whispered, her voice cracking over the words. She did not tell this man how many other bruises she had suffered from a multitude of sources before tonight.

''Ah, sweet wench, Sir Miles is a profligate character of which Whitehall has more than its share. You must beware of well-meaning courtiers.'' Then, when she drew away from him at his sage advice, he chuckled. ''Nay, fear not, tonight I'm safe as a castrated tabby. Come, wipe your eyes. Cry no more.''

Smiling, Jenny allowed him to dry the last of her tears; he was so kind, so gentle. ''You've been a good friend to me,'' she said, nervously twisting the damp kerchief into a spiral. ''Tonight I felt so alone, so betrayed. Until you climbed over the wall, I'd all but lost my faith in men. Tell me, how happened you to hear my sobs?''

"So piteous loud were they, no doubt they could be heard on the Strand." He drew her unresisting against the warmth of his chest and spread his cloak about her shoulders. "Warmer?" he asked, allowing his arm to add to that heat.

"Yes. I hadn't realized it was so cold."

"Sir Miles will answer to me if you take a chill," he began, his voice deepening in anger. "Where do you live?"

"In Swann Alley, off Cornhill."

"I know the place. 'Tis not far from Pasqua Rosee's coffee house."

"I don't know the coffee house."

"No matter—'tis in St. Michael's Alley. What of your family? Will they not be worried when you fail to return?"

The man's kindly questions invited Jenny to reveal a little more about the destitute nature of her existence; she also told him about Pet's immoral scheme to enrich the shop.

"Suspecting treachery, why did you come so willingly to Sir Miles' house?" he asked in a puzzled voice.

"Because I'm a fool! So benumbed have I felt since . . . since . . ."

"You quarreled with your lover," he interjected softly.

The word she had used had been "sweetheart," but Jenny made no objection to his correction. "Yes. I've little hope for the future, for my plans are all gone awry."

The gentle, dark-haired man affectionately stroked her damp cheek with the back of his hand. "Be not so unhappy," he urged, amusement plain in his voice. His dark face loomed close to hers as he said, "Think, your fortune could be awaiting round yon corner. Here you sit, weeping as if your heart is broken, bemoaning your lost love, when there are a thousand men who'd fall on their faces in the street if you as much as smiled at them."

"You make the future sound very promising." Jenny allowed herself to relax against his strength. God, how vulnerable she was to a gentle touch and kind words! Stiffening, she drew away from the heat of his body. Fragrance wafted from his clothing, mingling with a distinctive hot male scent; the arousing combination tugged her memory and Jenny shuddered.

"Are you cold?"

"No, 'tis only a remembrance that crossed my mind."

"What do they call you?" the man asked, brushing her tumbled hair away from her face.

"My name is Jennet Dunn . . . but they call me Jenny. What's your name?"

Did he hesitate overlong over the recounting, she wondered, as his warm, strong fingers deftly threaded strands of hair beneath her blue ribbons.

"William Jackson," he said.

"I'll call you Will—'tis the same name as my uncle's."

"Then mayhap you'll feel at home with me."

"Oh, I already feel at home with you. You are so kind to concern yourself with my grief." And to demand nothing in payment for that kindness, Jenny mentally added.

"Ah, but I cannot stand to hear a pretty wench weep."

"You said yourself you did not know what I looked like before you scaled the wall."

Will smiled at her reminder, his dark mouth curving to reveal a flash of even white teeth. A closer inspection of his shadowed face revealed a thin mustache, and Jenny was surprised to find him older than she had expected. From his prominent nose to his wide mouth ran deep, cynical lines; his eyes remained a dark gleam in his lean face.

"Ah, but I knew the possessor of such a voice had to be lovely" he whispered, drawing her head to his shoulder while he stroked her back. "Poor little Jenny, how badly life has dealt with you. I'm no stranger to suffering, or wandering, so we are kindred souls."

"Do you live next door?"

"Nay." He chuckled at her question. "I was merely visiting the lady who is married to Sir Miles' neighbor."

"Oh, then you're an expert at scaling walls?"

"To my own damnation," he agreed, his lean fingers toying with her abundant hair.

"Do you love this lady?"

"No . . . but she's very attractive."

Jenny smiled in the darkness, growing highly aware of the heat of his caressing hands. "You're a wicked man, Will Jackson, not very far removed from that scoundrel Sir Miles."

He laughed at her rebuke and nodded his head. "Yes, I'm afraid perhaps you're right. Yet, sweet Jenny, this lady welcomes me with open arms. I've no need of an aunt to arrange our rendezvous."

Stirring warmth aroused by Will Jackson's sensitive hands began to make itself felt; the sensation was growing so pleasurable that Jenny drew away from him in alarm.

"It must be very late. And how am I to leave this accursed place?" she asked quickly, trying to hide her confusion.

"The way I came into it."

"But the wall's spiked! There's glass atop it!"

Will Jackson spread out his strong lean hands before her. "No blood, no wounds. There are certain tricks to learn if you would climb yon wall. Come, I'll help you."

He led her to the shadowed corner behind the arbor, where he demonstrated that on the cornerstone were no crippling deterrents to scaling the height.

"Oh, had I known this place existed, I'd have escaped long ago!" Jenny cried.

"And I am fortunate you did not, for then we would never have met."

With Will Jackson's aid, Jenny scrambled to the top of the wall, finding a footing in the gnarled vines and trelliswork covering the masonry. At his insistence she crouched precariously on top of the wall awaiting his descent to the other side.

"Jump, sweetheart. Be not afraid, I'll catch you," he urged in a low voice, holding out his arms to her.

There was something so trust-inspiring about this man that Jenny did as she was bid, having no doubt he would fulfill his promise. A moment later she was cradled against the hard strength of his body, jarred slightly by the impact against his chest.

"There, safe and sound. Ah, what a delectable armful I've captured," he whispered huskily, slow to release her from his embrace. However, as Jenny stirred, impatient to be free, he obligingly slackened his hold. "Here, you must wear my cloak."

The black plush-lined cloak was soft and warm; Jenny snuggled inside its protective folds, for the wind blew chill as it whipped around the corner of the alley. The darkened graveyard of St. Mary-le-Bow loomed ahead, its marble slabs eerie in the moonlight. She gasped, startled by rustling in the foliage beyond the church railing. Jenny's companion, however, undaunted by the prospect of the materialization of an unearthly specter, merely chuckled as he drew her arm through his, the action imparting a welcome sense of protection. They passed the darkened church without mishap and headed in the direction of Cornhill, stepping briskly because the night was chill.

Mist rolled in from the river. The acrid bite of smoke stung their nostrils as the billowing grayness caught and held the output of many sea coal fires belching skywards.

"I sometimes have occasion to meet Sir Miles in my travels," Will Jackson told her presently. "For trying to seduce one so fair and innocent, he has earned my reprimand. A sharp word from me will soon put an end to his romantic notions."

Jenny smiled at Will Jackson's abounding confidence. From what she had seen of Sir Miles, it would take far more than a word from this gentleman in somber black to deter him from future attempts at seduction; nor was she quite as innocent as her rescuer supposed. But she did not wish to destroy his illusions.

By the time they reached the corner of Swann Alley, Will Jackson had Jenny laughing over his descriptions of some of Whitehall's more famous personages. Though she did not ask how he came by his intimate knowledge, Jenny assumed him to be a gentleman in service to one of the King's courtiers. In midstream, Will abruptly switched from recounting the idiosyncracies of court life to ask, "When will I see you again?"

Though it did not come as a total surprise, nevertheless his question caused Jenny's heart to thump erratically. So kind had he been, so gentle, and though she had not intended to become involved with him, the warm touch of his hands stirred a tingle of excitement in her blood. No doubt Will Jackson had a wife and, by his own admission, he had a mistress. There would be no other meeting.

"You have been most kind to me, sir . . ."

"Will."

"Will—but there it must end. We lead different lives. And though I will always remember your gallant rescue, there can be no more between us."

His wide, mobile mouth turned down at her firm refusal. "Ah, your cruel words wound me to the quick. What makes you sure we have no future? How can you know whether fate decrees our paths to cross?"

Humor twitched the corner of Jenny's mouth. "You are very eloquent, Will Jackson, but not near persuasive enough. I thank you for your friendship, but now I must bid you goodnight, and here, for if my aunt sees me with you, I'll suffer a second beating."

"Very well, as you wish, but you must keep my cloak. To remove it now would have the very direst of consequences."

"I can't, my aunt will know I've not come by it honestly."

"There has been nothing dishonest to our meeting."

"She would know I'd been with a man."

"But as that was her dearest wish, such knowledge will only make her happy. Keep it. You must not take a chill."

When Jenny would have unlooped the fastening, Will Jackson pressed her hands down. His hands were hot and the contact gave her a shiver of pleasure when he pinioned her arms at her sides. "I must go," she whispered, as he leaned closer. A lantern swinging above the tavern across the street shed a golden haze over his face, burnishing his black eyes with fire. And Jenny knew, if she did not leave immediately, Will Jackson was going to kiss her.

The moment for flight came and went.

"Jenny," he whispered, his breath stirring warmly against her brow, "you are very lovely. Can I not at least steal a kiss for my pains. A farewell kiss, if you must?" Then, without waiting for her assent, he pressed his hot mouth against hers in a gentle, arousing token of affection. "Goodnight, sweet wench. Now go, get you gone to yon haberdashery, unscathed by the wicked snares of worldly courtiers."

Though his words were mocking, he smiled as he spoke. Jenny blinked in surprise at his statement, finding the swift change in his attitude baffling. She was also surprised by the emotion that had surged through her legs when he pressed his mouth to hers, her reaction completely unexpected.

"Goodnight, Will Jackson. How shall I return your cloak?"

"I'll think of a way," he said, urging her to go.

With a parting wave, Jenny ran along the alley. At the shop door she paused, glancing back to see if he was still there. He stood beneath the lantern. When he saw her look back, he waved reassuringly, motioning for her to go indoors. Jenny was touched by his concern for her safety.

Unlike the last time she had come home in the early hours of the morning, no hostile reception awaited. The door was unlatched. As Jenny pushed against the oak panel, she heard Pet's lace-frilled slippers scuffling over the floorboards.

"Oh, Jenny, how late it is!"

Stiffly she endured Pet's eager embrace as she drew her inside the shop. "What hour did you expect me?"

So taut with anger was Jenny's question that Pet blinked and took a step backward. "Late, sweet Jenny, but not as late as this."

Though Pet tried to lock and bar the door quietly, the metal chains clanged and rattled, echoing through the silent shop. The door secure, she turned back to her niece, who stood immobile in the center of the shop.

"Where are your goods?"

"I left them at Sir Miles' house."

"Oh, well, 'tis of no matter," Pet dismissed as she eyed Jenny curiously. "That cloak, does it belong to a man?" she asked archly.

"Yes. But not to Sir Miles."

Pet's eyes narrowed. "How mean you?"

"I mean that your well-laid plans went astray."

"What!"

Unable to contain her anger any longer, Jenny cried, "How dare you send me there! How dare you make such arrangements behind my back? I've no desire to pander to . . ."

Pet slapped her face. "Shut your mouth! Do you want the whole household awake. Explain yourself."

"Sir Miles Russell tried to rape me . . ."

"Such words!"

"'Rape' is what I said. For, strange as it may seem, I did not welcome his advances."

"You refused him!"

"Not only that, I fought him. And I'm sorry I didn't draw blood on his arrogant face. 'Twas only by my wits I managed to escape."

Pet fell back in shock, her face reddening as she nervously clutched her throat. "Am I insane? Are you telling me you actually fought him? You dared attack such a wealthy man?"

Jenny ignored her aunt, not trusting herself with words. When she tried to pass her to go upstairs, Pet seized her arm.

"Answer me, you ungrateful slut! What of Sir Miles?"

"At this moment he's probably lying drunk on some tavern floor. You knew his wife would not be there. Don't lie to me!" Jenny cried as Pet opened her mouth to deny the accusation. "You sent me as an offering to that rake, the price agreed on, heaven alone knows . . ."

"How dare you say such things to your own aunt?"

"I say them only because they're true!"

"I did not know his wife was away," Pet shouted, fighting for breath as she tried to overcome her anger. "You fool! You stupid, ungrateful, little fool! How dare you treat your betters so? What am I to tell him? What can I possibly say . . ."

"Tell him I'm not sorry I hit him. Tell him I never want to lay eyes on his bloated, dissipated face again!"

"Now you've gone too far, too far indeed, you ill-mannered slut."

Pet swirled about, her hand raised. A whip snaked around Jenny's shoulders, and she gasped in pain as the lash stung through her clothing. But when Pet raised her arm, preparing to lash out a second time, Jenny seized her wrist. Fighting, scuffling, the two women fell to the dusty floor. Her self-control flown, Pet bit and scratched; she snatched handfuls of Jenny's hair, trying any tactic she could to gain control of the situation.

Tears of pain dimming her vision, Jenny fought desperately to possess the whip. At last, when she thought her strength was spent, Pet's fingers began to yield. With a cry of triumph, Jenny snatched the whip and flung it in the corner among the bales of fabric.

"Don't ever lay a whip to me again," she hissed, crouching over her aunt, who lay gasping on the floor, "nor make arrangements for the disposal of my favors. I'm in charge of my own body—no other. No man boards it unless I give him permission . . ."

"Oh, you slut, such vile talk . . ."

"Be quiet! I'm not done. All your kindness, all your concern over my impoverished condition led but to one end. At first I thought you such a loving woman; now I know you're nothing but a procurer for the King's court. Sell your sister if you wish, but you won't sell me!"

Pet's round face crumpled unexpectedly as great tears slid down her small upturned nose. "You cruel, ungrateful girl," she whispered. "You'd see your poor old uncle who's taken you in—a penniless creature and he already burdened with debt—you'd see him live in poverty without lifting a finger to help him expand his custom. You won't even try to cooperate . . ."

"I'll not prostitute myself to expand his trade. And that's really what you mean. No matter that you mask it with innocent words. Sir Miles paid you for my body and prostitution is the only name for that. Now, Aunt, I'm going to my bed. If you're wise, you'll not speak of this to Uncle Will, for though he wants to expand trade, I doubt he'd sanction running a brothel from his premises.''

The shock on Pet's face, bloated with rage and tears, did Jenny good. Why, oh why, had she not made this speech before? She would never have needed to endure Sir Miles' loathsome advances. Well, it was said now, stated in no uncertain terms.

''The man whose cloak you wear?'' Pet croaked, grabbing a handful of black plush.

''Is no one you can possibly know.'' Extricating herself from Pet's grasp, Jenny scrambled backward. Warily she stood, expecting a fresh assault, but her aunt made no attempt to renew the combat.

''So you are a slut! 'Tis but my selection of customers that sticks in your throat,'' Pet spat, her face ugly with hatred.

''My body is my own.''

''I doubt that.''

''Until I'm able to make my own way in the world, I'll work for Uncle Will. But never try to barter me again.''

''Get out of my sight, you ungrateful bitch!''

''Gladly.''

Picking up her skirts, Jenny sped toward the stair; she could hear Pet's labored breathing as her aunt staggered to her feet. Soon a pool of lanternlight followed her upstairs, but Pet did not attempt to speak to her.

Jenny was greatly relieved when she was safe inside her own room and heard Pet shut the door at the end of the passage. With the bed covers snug about her ears, she lay in the dark, tears trickling in her hair and running on the pillow. She had shed so many tears of late, she had thought herself incapable of more, yet these soft, strangely relieving tears expressed a degree of relief. Never again would Pet scheme to put her in a nobleman's bed. Tonight, on the floorboards of Uncle Will's shop, a battle had been waged. And she had been the victor.

For the next few days Pet treated Jenny with icy politeness. Though he could not overlook the strained relationship within his household, Will chose to leave matters where they stood, not being bold enough to inquire into the nature of the spat.

It was Tuesday of the following week when Pet raced inside the parlor, her plump face alight with excitement. Will, who was smoking his pipe before the glowing hearth, glanced up in surprise.

"Well, loveday, what makes you so happy this morning?" he inquired good-humoredly, immensely relieved to see his wife was her usual self.

"Oh, Will, I don't think I can tell you, so excited am I," Pet whispered, her voice trembling. She walked to the window and looked down on the street while she tried to compose herself. "What would be the most wonderful news you could ever hope to receive?"

Will smiled as he knocked his pipe against the grate. "Ah, that calls for a little imagination. I've been elected Lord Mayor, or maybe the rascally Dutch have signed a peace treaty, or perchance the selling price of ribbon's soared . . ."

"No! That's foolishness!" Pet snapped, spinning from the window. Her face had lost its radiant expression. "Something far closer to home, something wonderful happening to a member of your family!"

As Pet's gaze fell on her, uneasiness stirred within Jenny's stomach.

Will followed his wife's pointed gaze, laughing in surprise, as he said, "Oh, something nice about pretty Jenny. Very well then, wife—she's to marry a prince!"

"Oh, Will, be serious!" Pet flounced toward her husband, her hand raised to slap him. "Here's a letter requesting that Jenny bring a display of goods to . . ." Pet paused, turning to give her niece a glittering smile in an effort to win her over.

"Where am I to be sent now?" Jenny asked warily.

"Whitehall!" Pet shrieked, unable to contain herself any longer.

"Whitehall!" chorused Jenny and Will in unison. "The Palace?"

"Aye, the Palace. Know you another Whitehall, you addlepated fools? Whitehall, where dwells his Majesty. The Portuguese Queen wishes to view a selection of our best merchandise. She's especially interested in the new lace whisks."

Eyes round with shock, Jenny paled. "Me? I'm to show whisks to Queen Catherine?"

"The request especially asks for you. Word of your comeliness has already reached the court. Oh, Jenny, fortune's about to smile on us at last," Pet cried jubilantly, seizing Jenny's arm.

A warning expression flashed into Pet's eyes when Jenny would have torn herself from her embrace. "How could they have heard about me at Whitehall?" she asked, suffering the other woman's touch for her uncle's sake.

"As lovely as you are, niece, I'm not surprised," said Will generously, his soft round face alight with joy. "Just think of it! Royal patronage will make us a fortune! We can letter 'by appointment to her Majesty the Queen' on our sign. It'll increase business a hundredfold."

Uneasily Jenny wondered what new scheme her aunt had hatched; yet as Pet continued to bubble with genuine pleasure over the wonderful opportunity being offered them, she decided her aunt was as baffled as she about this latest honor.

"When am I to go to the Palace?"

"Tuesday next—now let me see the hour."

Pet took the folded parchment from her apron pocket and smoothed it out. After a few minutes' study, for she did not read nearly as well as she pretended, she thrust the summons into her husband's hands.

"Here, Will, read it. I'm all of a pother. I can make neither head nor tail of the thing."

Will took the parchment and held it close to the firelight. The day was gloomy, the heavy sky gray and overcast; inside this paneled parlor it was as dark as night.

"I'll fetch a candle," Jenny suggested, getting to her feet. She brought a tallow candle from the box on the dresser and lit it from the fire.

"Now we can see! What a clever wench you are."

Jenny smiled at her uncle as she peered over his shoulder at the official document, trying to decipher the curling, flowery script; it was a veritable work of art.

"Be that nine of the clock, Jenny?" Will asked, pointing to a phrase with his stubby forefinger.

"Yes, nine of the clock," she agreed.

"Ridiculous," Pet snapped from the window. Marching to the hearth, she snatched the paper from their hands. "Nine of the clock! I doubt her Majesty ever arises that early."

Will suffered his wife's displeasure, drawing thoughtfully on his pipe before he spoke. "She's a Papist. No doubt she arises early to attend Mass," he said after a few minutes' silence while Pet turned the paper this way and that, attempting to read the message.

Still unable to read the spelled number, Pet scowled. "Well, if you say so, husband, perchance she does rise early," was all she allowed as she handed the paper back to him. "Such excitement! When the messenger arrived, poor Doll fainted clean away, the silly bi . . . goose," she corrected hastily, her full cheeks flushed. Such extraordinary good fortune had made her careless. With an ingratiating smile for her middle-aged husband, Pet stooped to kiss his brow.

"Am I to go alone?"

"Certainly not," Will said quickly. "We'll send young Tim with you, niece. He'll be delighted at the chance to see Whitehall. And he's quite a promising lad—the best 'prentice ever I had."

"Tim!" Pet protested, her mouth tightening. "I'd thought . . ."

"As the oldest 'prentice it's definitely his place to go." Will was adamant.

"Yes, I suppose, but I'd thought perhaps . . . perhaps . . . Doll, might go," Pet finished lamely. She had actually hoped she would be her niece's chaperone. All her life Pet had longed for a glimpse of the court: the nearest she had come to attaining that dream was on her birthday, when Will had succumbed to her pleas and taken her for a stroll in Whitehall Park; she had worn her very best, hoping to be taken for a noblewoman.

"Doll! Heaven forbid! Though she's your sister, love-day . . ."

Will needn't have said more; even Pet had to admit her sister had many shortcomings. "Yes, I suppose it should be the lad. We can tire him like a page. Tuesday next! We've only a week to make his costume! And Jenny's too!" Eyes rounding in alarm, Pet spun about. "You've nothing presentable to wear to court," she gasped in dismay, clutching her pale hands to her ample bosom. "Oh, if only we weren't so poor!"

"Jenny's to attend as a tradesperson, loveday, let's not get carried away."

Pet shot her husband a scathing glance. "Well, I can see you don't intend to change, Will Dunn, court patronage or nay. Would you send her tired in a scullery maid's rags?"

"I thought the new blue taffeta most becoming," he interjected timidly, recognizing a building storm.

"That rag! She must have a far grander gown. I'll set to work on it at once."

With an excited cry, Pet flew from the room, her high-heeled shoes clattering noisily down the stairs as she sped into the shop to examine their wares. Though Jenny was an ungrateful, insolent little slut, she had the face and figure to charm a duke. The chit would make a successful match yet, Pet decided, her mouth set in determination. That little bitch would be well and truly tied to a nobleman whether she willed it or no! There was far too much at stake to allow the willful baggage any voice in the matter!

Chapter 14

The great day dawned clear with the snap of frost in the smoke-tinged air. Pale stars still glimmered in the heavens when the Dunn household arose, impatient to begin this auspicious day.

Jenny's new gown of moss-green taffeta had a loose over-skirt ashimmer with silver thread; her full breasts swelled invitingly above the low, lace-edged bodice. The gown's full balloon sleeves, puffing from a dropped shoulder line, were gathered at elbow and wrist with pink satin ribbon, while a dozen ribbon knots dangled along the sleeve seam.

Jenny shivered with cold in her fine new gown, having to sit still while Pet took great pains arranging her chestnut curls around a frivolous creation of wired pink and green ribbons. Beside them the sea coal fire sulked in the grate, puffing clouds of sulfurous smoke but adding little warmth to the frigid room.

At last, after much poking and prodding, accompanied by wails of despair and frowns of annoyance, Pet deemed her niece fit to make her debut. So much money and effort had she invested in this royal departure that she was sick with worry over the outcome. She must hope and pray the silly wench had wit enough to match her beauty, or their extravagance would end in hopeless disaster.

Standing back, hands clasped in ecstasy over her handiwork, Pet exclaimed, "You're truly lovely!" Her praise was sincere, for at the moment she had all but forgotten the enmity between them.

"Thank you, aunt." Jenny gulped in surprise, not expecting the compliment.

"Remember, our future hinges on today, so conduct yourself with care," Pet warned as she stooped to retrieve the cones of satin ribbon from the floor. "And for Christ's sweet sake, slap no one inside the Palace," she hissed, her face hardening. "As addlepated as you are, you foolish little slut, I declare, you'd slap old Rowley himself."

"I'm only going to show lace whisks to her Majesty," Jenny reminded coldly, her mouth tight.

"Aye, that too."

"Too?"

"The richest men in the kingdom surround the King, you dolt. And they're not blind!"

At that point Doll wandered into the room, announcing her presence by loud sniffles; when she saw how magnificent Jenny appeared in her finery, her thin face became a mask of envy. "Are you ready?" Doll forced the words, barely able to speak for the jealousy curdling her blood.

"Yes. Is Tim waiting?"

"Aye, the ugly little turd . . ." At a warning glance from her sister, Doll modified her speech. "Toad," she corrected, sniffling again. Frantically scrabbling in her full blue sleeve for a linen kerchief, and not being able to find it in time, Doll sneezed all over her sister.

Pet tried to brush the offending droplets of moisture from her fine magenta gown, muttering angrily beneath her breath; she did not give voice to her rage because Will had entered the room, eager to see Jenny in her new gown.

"You're a vision!" he exclaimed, glowing with pride. "Now, remember, Jenny, show her Majesty the best whisk first. Point out its exquisite workmanship and tell her how the soft style compliments the figure in a most flattering manner . . ."

"She's naught but a convent mouse. What cares she about her figure?" Pet interrupted impatiently, shooing her husband to the door. "You know, Will, I've been thinking about getting a new mirror for the parlor. There's a beautiful olive wood frame with oyster shell parquetry at the 'Change. And maybe some Turkey covers for the table. We'll be able to afford them now. Mayhap a settle with fringed India silk cushions—oh, how grand the room will look then."

"Grand and most expensive—but we'll see, we'll see," Will said as he beheld the mutinous expression on Pet's face.

The Dunns shouted their final message of good luck as Jenny stepped into the street with Tim at her side, a covered wicker basket filled with choice goods clutched in his thin arms.

Though her Majesty had only expressed an interest in lace whisks, Will Dunn had prudently included a glittering selection of his latest merchandise. It was likely the Queen purchased her trimmings and fabrics elsewhere, but there was always a chance she would be taken with his offering. A spirit of free enterprise prevailed in this land, and Will was eager to encourage such opportunities, especially when they enabled him to benefit handsomely.

"Remember, Jenny, show the swatches of fabric too," he called, stepping into the alley.

"Come back, she's old enough to remember by herself," Pet cried in exasperation. She had to drag on her husband's jerkin to prevent him following Jenny down the alley. Her mouth curled in scorn. What an old fool he had become since this summons arrived! Though the original purpose had been to display merchandise, the old dolt had completely overlooked the most advantageous aspect of the entire venture: once Jenny walked inside the Palace, fate stepped in; who knew what lecherous eye would light upon her soft white bosom and lovely face—and lighting, become ensnared, Pet added, with quickened breath.

"Remember to curtsy to her Majesty," Will shouted, thrusting his head around the door.

Jenny had reached the end of Swann Alley, and she waved in acknowledgment of her uncle's last-minute reminder. She was anxious to have this ordeal over, yet again she was not anxious to reach Whitehall. What if she tripped and dropped the goods at her Majesty's feet? And what was she to do with Tim? Surely he would not be expected to accompany her inside her Majesty's chambers?

They mingled with the stream of citizens hastening about their business on this crisp autumn morning. The wind blew cold on her neck and Jenny drew the black plush cloak around her chin, smiling as she recalled Will Jackson's kindness. When she returned his cloak, she must thank him again for his generosity; the warm garment was a welcome protection from the sharp blast sweeping off the river. When their next meeting would be, or if indeed there would be a next meeting, depended on Will's persistence. Though they had spent little time together, Jenny already felt she knew him, the pleasure of his friendship remaining long after his departure. Making snap judgments about a person's character sometimes proved dangerous, yet she was convinced he had her best interests at heart. To a friendless soul adrift in the great city, the knowledge she had at least one person who truly cared about her welfare was immensely comforting. She knew she was foolish to encourage a courtier's attentions, but he had been so kind and gentle toward her. And she could not ignore the spark ignited by his lips . . .

Tim tugged at Jenny's arm, breaking her chain of thought. "Coo, me stomach's all of a quake," he revealed, clutching his belly.

"Mine too."

"Do you think we'll see the King?"

"I shouldn't think he'd be interested in ladies' lace whisks."

Tim giggled. "He be more interested in what's underneath 'em," he stated with a wicked grin.

"That'll do, Tim." Though she felt obliged to admonish the lad, Jenny could not help smiling at his impudence. Tim was undoubtedly right in his observation. From what she had heard about his Majesty, anything female was fair game: King Charles had a prodigious reputation for snaring pretty young women.

"Wait a minute! Coo, me insides is coming out," Tim cried in distress before he dashed into the shadow of a building.

It took two more emergency stops before Tim's stomach had quieted sufficiently to allow them to continue. Pale and tongue-tied, the apprentice managed to calm his nerves before they reached their destination.

Not wishing to be reminded of her unpleasant interlude with Sir Miles Russell, Jenny chose the Watling Street route to the Palace instead of going by Cheapside. Tim confidently directed their journey, for he knew the city well. They paused to gape at great St. Paul's atop Ludgate Hill. The old church's steeple had long since tumbled in. During Cromwell's time the church's splendid interior had been ransacked, its hallowed walls providing shelter for merchants' stalls rather than the worship of God. Jenny would have liked to explore the dingy booksellers of Paternoster Row huddled on the far side of the cathedral precincts, but they had no time to digress. In the Strand stood a maypole where on Mayday milkmaids danced, bedecked with spring flowers. As they passed Tim listed the names of the grand mansions lining their route: Arundel, Somerset, York, Exeter, and Bedford House were more like sumptuous palaces than houses. On the left side of the street the houses had long gardens backing onto the Thames.

Whitehall Palace straggled for almost half a mile along the

river, more a hodgepodge of adjacent buildings than a single
grand edifice. The prospect of entering those hallowed precincts filled Jenny with excitement and alarm. When she
showed her official letter to the guard at the gate, they were
readily admitted, though the man acted somewhat haughty
toward them, complaining loudly about the early hour.

Tim turned around and stuck out his tongue, wagging his
hand as he rudely thumbed his nose at the liveried soldier.

"Stop it, Tim! Behave yourself!"

Tim was crestfallen at the thought of having behaved rudely, especially when he had intended to demonstrate his extreme
worthiness for so great an honor. "Sorry, I forgot meself,"
he apologized gruffly, peering up at Jenny from under a
thatch of corn-colored hair.

"That's better. Now come here, let's make sure you're still
presentable."

A tug here, a twitch there; Jenny fussed with the apprentice's suit in order to mask her own nervousness. Pet had
dressed Tim in a suit of good brown wool, her only conces-
sion to fashion being two knots of pink and green ribbon
attached to the garter holding up his new worsted hose.

When she could no longer delay matters, for close at hand
she heard the ominous tolling of the hour, Jenny stepped
briskly along the walkway. She was so nervous about meeting
the Queen that she barely noticed the beautiful park surrounding the Palace or the animals grazing there; all her thoughts
centered on her impending ordeal.

They finally entered Whitehall, its vast, echoing space
making them uncomfortably aware of the clatter of their own
steps. Through miles of winding corridors, escorted by a
liveried servant who did not disdain to speak to Jenny beyond
an initial supercilious comment about "jumped up trades-
people," they reached the Queen's apartments.

Instructed to wait in a narrow, chill anteroom, Jenny and
Tim stared in awe at the elaborate molded wall panels adorned
with gold; they gaped open-mouthed at the massive crystal
chandeliers glittering above their heads. To her surprise Jenny
found frayed curtains at the deep windows. This discovery
caused her to view the remaining furnishings with a more
critical eye; the seats of the gilded chairs flanking the double
doors were virtually threadbare, as was the red plush bell pull
dangling beside the door. Lavishly proportioned though Whitehall was, King Charles must lack sufficient funds to support

his luxurious lifestyle. Jenny was warmed by this observation; lack of money made the King seem less royal, drawing him nearer to the common man, for whom lack of funds was a daily struggle. Those street rumors about the King's servants and armies alike often going unpaid must be true, yet if all gossip was to be believed, impoverished though he be, Charles Stuart was by no means stinting in gifts lavished on his mistresses . . .

"This way."

Jenny gulped in surprise as she discovered a gaunt figure in black standing before the double doors. By the foreign inflection to her speech, Jenny knew the lady for a member of Queen Catherine's Portuguese retinue, yet her unbending, somberly clad presence greatly resembled that of Sir Miles Russell's housekeeper.

"Not you," the woman snapped, as Tim stepped forward to accompany Jenny. Without ceremony the wicker basket was plucked from the apprentice's unresisting arms. Vaguely waving a bony hand as she indicated the room in general, the foreign lady-in-waiting told Tim to wait there as she fixed him with a beady black stare, daring him to take another step forward.

"Wait here for me, Tim, I won't be long." Jenny gave the lad a warm, encouraging smile, though she felt as chilled as a January night beneath the withering gaze of this formidable lady-in-waiting.

As they neared a closed door at the end of another long corridor, the lady-in-waiting pointed accusingly at Jenny's cloak. Guiltily Jenny unlooped the fastening and swung the garment from her shoulders. Without the black plush cloak she felt disarmed, for it had been a mute reminder of its owner's kindness.

The Queen's chamber was small and totally unlike the lavish surroundings Jenny had assumed a Queen would inhabit. The young Portuguese Queen was seated beside a walnut table bearing an open bible and a guttering candelabra. So nervous was she of the encounter that Jenny felt as if she walked the circumference of London's boundaries as she crossed the dimly lit room. When she reached the chair where the small, dark woman clad in regal purple velvet sat, Jenny had the presence of mind to sink to her knees in a deep curtsy.

"I've been waiting for you," the Queen said in her light, heavily accented voice.

"Your Majesty, it is my humble pleasure to serve you."

Their eyes met and Jenny was surprised to find a glow of friendship in the Queen's soft brown eyes. Her plain, child-like face, marred by a short upper lip and protruding teeth sat ill above the wired standing collar of her heavy purple gown. Queen Catherine extended her small ringed hand for Jenny to kiss. And had not the dour lady-in-waiting impatiently gestured for her to rise, Jenny would have stayed on her knees gazing raptly at this little Queen.

"You must not be in such awe of me," Queen Catherine said kindly. She motioned for her lady-in-waiting to open the dark curtains. As the heavy brocade parted, beams of mild autumn sunlight speared the gloomy room, illuminating the dark-haired Queen in her carved walnut chair.

"Forgive me, Your Majesty, but I'm still very much in awe of you," Jenny revealed honestly.

The Queen smiled, her short upper lip drawing back to reveal protruding teeth, which she usually went to great pains to conceal. "You must not be. I forbid it! My husband has requested I view your lace whisks, for the quality of the goods from your shop has been highly recommended to us."

"Oh, yes, Your Majesty, they are of the very highest quality."

Catherine gestured impatiently for her lady-in-waiting to produce the basket of goods.

At the sight of Uncle Will's humble wicker basket Jenny's heart lurched: surely the Queen would find such ordinary goods too paltry to be pleasing. She swallowed, trying to mask her nervousness as she opened the hinged lid and withdrew a bundle of brightly colored merchandise. "This is the loveliest lace collar of all." She held out a fine-worked creation depicting delicate Tudor roses and oak leaves in a heavy ornate border.

With an exclamation of pleasure, the Queen accepted the whisk, holding the lacework toward the light as she admired its delicacy. "These symbols, for what do they stand?" she asked curiously, pointing to the design.

"They are the Tudor rose and the oak leaf of England, Your Majesty."

"Charles will be pleased to see me wear a tribute to my

adopted land, no? But how am I to wear it? There is no stiffening, no wire.''

''Allow me, Your Majesty.''

Jenny gently draped the deep collar around the Queen's narrow shoulders. ''It is worn loose, Your Majesty, not standing.''

''Ah!'' Queen Catherine patted the soft lace, smoothing it in place. Her lady-in-waiting curled her lip in disapproval, but was ignored by her mistress. ''Later this month I must attend a ship's launching—*The Royal Catherine* she's to be named—this collar I shall wear. Oh, but I'm always so seasick . . . it is not with pleasure I go.''

Jenny smiled in sympathy. ''Perhaps you will be more fortunate on this journey, Your Majesty.''

''Perhaps.'' Queen Catherine looked full upon Jenny, as if seeing her for the first time. She swiftly assessed her appearance, giving a small shuddering sigh as she said, ''Yes, just as I thought, you are very lovely. Perhaps if I were more beautiful, Charles would love me more.'' A sigh escaped the Queen's pale lips.

The sorrow suffusing Queen Catherine's sallow face pricked Jenny with pain. It was common knowledge that the amorous King was flagrantly unfaithful to his wife. Now that she too had suffered the pain of a man's faithlessness, Jenny's heart went out to the foreign Queen, so touchingly simple and childlike in her disillusion. ''Beauty fades, Your Majesty, it is what is in the heart that endures,'' she said kindly, wanting to reassure the Portuguese woman of her charms, yet respecting her intelligence too much to attempt flattering lies.

''That is true. But I'm sure your beauty will stay green for many years to come.''

''Thank you, Your Majesty.''

''What else do you have in your basket?'' the Queen asked as she leaned forward, breaking the uncomfortable silence that had briefly enveloped them.

Relieved to have their meeting on firmer ground, Jenny delved inside the basket to produce a handful of jewel-bright ribbons. The shimmering satin spread across Queen Catherine's skirts like a miniature rainbow. Choosing a handful of purple, brown, and gold satin knots, the Queen handed the ribbons to her lady-in-waiting before she turned back to Jenny.

''I'll wear your pretty ribbons to cheer my mood at Woolwich—the water will be bitterly cold so late in the month. Charles will be pleased to learn I've made a purchase from you. So often does he chide me for dressing like a convent . . ." the Queen paused, catching the warning eye of her stern mentor. "I'm saying too much. Go now, I'm well pleased with you."

"Oh, thank you, Your Majesty, y-you're m-most kind," Jenny stuttered. She barely remembered to curtsy so rapidly was she swept from the room, almost before she realized the audience was over.

When Jenny emerged in the chill anteroom young Tim was nowhere in sight. The lady-in-waiting brusquely returned her to the liveried servant who had brought them inside the palace. A nod of parting, accompanied by a brief curling of her thick lips, was the only condescension the Portuguese woman allowed before she swished back through the double doors, her heavy brocade skirts dragging across the floor.

"Old harridan! Like a bloody great cow she is."

Jenny blinked in shock at the lackey's words: so proper and stiff had he appeared that not once had she attributed human emotions to him. "Perhaps it's because she's foreign," she said.

"Foreign? Bloody Papist, that's what it is. Bloody Papists aren't human."

Not wishing to be involved in so treacherous a discussion, Jenny changed the subject. "Where's my apprentice?" she asked.

"Search me. Gone to sup, I s'pose. The same place you be bound." With these final words, nose correctly pointed at an angle toward the embossed ceiling, the man stepped forth, returning his charge through the endless maze of corridors.

The palace hummed with sound: voices and laughter came from behind closed doors as they passed, echoing through the twisting miles of corridors. The route the servant had chosen led away from the gathering, rather than toward it.

"Wait 'ere, girl, I've a message to deliver," the man growled, stopping before a closed door. "You be in this 'ere spot when I comes back, or so 'elp me . . ."

"I'll wait here."

Jenny grinned after the departing servant, who marched along, head held stiffly appropriate to his position in life; pompous though he was, the man had proved to be human after all. This room where she had been deposited was little more than a gallery with red upholstered chairs ranged in soldierly precision beneath a row of oil paintings in vast gilt frames. Jenny became absorbed in the portraits, reading the subject's name and deciding whether she would have liked them in life. There was a click at the door. She half turned, expecting to see the returning servant; the door stood ajar, but no one was there. Curious, she stepped toward it, starting with surprise when a figure suddenly materialized from the shadows.

"Will Jackson!"

" 'Tis gratifying to find you still remember me," he said as he glanced furtively along the corridor to make sure they were not observed.

"You surely did not think I'd forgotten you?"

He smiled, his mobile mouth curving to disclose even white teeth. "Nay, sweet one, I prayed you had not."

"I knew you held a position at court, for how else could you know so much about wicked courtiers!" Jenny smiled at him, discovering in the daylight that Will Jackson did not look exactly as she had supposed; he appeared tired and strained, yet her words made his dark eyes sparkle with laughter.

"How else?"

"It's disappointing to find you not in the least surprised to see me, when today I've been afforded so great an honor that I still cannot believe it."

"So pleased was I to see you, I did not question the event," he said quickly, motioning for her to join him in the gloomy corridor. "Come closer, sweet, then you can tell me all about this high honor."

"A royal summons came to the shop requesting I show lace whisks to the Queen. How she heard of Dunn's Haberdashery I've no idea, unless . . . you . . . did you . . . ?"

Will Jackson smiled. "You're too clever by far."

"That's why you weren't surprised to see me! I should have known! Oh, Will, I do thank you for the honor. The Queen's going to purchase ribbons also. My uncle will be beside himself—here, 'tis fortunate I wore your cloak, for I never expected to meet you here."

Jenny handed him the cloak urging him to accept the garment.

"Come with me, Jenny."

"I can't. I'm going to the kitchens where my 'prentice awaits."

"What an insult to take one so lovely to the kitchens. Your beauty should grace the grandest salon."

His compliments brought a warm flush of pleasure to her cheeks. "Thank you, Will, but the royal kitchens will be grand enough for me."

"Jenny, please come with me. We can picnic downriver."

"I can't, much as I'd like. I must return to the shop and give them my news."

"Please, Jenny, this is the only day I'm free. We'll have no more chances to meet like this. Besides, what harm can come to you on the river in broad daylight?"

What harm indeed? Jenny met his dark eyes, seeing impassioned intensity gleaming there. The memory of his kiss and of the stirring reaction caused by his hands renewed her caution. "You'll ruin my reputation. A wench does not go downriver with . . ."

Will Jackson tossed his dark head in laughter. "What reason is that? Your reputation—am I so scurvy a knave that you fear to be abroad with me? Can you not accompany me in broad daylight?"

It was Jenny's turn to laugh. "You are a devil casting aside all my maidenly excuses . . ."

"Not maidenly, I'll be bound," he added in an undertone, stepping closer. "Wenches have not so stormy a parting from lovers they have not bedded." At this sage remark he seized her hands, imprisoning her in the gloomy corridor. "I'll not take nay for an answer. I promise the 'prentice lad will be well taken care of. Why, Jenny Wren, I'll even provide you with an alibi staunch enough to satisfy your merchant uncle. What say you to that?"

"I still say I should not," Jenny protested weakly, highly attracted by his suggestion as the sheer magnetism of his personality reached out to engulf her. In Will Jackson's presence she felt young and carefree, transformed into that moonstruck lass who had dreamed of a handsome sea captain beneath the leafy chestnut tree. "I shouldn't come with you, Will Jackson," she whispered, shivering as he pulled her close. "But I've not always done as I should. I'll come downriver for a couple of hours, if you promise the alibi and 'prentice are both accounted for."

"I promise. Now, let's waste no more time." He pulled her with him down the narrow passageway, pausing as a door opened and voices echoed down the hall. "Quick, tarry not, lest we be discovered," he hissed, yanking her about so that she stumbled against him. He caught her, kissing her swiftly, a world of promise in his warm mouth.

After this helter skelter beginning, Will Jackson led Jenny a merry dance to the river stairs. Though speedy, their departure was of a highly furtive nature. He kept his plumed black hat pulled low on his brow to hid his face; doubtless his master did not sanction dalliance when he should be attending to more important duties.

"You are a wicked man," Jenny whispered, giggling as she tucked her hand beneath his muscular arm. Will was hastening her down the steps to the landing where a rowboat bobbed at its mooring. "You should be attending to the duties for which your master pays you."

"Too often must I attend to duty, surely I'm to be allowed a little pleasure in life."

"You hypocrite! Methinks you take far more than a *little* pleasure in this life, Will Jackson."

He laughed as he handed her aboard the swaying craft where a full picnic hamper awaited them.

"I was expecting you," he said in answer to her questioning glance.

Chapter 15

Though the warm sun had helped dispel the early morning chill, it was still uncomfortably cool on the water. When they had been under way a few minutes the sharp breeze dropped and Jenny unfastened her cloak. She lounged against banked velvet cushions with a sigh of contentment, watching Will ply the oars. He had removed his black coat and rolled up his shirt sleeves; muscles rippled in his arms as he stroked, easy and long, slicing through the murky water, his lean hands bronzed from exposure to the elements. Jenny wondered how a gentleman of the bedchamber, or some similarly related office, came by so athletic a physique. Perhaps he regularly accompanied his noble master on hunting forays, or shared with him an active sport. Jenny smiled with pleasure as she watched him, his lean face somber, his dark eyes soft as he rested, allowing them to drift on the shimmering water, the rowboat rocking gently in the swell of passing crafts.

"So you know Queen Catherine?" Jenny asked at length, anxious to discuss that very exalted personage, for she still found it difficult to believe she had actually spoken to the Queen.

"Yes, we're acquainted."

"I was surprised to discover I like her well, for I had thought to be afraid of her."

"And you were not?"

"No. But though she be Queen, I do not envy her."

"Why?"

"Her husband is unfaithful."

"Most husbands are unfaithful."

"But the King's unfaithfulness makes her sad because she longs to be beautiful enough to satisfy him."

"Perhaps no woman in the world is that beautiful," Will remarked, plunging the oars in the water.

"From what I've heard of his Majesty, I suspect you are right."

"And what have you heard of him?"

"That he has made cuckolds of every man at court."

"Ah, what prodigious energy our sovereign must possess."

His eyes twinkled as he looked down at her and Jenny sensed mockery behind his words. "I repeat only what I've heard. But, as you know him, perhaps you will reveal the truth."

"And perhaps I will not," he replied maddeningly. "Come, Jenny, let us not talk about so boring a subject. Kings are only half human at best."

"What do you wish to talk about?"

"You."

At that moment a floating mass of debris slapped against the prow of the boat, making her leap in alarm. Will Jackson rested the oars and reached over to grip her hand in reassurance.

"Be not afraid. I promised to take care of you, Jenny Wren, and I'm a man of my word. Now, pray tell me all about yourself."

While they rowed past the crowded banks of London town, heading toward the open green fields surrounding the city, Jenny told Will Jackson her life story. And though she had intended to omit certain unflattering details from the account, the truth unwittingly spilled forth, surprising them both by her candor. No part of her story appeared to shock him; it was as if life had already delivered such a preponderance of ill fortune he had become unshockable. When Jenny made a remark to that effect, he merely grinned.

Yet later, when he spoke, the laughter had fled from his dark eyes. "Life doesn't always reward men justly, as doubtless you've already observed. Sometimes, when one receives one's heart's desire, it's not quite all one thought it would be. Always, beyond the glory, lurks a two-headed monster waiting to devour us. So, you see, Jenny Wren, forearmed with such profound knowledge, I made a solemn pledge never to take life seriously for more than two hours at a stretch."

"Oh, you are laughing at me!"

"Nay, not at you . . . at life perhaps, but never at you."

"This unusual philosophy you have developed—tell me, is it shared by your master?"

"Definitely. In fact, it was from him I learned it."

Jenny digested this information. "Will you not tell me in whose service you are bound!"

"I cannot. Suffice it to say, dear heart, my master is both

the noblest and the lowliest of humans in this land.'' Beyond that confusing statement, Will Jackson chose to reveal no more.

The passing landscape of huddled warehouses and wharves changed to peaceful green meadows, dotted with grazing cows. Grand houses, their long gardens bordering the river bank, served as a gentle reminder of civilization. Never before had Jenny seen this peaceful aspect of the Thames; Southwark's stretch of river was a noisy, refuse-laden scum of barges and ramshackle crafts. It was unbelievable that this lovely scenery lay within walking distance of the largest city in England.

''Ah, you are sighing, is it out of happiness or discontent?''

Jenny smiled. ''Happiness. It's so lovely here. Thank you for bringing me.''

''Thank you for coming.'' He laid his black plumed hat beside him on the seat, and swept his lean hand across his brow, where black locks curled damply against his tanned skin.

''Is there no one here to betray you?'' Jenny asked impishly as she watched him cast the last of his defenses aside.

''Let us hope not.'' He smiled at her, his brown eyes soft. ''Come, sweet, we'll pull ashore here and picnic. Those willows will make a satisfactory windbreak.''

Though he said ''windbreak,'' Jenny knew instinctively he meant the trees would shield them from curious eyes. A pang of unease speared her breast. Here she was in the midst of the country with this man of whom she knew very little; so far he had treated her with kindness and respect, but he was still a courtier, a breed of men not renowned for honor.

After tying the rowboat to a gnarled tree stump, Will leaped ashore. He pulled the boat about, steadying it for her descent. Jenny half fell, half stepped, ashore. As she had known he would, Will caught her against his chest, where she became startlingly aware of his thudding heart. It took little imagination to envision their hearts beating as one. This time he did not imprison her in his embrace, but set her aside while he retrieved the picnic hamper.

Together they scrambled up the sloping bank to a shelf of ground that formed a seat beneath the overhanging tree branches. Here the silence was broken only by birdsong and the gentle slap of water against the muddy bank. In the distance, bordering the lush meadows, stood a grove of towering copper beeches; the sagging boundary fence was tangled with bindweed and silky plumed old man's beard.

Will unlatched the hamper and withdrew a wine bottle and several cloth-wrapped bundles. "You must forgive me if I appear greedy, but I'm an early riser and have not supped since before dawn."

"I've not supped since last evening, for I was far too nervous this morning to eat."

"Then we'll make short work of the delicacies. My man," Will paused, then rapidly revising his statement, he continued. "Tom knows all the kitchen wenches. 'Tis he whom we must thank for our banquet." While he spoke, he poured wine into a pewter cup and offered it to Jenny. "Malmsey, fit for the gods."

The heavy sweet wine was like none she had ever tasted before. Jenny adjusted the full skirts of her new gown, hoping stains from the riverbank would not ruin her finery; water spots already dampened the hem and marked the underskirt. Hopefully the gown would dry before she returned, for it would be no easy task to explain the damage to Pet.

Will handed her a venison pasty while he gnawed a turkey leg. The thoughtful provider of this hamper had even included fine linen napkins bearing an elaborate crest, yet when Jenny smoothed out the fabric, the better to study the insignia, Will snatched the napkin from her.

"Nay, you little spy," he cried. "Would you uncover all my secrets? Blast the man for his thoughtlessness," he muttered to himself as he hastily stuffed the snow-white linen in the corner of the hamper. "More malmsey?"

Unlike the heavy tinto she had drunk at Sir Miles' attempted seduction, this wine had no effect upon her save a warming, relaxing sweetness that spread slowly through her veins. Or yet again, perhaps the sweetness was caused by Will Jackson's presence. She sat up, stiffening against the thought. How foolish she had been to accompany him to this secluded place, to drink two cups of malmsey, to lounge beside him on the grass . . .

"Nay, be not afraid of me. Do not draw away, for I enjoy your nearness," he invited huskily.

"I must."

"Surely you do not find me repulsive."

"No."

"What then?" He thrust aside the wicker hamper with its half-consumed edibles. "Come, tell me what makes you shrivel like a spinster."

"I merely came on a picnic."

"And is this not a picnic?"

Jenny smiled; she was not naive enough to accept the innocence of his statement. "To picnic is *all* I intend."

Will reached for her shining chestnut curls, finding the texture smooth as satin beneath his fingers; her brow, her cheek, were down soft, her lips like rose petals . . .

"No, Will, please," Jenny protested, drawing away from the warmth of his tantalizing caress. "We've not finished our picnic."

"I have no further appetite for food."

Her indrawn breath rasped painfully in her throat as she stared at him. An intensity she had not seen before glowed in his hot dark eyes, the taut jawline, the tension in his long, athletic limbs, all warned her to beware. "Do you intend to seduce me, sir?"

He met her eyes and she saw amusement kindled there. "If that is what you wish."

"It is not my wish. In fact, I wish to return . . . now, while we're still friends."

"Friends?" he questioned, his brow creased.

"As opposed to something more . . . intimate."

Now his mobile mouth curved and Jenny knew she had been ill advised to make such a statement. "Then I'm not repellent to you?"

"I never said you were."

"But your firm decision merely to picnic made me think . . . but no matter, Jenny Wren."

Beneath the soft warmth of his caressing fingers, Jenny shuddered, knowing she should stop the passage of his hands across her cheekbone, along her chin and down her neck. At first she put up her hand and gripped his bony wrist, gently staying his caress—but that was only at first.

"Kiss me," he whispered hoarsely.

Their gazes locked. The burning fire of his deep brown eyes possessed her, arousing the slumbering passion in her soul. Without conscious thought, Jenny moved toward him; it was merely an inclination of her head, but it was all the encouragement he needed.

" 'Odd's blood, you little she-devil, you've tormented me

since first I laid eyes on you,'' he whispered, as his arms went about her.

No longer did Jenny protest they had come merely to picnic, nor did she remind him of his wife, nor of his mistress. Warm affection, extended so generously by this appealing courtier, sapped all her resistance. An unspoken message passed between them, the communication not of the mind but rather of the blood. She slid her arms about his wide shoulders, rejoicing in the hot, hard feel of him, in the pulsing life of this man who had befriended her. It was not merely as a friend she wanted him now; her blood drove her beyond reason, forcing her to seek him as a lover to heal the gaping wound in her heart.

"No, Will Jackson, you kiss me,'' she whispered hoarsely.

His dark eyes glowed with amusement and desire. Suddenly the electrifying heat of his mouth was on hers and weakening ardor rendered her helpless: her limbs, her heart, her blood, were possessed with a terrible ague. They kissed again and Jenny almost drowned in the heady engulfing scent of his body, so unaccustomed, yet so well remembered. The discernible pounding in his veins, the thunder of his heart, carried her to a primitive world of their own creation.

"Oh, Jenny, Jenny, I love you,'' he whispered against her ear, his breath hot and tantalizing. "I love you . . . want you.''

That rapid switch of declaration made Jenny's mouth twitch, the reaction reminding her that a part of herself remained aloof. Never again would she completely give herself to a man. The tremoring wave of passion surging through her limbs was a reasonable enough facsimile of love—aye, surely she loved Will Jackson well, or why else would she feel so perfectly attuned to his need? Molding her quivering softness against the hard enveloping muscle of his long frame, Jenny refused to further analyze her emotions. He made her feel wonderful; his nearness excited her. Love, want, it did not matter what she called so delirious a sensation. Kit loved her no longer. Yet this man, so hotly passionate in her arms, offered assuaging love; whether his sentiments were but a courtier's easy lies, she knew not. So bereft of love had she felt that Will's ardent words restored the flickering flame of her self-worth. For this magic hour beside the River Thames, their mutual passion became a treasured gift of love.

"You are so lovely. God, how I've been tormented by

dreams of you. I plotted to get you in my arms. There, I'm
undone—my guile, my deceit, unmasked. Oh, Jenny, Jenny,
say you love me in return.''

''Yes, I love you, Will Jackson, deceiving rogue that you
are with your picnics and your sympathy.''

He chuckled in delight at her reproof. Then holding her at
arm's length, he said, ''You must not berate me for my
dishonorable intentions.''

A chattering magpie darted from the branches overhead, its
pied markings flashing in the sun. Startled by the unexpected
sound, they collapsed in each other's arms, laughing helplessly, relieved to discover the harmless identity of the intruder.
Oh, what joy, what laughter, this man aroused within her.
Jenny desperately needed his wit, his gaiety, to dispel the
terrible pall of gloom shrouding her heart.

Their laughter dissolved into tension as they stared into
each other's faces. The naked truth blazed in the velvet brown
depths of his heavy-lidded eyes. Reaching out, Jenny boldly
traced his prominent nose, his heavy black brows; the throbbing warmth of his smooth, suntanned flesh excited her as she
continued her exploration, slipping her hand within the unfastened neck of his shirt, where dark hair, waywardly flecked
with gray, twined about her fingers.

Will glanced down as she curled a silver speckled ringlet.
''What an old man I am become.'' He laughed, but there was
a tinge of sadness in his voice. ''Thirty-four years of age,
yet I feel as if I'd already endured two lifetimes. Pretty
Jenny, make me forget the cares I've known.''

Because she found his words slightly unnerving, Jenny
made no light-hearted response; instead she slid her hand
deeper inside his soft cambric shirt, shuddering as she encountered the fiery heat of his hard chest as she sought to take
his mind from the haunting specter of the past. Will Jackson
was not always what he seemed: beneath his witty, suave
exterior lurked a darker self, rarely allowed to surface, yet
when it came uppermost, alarming in its intensity, his laughing mouth turned bitter and those cynical lines set hard as
granite in his lean face.

''Don't stop. You have my permission to explore further,''
he invited huskily as Jenny withdrew her fingers when she
encountered the resistance of the waistband of his breeches.
''In fact, my love, I find this entertainment immensely satis-

fying. Nay, do not cry modesty—you forget I'm privy to all the secrets of your soul.''

''Perhaps I should not have armed you so well.''

''Aye, perhaps you should not.''

He traced the low neckline of her green gown, sliding his smooth fingers beneath the edging, touching her swelling breasts. Her bodice lacing presented little challenge as he deftly opened her gown, shuddering with desire as he ran his lean fingered hands over her satin-smooth breasts. His rousing desire was swiftly transferred to Jenny, who thrilled beneath his expert touch; a terrible, throbbing ache possessed her flesh while she trembled for his kisses. Correctly gauging her eager response, he pressed his hot mouth over hers, his kisses growing deeper until Jenny lost herself in the hot probing delight of his tongue as he roused her to greater passion.

''I've felt so sad, so lonely—oh, Will you've been kind to me. And I'm sorely in need of love,'' she whispered, disarmed by his lovemaking.

''You already have my love,'' he whispered, tracing his burning lips in a fiery journey from her neck to her chest. His mouth gently possessed first one, then the other, of her roused pink nipples, his tongue a heated torment as she writhed beneath his caresses.

Jenny lay back against the fragrant riverbank, giving herself over to delight and passion and love. Birds twittered in the distance, their song a faint echo above the pounding of her blood. The intensity of Will's lovemaking created an unreal world. The hot, insistent pressure of his manhood exerted such force against her thighs that it threatened to ravish her through their clothing. Will stroked her full breasts, her back, his stirring hands speeding delicious warmth as he raised her skirts and fondled her firm white thighs. Impatient, he took her small hand and pressed it over the throbbing heat of his arousal, cupping her fingers about the swelling, imprisoning her there with his hand.

''Feel, I'm on fire for you,'' he whispered against her ear, trailing his hot lips down her neck. ''Seek me out. Be not so modest, wench.''

With hands that fumbled clumsily, Jenny exposed the embodiment of his passion, shuddering anew at the stirring sight. Though dim, the green light beneath this willow canopy was bright enough to acquaint her with the secrets of his body.

"How do I compare?" he asked in amusement.

Jenny glanced away, self-conscious to have been discovered in her comparison of all others to *him*. "How did you guess?" she whispered at last.

"'Tis only natural, sweet, and loving someone as fiercely as you have done, I would expect naught else. Yon fool lover who abandoned you is unworthy of your love. Spare no more thought for the past. Say you do not find me lacking."

"Never that," she admitted honestly, admiring the towering strength of his throbbing flesh in the green darkness of their willow cave. His ego was fed by her appreciation of his body, his passion the more inflamed. Slowly, winningly, he caressed her to greater heat, his expertise in arousal born of long practice. "Oh, Will, I'm hot for you," Jenny blurted with devastating honesty, "for your mouth, your arms, your . . .",

Smiling with pleasure at the torment torn from her ruby lips, Will sealed her words with his mouth. "Yield to me, Jenny," he urged hoarsely as he covered her with his pulsing length of sinew and bone, driving her into the hard-baked riverbank. His white cambric shirt gaped unfastened, her gown hung unlaced; their chests touched, wedding pliant flesh and hard crushing muscle. Jenny wrapped her arms about his neck, allowing herself to drift, enchanted by his husky voice whispering sweet vows of love and passion as that throbbing length of fiery heat probed demandingly between her legs. With his fingers Will gently parted her, needing little force to invade her body, for she yielded gladly, opening to him, anxious to receive the bounty of his passion.

A gasp escaped Jenny's lips as the searing entrance was made. Lest her ecstasy betray them, Will absorbed her delighted cries with his mouth as he engulfed her with his hard body. Slowly, deliberately, and with the utmost control, he moved within her. Jenny grasped his dark head, tangling her fingers in his hair. Their mouths ground together, but they felt no pain as passion, in all its well-remembered heat, possessed them. Hoarsely directing, though she doubted he needed instruction, Jenny finally yielded to desire. Like a rocketing flame she soared. Not once did he forsake her, knowing exactly what she needed. Together they strived until, with a burst of agonizing fire, their desires fused and melted as one.

Up from deep, sweet blackness she came, trembling, lonely. And he was there, holding her shuddering against his strength, cherishing her until the crisis was past.

"Ah, Jenny Wren, you were all I dreamed you'd be," Will confided ardently, his dark eyes lambent with spent passion, his wide mouth softly relaxed. "At this moment I love you intensely for the joy we've shared."

Contented, Jenny smiled, turning slightly in his arms. She kissed his lean tanned neck, her mouth gentle on his flesh. "Thank you, Will," she whispered, touching his face.

"Nay, 'tis I who must thank you, Jenny Wren," he protested as he lay back, totally at peace.

"You spoke truly when you said you loved me?"

"Truly."

She smiled again. Closing her eyes against the green daylight, Jenny drifted into a soft land of contentment; not until she felt the pressure of his hot mouth against hers did she return to the present. "You're a lusty knave." She chuckled as she trapped his hand against her breast, curving his long, elegant fingers about the swelling roundness. "Now you are imprisoned."

"Would that I might languish here a lifetime."

"And can you not?"

"Nay, for the hour grows late. Much as I hate to say it, love, we must return. "Odd's blood, mayhap a crisis has already occurred within my . . ." Will paused, glancing away from her searching gaze. "My master will be angry if he discovers me gone," he continued briskly. "Much as I want you to yield to me again—nay, not want, crave . . ." His hands trembled about her face as he brushed her spilled chestnut hair from her brow. "We'll meet again soon, for I cannot help myself."

As she gazed into his dark, intense face, Jenny recalled that this man had a wife, a mistress too. When her fertile imagination supplied a ready picture, she glanced away, disliking the painful reminder.

"What is it? Have I offended you?"

"No."

"Why do you look away?"

"I . . . remembered your . . . wife . . . and your mistress."

The pleasure dimmed in his dark face. And Will sighed. "Oh, so that is the terrible truth stealing your joy. Wives and mistresses are an unfortunate reality of life; they do not alter what we have felt for each other, the joy we have shared today. Your body and mine were created for each other. Our passion is so finely honed, 'tis as if we are one being. No wife or mistress can destroy so strong a bond.''

''It is painful bondage.''

He sighed and drew away from her to rearrange his clothing. ''All bondage is painful, Jenny Wren; have you not learned that?''

Tears filled her eyes as she stared at him, withdrawn, aloof. By mentioning his obligations she had destroyed the glowing aftermath of passion. Fool! Why must she ever torment a man with his responsibilities, with his past? It was the very reason she had lost Kit . . . Jenny closed her eyes as intense pain rocked her body—no, she must not think of him; never again would she think of him . . .

''Come, sweet wench, let us return.''

Jenny opened her eyes to find Will crouched beside her, his hand extended to help her rise; gone was that serious expression, the trace of reproof about his eyes. She accepted his hand, the tingling response when his fingers covered hers not going unnoticed. At his insistence, she allowed him to relace her bodice, enjoying the disturbing pressure of his knuckles against her breasts. The close proximity of so arousing a part of her body worked on his own; laughing, Will pressed her hand fleetingly against the long swelling beneath his clothes.

''Not all of me is bound by duty, as you can see.''

''I'll take comfort from the fact that he speaks for your inner self.''

''Of a surety you may do that.''

They kissed again and with a sigh he reluctantly disentangled himself from her arms. He stooped to gather the remains of their picnic. Jenny looked at the russet haze of beeches marching toward the horizon, memorizing the peaceful view. Forever would she remember this place! The gentle lap of water, the soft hazy light all formed an integral part of that memory, but most of all she would remember the fire and sweetness of Will's lovemaking. Perhaps they would never love again, for theirs was a doomed relationship from the start. She would not even ask him to swear fidelity. Their friendship, this plunge into ardor, had been a vital, necessary part of her return to life.

''Today you've made me whole,'' she whispered, seizing his arm and turning him to face her, ''and I thank you for it.''

''The pleasure was all mine,'' he replied huskily before he welded his hot mouth to hers, holding her close in a demanding embrace. ''But you speak as if today is the end, when 'tis only the beginning. I swear it's so. Believe me.''

Jenny smiled as she heard his sweet vow, wanting it to be true, but unsure of the validity of that hope. ''Come, 'tis a long journey ahead,'' she said.

Kissing her one final time, he led her down to the water's edge. The rocking craft tilted as he came aboard, making Jenny gasp, as she fully expected to be upended in the river.

The picnic hamper secured, oars at the ready, Will Jackson winked at her. ''Home, my lady?''

''Aye, lad, but do not make haste.''

''Why, are you not anxious to return to your forsaken tasks?''

''Nay. And if you hasten, you'll deny me the pleasure of watching you row.''

His indrawn breath, swiftly followed by a grin of pleasure at her candid statement, cheered her. Oh, Will Jackson was good, he was kind; he had loved her well. What then was missing? Why did she keep feeling as if something were wrong?

''That honest statement gladdens my heart. Perhaps someday, sweetheart, you will understand how much. I thought to travel slow, the more to gaze on you—little did I think to bestow mutual pleasure.''

Gathering her straying wits, Jenny smiled as she leaned toward him, her hand gentle on his face as she stroked his cheek, his mobile mouth, accepting his gentle kiss against her fingers. '' 'Twas a grave mistake to say such flattering things. I swear, I've turned you insufferably conceited.''

''Conceited—no, not that. I am ugly. God knows what any woman would find attractive about me, yet, I do confess to having certain talents.'' He grinned as he plunged the oars in the water, sending twin whirlpools eddying toward the bank.

''Talents?''

''Aye, sound not so surprised. Were you not delighted with my skill at lovemaking?''

Uttering a shriek of indignation for his overwhelming conceit, Jenny swung at him. Laughing at her assault, Will leaned far out of reach, neatly avoiding her blows. And growing mindful of their precarious position within the boat, Jenny subdued her attack.

"You insufferably conceited oaf," she stormed, trying to hide the humor tugging the corners of her mouth. "I would not be surprised to find your prowess proclaimed in a broadsheet for all London to behold."

And Jenny could not understand why he laughed so uproariously at her remark.

Chapter 16

Swann Alley buzzed with talk of Jenny's visit to Whitehall; neighbors came to gaze upon her exalted person as, time and again, she must describe in detail her audience with the Queen.

Will Jackson had remained true to his word to provide for Tim and give Jenny a plausible story to explain her delay, though her aunt and uncle were so beside themselves with joy over her elevation in the world that they would likely have accepted the first threadbare excuse she presented. The official explanation was that her audience with the Queen had been postponed to a later hour, thereby forcing her to wait for admittance. In the meantime, young Tim, well surfeited with luscious delights from the royal kitchen, had dozed contentedly before the hearth unaware of her absence. Jenny had convincingly played her part, not forgetting to berate the sluggardly prentice for detaining them further because he could not be roused from his nap.

Jenny's stolen hour beneath the willow fronds, when Will Jackson had pulsed hot with passion in her arms, remained a secret. Expert though Will's lovemaking had been, Jenny could not erase painful memories of another who had flamed her blood and whose shadowy presence tormented her still. As the days passed, that heated hour beside the Thames became so dreamily separated from reality that Jenny wondered if it had even taken place. Each time she pictured Will's dark, arresting face, he seemed to be part of an erotic vision she had created to satisfy the yearning in her soul.

Within the week smart Turkey covers for the dining table, a fine glass mirror with oyster shell parquetry, and a second-hand Mortlake tapestry in shades of green and blue arrived to enrich the Dunn parlor.

Will held his head in woe as the expenses mounted. "We'll be in debtor's prison come Christmas, you mark my words," he cried, when he could endure the torment no longer. "A lace whisk, a handful of ribbons—that's the extent of the royal purchase. And, wife, might I remind you, not even paid for yet . . .''

"How can you be so niggardly?" Pet demanded, her eyes like slivers of ice in her flushed face. "All these years your poor wife has longed for some decent furnishings. And now, when you have royal patronage at last, you begrudge me a few simple delights."

During such heated discussions, Jenny prudently withdrew. Unknown to Will, Pet had also ordered a set of carved walnut chairs to grace the parlor, but Jenny wisely did not reveal this latest extravagance to her uncle. "Sufficient unto the day," she repeated to herself as she shook the linen tablecloth into the street. Breadcrumbs descended on the cobbles, where a flock of sparrows swooped down to enjoy the feast.

"Wench, is this Dunn's Haberdashery?"

Startled by an unexpected voice at her elbow, Jenny glanced up to find a young man wearing a royal livery, squinting at the fading painted sign that swung above the door.

"Yes," she said, her heart skipping a beat.

"Then I've a message to deliver."

Numbly Jenny accepted the folded parchment, standing frozen on the doorstep while the royal messenger swept off his plumed hat and made a formal bow before he turned and strode down the alley. The stiff parchment crackled in her fingers as Jenny watched the man's bobbing red hat plume disappear around the corner.

"Coo, who was that?"

Doll pushed past her, straining for a glimpse of the grand stranger.

"A messenger from the Palace."

"The Palace! The Palace, did you say?" Will tripped over his own feet as he hastened across the uneven floorboards. An order, yes, that's what it must be—or payment for merchandise already delivered. Oh, wonder of wonders, salvation was at hand! He no longer need fear debtor's prison, nor must he quarrel with his wife about her extravagance.

Once the furor had died down within this twice-blessed household, Will spread the royal summons on the cutting table and studied its contents: Jenny was to make a second visit to Whitehall to display goods to Queen Catherine.

Pop-eyed over this latest development, Pet spoke with reverence when she said, "Jenny, dear girl, forgive me for my unkindness to you in the past."

Jenny smiled sweetly, accepting her aunt's peck on the cheek; it was amazing what miracles royal patronage had wrought.

"And this time ask her Majesty when we're to be paid," Will reminded, practical as usual.

"Will Dunn, for shame! Would you have poor Jenny humiliated? It's simply not done to mention money to a member of the royal family," Pet shrieked, scandalized that her own husband should be so crass, so uncouth, so . . .

"Well it should be mentioned! A man can't feed himself on promises," Will grumbled, as he slammed shut his red leather-bound ledger. This entire experience had been vastly disillusioning. Foolishly he had allowed himself to be carried on the crest of the wave of his wife's enthusiasm, imagining untold riches once they received royal patronage: so far, all that had come of the great event was one more unpaid bill.

"I'll mention the payment to her Majesty's lady-in-waiting," Jenny promised, in an effort to soothe her uncle's anger. "I'm sure it's been overlooked." Will's beam of gratitude made Jenny uneasy: she had not told anyone about Whitehall's threadbare upholstery and frayed curtains.

Sleet blew intermittently in the blustering north wind as Jenny hastened toward the Palace. This morning her audience with the Queen was not until eleven o'clock, so there had been no reason to rise at dawn. Tim trotted beside her, more than anxious to return to the wonderful feasts offered him belowstairs at the Palace. Though she tried not to dwell on the idea lest she be disappointed, Jenny wondered if she would see Will. He could have arranged this second summons to enable them to meet. Yet with this icy north wind raking the city streets, the massed gray cloud blanketing the heavens, there would be no idyllic picnic beside the river.

Jenny had given much thought to her relationship with the suave courtier, wondering if she had plunged recklessly into a love affair to salve the pain of Kit's desertion. Did her feeling for Will Jackson run any deeper than the passion kindled so readily in her blood? She had Kit to thank for teaching her how to respond exquisitely to a man's need. A wanton legacy from her unknown father, her hot blood had smoldered these years past, awaiting the spark of mutual desire. In the sweet vulnerability of passion, she had reciprocated Will's vows of love, despite the shadowy presence of his unknown wife and mistress, whose very existence somewhat tainted the abandon of her lovemaking. Jenny frequently reminded herself that a nobleman chose not his wife out of love but the selection of his mistress was an entirely different matter. Did Will seek to replace his old mistress with a new? It was not Jenny's intention to be branded any man's mistress, yet there had been one for whom she would have gladly swallowed her pride . . .

Tightening her mouth against the jarring memory, Jenny forced herself to speak to Tim. "Don't make yourself sick again," she cautioned him sharply as they walked along the Strand, congested with gilded horse-drawn coaches.

"I'll not eat so much marchpane."

" 'Tis kind of the cooks to feed you so well."

"Aye, and they said I might take a basket to me mum," he revealed breathlessly. "D'ye s'pose Master'd let me visit—'tis not me day off? There be over a month to wait for that."

Excitement spiraled through Jenny's stomach: the suggestion was a blessing in disguise! While Tim visited his family in Ram Alley, she would be free to share a stolen hour with Will. Today she would insist on coming to an understanding with him about the future. "If they offer again, you may accept. As long as I had to wait to see the Queen last time, you'll be home and back before I've shown a ribbon."

"Coo, Jenny, thanks. But what about the master?"

"I'll explain to him," she offered generously, not without a pinprick of guilt for her deception.

By the time they reached Whitehall the threatening clouds had thinned; patches of steel gray betrayed the sun's feeble presence. Within the elegant Palace gardens walked several warmly clad strollers, yet it was still too early for the majority of courtiers to be abroad.

On this, her second visit to the Palace, Jenny found neither her journey here, nor the walk through the lofty corridors, as long, for somehow familiarity had shortened the route. When the Portuguese lady-in-waiting appeared at the double doors to take Jenny to her Majesty, a liveried servant seized Tim by the ear and marched him away.

This morning Jenny did not wait to be told to remove her cloak. Without the benefit of Will's soft plush cloak, the Palace corridors were unpleasantly frigid; large goosebumps stood out on her arms and shoulders as she followed in the wake of Queen Catherine's joyless companion.

"Wait!" the lady-in-waiting commanded sternly, delaying Jenny's approach until she had first rapped on the door to announce their presence.

After a polite pause, the woman opened the door and walked inside the room. Jenny followed obediently, not raising her eyes from the trailing black skirts before her; when they neared Queen Catherine's chair, the lady-in-waiting bobbed a curtsy and stepped aside. Left suddenly unprotected in the center of the room, Jenny swiftly dropped to her knees, exhibiting a little more grace than she had managed at their former meeting.

"They tell us your name is Jenny," Queen Catherine said pleasantly.

"Yes, Your Majesty."

"Well, Jenny, we are most pleased with you."

"Thank you, Your Majesty."

"You may rise."

Jenny stood, allowing her gaze to come to rest on the Queen. Today Queen Catherine wore a pale blue silk gown with a scooped neckline softened by frothy white lace, the current English style far more becoming to her short-waisted figure than the stiff, more formal gowns she had brought from Portugal. Pale autumn sunlight spread a banner across the polished floor, illuminating the Queen's tiny blue-slippered feet. Beside her Majesty's chair lay a liver-and-white spaniel bitch, round brown eyes fixed intently on Jenny; the dog's tail wagged noisy acceptance of her royal mistress's visitor.

"Did you bring lace trimmings and ribbon? 'Tis what I requested."

"Oh, yes, Your Majesty. They are the very finest merchandise."

Queen Catherine nodded. She waved her small white hand, alerting the lady-in-waiting to produce the wicker basket. "Ah, yes, very pretty!" she exclaimed when the lid was opened to reveal a treasure of brilliant silks and satins. Turning in her chair, the Queen called, "Charles, come see the beautiful colors."

Charles! When Jenny heard that exalted name spoken, her head snapped about, her breath catching painfully in her throat. She had thought, with the exception of her lady-in-waiting, that Queen Catherine was alone. Now she noticed a tall masculine figure standing in the shadows beside the glowing hearth, his scarlet clothing a bright blur in the gloom. His

Majesty the King was present in his wife's chambers! Jenny's stomach pitched at the realization. This morning she was to see King Charles the Second, not as a gaudily decked puppet above the bobbing heads of a thousand cheering souls, but here, face to face, in the intimacy of his Queen's withdrawing room! The King clicked the lid of a gold box on the marble mantel before turning toward them. As the scarlet blur moved in the shadowed alcove, Jenny dropped to her knees, her heart thumping erratically as she listened to his brisk tread on the creaking wooden floor.

"They are beautiful indeed, my dear."

That deep, huskily amused voice pierced Jenny's soul. It could not be! It could not! Fearful of verifying her worst suspicions, yet knowing she must greet her King, Jenny raised her head. Her heart lurched as pain, strong as any physical blow, speared its fluttering, dying beat. The tall, dark-haired man clad in rich scarlet velvet laced with gold who stood, long elegant fingers resting casually on the carved back of Queen Catherine's chair, was no stranger.

"Welcome to Whitehall, Jenny," Will Jackson said.

Her breath left her body as she stared at him in disbelief. White as a ghost, Jenny faltered over her greeting, swirling close to unconsciousness as she met his laughing dark eyes. Her mouth opened time and again, but no sound came forth.

"Oh, poor girl, see how you've frightened her, Charles," the little Queen laughed, clapping her hands in delight.

"Frightened? Nay, how so? I am a most kind and loving monarch."

Kind, loving—aye he had been that. Jenny continued to stare at him while life revived in her icy limbs. "Your Majesty," she mumbled at last, discovering her tongue was too large for her mouth.

"Arise. Stand not on ceremony," he said kindly, and with some amusement, as his dark, heavy-lidded eyes hotly appraised her person.

Stunned, Jenny stood before the royal pair, hearing nothing, understanding nothing, as the Portuguese Queen asked for her husband's advice on the selection of colors to match her new gowns. Will Jackson, with whom she had unwittingly allowed herself to fall in love, was Queen Catherine's husband! Nay, not only that—Will Jackson was King of England! The King! And she had teased and fondled him, exchanging intimate, breathless . . .

"I've made my selections. You may seek refreshment."

Blinking as the Queen's sallow little face hovered into view, Jenny swallowed. Her witless mumble lost, she clumsily retrieved her basket and stumbled backward, barely remembering to curtsy when she reached the door. Her only thought was for flight. As she raised her stricken face, flushed with shame, humiliation, and betrayal, Jenny held King Charles' hot-eyed gaze. And so filled with reproach was her parting glance that he understood what devastation he had caused with this morning's surprise meeting.

"Wait here," the Portuguese lady-in-waiting commanded as they emerged in the chill long gallery to find it deserted. Clucking beneath her breath, the woman stood in the doorway unsure of what to do; she tapped her shoe impatiently on the floorboards as they awaited the serving man's return. "Wait here," she repeated after a fruitless ten minutes, pointing to a spot on the floor several feet before the double doors. Then, without further ado, the lady-in-waiting turned and hastened back the way she had come.

The throbbing ache in Jenny's throat threatened to choke her; pain, so acute, she gasped, struck her chest. Oh, God, how deeply he had deceived her! And she, unknowing he was the King, had laughed and teased and loved him with unabashed delight . . .

"Jenny."

She stiffened as she heard him speak her name, but she did not move toward him.

"Jenny."

His voice became more insistent, a trace of anger in the stern summons. A petrifying thought struck her: the King commanded; he could not be ignored. Woodenly she moved, her heart leaden in her breast. Like one long dead, she stared at his velvet-clad magnificence, bright in the gloomy corridor beyond the side door. And her heart splintered afresh for the painful knowledge of his deception.

" 'Odd's fish, look not at me like that," he dismissed impatiently, reaching forth to grasp her sleeve. Ungently he yanked her toward him, glancing about furtively to make sure they were not overheard; in the background came the buzz of many voices interspersed with laughter.

"You lied to me!"

"Nay, my vows were not lies."

"You lied to me!"

He pulled her close and she shuddered at the realization that she was imprisoned within the King of England's strong arms. His gold-edged red velvet coat felt softly repugnant against her bare skin.

"Jenny, stop being such a little fool," he hissed in anger. "Think you for one minute you would have felt the same about me had I told you who I really was? Where would have been the laughter, the sweetness of our love? It would have been all, 'Yes, Your Majesty, no, Your Majesty'—nay, probably not 'no'—a wench is easily biddable by he who possesses the throne. I did not want that from you. Can't you understand?"

"I want to go home."

"Stop it! Look at me."

Swallowing the painful lump that rose in her throat, Jenny demanded, "Is that a royal command?"

"Yes."

Trying to brazen out her shimmering tears, she looked up at him; laughter had fled from his dark eyes, granite-hard lines etched deep on either side of his mouth, no longer softly mobile, but straight and bitter.

"I'm not fool enough to willfully disobey my King."

Angrily he shook her, darting another glance behind him as the laughter grew louder and a door slammed. "I'm not a man of violence but, so help me, at this moment I long to give you a taste of my fists . . ." His indrawn breath shuddered through his chest as he glared at her. "What happened to the beautiful love you bore me?"

"That love belonged to Will Jackson!" she spat, trying to wrench free of his grasp, but his bruising fingers trapped her there.

"Many times have I used that name in my wanderings. Will Jackson, Charles Stuart, whatever name I use, I'm still the same man. You did not love the *King* of England, you fool wench, you loved the man . . ."

"You're right, I never did love the King of England," Jenny repeated grimly, in rage and pain. She had the good sense to keep her voice lowered as, despite his blazing anger, did he.

"Must I lose you because I'm not he?"

"You deceived me!"

"Not when I said I loved you."

"And your wife, your Queen, what of her?" Jenny demanded, trying to still the tremor in her legs.

A cynical smile stole across his mouth. "Will Jackson had a wife, a mistress also, yet you did not object to lying with *him*."

Ashamed, Jenny could not meet his eyes. "Will Jackson loved . . ."

"Stop it! Will Jackson does not exist. Charles Stuart loved you. Charles Stuart comforted you. Charles Stuart made you pant . . ."

"Stop!" groaned Jenny, making a valiant effort to work free of his grasp. "Isn't it shame enough that I . . . that I . . . without regard for your exalted person . . . without even suspecting you . . ." Tears engulfed her and she could go no further.

"That's why I enjoyed your every touch—because you didn't know. There was nothing self-serving to your caresses, no dreams of coronets, or mansions. You loved me as a man."

"But you are the King!"

Drawing her closer so that his hot breath hissed into her face, he whispered fiercely, "Is not the King a man first?"

Tears spilled down her flushed face as Jenny glared up at him; anger, betrayal, and pain for her loss swept through her body in a trembling wave. "When I . . . when we . . . never once did I give you due respect. Had I but known—oh, how ashamed I am, now . . ."

"Respect!" he rasped. "I get respect from archbishops and Lord Mayors. 'Tis not what I want from you."

"What do you want from me?"

"If you must ask, then you're more fool than I thought."

Anger spiraled through her pain. Jenny glared at him, contemplating slapping his face before horror for her traitorous thoughts stole the blood from her cheeks. "Your Majesty, I'm but your subject to command," she murmured, unsure if she spoke out of mockery or fear.

Grabbing her about the back of the neck with his free hand, he pulled her even closer. "Very well then, mistress, I shall command thee."

His rough growl was foreign to her ears: Will Jackson spoke only soft and beautiful sentiments. But she had forgotten—Will Jackson no longer existed. "Whatever is your Majesty's wish."

His black eyes burned hot as coals, but the emotion was not of passion. As he spoke, Charles gripped her neck and her narrow waist, his long, bony fingers gouging her soft flesh until tears of pain pricked her eyes. "My wish, sweet wench, is that you retire to Sir Miles Russell's mansion and await me there."

"No!" Jenny shrank from the order. "I cannot!"

"Think you I intend to share my prize? I assure you, the profligate knave is safe in Buckinghamshire. But his name and his house will serve me well. 'Twill also spring delight in the fluttering heart of your scheming aunt."

"Oh, no, please . . ." Jenny hung her head, devastated with pain for all her lost dreams.

"You will do as you are told."

Blinking back hot tears, she looked into his face, forcing her legs to halt their quivering collapse. "And when I am there?"

"Must I explain in detail?" he asked sarcastically, a quiver of amusement lifting his wide mouth.

"Oh, how could I think . . . how . . ." she bit back her words, appalled to realize it was her monarch who towered above her, in whose demanding grip she struggled. "You seduced me. There's no other word for it."

"Have you not heard—I'm an expert at such sport."

"You lied to me! You deceived me! And yet still you expect me to greet you with open arms because you are the King."

"Nay, *despite* that fact, my dear. Come," he urged, as his punishing grasp slackened, "change not toward me because I'm not plain Will Jackson. Is it not worthier to know it is by Caesar thou art fucked?"

Jenny found herself thrust aside as he strode away without a backward glance. Trembling, fighting tears, she leaned against the paneling, finding the wall ice cold against her burning face. She gave vent to a flood of grief for yet another dream shattered beyond repair. Now she understood his furtive glances, his anger over the inclusion of that crested linen in their picnic basket. How close he had come to betrayal. As for his gale of laughter over her joking suggestion that he might advertise his assumed prowess at lovemaking in a London broadsheet—Charles Stuart's healthy libido was the subject of a multitude of bawdy limericks . . .

"This way, mistress. And make haste."

Rocking back on her heels, Jenny drew a painful, shuddering breath. A small man, dressed in a plain black suit, stood before her, indicating the door at the end of the corridor.

"I'm preparing to leave," she uttered thickly, drawing the black cloak about her shoulders, hating it because it was *his*. "I was not aware there must be haste . . ."

"Nay, *stealth* is the word, mistress," the little man said, his thin mouth quirking in a smile.

"Stealth?"

"A conveyance awaits to transport you."

"Thank you, I can walk. Besides, I have a 'prentice lad. . ."

"The lad will be well looked after. I urge you, mistress, to do as you are told."

Eyes rounding in shock, Jenny gradually realized what she was being told. "Am I being commanded to take the carriage?"

"It is an apt way to describe the order—yes, I would say so."

"And if I refuse?"

"You are too wise for that," the man said with a smile. "Come, follow me."

While Jenny followed the soft-footed courier, a thousand reckless ideas swirled through her head: she would refuse to obey, for surely, in affairs of the heart, a King had no more right to order than any other man. But as her anguish subsided, Jenny realized the validity of his Majesty's argument: the love she bore Will Jackson still lived, despite his false identity. And her lover's exalted station could never erase that abandoned exchange.

A knife-sharp breeze blew from the river. Gone were those faltering golden rays of sun; the gray sky hung heavy, the threat of impending winter descending like a pall over the city. And the chill of discovery in Jenny's heart matched the shrinking warmth of the dying season. Such easy, sensuous things she had said to Will as she delighted in intimate caresses—the reminder flamed her cheeks with scarlet. He was the King and she had treated him as if he were a royal groom!

"Here, Mistress Dunn, your carriage is waiting."

Swallowing the lump in her throat, Jenny nodded her assent. The little man opened the door of the heavy, unmarked conveyance and assisted her inside its velvet upholstered interior. The door closed; a command was given and the heavy vehicle lurched into motion.

With tears trickling down her cheeks, Jenny stared through the small square window at the disappearing royal park where, beneath the autumn bright trees, a pair of golden spotted deer browsed among a herd of cows. What new fateful turn was her life about to take? She would demand the driver stop the coach—she could do that, but Jenny knew such a defiant move was unwise. Kind, gentle, forgiving Charles Stuart might be, yet the anger betrayed beneath the surface of his speech delivered in an undertone in the gloomy Whitehall corridor reminded her of the darker side of his nature. Was the King capable of punishing a woman who refused his suit? Perhaps in all matters save passion, his generosity served him well. With plain Will Jackson she had fallen in love. Born out of loneliness and need, forged in the white heat of passion, her attachment had been for a common man; the discovery that the man was also the King had thrown her emotions into raging turmoil.

A thick gray mist swirled up Cheapside, wisping in doorways, wreathing about chimneypots, collecting the sulfurous haze of sea coal smoke to cherish for its own. Jenny stared through the window, watching a haloed lantern across the street until the yellow glare dimmed to extinction. The clop of horses' hooves, a slamming carriage door, stung her to awareness: King Charles stood below.

She allowed the heavy wine velvet curtain to fall in place. Nervously smoothing the full skirts of her borrowed amber satin gown, fiddling with the fall of thick cream lace at mid-arm, she tried to compose herself. Tonight was to be her baptism of fire. Not since yesterday had she seen him. Her anger, her humiliation, both bitter goads, had produced in him an uncharacteristic flare of temper. Would that demanding monarch, or the tall, dark man with the laughing eyes with whom she had fallen in love, walk through the doorway?

Jenny swallowed the rising lump in her throat and she checked the refreshments on the walnut side table. Earlier in the evening a servant had brought a teardrop crystal decanter of spiced hypocras and a silver plate of honey cakes. Sweets to sweeten her royal lover's mood, she thought bitterly, as she nervously rearranged the Venetian wineglasses with their golden rims. Yesterday, when the carriage had delivered her to Sir Miles Russell's modest mansion, she had been wholly distraught over the revelation of her lover's deception. But that had been yesterday. Many hours had elapsed since then, giving her ample time to review the current situation. Her pain and grief had crystallized into a cold summation: either she resumed her love affair with the King, accepting all the accompanying difficulties of her official birth as royal mistress, or she told him the elusive flame of passion was spent. Agonizing though the decision would be, Jenny's sense told her the latter was by far her wisest choice.

Last night a letter had been delivered to Dunn's Haberdashery informing Uncle Will and Aunt Pet of their niece's intention to take up residence in Sir Miles Russell's esteemed household. Needless to say, no specific reason was given; Pet's active imagination would readily supply an answer. God, could Pet but know the truth! How her eyes would widen, her lips part as she became hysterical with joy. But the truth was not to be revealed just yet. All London would accept Jenny as Sir Miles Russell's new mistress, this convenient arrangement concealing, for a time, her clandestine attachment to the King. While enjoying the protection and sanctuary of Sir Miles' home, she would be readily available to her monarch . . .

"Jenny."

The King walked inside the room unannounced; his face lay in shadow as he stood far out of the pool of light cast by the branched silver candelabra on the table.

"Your Majesty." Jenny dropped a stiff curtsy, fighting the suffocating pounding of her heart. At first she did not raise her eyes, but curiosity eventually drove her to look at him.

"Ah, so at last you've found the courage," he mocked, as their eyes met. "I thought I was to be treated to a perpetual view of your lovely curls."

Tongue-tied, Jenny did not reply. Tonight, Charles—aye, she must be prepared to call him by his own name, or yet again, perhaps she should address him merely as 'Your Majesty'—tonight, Charles wore a gray moiré suit piped in red velvet and trimmed with gold braid. At his neck frothed a lace cravat to match the billowing froth protruding from his red turned-back cuffs. White stockings clung like a second skin to his long muscular legs; rosette garters of gold matched the trimmings on his square-toed black shoes. For the first time priceless jewels glittered on his slender fingers. And though he wore not his crown, nor carried his scepter, Jenny could not forget he was the King.

"Forgive me, Your Majesty," she faltered, searching for the right words and not finding them.

"Forgive you—nay, I forgive you nothing. Stand, you scramble-brain; are you to spend the entire evening on your knees?"

Guiltily she stumbled to her feet, fighting that shuddering heartbeat that threatened to take her breath. Once more she met his eyes, but it was too dark to distinguish with what emotion that brown depth burned. "Would you take refreshment, sire?" she asked, belatedly remembering her manners.

He nodded his assent.

Jenny walked to the side table to pour the hippocras; when she turned, he was standing before the hearth, holding his hands to the blaze.

"Thank you, wench."

Jenny sipped the spiced wine, finding its cloying sweetness nauseating. She offered him a honey cake and he accepted it, popping the tiny cake whole into his mouth.

"Christ, is this to be the extent of our meetings from this time forward?" he demanded gruffly, setting down his glass none too gently on the black marble mantel.

"I've done as you commanded." His eyebrows raised in warning, but Jenny continued recklessly, finding that once she had unbridled her frightened tongue, it wagged out of control. "I came to this loathsome place to pose as that creature's light o'love. I obediently signed a letter stating my new affiliation and ordered it delivered to my relatives. And now, Your Majesty, I am here, waiting on you as a dutiful hostess should, by offering you wine and sweet cakes. We are being charmingly polite as befits a sovereign and his subject . . ."

Charles gripped her upper arm, his fingers biting into her flesh. "Shut up!" he commanded, his face menacing. When Jenny opened her mouth to continue, he clapped his large hand over it, pressing the words back. "Now you listen to me, Mistress Dunn. Never have I needed to ensnare an unwilling wench to warm my bed. If you find this situation so loathsome I'll gladly release you from bondage. It was not my intention to hold you prisoner here, nor to entrap you for my bodily delight. Do you understand what I am saying to you?"

Jenny twisted away from his hand, freeing her mouth. He did not stop her as she pried his fingers from her arm. "Aye, 'tis understood. I'm not quite the dolt you imagine," she cried, momentarily forgetting herself. As his mouth quirked in that sardonic smile she knew so well, Jenny caught her slip and hastily added, "Your Majesty."

Charles inclined his head slightly, acknowledging her correct use of his title.

"What does the future hold for me? At least I'm entitled to know."

"Whatever you wish. You are not my slave."

"But I am your mistress?"

"Only if you wish it."

"I do *not* wish it!"

Angrily he swung from the fireplace, his dark eyes flashing. "You are being foolish! 'Odd's fish, what matter the name I use? You were ready enough to let me take you when you thought me an insignificant lackey. Did you not swear you loved me?"

Jenny dropped her gaze from his, finding tears prickling beneath her lids. "Yes, I did say that."

"They why this unexpected change in affections? God knows, most women would be only too delighted to jump into the King's bed . . ."

"That was never my wish and well you know it."

"Why then that quivering affection for penniless Will Jackson, and nothing but cold anger for the monarch of this land? Tell me that, mistress, for surely you will have some cockeyed logic to account for your inconsistency."

Eyes blazing, Jenny took a step toward him; too close to despair, too tense, too hurt, had she been of late to exercise much caution. "I loved Will Jackson for what I thought him to be. He cherished me. When I was broken-hearted, he comforted me. Never once did he reveal he was not as I supposed. And, though you taunted me with it, I did not lightly discard the knowledge of his wife and mistress. I salved my conscience with the thought that perhaps he had not chosen the lady who shared his name, but married merely to cement some family . . ."

"And do I not share that same fate?" Charles demanded in anger. "Catherine of Braganza brought with her copious possessions my empty coffers ached to hold. Think you it was a love match? That poor, convent-bred wench had not the first idea how to be a woman. Think you that I, Charles Stuart, would have chosen such as she to share my throne had I been allowed the freedom of choice?''

Jenny met his angry glare, trying to blink away tears that would not be held back, but spilled treacherously down her flushed cheeks. '' 'Tis not your Portuguese Infanta who causes me the most pain, Your Majesty, but my Lady Castlemaine, Frances Stewart, and a dozen others, from actresses to countesses, who are privy to the secrets of your body. I will not join so illustrious a line of whores!''

A sneer curved his lips. "Whores are they? And what of that wench who writhed in ecstasy with impoverished Will Jackson beneath God's clear blue sky? What hallowed title does she crave to be called?''

'' 'Tis not to be called whore! Royal or nay, the word is the same. When I gave myself to him . . . to you . . . it was out of need. I reached out and accepted what you gave. Being privy to my recent pain, you took advantage of my weakness. You lied to me. You deceived me. Never once did you betray who you really were. You let me treat you like a royal groom, making free with . . . with your . . .''

He grinned as she sought a polite word for the thought that jabbed through her brain. "My body delighted in the freedom of your hands, Mistress Dunn, for I have not educated it to understand such pleasure was not meant for kings. Tell me, had you known who I was, would you have shrunk from caressing my most treasured and intimate . . .''

"Yes!" she cried, stopping him before he put a name to it. Already she had learned enough about her royal master to know he was a man of the people; long years of poverty had well acquainted him with the common vernacular of servant and guard. Somehow, to hear him speak such words would shatter a little more of her self-imposed barrier, destroying that pedestal on which she strove to place him. Will Jackson could use forthright language; King Charles must not!

"You are a liar!"

Her indrawn breath rasped painfully in her chest. "What did you say?''

"I said you are a liar," he growled, stepping toward her. "Speak not such empty-headed twaddle, wench. Next you'll suggest the royal prick is plated in gold. I'll have no more of your hypocrisy! Either you want me, or you don't—I'll not spend the rest of this damnable cold night arguing the point.''

Pain throbbed through her body as she stared at him, hard, withdrawn, neither gentle Will nor royal Charles. Those high-flown denials of the position he offered dwindled to naught beneath the burning gaze of his dark brown eyes; her intentions, however well meant, disintegrated beneath the overwhelming power of his masculinity. Jenny's legs began to tremble.

"Well," he persisted, giving her a gentle shake to rouse her from her reverie. "What is your answer to be?"

"You have not stated my choices, Your Majesty," she said, not wanting to inflame him further, but quite unable to stop.

Muttering an oath beneath his breath, he released her and turned away. For a few minutes he stood withdrawn before the window, pulling the curtain aside to gaze into the mist-choked street. At last he turned, sighing for the mistrust which had come between them.

"Jenny, when I said I loved you, I meant it. When I said I wanted you, I meant that too. The only thing I lied to you about was my identity and I have already explained my reasoning behind the lie. As a simple man to a maid I ask you now: Wouldst thou lie with me, Jenny Wren, for my blood burns to possess you?"

Those impassioned words, delivered in his deep, intense voice, served to totally disarm her as no royal command could have done. Tears dimmed her vision as Jenny stared at his tall dark figure, unmoving before the closed velvet curtains. The silence in the room was all-enveloping. A crash of splintering sea coal sent a burst of sparks up the chimney, but still they did not speak. As she continued to stare at him, transfixed, his wide mouth lifted; his ill humor disintegrated like magic. Charles held out his arms, pleading with her to accept him as an equal.

"Aye, Will Jackson, I'll lie with you," she said.

Jenny moved those steps that had seemed a thousand miles, their bodies separated by a mountain of anger and distrust. His embrace was eager and hot as he imprisoned her against his body. His mouth came down, devouring hers. All the heat, the warm affection of the man she knew was in that kiss and Jenny blinked, staring up at him, finding his dark brown eyes glowed orange in the reflection from the blazing hearth.

"Oh, Will," she whispered, trembling in his arms, on the verge of tears of forgiveness and relief. "Still do I love you."

A sigh shuddered through his body, relieving and profound. "Bless you, wench, bless you," he whispered, his lips against her hair. "But you must not call me Will. My name is Charles. Say it. Let me have the pleasure of hearing your sweet voice speak my name."

"Charles," she said, finding it strange to speak to him so. "At first I may forget at certain . . . times." She smiled, rejoicing in the answering response she read in his eyes.

"At those times you are forgiven anything, sweetheart," he vowed, slipping his hands over her back, speeding blissful warmth to her body with his caress. Charles traced his finger along her nose and across her high cheekbone, allowing the tantalizing warmth to dip to her neck, her breast. The warm globes of her breasts shone golden in the firelight as he exposed their beauty, his hands clumsy with her bodice lacing in his desperate need.

Jenny shuddered as Charles bent his dark head and swept her breasts with his mouth. Her hands moved forward to encircle his neck until she remembered he was the King; Jenny stopped her impetuous movement.

"Nay, there'll be no false modesty, you vile wench," he hissed, raising his face from her breasts. "Nothing between us has changed. Your King commands you to caress, to hold, to torment, to give him all the delight you unstintingly bestowed on poor Will Jackson."

She hesitated a moment longer, until, impatiently, he snatched her arms and placed them about his neck. Jenny blinked, fighting the startling knowledge that surged through her brain: she embraced the King of England! The strong, sun-bronzed neck about which her arms were twined belonged to he who was born to wear England's crown; the dark head, which she now caressed, running her fingers through his thick black hair, was where that priceless jeweled creation rested.

"You are the King!" she breathed in awe, her lips gentle against his neck. "You are King Charles and I called you a conceited oaf!"

Charles chuckled in delight at the shock in her voice. "Aye, and right merrily did I enjoy it." He moved her backward toward the hearth, where the warmth from the fire engulfed them.

Jenny shuddered as the blood surged recklessly through her veins while he fondled her breasts, his lips searing against her cheek. "I am exalted," she breathed in awe, still somewhat bemused by the events that had befallen her.

"You are addled," he snapped, shaking her gently before pressing her against the rousing passion stirring beneath his splendid garments.

His brisk observation served to break the spell. "Charles, Charles Stuart," she repeated, almost to herself, "does he love a wench as grandly as did poor Will Jackson?"

Charles smiled down at her as, with a quick movement, he brought her from the floor, lifting her, positioning her upon the insistent thrust of his body. Impaled thus, she squirmed pleasurably upon the heated weapon that threatened to bore through her clothing. "There is but one way to learn the answer to your question," he invited huskily.

Warmly arousing, his tantalizing suggestion hung in the room. Jenny shuddered as perfume, mingled with the hot arousing scent of his flesh, arose from his garments: musk, cinnamon, and rose bound her in an ecstasy of sweetness. Eagerly she sought his mouth, finding it temptingly responsive beneath her own.

"Well," he whispered when their lips parted. Swiftly he slid her from that thrusting temptation, setting her back on her feet. "Would you keep me forever in suspense?"

Jenny smiled at him, resting her head against his broad shoulder. "Whatever I thought you to be, 'twas never this," she confided. "Yet, in truth, what you are and what I thought you were matters not a whit. Your kiss, your touch are still the same. You are the man I love, despite your noble birth. I'm sorry for being such a shrew, but I was sore affronted at having been taken advantage of . . ."

He snorted in disgust, halting her speech. "Taken advantage of! You rogue, surely it is I who was taken advantage of—ensnared by your arms, your kisses, you wicked witch of Swann Alley. How dare you suggest . . ."

Pressing her fingers against his mouth, Jenny silenced his indignant speech. "Am I forgiven as I forgive you?"

"Put that way, I can hardly deny the favor," he whispered huskily. "Now, wench, you are doing a deal too much talking. Come, your hand." Charles took her small hand and pressed it firmly against the stirring presence beneath the lush gray fabric. "Would you torment me any longer? Yield to me, Jenny Wren, now, here. How soft is the rug before yon hearth? Think you it gentle enough to cradle a King and his love?"

"When that King first tasted his love on the hard riverbank, yes, I would say 'tis soft enough," she whispered, shuddering at the leaping response beneath her hand. She slid her tongue tantalizingly across his lean cheek as she invited, "Come, then, my love, repledge my faith in you. Love me, Charles, make me happy again."

He covered her face with kisses as he bore her to the red Turkey rug before the hearth. Yet still, even now, when she reached for the buttons on his lace-bedecked shirt, Jenny hesitated, far too conscious that the fine garment belonged to the King. Impatiently, he nudged her to continue to undress him, anxious to repeat the exciting experience they had shared that magical afternoon beside the Thames.

The fire was warm against her bare flesh, the soft glow fusing with her inner heat until Jenny was consumed with fire. The tantalizing taste and feel of his mouth was all over her, tingling through her belly, her thighs, her chest: no longer did she remember this man was the King; as he expertly aroused her she knew only that he was her lover. Delighting in her caresses, Charles shuddered with passion as Jenny kissed the hard length of his body, trailing her soft lips from the hollow of his neck to his belly.

When at last they were so aflame they had come dangerously close to the point of no return, he rolled her to her back. As he drew from her, Jenny felt a sense of loss. Charles gazed down at her lovely, curving body, gleaming like molten gold in the firelight. Her limbs throbbed as she breathlessly waited for him to continue, and her passionate reaction served to increase his excitement. Jenny touched his hard lean flanks, his flat belly while he remained suspended in the wonder of the moment; until, sensing her impatience with his inaction, he smiled down at her and asked, "Art thou ready, sweetheart?"

Jenny returned his smile, the taunt he had flung at her in the gloomy palace corridor flashing through her mind. With whisper-soft fingers she caressed the swollen length of his towering flesh as she said, "Aye, ready for you to make good your threats—Caesar."

His wide mouth dissolved in laughter as he recalled that statement spat in terrible anger. With one quick thrust he entered her, making her cry out in delighted surprise. "I intend to love you instead, Jenny Wren," he said.

Chapter 17

Sir Miles Russell returned home during the first week in November and, though greatly surprised by the unexpected turn of events, he was far too wise to question his sovereign's actions. He owed his King a number of favors; this was to be the first repayment.

Jenny stiffened as Sir Miles bowed formally and kissed her hand, his unwanted touch stirring unpleasant memories of their last meeting.

"Sir Miles."

"What pleasure it is to return from an extremely boring sojourn in the country to discover so beauteous a creature awaiting me in my own drawing room," he murmured as he released her hand.

"I trust his Majesty has already spoken to you of his plans?" Jenny asked icily, disliking the intimate manner in which Sir Miles was surveying her. His probing blue gaze slid rapidly from her face to the tempting display of flesh barely concealed beneath the pink lace whisk at her bosom.

"You may rest assured he has. But, my dear, if we are to continue the ruse our King demands, surely we must not be so icily distant toward each other. Won't that make people question our loving relationship?"

Though Jenny hated to agree with him, she knew he was right. "Perhaps had you behaved more like a gentleman toward me at our last meeting, Sir Miles, I would not find this enforced civility such an imposition," she concluded coldly.

"You are to be congratulated, my dear, your speech has become most ladylike . . ."

"Stop your mockery! Have you not even the grace to apologize for trying to rape me?"

"Grace? Under the present circumstances it would be more appropriate to say 'good sense.' After all, my love, Carolus Rex is now your protector."

"You odious . . . let me assure you, the selection of this

239

house was none of my doing! Had I been given the choice never would I have sought to lay eyes on you again!''

Sir Miles smiled, his bulbous blue eyes turning glassy. "Ah, you leave me no illusions. Dear wench, a thousand pardons for having the effrontery to assume your body was for sale. I was unaware there was but one man in all England who possessed the proper credentials . . .''

"You may be the first to know I did not choose the King for my lover.''

"Nay, for ever *he* seeks to do the choosing.''

"That's not what I meant. When I met his Majesty, I did not know him for the King.''

Sir Miles smiled knowingly: he was familiar with Charles Stuart's delight in playacting. "Then, my dear wench, what a marvelous stroke of fortune that discovery must have been.''

Jenny abruptly turned her back on him, longing to retaliate, but uncomfortable in the presence of a servant who had brought his master a decanter of wine. For the man's benefit she accepted a glass of tinto from Sir Miles, forcing a frosty smile of acceptance after he quirked his eyebrow in censure of her set countenance. When the servant departed, she swung about to face him.

"Sir Miles, though I'm under your roof, I'm not here for your amusement.''

"Old Rowley's not one to quibble about sharing his mistresses,'' he countered, his bulbous eyes lit with a suggestive gleam. "Surely . . .''

"Beyond our public appearances I intend to have absolutely nothing to do with you. And you may rest assured, those functions will bring no joy.''

"If you do not wish to anger your royal lover, those public functions you refer to so despisingly must at least appear to bring joy, dear lady. Amiable though he may be, Charles Stuart is not without his tempestuous moments.''

"Agreed, but I intend to keep those functions to an absolute minimum. Each hour I must feign affection for you will seem like purgatory.''

Sir Miles, preparing to take his leave, bowed stiffly over her extended hand. His full lips pulled back in a sneer as he said, "Assuredly, my love, your merest wish is my command.''

Jenny nodded, her mouth tight. "I expect no less than total cooperation from you.''

He paused, his hand on the door handle as he remarked casually, "Oh, by the way, my love, a relative sits below anxiously awaiting your pleasure."

"Relative?"

"Mistress Dunn, that artful schemer, has come to congratulate you on your immense good fortune. I shall have her sent up."

A wave of panic assailed her. Jenny had no desire to chat with Pet; the ordeal of needing to pretend affection for her supposed lover filled her with dread. But it was too late to feign indisposition; even now she could hear the hurried clatter of Pet's high-heeled shoes on the polished stair.

"Mistress Pet Dunn," announced the serving man.

With a flurry of rustling skirts, Pet sailed inside the room, dismissing the servant with a disdainful wave of her gloved hand.

"Jenny, my love! Oh, how it does my eyes good to look upon you," Pet cried, running toward her, arms outstretched.

"Hello, Aunt Pet." Jenny endured her embrace, slipping her arms about her aunt's plump body in a half-hearted gesture of affection. "I wasn't expecting you."

"Not expecting me! Fie! Do you think I could stay away a moment longer?" Pet cried shrilly while her gaze roved greedily about the finely appointed drawing room. "I'm broken-hearted to think you didn't invite me before now, but considering how excited you must be over your good fortune, I'll forgive you."

Pet darted across the room to examine the blown glass ornaments on the beechwood side table; the purple embroidered chair covers and matching heavy damask draperies also became objects of close scrutiny. As Jenny watched Pet so absorbed, she longed to tell her the truth, yet such devastating honesty was out of the question. "How's Uncle Will?" she asked at last, forcing a smile. "Did he not come with you?"

"He's well," Pet answered vaguely, looking away from Jenny's direct gaze. She fiddled with the lid of the bible box of cedar inlaid with olive wood, feigning immense interest in its design.

"He does not approve."

"He'll come round in time, have no fear. Will's somewhat straight-laced in his outlook, that's all. But he'll come round, I'll see to that. Why, he can't afford not to, can he?" Pet smiled craftily, her plump cheeks flushed with excitement.

"You'll be finely clad, you'll have jewels, you'll attend balls and parties with the cream of London society; oh, Jenny, how lucky you are! Never in all my life did I dream you'd bring us such great fortune."

"Fortune?" Jenny repeated, wondering at her aunt's remark.

"We're changing our sign to Will Dunn Esq. Mercer and Haberdasher, by appointment to her Majesty the Queen. The entire court will soon be at our feet. That's if you, my love, encourage them to shop where you shop. You can become a leader of fashion. And your fresh beauty will soon outshine that prize whore, Barbara Palmer. Why, even his Majesty may look with favor on you 'ere long—look not so bewildered, he ever has an eye for a new face. As Sir Miles will pay our bills without question, your fabric can be purchased from us. Your tailoring also can be contracted by us . . . oh, Jenny, just think, we'll be the most prosperous shop in all Swann Alley—nay, in all Cornhill!"

Pet sailed across the room. Unclasping her ruby plush cloak, she carelessly allowed it to drape open to reveal the sumptuous brown fur lining; beneath the luxurious cloak, Pet wore a brown velvet gown laced with gold. Both garments were new acquisitions.

"How grand you look."

Pet preened at her niece's compliment. "Thank you, my love. As usual Will complained about the cost, but he cannot expect me to go about clad like a drudge, not now that we're on the verge of prosperity. Besides, I'm on my way to a business engagement. A wench I know at the King's Head is a friend of Sam Pepys of the Navy Board. With all this talk of war, the navy's assumed vast importance. The docks are humming with activity, fitting out vessels, loading provisions—anyway, Peg's arranged for me to sup with him while we discuss supplying the navy with cloth." Pet smiled smugly as she patted her fluffy blond curls. "Peg says Sam's got an eye for comely women—a few promises, a handclasp, and who knows what favors I might secure."

For well over an hour Pet stayed, relating the latest street gossip about Lady Castlemaine, the Duke of York, and even the King himself, casually using their Christian names as if they were the best of friends. After downing two full glasses of rich tinto, Pet grew even more talkative until her chatter was abruptly halted by the strident chimes of the painted French clock on the mantel.

"Twelve! Oh, but it can't be! I must rush. Let us allow bygones to be bygones, my dear Jenny. I'm delighted you've shown such good sense at last. I declare, I was losing faith in you. Have no fear, Sir Miles' good lady will give you no cause for alarm, for I heard from a reliable source that she lies bedridden in Buckinghamshire—now, remember, my love, make all your purchases from your Uncle Will. Such kind thoughts will greatly restore his humor."

So saying, Pet kissed Jenny on the cheek; then, gathering her gloves and cloak, she rang the bell for the servant to escort her to the door.

Jenny watched her aunt descend to the street, head high, nose in the air as if she were a grand lady. At the corner of the bisecting street a great heap of branches had been assembled to be burned this fifth of November in annual commemoration of Guy Fawkes night. A misshapen effigy of the notorious conspirator who had attempted to destroy the Houses of Parliament perched atop the pyre, a placard hung about its neck. Curious, yet hardly deigning to acknowledge such common entertainments, Pet slowed her steps to read the scrawled handwriting on the placard. Behind her back a couple of ragged urchins, who had watched her leave Russell House, danced about, pulling faces and chanting derogatory epithets.

Instantly dropping her haughty pose, Pet seized a branch from the bonfire and laid it about the boys' ears, her face flushed crimson with rage. Though Jenny could not hear her aunt's accompanying words, she doubted they were in the least bit ladylike. Pet's easy fall from the pinnacle upon which she had placed herself made Jenny smile. Never would Pet rest in her relentless ambition to appear rich and noble. How much nearer to glory she had come than she suspected. If Pet had the slightest suspicion Jenny's lover was the King himself, she would probably contract to buy a mansion.

After her aunt mingled with the crowd beyond St. Mary-le-Bow's dark stone edifice, Jenny turned from the window. It would be no inconvenience to purchase her future needs from her uncle's shop. Jenny was reluctant to fan the flames of Pet's greed, yet for Will's sake, and in repayment for his kindness during her time of need, she decided to make the bulk of her purchases at Dunn's of Swann Alley.

* * *

The ordeal of her first public appearance as Sir Miles Russell's mistress was over. Jenny sighed with relief when they drew up outside the Cheapside mansion. Glad of her fur-edged cloak as a blast of cold air met her, she dismounted from the lumbering coach emblazoned with Sir Miles' coat of arms. Far above the uneven rooftops stretched clear, star-pricked sky, while here, between the buildings, hung a sooty haze, reducing the surroundings to somber shadows. With the acrid sting of sea coal smoke sharp in her nostrils, Jenny allowed Sir Miles to escort her up the shallow steps to the house.

"Congratulations! No one would have guessed we are less than friends," he remarked, as they warmed themselves before the blazing hearth in the back parlor.

"To present such a picture was my intention."

Sir Miles poured a cup of mulled wine and handed it to her. "'Tis a pity his Majesty was otherwise engaged, he would have been delighted with your performance. Why, my love, someday you might tread the boards of the Duke's Theater, so accomplished an actress have you become."

Jenny managed a faint smile, though Sir Miles' reminder of Charles' defection from the dinner party at Lord Benbrook's townhouse made her heart ache afresh with the knowledge of the nature of his more pressing engagement. "His Majesty will have an opportunity to observe my skill at a later date," she said stiffly.

"Aye, if the royal whore doesn't detain him again. Could it be that she suspects his attention to be wandering? Methinks not only has she word Charles pants over pretty Mrs. Stewart, but perchance she's heard some whisperings of a secret light o'love who has recently set his blood aboil."

"What do you mean by that?"

Sir Miles smiled, his bulbous eyes gleaming maliciously above the gold-edged rim of his glass. "Barbara Palmer may be a whore, but she's no fool. Surely you don't think you're the first wench our sovereign has skillfully hidden away for his amusement. And, my love, you will certainly not be the last."

Jenny was too vulnerable to accept this speech for what it was; tonight the reminder of Charles' unfaithfulness speared her heart. "If you think I'm unaware of his Majesty's roving eye, Sir Miles, you must think me a total fool."

"God knows, all London's privy to his adventuring. I

merely seek to remind you he pines not the night away. When, and if, he wishes to board you, he knows exactly where to find you. Here you wait, soft and pliable as a well-worn shoe . . .''

"Good night, Sir Miles, your conversation bores me,'' Jenny said, nervously smoothing the crystal embroidered skirts of her rose-pink satin gown.

"You're fool enough to think he loves you.''

"My private emotions are none of your concern. In providing a convenient lodging, you purchased nothing of myself,'' she reminded as she walked stiffly to the door.

"You're only a new plaything to him! Never was it his intention to be faithful. Nor does he expect faithfulness from his women. He's no hypocrite.''

To her alarm Jenny discovered the door handle turned uselessly in her clammy hands. Growing desperate, she rattled the brass knob, shutting her ears to Sir Miles' cruel taunts. Whirling from the door, she held out her hand, her eyes flashing in anger as she demanded, "Give me the key!''

"Never. Once I contracted for you, sweet bitch, and you never did honor the bargain.''

They struggled before the embossed door, Sir Miles wrenching cruelly on Jenny's delicate wrists as he sought to imprison her against his body. The cold hard centers of the buttons on his coat pressed sharply into her soft breasts. Desperately Jenny craned her head back to avoid his moist lips as he tried to kiss her. Her efforts were in vain as those possessive lips clamped over her own, devouring like a savage beast; a mingled repulsion of tinto, stewed oysters, and pickled onions invaded her tongue-ravaged mouth.

"Think you I sat beside you, that I offered you tidbits, and simpered like a half-wit just to come home to a cold bed?''

Jenny managed to free her hands. Lacing her fists, she delivered a mighty blow on top of his head. The heavy layers of his full-bottomed periwig cushioned the force of her rage; his hat had already fallen to the carpet and been trampled underfoot. Her resistance angered him rather than inflicted pain. Abruptly Sir Miles grabbed Jenny's flailing arms, his fingers imparting a trail of bruises on her soft flesh. The cold wooden door pressed into her back as he forced her against it, positioning her, his fumbling hands busy with her voluminous skirts.

Jenny sobbed and fought, hating him both for his actions

and the cruelty of his taunts. Though his demanding hands moved to her thigh, she clamped her legs tight, halting his invasion; when his attention strayed to her bodice, Jenny drew up her knee, prepared to deliver a crushing blow to his vitals. But alerted to her intention, Sir Miles twisted away.

"There's nothing you can do, or say, to dissuade me. So, if you value your new finery, you'll remove it before I'm forced to strip you," he snarled, his face purple with anger.

Tears of rage burned in her eyes as Jenny experienced a stunning feeling of impotency. The ordeal of pretending affection for hated Sir Miles, coming so swift on the heels of her knowledge that Charles preferred to dine this night with Lady Castlemaine, had robbed her of emotional strength. A wave of disabling weakness swept through her limbs as she struggled ineffectually against his flowered brocade suit.

"I'm no match for your strength, as well you know, you odious creature. If it is your pleasure, then take me on the floor as you're accustomed to service the sluts of your acquaintance, for I doubt any *lady* knows aught of your lovemaking." Jenny's taunt was rewarded by a flicker of shame crossing his reddened face.

"I did not want to steal between your legs, wench," he protested gruffly. But though his words seemed apologetic, Sir Miles did not slacken his grasp.

" 'Tis the only way you'll get there."

Angrily he shook her, banging her against the door. "Your attitude demands such action. Can you not at least be cordial?"

"Cordiality is not an emotion engendered by rape."

"Charles has his other women. You're not expected to remain celibate. Come, you're lonely, even I can see it. Be not lonely, wench. I would fain erase all that has gone between us and provide you with loving companionship. He does not love you—he will not care."

"I care!"

With flaring nostrils, Sir Miles stood his ground a moment longer, his breathing becoming ragged. "Bitch!" he spat at last. "Then we shall do it my way."

Jenny fought against him, trying to evade his mouth as his soft, fleshy lips smothered hers. When he pried open her clenched teeth, Sir Miles' full lips snagged a moment beneath the sharpness: Jenny bit hard.

" 'Swounds! You vicious hellcat!"

Sir Miles fell back, his lower lip streaming blood. The crimson splashed on the fine Turkey rug and stained the frothing lace at his neck. His pale eyes gleamed brittle as glass as he stared at the gushing blood his kerchief failed to quench.

"Give me the key! I promise you his Majesty shall hear of this. And I shall spare him no details. No doubt your wound will be proof enough I speak the truth. Now give me the key. If you ever lay hands on me again, you'll regret it for the rest of your days."

Jenny's angry threat hung in the quiet room as they glared at each other.

With a snarled oath, Sir Miles took the key from his pocket and flung it at her. "Take it, you street whore. God damn you for your treachery. I'll be the laughingstock of the city."

Jenny retrieved the key from the hem of her skirts and hastily unlocked the door. In a flash she was in the corridor and up the stairs; Sir Miles' angry voice drifted after her, but she was confident he would offer no pursuit.

Thankfully Jenny closed the door behind her, turning the key that sealed her sanctuary from invasion. A welcoming fire blazed in the small suite overlooking the bare garden. Shivering both from cold and shock, Jenny huddled before the hearth, stretching her icy hands to the blaze. After tonight she doubted she need fear Sir Miles' unwelcome advances. The bite she had inflicted would indeed cause much amused comment when he went to court, for there was no simple explanation to be given for such a wound. But her victory brought with it no pleasure. Though uttered out of spite, nevertheless his cruel taunts had struck home. Charles was unfaithful—perhaps, at this very moment, he nestled in Barbara Palmer's soft white arms, his body buried deep within hers. As Jenny pictured that scene a wave of nausea spiraled from her stomach to her throat and she clutched her body, shaking her head in an effort to rid herself of the hateful picture. When she first accepted his love Jenny was aware the King was not known for constancy, yet considering the depth of their shared affection, naively she had expected him to change.

Rousing herself from the fog of self-pity that was rapidly invading her mind, Jenny walked into the bedroom. She would not ring for the maid to help her undress: many years of ministering to others deterred her from rousing the girl from her warm pallet on this cold autumn night. Besides, she had not grown so idle she must have assistance to undress.

Tears dimmed her vision as she unlaced and unhooked, struggling to divest herself of her fine satin gown. Six sumptuous new gowns hung in the inlaid cupboard; a mountain of ribbons, feathers, and silk flowers lined the drawers of the walnut chest. Usually generous after lovemaking, Charles had promised Jenny a jeweled necklace as a Christmas gift. Yet satin gowns and jewels, beautiful though they were, were a poor substitute for happiness.

Lighting a taper at the hearth, Jenny walked to the double-doored inlaid walnut cupboard where her new finery was stored. She flung open the heavy doors and held the taper aloft; a pool of light splashed the shimmering velvet and satin with gold. Like a pirate's treasure, paste jewels and gold lace winked among the billowing yards of sea green, purple, crimson, and pink. To own such beautiful gowns, to be singled out for favors by the King, was surely a woman's dreams come true, Jenny thought, a growing ache in her throat, all her dreams—save one.

An unbidden memory of Kit stirred anger and pain within her breast. She closed the cupboard, banishing that scintillating rainbow from view. Men were such unfaithful creatures! Acceptance of that truth should not have come as so great a blow, for she had reached that conclusion long months ago. What of Kit, with whom she had imagined sharing the rest of her days? He had deserted her for another. And though her pain was of long standing, Jenny still could not dwell upon it with indifference. First she had been deceived by handsome dashing Kit, then by kind-hearted Will Jackson, whose identity existed not at all. Both were virile, exciting men; to have demanded faithfulness from either of them was too much to expect. Yet, fool that she was, once her heart had been committed, she had expected just that. Fool! Fool! Her idiocy knew no bounds. A reckless sea captain who sailed to mysterious foreign ports and Charles, King of England, were the two men to whom she had entrusted her precious, fragile heart. They had both discarded her devotion as casually as they changed their clothes!

The vast Palace ballroom blazed with light. Walls of gilt-edged mirrors reflected the golden shimmer of crystal chandeliers suspended from the lofty ceiling, where candles dripped hot streams of wax onto the heads and bare shoulders of those gathered below. Beribboned garlands of evergreens festooned the room; scarlet, green, and gold damask cloths covered the trestle tables where the refreshments were laid. Despite the intermittent snow flurries drifting past the deep, uncurtained windows, the room temperature was that of midsummer. This lavish Christmas masked ball was the first Whitehall function to which Jenny had been invited. Ostensibly she attended the ball as Sir Miles Russell's mistress, and in that capacity was viewed with open interest by the assembled courtiers and their ladies.

Tonight Queen Catherine wore white watered taffeta stiffly embroidered with pearls, her dark hair dressed in a becoming new style and adorned with loops of pearls. Jenny thought her most attractive. But Charles' Portuguese Queen was not the star of the evening. Though her well-known face was concealed beneath a silver mask edged with diamonds, the notorious Countess Castlemaine actually ruled the glittering assembly, laughing, flirting, graciously accepting the homage of smitten admirers as if she were the Queen instead of the diminutive figure in white whose sallow face revealed her sadness. Because of Barbara's notoriety, Jenny was able to gaze upon Charles' chief mistress with less jealousy than she would have imagined; it helped to think of the court beauty as a national monument instead of a woman. Here at last was the fabled creature about whom she had speculated so avidly in the dingy taproom of the Rose and Crown, never for a moment expecting to attend a court function as her equal. Purportedly Barbara had Charles wrapped about her little finger; so great an influence had she over him that Lady Castlemaine had once aspired to be named Queen; she had never forgiven her royal lover for his omission.

"My dearest lady, your form is divine. Would that I might glimpse your lovely face," whispered a husky masculine voice at Jenny's elbow.

A young man in glittering silver brocade, a full red periwig flowing from beneath his silver mask, paid the flowery compliment. Already his hand rested possessively on her arm.

"You will forgive me, sir, if I do not unmask. They say mystery is an added aphrodisiac," she offered gaily, withdrawing her arm as she looked around for Sir Miles to come to her rescue. Jenny hated having to signal to him, for she had no desire for his company, but in order to convincingly play the role the King desired, such a signal must be given.

Fortunately, Sir Miles was already aware of the sparkling young gallant's amorous intent.

"Sir, allow me to introduce you to wenches who are in search of a lover—this lovely creature is already mine," Sir Miles drawled smoothly as he reached Jenny's side. His hand rested hot against her waist, the moist unpleasantness penetrating her lavender satin gown. Jenny smiled brilliantly as she knew she was expected to do now that her lover had rescued her from the unwelcome attentions of this stranger. The red-whigged gallant bowed stiffly and excused himself, not anxious to clash with the influential middle-aged courtier.

"When will his Majesty arrive?" Jenny asked, keeping her voice low.

Sir Miles shrugged. "I expected him to be here already. See, Barbara's anger mounts by the minute. At least, my dear, tonight you can rest assured he's not dallying with her."

This malicious assurance was not intended to comfort. Jenny smiled coldly and stepped away from him, but Sir Miles detained her arm.

"Nay, dance this coranto with me. At least until our sovereign arrives, we must appear to be the very closest of companions."

An exhaustive program of dancing lessons these past weeks had increased Jenny's confidence in her ability to dance in public. Monsieur Simmette, the dancing master appointed by Charles to prepare her for social functions, was effusive in his praise of her natural ability. Amid the running, gliding steps of the coranto, Jenny's final discomfort evaporated. Too much attention must she pay to these unfamiliar dance steps to allow herself the indulgence of self-pity. Just as the music ended, a flurry at the far end of the ballroom alerted the assembly to the arrival of their King.

With fluttering heart Jenny turned and, before she sank to the floor in a billowing curtsy, she had a clear view of Charles, head and shoulders above his two companions, striding inside the brightly lit room. His suit of ice-blue satin edged in magenta velvet, beribboned and laced in silver, made his complexion appear even swarthier. A mountain of plumes sat atop his black hat, spilling over the brim in swirls of fluffy blue and magenta. Like dipping flowers, the ladies went down, their billowing gowns a myriad garden of color. Pausing to exchange an occasional greeting, the King moved rapidly through the parted dancers, chatting amiably with his two companions whose identity Jenny did not know. When he reached her, he paused, his dark gaze flicking first to Sir Miles Russell as if seeking assurance that this was indeed his love beneath the sparkling silver mask.

"So this is your lovely lady," the King said, chuckling as he reached for Jenny's arm and raised her to her feet. "You are to be congratulated, Sir Miles, on your immense good taste."

"Oh, Your Majesty," Jenny gasped in genuine surprise, hardly expecting to be singled out so publicly for his attentions. Unknown to her, Charles was not secretive for long about the paths in which his heart lay.

"What beauty! And, as yet, I have not even seen her face," he added, as Sir Miles bowed low, a dull flush lighting his sagging features.

A gale of laughter greeted the King's sally. And, still chuckling, he moved on without a backward glance, leaving Jenny flushed and nervous as she wondered whether to resume her curtsy or to remain standing.

The King stopped before his dark-haired Queen; taking Catherine's hand, he raised it to his lips, proposing she join him in leading the bransle. The sheer joy suffusing the Queen's sallow face brought Jenny close to tears, for she well understood Catherine's pain. Hastily blinking back the moisture, she moved forward to watch them dance. While the two dark-haired figures moved in perfect rhythm to the music, Catherine gazed with rapt attention into her husband's swarthy face. Poor little Portuguese Queen! Catherine of Braganza dearly loved her virile, unfaithful husband, and though Charles showed her great kindness, never would she be foremost in his affections.

At the appearance of her royal lover, Lady Castlemaine had unmasked, not expecting the King's snub. When, instead, he asked his Queen to dance, Barbara boiled with anger. Her lovely face was a study of bad temper: her full mouth pouted unbecomingly; her heavy lids were lowered over her fine eyes; and even her delicate nostrils flared like an ill-natured nag's. A dozen laughing couples joined the royal pair, forming a brilliant circle on the dance floor, but still Barbara refused to become part of the carefree throng. She stood near the door glowering into her glass of white wine, smoldering with resentment over the King's indifference.

The gay dances followed each other in heady succession

while the room grew warmer and the candles burned lower. Jenny partnered Sir Miles until he handed her to a portly courtier in a tightly curled brown wig. Before he departed for the refreshment table, he confided to her that the man was a high court official. While they danced, the man ogled her, relaying choice snippets of court gossip in a gravel voice. The chitchat soon became an unintelligible monotony as mounting age and corpulence robbed her partner of breath, causing him to gasp out his stories while he steered Jenny back and forth in accompaniment to the lively music.

At last, begging off more dances, she retreated to the steaming windows. Infinite black sky stretched beyond the pane; a faint frosting of snow drifted against the windowsill. In the wall's full-length mirrors Jenny quickly checked her appearance, noting her flushed cheeks and the wayward strands of chestnut hair escaping from her elaborate coiffure. Her lovely gown of deepest lavender satin billowed from her slender waist like a flower in full bloom; yards of lace flouncing trimmed the full skirts and edged the elbow-length sleeves, while at intervals the lace was caught up by small ribbon nosegays of lavender and pink, fashioned to look like posies with leaf-green satin leaves. Though she had admired her shimmering reflection in the full-length Venetian glass mirror in her bedchamber at Russell House, Jenny still found it hard to believe she was this dazzling creature. The lavender satin made her smooth skin appear even creamier, the delicate color bringing out the many shades in her bright chestnut hair. Lavender and pink posies caught up with imitation pearls adorned her elaborate hairdress, which had taken more than an hour to arrange. The French maid appointed by Charles, being highly experienced in ladies' hair fashions, had excelled herself tonight.

"Exquisite!"

Startled, Jenny raised her eyes to encounter a pair of soft brown eyes laughing into hers. Charles had come to stand behind her, approval for her lovely appearance readily apparent on his lean face. "Oh, Your Majesty," she gasped in surprise, beginning a curtsy, but he gripped her elbows, forcing her to remain upright.

"Nay, stand not on ceremony with me, wench," he said, his deep voice huskily inviting as he swept the reflected image before him with an admiring gaze.

Only then did Jenny become conscious of the sea of unfamiliar faces forming a curious semi-circle at a discreet distance behind him. Perhaps no one was close enough to hear his words, but Charles was taking no chances of betraying what, for the moment, proved to be a very amusing deception.

"Will you do me the honor of dancing with me, Mistress Dunn?"

"Certainly, Your Majesty, it will be my pleasure."

Charles' hand was hot on her arm as he led her to the center of the vast ballroom. A thousand eyes focused on the pair as the King raised his hand and signaled for the musicians to begin their piece. Such an accomplished dancer was Charles Stuart that when he took the floor even the ladies rose to watch him. The fact that he had singled out this unknown beauty for so great an honor merely increased the observers' interest: speculating on her background, asking, guessing, even fabricating facts, the guests set the ballroom buzzing with a mounting wave of sound.

"Be not afraid, sweet," Charles whispered, tightening his hand on her arm. "You dance superbly."

Gratefully, Jenny smiled at him, knowing he sought to put her at ease. As they whirled past the Queen seated on a gilded chair, Jenny wondered if her Majesty guessed that this sumptuous creature in lavender satin and the awestruck vender who had presented a display of ribbons in her chamber were the same. The gossips said Queen Catherine was well versed in her husband's infidelities, yet Jenny hoped this liaison remained a well-kept secret: the kindness displayed toward her by the foreign queen was ill repaid by wantonness with her erring husband.

"How long it has been since we've been alone? Is it ten days?"

"Nay, twelve, Your Majesty."

Charles smiled at her correction. He was not masked and his well-known saturnine countenance reflected his every emotion. "Then, sweet wench, we can allow so shameful a state of affairs to continue no longer. 'Ere that total become thirteen, I shall *join* you." And the suggestive gleam in his hot, dark eyes betrayed the exact meaning behind his emphasized word.

With quickened breath, Jenny tried to concentrate on the dance; several times she faltered, unable to count the measures for the excitement whirling through her body. She was too prudent to remind him how often he had been denied her company, not because she had not welcomed him, but because he found another's arms more inviting.

When the dance ended, he bowed elegantly over her hand, turning it uppermost to press a hot, ardent kiss against her palm. The gesture, though public enough, sent a quiver through her arm. And Jenny's reaction to King Charles' gallant tribute did not go unnoticed.

During the following round of bransles and corantos, Jenny nibbled a venison pasty, washing it down with a glass of mild sweet white wine that bubbled up the back of her nose.

Once again Charles swept through the rapidly parting throng to single Jenny out for attention. Their gazes met and fastened above the sea of heads, an unspoken message passing between them. Out of the corner of her eye, Jenny glimpsed Barbara's furious face, eyes flashing, nostrils dilated in rage over her lover's continued indifference.

"Mistress Dunn, will you dance the new French dance with me?" This time Charles held out his slender, olive-skinned hand as he gave his invitation. Jenny shuddered as he clasped her fingers.

They took the floor alone, their dance an exhibition upon which all attention was riveted. This was a new French measure, taught to Jenny only three days ago by the gushing little French dancing master who had not revealed the reason behind the express lesson. Now Jenny understood why Monsieur Simmette was so anxious for her to excel: the instruction had been by royal command! Charles' dark eyes sparkled with laughter as he heard the gasps of excitement rippling through the assembly over the dance, which had not been seen before at court. Already mental notes were being made to seek out Mistress Dunn's dancing instructor, as first one, then another, of the ladies swayed where they stood, copying the gay rythym of the dance. Even Lady Castlemaine, who would have preferred to feign indifference, eagerly absorbed the measure of those unfamiliar steps in order that she too might excel in the new French dance.

An exclamation of surprise followed by a noisy round of applause greeted the ending of the dance. Whether the official finale to the measure was thus, Jenny did not know, but as the final gay notes came to an end, Charles swept her into his arms and pressed an ardent kiss on her lips. A wave of gasps, nudges, and raised eyebrows followed the incident as he led

Jenny back to her escort, who waited beside the refreshment table, a full glass of wine in his hand.

"Sir Miles, I thank you most heartily for allowing me the pleasure of your lovely lady's company."

"I am honored to know I have pleased your Majesty."

"Look after her well."

"That is my intention, sire." Sir Miles bowed stiffly.

Momentarily shielded from curious gazes as he turned, Charles winked at Jenny, the promise of what was to follow later tonight reflected in his hot dark eyes. Then he strode away amid the clamor of excited courtiers who were demanding to know who this beauty was and how she had learned the new dance ahead of the court. Good-naturedly, Charles fended off their inquiries, refusing to divulge any information about the mysterious lady, even feigning total ignorance of her appearance; yet those who knew him well did not for one moment believe his protestations. Before long the story was circulating that the object of his Majesty's current infatuation had been known to him in France: this theory was doubly satisfying, for not only was it a neat explanation of Jenny's knowledge of the latest dance, but it also explained why none of the courtiers had previously known of her existence. When one somewhat jaded rake revealed he had it on good authority that Sir Miles Russell's beautiful amour was lately a seller of ribbons from Cornhill, he was immediately shouted down. The glittering throng preferred not to believe so ordinary an explanation. But the rake's second observation, that 'ere long it would not be to a bed in Cheapside that the beauteous creature would retire, was unanimously accepted.

"We shall leave in a few minutes," Sir Miles told Jenny in an undertone. The King had departed early, pleading an urgent private meeting with a member of his council, much to the disappointment of those hangers-on who had sought to follow him.

"Are we to go home?"

"Nay, you thick-headed jade," Sir Miles sneered, "not *we*. *I* shall go home—you are to be offered another diversion."

Their conversation was interrupted by a woman's shrill, demanding voice. "Sir Miles, how dare you keep your plaything hidden? Unmask her so we may all behold her face. Let us see if her beauty lives up to its promise."

All eyes focused on the imperious figure of Barbara, Countess Castlemaine, resplendent in black and silver, glittering with jewels, her lovely face twisted with jealousy as she sailed toward them, angrily tapping her fan against the palm of her hand.

"This is a masked ball, my Lady Castlemaine," Jenny replied, stepping forth without giving Sir Miles a chance to speak.

"You are refusing to unmask?"

"Yes."

Barbara bit her lower lip, trying to keep her temper in check. "Why seek you to entrap his Majesty when you already have a lover?" she demanded in an undertone, but her temper kept her voice loud enough to be heard in the quiet that enveloped the room.

"I was not aware of any rule allowing only one lover per lady."

A gale of laughter greeted Jenny's sally. Lady Castlemaine stepped closer, her fists clenched. "You've a ready wit, wench. Take care, lest your tongue be your downfall."

"Nay, Barbara, seek not to quell her voice, for 'tis charming to hear," drawled a young man in a flowing golden wig. He stepped forward, heavy-lidded blue eyes scanning the lovely adversaries; despite his youth, all the telltale marks of indolence and dissipation were reflected on his face.

" 'Twould behoove you to quell yours, my lord Rochester," Lady Castlemaine spat viciously, momentarily forgetting Jenny as she rounded on him. "Think you I'm not familiar with your poisoned pen that scandalizes me without shame as if I were some Drury Lane harlot!"

"My dearest Barbara, when you stop behaving like a Drury Lane harlot, I'll sheathe my wit and write flowery odes to your purity."

Amid much cruel laughter Lord Rochester bowed and took his leave, leaving Lady Castlemaine speechless with rage. For a moment she stood motionless, her face working, words of retaliation unfound until her tormentor was too far away to hear them. "A pox on the bastard!" she cried, flouncing off, the yards of her silver-laced gown sweeping angrily over the polished floor. "I consign both him and Sir Miles' simpering little bitch to hell!"

Those guests close enough to hear her utterance laughed; those too far away to hear were soon acquainted with Lady

Castlemaine's retort. So angry was Barbara at being ignored and publicly humiliated that she stalked from the ballroom, bound for her apartments above the Holbein gate.

In the wake of Lady Castlemaine's departure, Jenny grew increasingly uncomfortable. Her every move was avidly noted by the curious eyes of this glittering throng of jeweled parasites, who whispered behind their hands, laying odds on the speed with which Charles Stuart would take her to his bed. At last, Sir Miles, feeling a respectable time had elapsed since the King's departure, told her to follow him out of the ballroom. Jenny walked behind him, dwelling on her brush with Lady Castlemaine, whom, though it had not been her intention, appeared to have become her enemy. Because Barbara's penchant for revenge was well known, Jenny's unease mounted: such a powerful enemy could prove dangerous. Without scruple, Charles' mistress frequently schemed to bring about the downfall of those who crossed her path.

"We're to be met here," Sir Miles said, breaking Jenny's uneasy chain of thought.

Within minutes Charles' manservant appeared, hastening down the chill hallway where they waited, unspeaking, listening to the waves of laughter echoing from the ballroom; though it was nearing midnight there was no sign of the revels coming to an end.

"Mistress Dunn, follow me."

Sir Miles nodded his assent. "Yes, go, my love, the royal stud awaits," he quipped sarcastically.

The little man in the dark suit hastened before her. As they passed a lighted sconce flickering vast shadows across the gilded paneling, Jenny recognized him as the messenger who had taken her stealthily to the coach on that fateful day she departed for Russell House.

"Am I being taken to the King's chamber?" she asked, hurrying to keep pace with him.

"Mistress, you must learn not to ask questions," came the stern retort.

Duly chastised, Jenny proceeded in silence. They ascended a narrow, winding flight of stairs, their movements furtive until they reached a closed door. The King's trusted servant tapped on the door to announce their arrival, then he gestured for her to enter the room.

The gloomy room was lit by several flickering candles in

tall gilt sconces. As she entered a flurry of yapping, furry bodies hurtled toward her; the royal spaniels had come to inspect their master's latest amusement.

"Down, there's a good girl." Laughing, Charles appeared from the shadowy recesses beside the hearth to retrieve the wiggling, yapping bitch who had placed her front paws on Jenny's satin skirts. Two other dogs circled her, their voices shrill and excited as they scented out this threat to their master's affections. Good-naturedly, Charles shooed the dogs outside, calling, "Tom, be a good fellow and take them away. Their concern for my safety might prove distracting."

At last the door was closed and they were alone. Nervous to be inside the King's bedchamber, Jenny waited stiffly beside the door for his command. Charles had already removed most of his finery and stood before her in shirt and breeches. His heavy black periwig reposed in majestic splendor on the wig stand on his dressing table; his own short black hair curled thickly about his brow.

"Well, are you turned mute?"

She blushed, feeling foolish. "No, 'tis just that I've never been here before . . . I mean . . ."

Smiling at her, Charles reached out and gently drew her into his arms. "Hush, poor child, be not afraid of your wicked King. What think you of my kiss this evening? Did you not enjoy it?"

"Nay, for I was too aware of all those watching eyes."

"I intend to remedy that. Here there are but two watching eyes, and they, sweet wench, are hot with need."

So saying, his mouth came down hard on hers, the fervor of his passion causing her to squirm pleasurably within his strong embrace. Charles chuckled a moment later as his body responded magnificently to the challenge of her nearness. He kissed her again thoroughly, his mouth exploring hers, drawing every drop of response from her dew-soft lips.

"I've been so lonely without you," Jenny whispered, giving herself up to the hot safety of his embrace. She rested her head on his square shoulder and uttered a deep, contented sigh. He did not say he too had been lonely; she was grateful for his honesty.

"You need feel lonely no longer, Jenny Wren. And if I'm to live up to my promise to join you 'ere the clock strikes twelve, we must make haste."

His husky invitation made her smile. Apart, she ached with

pain at his infidelity, yet when they were together, Charles had the extraordinary talent to make her feel she was the only woman in his life. It would have been too painful to have been reminded at every turn of his unfaithfulness; this way, for the passionate hours they shared, she could delude herself into thinking he was wholly hers.

"Oh, sweetheart, I do not intend to hold you to that vow. First you must love me, slowly, beautifully . . .''

"That's no hardship. 'Odd's blood, how delectable you make it sound.''

"And it is delectable, is it not?''

"With you it is paradise.''

Aware of the heat of his body searing through the fine lilac satin of her ballgown, Jenny yielded to the temptation of his touch. Charles drew her with him to the large red velvet-curtained bed resplendent with the gold-embroidered arms of England. Here, on this royal bed, their bodies would be united: Charles, King of England and Jenny Dunn, late of the taproom at the Rose and Crown. How strange were the circumstances that had led her to this place and how fearful that road. Six months ago she had not dreamed she would be inside Whitehall Palace this Christmas, locked in the strong arms of the man who wore the crown. The King! A wave of shock rocketed through Jenny's body at her sudden realization of the truth behind Rosa's prophecy: that shadowy royal presence had not been Manuel, king of the wandering gypsies, but the monarch of this realm!

"What is it, sweet?'' Charles asked, eyeing her curiously as he saw a glimmer of something close to fear in her lovely face.

Jenny reached for him to reassure herself of his reality. Eagerly she sought the hot substance of his shoulders, the sinews in his arms, the hard square set of his frame beneath his fine, lace-trimmed cambric shirt.

Grinning at her actions, Charles whispered, "If you've a mind to feel me, wench, don't stop there.''

Jenny smiled at his wicked invitation, but she shook her head. "Not until I've told you what stilled my pleasure.''

"Then tell me, keep me not in suspense.''

"A gypsy woman foretold I would form a close attachment with a king. Not until this moment did I realize that prophecy has been fulfilled.''

Charles smiled tenderly at her, brushing the back of his

hand across her soft cheek. "A close attachment is exactly what I seek from you, dear heart."

"Then, Your Majesty, that is exactly what you shall have," Jenny promised huskily. With trembling hands she caressed his face, thrilling to the touch of his hot swarthy skin beneath her fingers. "You are my King but you are much, much more than that."

At her tender words an expression of delight crossed his dark face. His passion rising, Charles stroked the swell of her breasts beneath the expensive lilac satin. Eventually, growing impatient, he turned her about and began unhooking her tight-fitting bodice. He soon peeled away the shimmering fabric to reveal the bounty of her white breasts, lush and full, erotically inviting in their frame of lilac sheen. With a shuddering sigh of contentment, Charles lay back against the mountain of soft down pillows, drawing her atop him; now Jenny's breasts hung before his face like tempting, forbidden fruit, ripe for the taking. In an agony of desire, he shuddered again, keeping his hands gentle as he fondled that delight, monitoring the pressure lest he hurt her, for he knew she was not yet aroused beyond the point of feeling pain.

His mouth swept across her flesh, tingling life and passion through Jenny's veins. Gentle, yet demanding, he tongued her nipples. Tonight Jenny wanted to enjoy the full pleasure of his lovemaking, to accept his caresses, his kisses, without the need to respond. But such foolish intentions lasted only until he pressed against her, the arousal of his body not to be denied; only until he uncovered the surging darkness of his passion, too impatient to wait for her to make the move, too desirous of her caresses to endure the unrequited torment a moment longer. The liquid fire of her arousal was painful, consuming. Charles Stuart was an accomplished lover: with his hands, his mouth, his tongue, he awakened every inch of her body. Jenny trembled beside him in the hallowed island of red velvet and glittering gold, giving herself up to sensations of the flesh. As she touched and caressed him in joyful exchange, she realized those bawdy limericks penned about both his skill and his physical endowment came very close to the truth.

As he often did, Charles paused in his lovemaking, drawing back from her, the more to gaze upon her perfection. By now Jenny's lavender gown lay in a brilliant heap across the chair, spilling its lacy profusion to the dark red Turkey carpet; his shirt and breeches lay beside her gown. Anxious not to interrupt the delicious sensation of her hands, he urged her to continue the intimate caresses she had begun, shuddering again at the pleasure of her touch. When Jenny smiled at a thought that crossed her mind, he smiled back, his thick, dark eyebrows raised in question.

"What gives you humor, wicked wench?"

"I was thinking, Your Majesty, what a great gypsy king you would have made." But though he pressed for an answer, Jenny laughingly refused to satisfy his curiosity. "Nay, for you're already so conceited, 'twould merely fuel your pride."

"You little scramble-brain, you'll call me conceited once too often," he warned in mock severity. "For such slander you can be sent to the Tower."

"And willingly would I go, Your Majesty, if only you will accompany me."

" 'Odd's fish," he muttered, suddenly turning serious, "if I thought 'twould guarantee I could keep you beside me, gladly would I go."

And Jenny trembled beneath the sweeping caress of his hands. Gone was the half-amused, half-tormenting, time of their lovemaking. Passion turned him grim as he shuddered against her, his hands, his mouth, his manhood seeking an immediate response from her shapely body. Jenny gave that response, losing herself in the sweeping fulfillment of passion as she allowed it to consume her senses. No more thoughts about his infidelity or his lack of provision for her future, no more thoughts about Barbara and the dozen others who had lain in this very place came forth to dim her pleasure. Jenny remembered only that the man in her arms was her lover, not her King.

Bodies united in a fiery thrust, their mouths opened wide, hot and eager, their tongues meeting and probing the furnace below. In this trancelike erotic dance Jenny automatically responded to Charles' unspoken directions. Expertly he moved within her, drawing the utmost response, playing her as a finely tuned and priceless instrument. Jenny's heat mounted until she felt as if this vast bed was a sea of fire upon which she was to be sacrificed. Her King was a magnificent lover—and at this moment he was hers alone. Waves of searing pleasure gripped her, and then she plunged, tumbling over and over into warm rich blackness. But there was no loneliness or pain, for once his own storm was past, Charles held her close, cherishing her against the throbbing life of his virile body, assuring her of his love and devotion.

In the cold blackness before dawn, Jenny was bundled into an unmarked coach and driven back to the Cheapside mansion where she lived a lie with Sir Miles Russell. Her body still throbbed with languid satisfaction, but her heart ached for the one thing she wanted from Charles, which he was incapable of giving.

Chapter 18

Jenny was seated in the sheltered arbor of the garden behind Russell House. A mild spring breeze stirred shimmering hazel catkins from an invading bough of the neighbor's tree, setting thin, gray shadows dancing across the wall. Fragrant blue hyacinths marched in soldierly precision about the perimeter of the narrow, winter-browned lawn; the novel Dutch blooms were highly sought after for their fragrance, best enjoyed in the damp morning air.

Last week Sir Miles had departed for the country and would be absent for the rest of the month, a blessing for which she was immensely grateful. By the new year Jenny had hoped she need not remain in this household, yet Charles had not chosen to set her up in a residence of her own. Whether he believed their secret too well kept to necessitate the move, or whether it was more because he had no wish to cross Lady Castlemaine, Jenny did not know. When they were together nothing seemed to have changed, despite the wounding gossip of his many amours; currently his name was linked with those of several Drury Lane actresses.

Jenny rose from the bench to pace the path. Was it because this was where she met him that Charles' swarthy image always danced before her in the garden? Disturbing thoughts of her fickle, high-born lover returned time and again to plague her. All winter they had enjoyed each other, neither more, nor less, than before. When she cautioned him about those painful rumors, he laughed and said that if she believed all she heard he would need the desire of ten men. Yet Jenny remained unconvinced by his jovial dismissal.

In January she had skated with the King on the frozen pond in the royal park, he being most gentle in his instruction of the art he'd learned in Holland during his many years of exile. He had kissed her, soothing her hurt when she fell, their open affection observed by countless courtiers who sped by on that frosty day. When she accompanied the King to the Duke's Theater to watch Nell Gwynne, Jenny sat in the royal

263

box, thereby further enraging Lady Castlemaine. Charles had even introduced her to his brother James, Duke of York, on the occasion of the Lord High Admiral's return from the fleet lying off anchor awaiting the next move in the war with Holland, now officially declared.

Riding lessons followed dancing lessons, the better to prepare Jenny for her introduction into society. The need to sit straight in the saddle, her hands, her knees, placed correctly, her head held high, was a far cry from the barebacked routine she had performed at the Southwark Fair. When at last her equestrian seat was acceptable, Jenny received a beautiful riding costume copied from a gentleman's dress, this latest fashion being all the rage among the court beauties. Dressed in her snug-fitting red wool coat and plumed red hat, Jenny had ridden beside the King and the Duke of York one memorable winter morning when the cold wind reddened her nose and stung her cheeks.

But for all these obvious demonstrations of the esteem in which he held her, Jenny remained as unsure of Charles Stuart as she had been that first night she joined him in the royal bedchamber.

Lavishly outfitted and schooled in social graces, Jenny had been prepared by his Majesty to enter Restoration society. In truth, a pretty face and figure with wit enough to amuse him was all Charles Stuart demanded in a woman; far more was needed to protect Jenny from social embarrassment. He was too kind-hearted to want her to suffer humiliation before his courtiers. As Sir Miles' official mistress Jenny was socially acceptable; as the King's probable mistress she was included in a multitude of invitations; but no one welcomed her for herself. Mistress Jenny Dunn had ceased to exist! Only as an extension of the powerful man with whom her name was linked did she survive socially.

The King never discussed affairs of state with her. All news of current events Jenny obtained from street gossip and the London broadsheets. Nor did Charles ever discuss his other women. On the few occasions she had grown bold enough to mention Barbara, or Frances Stewart, or any one of the multitude of others with whom his name had been linked, Charles sighed disapprovingly and grew stern. And, if she persisted, his humor grew increasingly thin. Being no fool, Jenny learned to accept that part of himself he allowed her to know and tried not to dwell on the rest. Her current position provided scant security: she was the King's mistress, but not officially termed as such; he vowed he loved her truly for her guileless disposition, yet time and again she heard of his adventuring in another's arms. Too late, Jenny had come to learn what it was to exist on the whim of a man's desire. It was an existence she liked not.

Before the weekend she received an unexpected invitation to join the royal party at Newmarket for the first race meet of the season. His Majesty, chafing to experience the thrill of the sport he adored, had cast aside the worries of his throne for one glorious week of pleasure uninterrupted by sober reminders of impending doom. Despite the bad news from the fleet, the general gloom of a nation at war, the hotly contested issue of Tangiers and the empty state coffers, the court generated a mood of reckless gaiety. King Charles had spent too many years in poverty, and those who would be his friends were wise to remember it. Wit, laughter, and amusement were escapes in which the King hid his bitterness. So the sumptuous, full-bodied women and the profligate rakehells of this Restoration court sought to provide diversion, the more to win the reward of their sovereign's favor.

The whole laughing, uproarious brigade sallied forth for Newmarket, accompanied by their wives, their mistresses, and enough baggage and servants to sustain a traveling army.

Never having attended a horse race, with the exception of the primitive events staged by the gypsies, Jenny was excited by the cavalcade of color and the contagious excitement of the crowd.

The King wagered heavily on his favorites. So lucky was he in his bets that he challenged a nobleman newly arrived from Ireland to race for a silver cup. The crowd was agog with praise for this rich lord's string of excellent horseflesh bred on his Irish estates. His Majesty had at his disposal the best animals from the royal stud. The race for the King's Plate promised to be a rare spectacle.

On this mild, spring afternoon, fresh with the scent of growing things, Jenny sat in the stands with the King's party. Newmarket Heath stretched before her, patches of vivid color staining the pale new grass. The jockeys' brilliant racing silks complimented the satin-smooth coats of their mounts. Some of the finest animals in the world, bred both for speed and beauty, jostled each other in the paddock, impatiently awaiting the third race of the day. About the splendid horses and their diminutive riders surged a peacock-bright throng of courtiers, all wagering heavily on the outcome of the upcoming event.

"Place a bet on the gray, sweeting," Charles urged, as he changed seats to sit beside her. He kissed her cheek and whispered knowingly, "He'll outrun the other nags by a mile."

Jenny did as he suggested and won twenty guineas. She put the gold coins in the beaded leather purse attached to the waist of her full-skirted amber gown. This satin dress had been made by her aunt, who had a gift for design. And though she frequently ordered fabrics and notions from the shop in Swann Alley, Jenny had never resumed her relationship with her aunt and uncle, for she felt uncomfortable in their presence.

The warm sun crept across her back, penetrating the soft fabric of her amber plush tippet. Jenny was surprised to feel Charles' hand stealing beneath the garment to fondle her breast.

"Nay, do not react, 'tis our secret," he whispered, as he wickedly teased her earlobe with his hot tongue. "Will you wish me luck, sweetheart? Soon I'm to ride against Lord Ross, damn his soul, for he's a splendid horseman. My nag should best his, yet I'm suspicious of this string of bloodstock he brings from Ireland. They say 'tis the best horseflesh of the century. The gray that won you your guineas is his—but not for long. That nag will be mine 'ere the day's out."

The surprise of having the King's undivided attention lightened Jenny's heart. "Of course I wish you luck. Fear not, Your Majesty, there's no finer rider in all England."

"But what about Ireland, wench, what about Ireland?" Charles laughed as he slid his arm about her narrow waist. "You're a good wench. And you gladden my heart. I'm of a mind to return this night and decline the grand ball at Lord Amersley's."

Jenny swallowed. Barbara was a house guest at the country mansion. Was Charles' desire to return to London his way of suggesting he wanted to spend the night with her instead of Lady Castlemaine? "Am I misinterpreting your message?" she whispered, her breath fanning his lean cheek.

"Not for one moment." And his dark eyes softened as he smiled tenderly at her.

A raucous burst of laughter destroyed their intimacy as the beribboned, brilliantly garbed courtiers returned to their seats after placing bets on the outcome of His Majesty's challenge to Lord Ross. Soon Charles was surrounded by his friends, who patted him on the back as they urged him to "ride like hell." A more formal sovereign might have rebuked his courtiers for their familiarity, but Charles Stuart merely joined them in laughter before he sauntered toward the paddock, his red plumed hat bobbing in the sunshine.

The beautiful Suffolk countryside was rapidly greening, as plentiful spring rain had brightened the grass. And though the weather was still treacherous, sunny days being followed by chill rain, the promise of the infant season was already unfolding. What new uncertainties would this year bring? Jenny thought with melancholy. Life lived at so precarious a level was without substance. Charles provided her with little sense of security. Today he whispered she was a good wench, suggesting by word and caress that he had missed their lovemaking, yet tomorrow he was just as likely to entertain another of his "good wenches," sparing little thought for the lonely guest in Russell House.

"They're off!"

The cry shocked Jenny out of her lethargy. Eagerly she thrust those disturbing thoughts to the back of her mind as she craned forward, the better to see the two men pounding across the empty heath. The King took the lead on a great black stallion, its magnificent coat gleaming like silk in the pale afternoon sunlight. Man and horse, muscles straining, pulled for all they were worth amid the shouts and cheers of the spectators. Slowly, and with the utmost ease, his opponent's chestnut gained on the royal mount. The chestnut's nose drew even with that proud black satin tail; they galloped neck and neck. The quickened pace whipped the plumed hats from the riders' heads, sending the expensive creations bowling gaily along the rail.

Jenny held her breath, tense with the excitement of the moment. As she watched the two riders nearing the finish, crouched in their saddles like professional jockeys, a chill ran along her spine. Her gaze strayed from Charles' swarthy presence to the fair man riding beside him, his golden hair streaming a banner in the wind; the man's lean, tanned neck was exposed to the air as the wind ripped open the buttons of his lace-trimmed cambric shirt. Something about that rider struck a poignant note within her soul. No sooner had Jenny accepted the source of her memory than she also had to accept the pain of that reminder: the Irish lord had the same coloring as Kit. During the months since she had last seen him certain men had the ability to still her heart when, for an instant, they reminded her of him. Bright golden locks, the brilliance of light blue eyes, a shared feature, a certain mannerism, could stun her until she realized the man was a stranger. Not once had she seen Kit since that terrible night they parted beneath the tavern lantern; Louise de Brand's lovemaking must suit him well.

Bitterness hardened her mouth as Jenny fought to dispel the painful memory. The horses had already passed the finishing post and she did not know whose mount had won. But in a moment it was not difficult to ascertain the winner, as the eager supporters crowded about the pair, waving their hats and cheering in tribute to the hard-fought race. The King had not won. Before the noisy courtiers surrounded him, Jenny saw Charles slap his opponent's broad shoulder, congratulating him on his victory, a smile on his dark face.

A fierce pounding began in her temples and Jenny closed her eyes, blanking out the colorful scene below. If only she could exchange the noisy racecourse for her quiet room.

Jenny fought her way down the steps from the wooden stands, going in search of a soothing drink to ease her parched throat. The mug of strong ale was coolly refreshing. All around her jostled the noisy courtiers and their women, disregarding her after the first polite greeting, for they were still not sure in whose bed she reigned. Lady Castlemaine had not chosen to acknowledge Mistress Dunn, therefore they too must abide by her decision.

With a start Jenny noticed Sir Miles heading toward her with a group of gentlemen. She had no desire to be trapped into playing his beloved this afternoon, so she turned into the crowd and quickly disappeared from sight, retracing her steps to the stands.

Several ladies tittered and whispered about the latest court scandal, huddled in the corner of the stands. Both smiled charmingly at Jenny, their false friendship dropping like masks once her back was turned. That she had now become the object of their spiteful tongues Jenny did not doubt.

By the time the races were over, the March wind had risen and struck chill along the half-empty tiered boxes. The late afternoon sun hung low in the pale sky as Jenny gathered her few belongings and made her way from the stands. King Charles had beckoned for her to join him several minutes before, but he had been surrounded by the others and she had declined to join his friends.

"Jenny! Mother of God! It is you!"

The familiar husky voice stopped Jenny in her tracks. Turning slowly to behold the speaker, she felt faint, her voice strangling in her chest as she gasped, "Kit!"

He stepped forward, after glancing about to make sure they would not be overheard. "Did you not know it was me?"

"You? When?" she repeated stupidly, blinking to clear her hazing vision.

"In the race against his Majesty."

Jenny swallowed. Now that she regarded him more closely, she recognized the distinctive blue and red suit worn by the winner of the King's Plate. "They said you were Lord Ross," she protested accusingly.

"Aye, and so I am."

"From Ireland?"

"Yes. Remember, I told you of an inheritance I hoped to gain. Well, God be praised, it came just when I needed it most."

They stared at each other unmoving, seeking out each detail of the other's face, searching for evidence of deep emotion.

"I trust you've been well, Lord Ross," Jenny managed coldly, coming to her senses at last. She took a step backward; he stepped forward.

"Christ, is that all you have to say to me?"

"What should I say?"

"After all this . . . you should damned well say you're sorry," he growled, his face hardening. "All this time with no idea where you were, no answer to my letter."

"What letter? Oh, 'tis easy now to say how you yearned for me, how you wrote great reams of affection and somehow, someway, the missives went astray. Well, you need not waste your imagination on me, my lord, for I am far wiser than when you saw me last. No longer does it matter."

"Not matter!" he cried, his hand gripping her arm. "I think it matters. And you will give me satisfaction, even though it be the last time we meet. I will know what is in your heart!"

"There's nothing in my heart."

"You lie!"

"Nay, 'tis you who are the liar."

Kit's face darkened, his eyes turning cold as steel. "Once I warned you about your errant tongue . . ."

"Your warnings, your threats, your promises, mean no more to me. Now, unhand me, before we are seen."

"Aye, I'll unhand you. Are a thousand laced gallants to come to your rescue, mistress? For, by God, such as you does not come to Newmarket Heath aselling ribbons. Why are you here? And with whom?"

"We no longer owe each other explanations, my lord. Everything that was between us is over."

Kit's handsome face was a mask of tight-lipped anger. As Jenny gazed at him a wrenching pain gripped her heart and she faltered on the heath, her knees doubling beneath her weight. Myriad colors danced before her eyes, voices swirled, yet through that nightmare his face remained clearly focused, his anger reaching out to smite her.

"I must go," Kit said abruptly, noticing a companion threading his way through the crowd, beckoning to him. "Meet me in twenty minutes in the paddock."

"Nay, my lord, never again shall I meet you."

"You'll do as you are told, dammit! At least you owe me an explanation, if nothing more than to tell me again to my face that it's over between us."

Jenny could not meet his gaze. The memory of his lips, the tender light in his eyes, speared her with longing. "Very well, my lord," she agreed at last, her voice barely audible above the noise of the race crowd. "Perhaps you are owed that much. I'll meet you within the half hour."

"Do you promise?"

"I promise."

A party of enthusiastic well-wishers swamped him then, turning Kit about, sweeping him away in their noisy midst. Jenny stood unmoving, trying to accept the terrible pain his unexpected appearance reawakened. Forever he caused her pain. Long months ago she had tried to convince herself she was immune to his charms; his deceit, his treachery mattered not, for she was beloved of the King. But it wasn't true. Kit affected her as no other man could.

Blindly she turned, colliding with a tall figure who loomed behind her.

'' 'Odd's fish, wench, look where you're going,'' said King Charles.

Like a drowning soul Jenny seized the slender thread of their relationship, pulling herself to safety, despite the tempest raging within her soul. She grasped his extended arm; laughing, close to hysteria, she forced the emotion to dispel grief burning treacherously close to the surface.

'' 'Tis too many cups of ale, Your Majesty. I declare, my very vision mists,'' she cried gaily, riveting her entire attention on the tall dark man whose identity blurred into a pillar of wine-red velvet and silver lace.

The gentlemen surrounding the King laughed in amusement at her explanation, but Charles eyed her with a puzzled gaze. ''Then, sweet wench, allow me to escort you safely to a carriage,'' he offered, taking her arm and turning her about.

''Oh, Your Majesty, you're most kind, but Sir Miles . . .''

''Sir Miles won't mind sharing your company with me, for he's ever wont to please his King.'' Charles smiled at her, pleased to learn she still played the public role he had chosen for her. ''Come, mistress, we must be gone, for the wind turns sharp.''

The short walk to the coach was a blurred misery of false laughter and desperate gaiety. Jenny wondered how she managed to traverse the distance. Suddenly, as they neared the place where the coaches stood, she remembered that Kit awaited her in the paddock; her heart wrenched at the thought. She could not tell the King she had an assignation with another man. What could she possibly say to him?

''Your Majesty, I cannot leave just yet. I've some unfinished business with . . .''

''Nonsense,'' he dismissed heartily, gripping her arm. ''If we leave now we'll be in London in time to sup,'' he added in an undertone, his breath fanning her chilled ear as he leaned close, the hot spiced scent of his flesh and of his fine clothing enveloping her. ''You've played the innocent long enough. See, they've all but left us.''

True to his word, only three courtiers walked with them; the others had raced for their coaches and their mounts. Her mouth turned down in pain for yet another broken vow between herself and the handsome sea captain. Kit Ashford had already caused her much heartache; she marveled she could spare a kind thought for him, let alone admit to so much more.

As they passed Jenny glanced toward the paddock hoping to spot him, hoping he would see she was now bound to accompany the King to London. But Jenny could distinguish little through the milling throng at the rail.

"'Odd's fish, do I detect reluctance on your part?" Charles asked, a puzzled frown knitting his dark brows.

Jenny squeezed his arm in reassurance, her heart pitching over the discovery of how readily she was betraying herself. "Nay, 'tis but a surprise. We are usually so discreet."

Charles threw back his dark head and his laughter pealed out. "Ah, so now we have it. A case of latter-day modesty, is it sweeting? Have no fear, after today there will be even more tongues wagging. Does she, or doesn't she? they already ask. Have you not heard them?"

"They take care before me."

"But not before me. They've the audacity to ask if I've had the measure of you and if the taking was sweet."

"And what do you tell them, sire?" Jenny asked, as he handed her inside his coach, resplendent with the noble arms of England.

"I tell them nothing. You can't imagine how much it infuriates them."

The door slammed and Charles winked at her, his hand hot in hers.

"Are we traveling to London tonight? I'd thought we were to attend Lord Amersley's ball." Jenny had already guessed his answer, but she must ask. If they dined at Lord Amersley's she might find the winner of the King's Plate an honored guest; perhaps then she could explain to him why she had not kept their agreement to meet in the paddock.

"I told that group of ne'er-do-wells we'd sup there, but I can tell you, Jenny Wren, that I've already changed my mind. What a fickle, changeable soul this Charles Stuart be. Never can he make up his mind for two minutes at a time." And he bent his dark head to hers, his mouth hot and ardent.

Beyond his plumed hat the Newmarket racetrack sped past, green and spattered with myriad colors. Somewhere on that matted turf Kit waited impatiently for her to fulfill her promise, unknowing she had little choice but to obey her King. Her failure to keep their tryst would be construed as lack of affection, his assumption untrue, yet perhaps it was the wisest solution to the dilemma. Kit belonged to her past. Their love had taken place long ago and never again could the delight be rekindled.

For the first time the sweetness of Charles' expert kisses failed to arouse her as they sped through the gathering dusk toward London.

The sun dropped beyond the horizon, disappearing behind a grove of gaunt oaks. Kit paced impatiently, glancing about at the dwindling crowd, hoping for a glimpse of her amber gown. For over an hour he waited, and though his sense told him she would not come now, he clung desperately to that promise she had made. The rising wind tossed the red plumes on his hat and stole inside the gaudy, unbuttoned coat draped elegantly on his broad-shouldered frame, to spear his flesh with icy needles. By God, he was not going to lose her! He would not allow her to be swallowed in that nameless, faceless crowd, dancing attendance on some unknown nobleman. While he waited he had reached the painful conclusion she was kept by a nobleman—a haberdasher did not dress his women so fine. But though he had reached that conclusion, the pain of his assumption was almost more than he could bear. Like a fool he still made feeble excuses, suspecting the worst, yet wondering if she could possibly be here with her family . . .

"Kit, good fellow, are you to spend the night on the track?"

Abruptly he turned to face the jovial speakers: Harry Kent and Baptist May, Keeper of the King's Privy Purse, approached him. Though it pained him to make the effort, Kit forced a smile.

"I'd thought to meet someone here, but it appears I've been taken for a fool."

Baptist May smiled in sympathy. "Well, I'm to London. They tell me his Majesty has tricked us all by taking the London road. God knows what adventure drives him posthaste to Whitehall." His heavy face was somber as he turned about. "Stay if you wish, my lords, 'tis perhaps merely a wild goose chase."

"Go ahead, Bab, I'll join you shortly. First I must sup. A good meal washed down with sack would be a fitting ending for the day," said Kit, attempting to master the rage that speeded his heart and tensed his frame.

"I'll stay with you, you lovesick fool," offered Harry Kent, raising his eyebrows at the Keeper of the Privy Purse. "Go about your duty, Bab, let none say you're lacking in concern for your noble master."

Kit turned aside from the other two men, who continued to quip and joke until Baptist May finally took his leave, hastening toward his coach to follow the King. Hot anger radiated through Kit, yet it was not merely anger that turned his mouth bitter; pain, disillusion, and spurned love flooded through him.

"What does this filly look like?"

"How do you know 'tis a filly?" Kit asked, a frown knitting his brow as he scanned the dwindling knot of brightly dressed people still trickling over the racetrack.

"An unkept tryst with a shapely filly is the only reason you'd be standing here in the chill night with that injured air about you. Tell me her name. Perhaps I can assist you in finding the baggage so we may repair to the closest tavern and sup."

"You do not know her."

"How can you tell? Believe me, my friend, most of her Majesty's maids—God, what an inappropriate title—are known to me. Handsome I may not be, but there's no denying I've certain winning ways."

Kit forced a smile in reply to his friend's comment. "Nay, she's not one of the maids of honor. She's but a wench I know and love. And though she told me it was over between us, I couldn't accept the truth. I see she meant it."

" 'Swounds, you've a face to sink a battleship. Take heart, dear Kit, there are a dozen others who'll come willingly to your call. You've no need for monkly celibacy this night, not as long as you count me amongst your friends. But her name, man, tell me, if only for my own information. I would fain see the filly who can cause you such distress."

"Her name is Jenny. She's the loveliest of creatures. Abundant chestnut hair, skin like pearls, eyes gray as the winter sky. Her form is . . ." Kit caught the amused expression on his friend's face and he halted his rhapsody. "You must think me addled," he concluded gruffly.

"Smitten, but 'tis a worthy state. Yet this wench of whom you speak—you're wrong in thinking I do not know her. Is she not Mistress Dunn?"

"Aye, but how . . . how do you know her?" Kit demanded, gripping Harry's arm.

"There are few in London who have not heard of her. Can it be you don't know?"

"Know what?"

"She belongs to Sir Miles Russell."

Kit stared at Harry Kent's face until his blunt features blurred into a red haze. "I don't believe it!" he said at last, his voice little more than a strangled croak.

"Well, believe it or not, my friend, 'tis to his house she returns. Some say the King himself dips into the well, but he's been so secretive about the affair that one can only speculate. Assuredly he yearns to possess her, yet whether the minx plays him like Mrs. Stewart, 'tis hard to know."

"No!" Kit cried, his fists whitening as he stared at his companion.

"Aye, 'tis true. She's known about town as Sir Miles' light o'love, though bedamned if he appears very joyful about the matter. I'm sorry, Kit, old friend, but your chestnut filly's played you false."

For a long time Kit stood unmoving, his fists clenched, his legs tense as a coiled spring. Jenny bought and kept by that profligate creature! It was not true. It could not be true. Perhaps it was merely a rumor. God knows, the court was fueled by rumor and innuendo . . .

"Come, Kit, let us drown our sorrows. There's naught you can do about it," Harry said at last, worried by his friend's silence. "Had you not been so long in Ireland you would have heard. But no matter. We've all been overthrown sometime. 'Tis not the first, nor will it be the last."

Like a blind man, Kit Kent, moving numbly across the paddock. Overhead pale stars pricked the darkening sky. To imagine Jenny enfolded against that lecherous creature, old enough to be her father, brought bile into his throat. Pain, anger, frustration welled into a wave of vengeance as he strode across the scrubby heath. Though he may never regain her love, he would have satisfaction, he vowed. As it was said of the Italians, he too possessed the ability to feed on cold hate. Not forever would Sir Miles Russell sleep safe. Somehow, someday, he would be made to pay in full for his pleasure!

Chapter 19

The spring and early summer of 1665 were hot and unusually dry. The suffocating spell was broken briefly on the night of June 8 by a tempestuous storm. In the wake of this night of violence came the long-awaited word from the fleet; soon all London rang with the news of a great English victory against the Dutch! The fleet had battled off Lowestoft, temporarily crippling the Dutch navy. English losses were mild, though several key naval men, the foremost being the great Earl of Marlborough, were killed. Londoners celebrated the joyous news in grand style with bonfires and firework displays. And King Charles designated June twentieth as the official day of thanksgiving for victory over England's enemies.

The news of the fleet's supremacy over the Dutch was welcome; news of another sort was not. On the heels of victory the dread bubonic plague erupted within the city. Red crosses marking plague-infested dwellings appeared on doors in Fenchurch Street, and though since April the bills of mortality had recorded isolated plague deaths in the shanties huddled beyond the walls, evidence that the malady had spread to the heart of the city brought fear to the staunchest breast.

Jenny received the alarming news from her French maid, Marie, when she brought her morning chocolate in the new red chocolate set, which had been a gift from the King.

"Madame, the plague is spreading," Marie recounted fearfully, her round dark eyes fixed on her mistress's face.

"They say there's always plague in summer. The hovels beyond the walls are hotbeds of it."

"But 'tis spreading from the 'Liberties,' Madame. Two houses . . ."

"You mustn't be afraid, we're safe here," Jenny assured, patting the French girl's plump arm. "Now, have you pressed my gown for this evening?"

"*Oui*, it's like new," Marie said with pride.

"Thank you, Marie. You may go."

The dark-haired maid curtsied and left the room.

Jenny's stomach pitched as she thought of the spreading plague. Inside Russell House they seemed safe, yet beyond these windows lay the filthy London streets, reeking to high heaven in the torrid heat. Filth was a way of life within the city: the cobbles were slimed with sewage, renewed daily by generous applications from household chamberpots, with butchers' offal, with the effluent from the tanneries and soap factories.

It was futile to agonize over a situation beyond her control when a stomach-churning ordeal loomed far closer: tonight she was to preside over Sir Miles' dinner table while he feted influential friends in celebration of the recent naval victory. It was an occasion to which she did not look forward.

Yesterday Marie had repeated gossip that Lady Castlemaine was with child. The identity of the seed swelling within Barbara Palmer's belly remained a mystery, yet Jenny's heart lurched when she attached a ready name to the infant's sire. Of late, Charles had patched up many of his differences with Barbara—'twas common knowledge he had been in her bed the night they brought him word of the English victory. Both snippets of gossip had begun a hot tide of nausea in her belly. Whether he bedded Barbara or not, the King's affection for her remained unchanged. During those long, lonely nights when he chose to dally with another, the assurance brought scant comfort.

The polished walnut dining table gleamed with fine crystal and engraved silver; a low, oval vase of massed cerise roses complimented the pink lace table cover. Because of the sultry evening, the deep windows had been flung wide to admit the breeze stirring languidly between the buildings. Unfortunately, the open windows admitted far more than the pleasant breeze; tonight the London streets stank like an open sewer.

Jenny held a nosegay of spicy pink carnations to her nose as she glanced over the table to assure herself it had been laid according to Sir Miles' directions. The silver lace-edged neckline of her stylish gown of softest sea-green silk was deeply scooped to reveal the creamy swell of her bosom. In the dark perfumed valley between her full breasts nestled an oval topaz surrounded by diamonds, the beautiful pendant a Christmas gift from the King. Charles had looped the jeweled gold clasp about her slender neck so lovingly, praising her beauty while comparing the amber fire of these rare gems from the Americas to her silky chestnut hair. How wonderful had been their coming together! In the golden fireglow their hearts, their bodies, had pulsed as one—the following night he had slept with a Drury Lane actress!

Abruptly Jenny forced her mind from such painful thoughts. Charles loved her in his fashion; it was her misfortune that it was not the fashion in which she desired to be loved. Lately her thoughts frequently strayed to that spring afternoon when the King had swept her away from Newmarket Heath. That was the last time she had heard from Kit. Aware of his deep involvement in the engagement against the Dutch, Jenny had risked betrayal of her concern by inquiring about his fate. Her informant had assured her dashing Lord Ross was very much alive; in fact, his praises were being sung throughout the land because of his heroic rescue of his Majesty's flagship.

Jenny had fully intended to keep her promise to meet him in Newmarket Paddock. Fool! One glimpse of his handsome face and she had turned soft as butter: the sight of his broad-shouldered figure, of his strong, slender hands awakening such precious memories had made her blood race with wild delight. Kit Ashford was as handsome as a god, but for all that he was unfaithful. He lied as easily as he breathed. No doubt the women who were privy to his arousing mouth and great sexual prowess were legion. What she might seek to overlook in the King she could never forgive in he who had stolen her heart!

Jenny stood beside Sir Miles to greet their guests. Wearing a false smile, she curtsied prettily as she bid them welcome, conscious of his hand biting into her waist, turning her this way and that, pulling, pushing, as if he manipulated a puppet. Many an admiring glance was cast in her direction by these courtiers turned seamen, who lavishly praised Sir Miles for his excellent taste; their well-meaning praise successfully reduced Jenny to the state of chattel.

When the guests were settled comfortably with their wine glasses, one place remained empty. Turning to Sir Miles, Jenny asked, "Is this guest not coming?"

"Not coming! The honored guest of the evening! He saved a crippled vessel from falling into Dutch hands. His name's become a household word, you stupid wench," Sir Miles snapped, irritably flicking the sleeve of his pearl satin coat.

"Perchance he's been detained. Offer another round of tinto.
We'll wait."

Jenny complied with the host's wishes. The elegantly dressed
courtiers, who had for the most part come without their
ladies, laughed heartily over amusing anecdotes as they grew
increasingly tipsy in the dim, overheated room. The only two
women present chatted in the corner, ignoring Jenny as if she
were part of the furnishings.

If she did not get a breath of fresh air, Jenny felt she would
suffocate. The gold fringe on the edge of the sapphire velvet
draperies stirred in the fitful breeze puffing erratically about
London's ancient timbered dwellings this oppressive twilight.
Clutching her pounding head, Jenny leaned far out over the
street to catch the wayward breeze. Her attention was attracted to a hackney disgorging its well-dressed occupant
outside the door; Sir Miles' laggard guest had arrived.

Jenny was still standing at the window when Sir Miles
rushed forth with effusive praise for the bravery of this honored latecomer.

"By the Christ, all England should get down on their knees
to you, my lord. You were the hero of the day! London still
rings with your praise. Welcome, welcome to my home. I'm
honored to have you accept my invitation. Not being the best
of friends in the past, I doubted you would remember me."

"On the contrary, Sir Miles, your name is very well known
to me."

Despite the smothering heat, Jenny froze before the open
window. Her hands whitened as she gripped the window
ledge. That voice! Oh, God, no, don't let it be he, she prayed
desperately, don't let him find me here. Don't let him assume
what I know he will . . .

"My love, won't you greet our guest?" snapped Sir Miles
as he pointedly cleared his throat to attract her attention.

Jenny moved the short distance between them on leaden
feet. Like a mechanical doll, she dipped a curtsy before him.
Tonight Kit was dressed as a court gallant in lavishly embroidered gold silk, a froth of fine creamy lace at neck and wrists;
his plain felt hat sported a glittering jeweled hatband to match
the winking square buckles on his highly polished brown kid
shoes. Without his customary knee-high boots, Kit's strong,
muscular legs appeared almost naked. It was at his legs Jenny
stared, dreading the moment she must rise to face him.

"Ah, such a beautiful lady. You are most fortunate, Sir

Miles. Many men have searched the world over and not found one so fair," Kit said gallantly, a sharp edge to his compliment, undetected by all save Jenny, who quailed before it.

"I thank you for your kindness, my lord. Yes, my sweet Jenny is indeed a treasure."

And only Jenny heard Kit's rapid intake of breath at those tender words of praise. Slowly she rose to face him, her heart lurching with pain at the embittered line of his mouth. When he bent to kiss her hand, Kit's hard lips were chill against her flesh.

"Welcome, Lord Ross," Jenny murmured dutifully.

Eyes narrowed, Sir Miles glanced sharply at her. "You know each other?"

"I watched his lordship ride against the King at Newmarket," Jenny explained hastily, not anxious to reveal her former relationship with the famous Captain Ashford.

"Ah, yes, and 'twas a fine performance, Lord Ross. His Majesty takes great pride in his riding skill. You're to be congratulated—but come, enough talk, let us sup."

And Sir Miles signaled for the meal to begin.

Through the endless courses of rich food, Jenny labored, her mouth dry, her taste flown. The chilled beef soup, served off delicate china plates, she passed without tasting; a bite of succulent veal, a nibble of pigeon stewed in Malaga she forced between her stiff lips. To add to her discomfort Kit was seated directly across the table from her at Sir Miles' right hand. Their eyes met frequently, until one or the other hastily ended the communication. Kit hardly touched his dinner, blaming the oppressive heat for his flagging appetite when his host looked askance at his untouched plate of food.

A molded ice, a feat in itself to produce after the day's oppressive heat, was borne triumphantly to the table on a silver platter by Sir Miles' chef. The shiny pink concoction, molded in the shape of a medieval castle, created a great stir of approval among the guests. Jenny toyed with her engraved silver spoon, stirring it aimlessly about her crystal dessert dish while the solid mass dwindled to pink liquid. She sipped the pinkness from her spoon, finding the cool liquid soothing to her parched throat.

At last the torment was at an end. With darkness the breeze had intensified, so Sir Miles suggested that his guests repair to the cool garden, where wine, cheese, and biscuits would be served. Though he looked daggers at her, Jenny declined to join the party. Tonight she had discovered she no longer cared what Sir Miles thought, or did. Too often, of late, in her desperate effort to please Charles by living this lie, she had been overly conscious of outward appearances. Now her head throbbed as if it would burst, her pain multiplied by the ordeal of Kit's presence. Each time he looked at her with that angry, challenging stare she was gripped by a chill of foreboding.

Jenny snuffed the guttering candles on the dinner table, plunging the room in gloom. It was a relief to be alone at last; now, if she wept, no one would remark upon it. Yet curiously the throb of tension pounding like a muffled drumbeat in her brain did not produce tears. Faint laughter and voices drifted from the garden, where the well-surfeited seafarers held forth with embellished accounts of their bravery, offering numerous suggestions about how his Majesty could permanently eliminate the Dutch problem. Though Jenny did not hear his voice, she supposed Kit too held forth, pouring out his daring exploits to enchant the two ladies, who were probably hanging on his every word. Jenny stood still, rigid, as she pictured the scene. Captain Ashford had years of experience at enchanting ladies; those two plump partridges should prove easy game.

But she was wrong. A sharp click sounded behind her, and Jenny glanced up to see a man's shadowy presence in the doorway.

"I thought you'd be here," Kit said gruffly.

Jenny swallowed, panicking as she realized she was trapped. How she longed to flee from this confrontation, yet he stood between her and the door. Jenny contemplated pushing past him, but she was surprised to discover she had not the energy for flight.

"I did not expect to see you here tonight," she said quietly.

"Of that I'm certain."

"This is not what you think."

"How do you explain your current condemning position, Mistress Dunn?"

"I don't love him. I don't even like him," she protested tearfully. "Oh, Kit, you don't understand."

"I'm not that much of a fool! I understand well enough. At least it explains why you didn't meet me, though the reason behind your empty promise is still a mystery."

He came to stand beside her as she slumped on an embroidered footstool, her throbbing head in her hands; it was immensely distracting to find his strong muscular legs brushing her sea green skirts.

"I was prevented from meeting you that day, but it had nothing to do with Sir Miles. His Majesty commanded me to return to London."

"Now you're the liar!" Kit snarled, not stepping back when her head snapped up.

Through a mist of tears Jenny stared up at his set features, barely distinguishable in the thickening light. During the torturous hour they had supped she had been forced to endure the pain of seeing his handsome, arrogant face across the table, knowing they were irreversibly estranged yet recalling all the sweetness of their love.

"Please, Kit . . ."

"Please, Kit—think you I'm a simpleton! 'Tis plain enough whose bed you share. A man does not deck a woman so fine and keep her under his roof for naught. When first I was told you were his mistress, I couldn't believe it. I only accepted this invitation to learn the truth."

"And you still don't know it!" Jenny cried, leaping to her feet. "Speaking of truth, perhaps now I too can have my share of it. Why did you leave London without a word? Was the great love you bore me so easily quenched that a heated exchange of words was sufficient to damp the flames?"

"What are you talking about?"

"When you fled the city with your Frenchwoman. Oh, you didn't know I was aware of your despicable treachery, did you?" she challenged sarcastically as she heard his indrawn breath. "Well, my dear Lord Ross, I came to your lodging all bathed in contrition, intending to ask your forgiveness. You'd do well to look upon me now while still you have the chance—such a total fool does not come twice in a lifetime."

"You talk like a lunatic! But look well on you I shall, for what I must say needs light." Against her heated protests, Kit relit the candles on the dining table, shielding the wafting orange flames with his hand as they bent in the night breeze. "Now, Mistress Dunn, while looking me full in the face, tell me you will have no more of me."

Jenny stared into his grim countenance, freshly aware of her tear-stained face, where ravages of tension and grief had tightened her classic features; once she would have shielded such ugliness from him, but that sweet vanity was a thing of the past.

"Despite having to share you with that foreign woman, I was prepared to do so because I believed the deep love you bore me made it worth enduring pain. That was before they told me you'd left without a word. Only then did I realize what a blessing my jealousy proved to be by allowing you to leave without bothersome entanglements. And for all this time, until you appeared on Newmarket Heath, I heard not a word from you, my darling."

"Did you not get my message?"

"No message ever came."

"That's impossible! I sent a young lad," Kit broke off as a brittle doubting smile uplifted her full red mouth. "I speak the truth!" he cried.

"Of a certainty, my lord, naught but the truth," she mocked.

"My uncle died and I was called away to Rosshythe to settle the estate. That's the reason I left so suddenly. But it was not without first letting you know."

Still that smile. Kit grasped her arm, his nostrils flaring.

"Do you seek to beat me?" Jenny hissed, wrenching away from him.

"Nay, for your aging lover will surely come to your rescue."

"He's not my lover!"

Now it was Kit's turn to smile. His mouth twisted scornfully as he said, "Forgive me, mistress, that fact had slipped my mind."

"Leave me! There's nothing more for us to say to each other."

"Nay, not yet, not until you've told me to my face what I desire to know."

"And what is that?"

"Whether you love me?"

"What does it matter? You have Louise de Brand for comfort. Must your vanity be served by my feeble protestations of love . . ."

"Always it's Louise de Brand! By the Christ, can you not get it through your addled brain we're not now lovers!"

"Not now! Oh, my lord, what a change. The last time I heard that pretty lie you stated you were never lovers . . ."

Kit seized her arms and shook her, his face dark with anger. "Enough!" he cried. "Louise was a pretty woman with whom I idled away my time long before I met you. And she was not the only one. Now, you have the truth, are you satisfied?''

Tears of rage stung Jenny's gray eyes. ''Satisfied? Think you word of your infidelity would delight me?''

''I thought perhaps it would delight you in the manner in which I was delighted when I heard of yours.''

They glared at each other. Tense with pain, Jenny wanted to strike him, but he imprisoned her hands at her sides. She kicked him, bruising his shins with the hard sole of her shoe. ''Must I tell you a thousand times this is not what it seems?''

Rage and passion made him rough as Kit imprisoned Jenny against his hard muscular body and he buried his hands in her hair, dragging her head back until his hard mouth branded her trembling lips.

Near to swooning in the sweet agony of his embrace, Jenny steeled herself to remain aloof, denying the softening emotion flooding her veins.

He uttered an oath of fury before he flung her from him, sending her stumbling into the table. ''So, things are not what they seem! Well, now I have my answer, Mistress Dunn. The coldness of your arms tell me all I wanted to know.''

In the deathly quiet following his heated outburst, Jenny heard the murmur of approaching voices as Sir Miles and his guests came indoors. ''Can we not discuss this when we are both in our senses?'' she gasped in desperation, loath to destroy all the sweetness there had been between them.

''Nay, mistress, I'm in my senses well enough tonight. So we are finally done with each other. I cannot say it causes me great pain,'' he lashed out cruelly, his face hard as granite. ''At least now I know where I stand. No longer need I hark back to something which is long dead.''

Jenny's breath strangled in her throat at the terrible finality of his words. ''Please,'' she whispered, fighting the trembling weakness in her limbs, ''oh, please believe me when I say Sir Miles is not my lover.''

His scornful laughter filled the room. Jenny longed to reveal the trap in which she found herself, longing to tell him it was not Sir Miles, but royal Charles who held the key to her bedchamber. Yet even that admission would not alter things: in Kit's eyes, whether her lover be king or lord made little difference.

''Goodbye, my love. Hark, is that not your aging lover

approaching? He, who has bedded more women than sand on the seashore. Come, dry your eyes, it would not do for him to see you so distraught.''

Hate, anger, pain flooded her body. Jenny stared at Kit's handsome face, finding his penetrating blue eyes gleaming cruelly in the candlelight. How she had ached for his touch, yearned for the sound of his voice; now he confronted her as a hated enemy.

''Are you done taunting me?''

Kit did not reply as he stepped toward the door. Turning for a final parting glance, he found her achingly lovely. The desire to accept her invitation to meet again came uppermost in his mind; he longed to take her walking through the blossoming trees in Foxhall Gardens in a final desperate attempt to rekindle their love. Never before had a woman moved him to such deep passion, nor had any other made him suffer the pain he had endured these months past while he wrestled with the knowledge that she had discarded him for another. By God, she was naught but a tavern wench! Yet he would gladly exchange her for a dozen princesses of the blood royal. Torn between the dictates of his heart and head, Kit hesitated, until a fresh surge of jealousy and wounded pride effectively stayed his voice.

''Why, my lord, are you leaving us?'' Sir Miles asked in surprise as he collided with Kit in the doorway, his heavy face flushed with wine. Behind him streamed his guests, whigs askew, neckcloths unfastened, their faces rosy with an overabundance of fine tinto.

''Aye, Sir Miles, I am.''

''But the hour's still early,'' Sir Miles protested as he came inside the room. His gaze riveted on Jenny's tear-stained face. ''What's this?'' he demanded gruffly, his jaw tightening.

''This, my dear Sir Miles, is an ungrateful baggage. Both she, and your home, lack sufficient hospitality to keep me here a moment longer.''

A sharp intake of breath came in unison from the guests, who, though tipsy, were nonetheless sober enough to understand the deliberate insult.

''Perchance my hearing's not as sharp as it once was, my lord,'' Sir Miles growled. ''I must have mistaken your words?''

''Nay, your hearing is adequate. I repeat: I find fault with your home, your mistress, and most especially with you.''

Eyes brimming with tears, Jenny stared in horror at Kit. Lines of grim determination hardened his handsome face, prematurely aging him; his dark gold hair formed damp ringlets across his brow. Kit emitted such an aura of stark emotion that it charged the air with tension. He spoke not out of drunken foolishness; his unprovoked attack on Sir Miles Russell was a calculated move to involve the nobleman in an affair of honor that would be settled in only one way. And Jenny shuddered at the probable consequences of his heated outburst.

"How dare you!" Sir Miles spluttered, his bulbous blue eyes stony in the flickering light.

"Have you forgotten? I'm famed for my audacity. 'Twas that quality which allowed me to skuttle an enemy vessel and save his Majesty's flagship—the very reason you invited me here to sup." Kit snatched his gloves from the side table, and stepping close to Sir Miles, he fixed him with an angry glare. "We have a score to settle, sirrah."

The cold challenge sobered Sir Miles. Blinking in disbelief, he took a step backward. "Nay, I've no quarrel with you, my lord. The night's hot, the wine strong. Sleep on it. I will accept your apology on the morrow."

A murmur of approval greeted Sir Miles' reasonable suggestion, but Jenny knew his words were in vain. A band of angry color mounted in Kit's face; he glanced at her one final time, as if to reassure himself of the need for action, then he spun about and slapped Sir Miles across the face with his lace-trimmed gauntlet.

"Now will you give me satisfaction?"

"You blackguard! No one insults me and lives to boast of it! Aye, I'll meet you. Name the time and place!"

A clamor began in the room as the concerned guests sought to dissuade the two angry men from participating in a senseless duel.

"His Majesty finds little favor with dueling."

"Make amends. Come, 'tis not too late. Tinto be a potent drink."

But the two adversaries remained stony throughout the friendly cajoling.

"Gentlemen, please go home. You must forgive me for my lack of hospitality, but my humor wears thin," Sir Miles announced grimly.

The guests finally departed, casting backward glances at

the two hostile men who faced each other in the center of the elegantly appointed room.

"When will you give me satisfaction?" Kit demanded, once the others had left the room. As he crammed his hat on his head, he warned, "I'll not wait indefinitely."

"You shall have satisfaction on the morrow, if it suit."

"Aye, the morrow suits me well enough. In St. James' Park at early light. Ready your seconds."

"You can be assured *I* will be there," Sir Miles snarled, his face dark with anger. "You've insulted me, my lord, and for that you shall die."

"Stop it, you fools! Can you not see this for what it is!" Jenny cried, as she forced herself between the glowering men. "This quarrel is deliberately provoked. He takes issue with you over me," she told Sir Miles, battling to keep tears from her voice. "Oblige him not."

"Over you? I don't understand."

Kit's lip drew back in scorn. Jenny's bid to introduce sanity into the proceedings merely reinforced his belief in her intimate relationship with Sir Miles Russell. The pain of this thought goaded him beyond endurance. "I believe a man should at least know for what reason he is going to die. Before she came to your tired bed, Sir Miles, we were lovers." Then Kit turned and strode from the room.

"By God, that's rich! What a jest! Challenged over a woman I've never once possessed." And Sir Miles began to laugh until tears trickled down his sagging cheeks.

"You fool! You're no wiser than he!" Jenny cried, as she raced to the privacy of her room, where she gave vent to the overwhelming grief that consumed her throat with fire.

The next morning the two noblemen met to settle their debt of honor. The cloudless blue sky shimmered with the promise of another hot day. A dawn chorus of birdsong drifted from the heavy-leaved trees, breaking the summer morning stillness of St. James' Park. So soon after dawn was it that only one early morning stroller passed the group of men waiting beneath the shadow of the oaks, and knowing not their deadly purpose, he walked on.

As the sun rose higher, Kit grew impatient. The King often took his spaniels for an early morning stroll; what misfortune it would be to suddenly confront his monarch, bloodied sword in hand. "Are we never to begin?" he snapped to his younger brother James, who had eagerly agreed to act as his second.

"Have patience, my friend," interjected Harry Kent, who had also accepted the honor of acting as his second, but with far less enthusiasm. "Can you not wait to die?" he asked, his face grim.

"I assure you, Harry, I have no intention of dying."

"Sir Miles is a formidable swordsman."

"And so am I," replied Kit, flexing his narrow sword blade, the glittering steel flashing in the early sunlight.

While the combatants went about their deadly preparations, several coaches drew up beneath the shelter of the trees, but their occupants made no attempt to stop the duel. All courtiers privy to this quarrel had refrained from mentioning it to their King: once the duel was fought it would be up to the victor to attempt reinstation with his irate sovereign.

Jenny alighted from a hackney. After paying him, she waved the driver on. Clad in an enveloping dark cloak, she stood in the shadow of the trees so as not to draw attention to her presence. Shivering with a mixture of cold and terror she watched Kit pacing the ground, measuring distance and calculating his thrust. The slim young man beside him she recognized as his brother James, who had been pointed out to her weeks before as Lady Castlemaine's latest lover. James was a shorter, younger version of his dashing brother; because of his extreme youth, those distinctive Ashford features that tugged her heartstrings with bittersweet memories were, as yet, softly unformed.

Had Jenny thought this tragic duel could have been prevented, she would have flung herself between the participants; yet such dramatic action was pointless. Denied this bout, Kit would merely arrange another, for so bent on vengeance was he that no breath of sanity entered his plans.

The antagonists grew increasingly anxious as the sun traveled higher in the sky while the seconds and the physician in attendance continued to argue over technicalities.

"Are we ready?" Kit growled, spinning on his heel.

For a moment Jenny had a clear view of his set face. The shock of seeing his handsome features in so grim a mask began a trembling ague in her limbs. She clutched her cloak about her, trying to still the tremors. This might be the last time she would see Kit alive!

"Come then, my lord, let us get to it."

The determination in Sir Miles Russell's voice struck a

wave of fear through Jenny's heart. In contrast to Kit, who wore a plain cambric shirt and dark breeches above his bucket-topped boots, Sir Miles was clad in pearl-gray satin breeches and a lace-trimmed shirt; a second held his embroidered gray coat and silver-plumed hat. Quite clearly Sir Miles expected to win this duel, for he wore fine clothing in preparation to receive the congratulations of his friends after he had put down this hot-tempered sea captain.

Now the seconds, the black-clad doctor, and a small group of friends who had gathered for an uninterrupted view of the contest retired to the safety of the trees.

The two men stood alone in the sun-splashed clearing. No greeting was exchanged, merely stony glares seething with hostility. It was said the Queen's ladies swooned in ecstasy when men quarreled over their attentions, but the knowledge that two men dueled over her only chilled Jenny's heart. She had despised Sir Miles for some time, yet she had no wish to watch him die at the hands of her beloved . . .

Shock radiated through her body as the thought registered. Her beloved! Was that really how she considered Kit, even now, after all that had gone between them? No, it was not true! She hated him for all the pain he had caused her. No man who had truly loved a woman would have been so cruel . . .

"En garde!"

The barked command riveted her to the present. Like a deadly dance the two men moved, Sir Miles not quite as agile as his opponent, for advancing years cut short his wind and dulled his movements. Once, twice, the swords clashed, echoing through the parkland. A great twittering black cloud of frightened birds rose in search of sanctuary. Kit's foot slid on the dew-wet grass and Jenny cried out in anguish as she pictured his opponent's silver blade piercing his heart. No novice to bouts of sword play, however, he quickly regained his footing. Swinging about, Kit cleverly forced Sir Miles into the direct sun; as the great golden disk sailed above the trees, its slanting rays burned the grass with light. Blinded by the sudden, unexpected glare, Sir Miles faltered, enabling Kit to close in for the kill. Too eager was he, too sure the sun was in his favor, that Kit grew careless. Sir Miles bellowed in sudden triumph as his blade punctured the fleshy part of Kit's shoulder, unleashing a great spurt of blood over his cambric shirt.

"Ah, youth has its disadvantages, after all. You grow too

careless, my lord,'' taunted Sir Miles, thinking to drive his opponent to further rashness.

Kit tried to ignore the hot pain in his arm. He suffered Sir Miles' gloating taunt in silence, saving his breath for the encounter. Parry, thrust, the blades flashed bolts of fire from the shafts of sunlight spearing the wet grass. Though his arm burned like hell, Kit knew he could not stop: one moment of inattention could be his downfall. Sir Miles Russell had not come by his reputation as a swordsman lightly; long years of action on the battlefields of the Royalist cause had prepared him well for today. Nevertheless, the stamina of youth was on Kit's side. Already the other man was winded, his sagging face flushed, his mouth gaping as he fought for air. Once more Kit cleverly maneuvered his opponent to face the sun. And this time he followed through with his advantage. The instant Sir Miles narrowed his eyes against the glare, Kit stepped closer, surefooted on the slippery grass. As Sir Miles raised his sword, momentarily blinded by the explosion of white light as sun hit steel, Kit drove hard into his midsection. His blade jagged upward beneath the ribs, encountering soft yielding flesh; an inch to the right and his sword would have deflected off the ribcage. For a moment Sir Miles turned glassy-eyed with shock before his mouth widened in a scream of agony as he crumpled on the ground.

Sir Miles' seconds ran to assist him, followed closely by the doctor in his flowing black cloak. The seconds crouched beside their man, attempting to staunch his pumping blood with wads of linen, while Sir Miles thrashed about, bloodying the turf.

Kit watched, breathing hard, a tremor of mingled triumph and unease radiating through his tired body. He had killed him! Though Sir Miles still drew breath, Kit had fought enough men to know such a wound would prove mortal. And though this was revenge he had burned for, fulfillment bore not the sweetness he had imagined. Far from elation, he knew empty numbness as he viewed his fallen foe, so pathetically small and impotent beneath the towering trees of St. James' Park.

''He's gone,'' one of Sir Miles' seconds announced grimly as he straightened up. ''You've murdered a man, my lord. What think you of that?''

''Had I been the one who fell, methinks you would not have been so concerned?'' Kit countered, his pale eyes nar-

rowed. Already an ugly rumble could be heard as men climbed
from the coaches to investigate the fate of their fallen friend;
needless to say, Sir Miles Russell's supporters were aging
toadies from Whitehall.

"His Majesty shall hear of this," announced one of the
men indignantly, as he glared hostilely at Kit. "He has
forbidden pointless dueling."

"I assure you, sir, this was hardly a pointless duel. There
was an abiding factor to be avenged."

"So you say, but we know naught of it," challenged
another.

"There's a lady over whose affection we took issue,"
retorted Kit, turning on his heel. "Besides, were it any of
your affair, gentlemen, 'twould have been one of you, not he,
spitted on the end of my sword."

The men drew back, warned by the passionate anger blazing in his face. This new Lord Ross was an unknown quantity.
And though much praise had been sung about his recent
heroic feats at sea, despite his long-standing friendship with
the King few knew him personally.

Clasping his pumping wound, Kit turned toward his own
seconds, who did their best to stop the bleeding. Two, three,
linen cloths were discarded, all bright with blood. Kit swayed,
clutching the gnarled trunk of a nearby tree as faintness
assailed his senses.

Jenny stood in the shadow of a coach drawn up at the end
of the trees, tears of relief running unchecked down her
cheeks. Grave concern for her beloved's safety propelled her
forward. What did it matter now if he knew she was here?
What did it matter if he grew angry with her? He bled
profusely and her heart ached for his pain. She would nurse
him out of regard for the love he had borne her in the past.

With a gasp of surprise, Jenny leaped out of the path of a
coach careening across the grass. Almost before the vehicle
stopped, the door flew open and, amid a flurry of bright blue
skirts, a woman half fell from the coach. With voluminous
skirts held above her ankles, the black-haired woman raced to
assist the bleeding man leaning against the tree.

"*Chéri*! Oh, how you bleed!"

That hysterical feminine voice effectively stayed Jenny's
steps. She fell back, hoping she had not been seen. As if from
a physical blow, she recoiled as the dark-haired Frenchwoman
enfolded Kit in her shapely white arms, cooing to him,

whispering endearments in her own language as she urged him toward her waiting coach. Louise de Brand had come to save her lover; no longer had he need of Jenny's ministrations. What perfect irony that Kit had killed a man over a woman he no longer loved!

The four bays snorted and grew restless, alarmed by the stink of blood as the wounded man approached the coach.

Her forehead was clammy as Jenny leaned against a nearby tree, fighting an overwhelming wave of nausea. Though it was almost more than she could bear, she continued to watch the scene unfolding before her burning eyes. Weeping as she helped James shoulder his brother's weight, Louise de Brand settled Kit inside her coach. It was her silk scarf that bound his wound. After issuing a shrill command to the coachman, Louise slammed the door. The vehicle lurched forward, scattering the straggling spectators who had gathered to view the spectacle. The last Jenny saw of Kit was the rear of the ebony vehicle lurching through the trees at breakneck speed. The coach had barely disappeared when a cry of alarm went up from the gentlemen surrounding Sir Miles' body.

"His Majesty approaches!"

With a gasp of dismay, Jenny quickly spun about; to face Charles was the last thing she wanted to do. The royal party was already passing the lake. With her cloak pulled close about her face to shield her identity, Jenny walked rapidly in the opposite direction. Tears trickled down her cheeks and dripped inside the neck of her cloak. Even today, when Kit was wounded and weak from loss of blood, it had not been she to whom he had turned; like the angel of mercy, French Louise had appeared from nowhere to offer comfort.

Chapter 20

All London buzzed with accounts of the duel fought between Lord Ross and Sir Miles Russell. The threat of legal action over the well-known nobleman's death was not lessened by the fact it had been a dispute between rival lovers.

Through it all King Charles remained silent. The gossips pronounced him angry both over the duel and the effrontery of the duelists, who had dared to clash swords in St. James' Park virtually within sight of the royal party out for their morning walk; then again, those who recalled his Majesty's strange antagonism of late toward Sir Miles and his lifelong friendship with the hot-headed naval hero doubted that the King would press for punishment of the crime.

Jenny stayed in seclusion within somber Russell House, retreating behind the heavy draperies that custom dictated should be drawn out of respect for her recent bereavement. As the days stretched into weeks, her unease mounted. She would have welcomed some communication from the King to set her fears at rest, but the Palace maintained an official silence on the matter. And though she suspected Charles was angry over her unfortunate involvement in the scandal, he was apparently in no hurry to confirm her suspicions.

One sultry July afternoon Jenny sat in the walled garden beneath the shade of the neighbor's hazel, making a feeble attempt to embroider a lawn chemise with blue forget-me-nots and pink daisies. There was not a breath of air. The fragrant roses, now in glorious bloom, could not mask the stench of the city streets permeating even this green oasis. While she sewed, poignant pictures of happier days flitted through her mind. Was her romantic life always to be a turmoil of fierce emotions? By her unfortunate choice of men she appeared to have set such a course. Though she usually tried not to think about Kit, today she spared him a few compassionate thoughts. Deceiver and liar though he was, he must still bear her some love: why else would he deliberately challenge a man to a duel over the disposal of her favors? Few were privy to her

former liaison with him. Anger and false pride Kit possessed
in plenty, yet there had been no need to demand satisfaction
to salve his honor. Could she dare hope jealousy and pain
over her seeming infidelity had spurred him to that reckless
challenge?

Eventually Jenny laid aside her embroidery, unable to concentrate on the bright blue flowers. Though the pain had been
great, she had finally accepted her loss of Kit's love; she
could also accept her slide from favor in the King's eyes. If
need be she would set out on her own, using her skills as a
seamstress to support herself.

Her unresolved position in life was not Jenny's only concern as the scorching summer progressed. The city mortality
bills rose rapidly and mounting fear of the plague gripped rich
and poor alike as deaths were counted in the thousands during
those early weeks of the hot, sultry July of 1665. Jenny's
unaccustomed listlessness filled her with alarm. What if she
had contracted the terrible sickness? All precautions had been
taken by her household, yet none knew the method of trans-
mission of the current scourge. A belief that the plague was
spread by cats produced a campaign to eradicate the city's
felines, but the only apparent effect of their removal was an
increase in the rat population.

"Madame."

Her maid stood before her clasping and unclasping her
hands in great agitation. "What is it, Marie?" Jenny asked,
her stomach pitching as she wondered if Charles had finally
broken his silence.

"There are three visitors to see you, madame."

"Show them into the garden."

"They . . . they wish *you* to come indoors, madame."

"Who are they that they dare command me in my own
home?"

"They are Sir Miles' relatives, madame."

Inwardly Jenny quailed; long had she awaited this visit.
With Sir Miles Russell dead, she had no claim to the shelter
of his house. Fate had rendered meaningless even a King's
grand lie. "I'll come at once," she said.

They were awaiting her in the parlor, a pigeon-chested
dowager in a flowing puce gown and two young men, arrogant
and richly dressed.

"So you're the greedy baggage who's been milking Miles

dry!'' shrilled the woman, her mouth set in an aggrieved line amid her many chins.

Though she had intended civility, Jenny stiffened beneath the unwarranted attack. "Whom do I have the displeasure of addressing?" she demanded, dispensing with the customary polite greetings.

"I'm Parker Russell and this is my brother, William. And you, mistress, have just insulted our mother," snapped one of the young men, his pasty face surly.

"Not until she insulted me."

The dowager in puce bristled as she stepped forth, prepared to do battle. "How dare you speak to us like this? We're the rightful heirs to this house. Poor, dear Miles' wife, my sister, expired at the terrible news of his murder. Now everything goes to us." Though she strived for a suitably grief-stricken air, the woman could not prevent a gleam of triumph from lighting her small, colorless eyes.

"How fortunate for you," said Jenny, her voice brittle.

"You're no longer welcome here," growled Parker Russell. "I'm my uncle's heir and I'm ordering you out before sunset. We'll not support an immoral creature off the streets. Take nothing besides the clothes on your back."

"Perhaps you disbelieve the popular rumors about the actual object of my affections," began Jenny. The rapidly changing expressions on their faces revealed their knowledge of the gossip linking her name with that of the King. "I can assure you, nothing I possess was actually bought for me by your uncle."

The trio gasped, anger and indignation coloring their faces as they realized what she was saying.

"You're a liar," snapped the younger man, his face flushing pink. "If my uncle did not provide for your wantonness, pray tell who did?"

"At the moment I'm not at liberty to reveal his identity." Jenny's knees shook beneath the buff silk skirts of her afternoon gown. "Allow me a few hours' grace and my maid will have my possessions packed. Have no fear, I shall take nothing belonging to your uncle."

"Your very clothes belong to us!" cried the woman, panting in anger. "Don't you so much as take a feather out of this house."

"You are wrong. My gowns belong to me."

"It's a lie! Such ingratitude after poor Miles took you in and showered you with luxuries—you, who are nothing more than an ill-bred baggage off the streets . . ."

"There was never any pretense of affection between us. Your brother-in-law provided my shelter at the suggestion of a certain . . . friend."

Jenny longed to tell them it was the King who had commanded her to this house, but she dare not. Already she had come dangerously close to betraying their relationship in the broad hints she had offered in explanation to Sir Miles' relatives. Were she to reveal the truth, Charles would be furious. Still enjoying his leisurely deception of his courtiers, he would never forgive her for spoiling his game.

The two young men stepped between her and the door. Angrily Jenny shook off their detaining hands. "When I've packed my possessions, I'll be gone. And it will be long before nightfall. No doubt I could fight you for my right to this house, as many others would do, yet because I abhor every inch of this detested place, it will be my greatest pleasure to depart from it."

So saying, Jenny turned her back on them, ignoring the angry outburst that followed her up the stairs.

On the first-floor landing Marie huddled against the banister, her brown eyes round with fright. "Oh, madame, we're to be thrown into the street," she wailed. "Oh, please, go to his Majesty, tell him of this insult."

Jenny shook her head. "No. I won't clamor for favors like the others. Surely the King is aware of my situation. Had it been his intention to provide us with alternate lodgings, he would have done so. Have no fear, we'll not starve. My aunt and uncle will take us in until I find a place." The brave statement instilled confidence in the plump, dark-haired French girl, but the thought of returning to Swann Alley in such greatly reduced circumstances filled Jenny with dread.

All Jenny's possessions had been gifts from the King; what a grand gesture it would be, in view of his current indifference, to throw out the shimmering finery. But she could not afford to indulge in such a foolish gesture: There was a ready market for used finery, and though she did not dwell on the morbid thought, in the months to come these gowns could make the difference between life and death. Bitter disillusion tightened Jenny's mouth as she helped Marie fold and smooth the shimmering fabrics. Was this the extent of the King's love for his "good wench"? Would he see her turned out into the plague-ridden streets? Did Charles' continued silence mean their relationship was over?

Marie went outside to summon a hackney. Between them they carried the two trunks and a canvas valise down the long flight of stairs; Sir Miles' arrogant young heir forbade the servants to aid them.

Jenny departed Russell House with the resounding slam of the front door ringing in her ears. Head held high, she maintained her composure, though her stomach sank as she gave the Cornhill address to the hackney driver. Poor Marie looked so tearful and woebegone that Jenny slid her arm about the girl's narrow shoulders in reassurance. She must be strong, if only for Marie's sake.

"I'll offer to work for our board. And you sew such a fine seam, Marie, that I'm sure there'll be a place for you also," Jenny assured kindly.

"Madame, if I may say so, you should be ordering this coach to Whitehall," Marie declared, her dark eyes flashing as she climbed inside the battered conveyance. "I don't understand the unkindness of allowing you to be put out in the street. A King he may be, but . . ."

"That's enough!"

Eyes downcast at the rebuke, Marie remained silent as the hackney swayed and rumbled over the cobblestones, lurching its way toward Cornhill.

Her maid's sentiments so closely mirrored her own that Jenny could not allow them to be voiced. She too smarted at her royal lover's indifference, but she had other, more pressing concerns. Pet would rail at her for her stupidity in allowing so lucrative a position to slip through her fingers; Doll would gloat over her downfall; and most likely Uncle Will, ashamed to acknowledge one who had fallen so far from grace, would avoid her.

"Why are we stopping?"

It was far too soon to have reached Swann Alley. Jenny peered through the murky coach window to find the narrow, unfamiliar street deserted. This was a shabby, impoverished district where beggars crouched in doorways, their faces a mass of sores; so still were they that Jenny doubted they were even alive. Several mangy curs picked through heaped refuse in a narrow alley leading into a darker, more forbidding court. The crush of people quitting the city had made the driver seek less traveled byways to avoid congestion. To her horror Jenny saw primitive red crosses painted on doors within yards of where they sat.

"Driver!" she cried shrilly, rapping on the pane behind the box where his dark bulk obscured her vision. The man ignored her. One of the horses let out a frightened whinny, the sound beginning a tremor of fear down Jenny's spine as that dull bulk teetered sideways and thudded onto the cobbles.

Urging Marie to stay inside the hackney, Jenny hurried to investigate. "Driver, what ails you?" she demanded, her voice shrill with fear.

There was no reply. Gingerly Jenny shoved his inert form with her foot, rolling him on his back. The hackney driver lay unmoving in the fetid kennel dividing the street, his thick features suffused with a rosy rash, his shallow breathing little more than the rapid grunt of a laboring animal; a trickle of slime ran from his slack mouth. With an exclamation of horror, Jenny leaped back. The man may not have succumbed to the plague, but his symptoms were so ominous that she was taking no chances.

"Madame! Madame! What is it?" shrieked Marie, rushing to her side.

Brusquely Jenny said, "Come, we'll travel on foot."

Trembling and weeping in distress, Marie helped her mistress haul down the trunks and the canvas valise from atop the hackney. All the while they cast fearful glances at those huddled waifs in the doorways, but apart from a few feeble cries for help, the bundles of rags heeded them not.

The valise had to be left behind; it was all they could manage to stagger beneath the weight of the leather trunks. Anxious to quit this horrid street, Jenny shuddered as she read the crudely scrawled inscriptions beneath those ominous blood red crosses: "Lord have mercy upon us!" Adding her own heartfelt prayer to those sentiments, she urged the weeping maid to more speed. Jenny counted six more doors marked with red crosses. The forbidding sight chilled her. The very air they breathed was tainted with the plague; those beggars, the hackney driver, even the rotting carcasses of bloated rats floating in the fetid liquid trickling down the central kennel were sources of contagion. Fear sped Jenny faster and faster along the uneven cobbles, until Marie begged for mercy, unable to keep pace with her mistress's stride.

Each increase in the mortality bills had put more citizens to flight, their belongings stacked in ramshackle carts, creating the largest traffic jam Jenny had ever witnessed. On all sides irate people bellowed and shook their fists over the delay, desperate to quit plague-ridden London. Yet for those who already tossed feverishly among their treasured possessions, flight was in vain. Death traveled with them.

Each passerby, each door painted with an ominous red cross, increased Jenny's fear. Driven by desperation, she virtually ran to Cornhill. So anxious was she to be shut of these infected streets that she paused only long enough to make sure her sobbing maid followed. Not since the morning of the duel had Jenny walked these streets, and though the servants had mentioned growing panic among the populace, she had assumed their tales to be grossly exaggerated. It was a shock, therefore, to discover those fearsome accounts were true. Not only were shapeless forms huddled in squalid, nameless streets, but here, in this more affluent neighborhood, those same bundles of rags blocked alleys and porticoes. Everywhere she looked ominous red crosses splashed the doors like blood.

At last, the welcome sight of Dunn's Haberdashery came in view. Of late, trade in this plague-ridden city had lessened to a mere trickle, but, ever hopeful, Will Dunn had declined to shutter his business. Jenny was grateful for her uncle's greed.

"Here, Marie, you can put down the trunk."

Thankfully the maid allowed the heavy trunk to slide to the cobbles, her arms and hands numb from the weight. "Is this where your family live?" she asked in surprise, glancing at the old black and white timbered dwellings.

"Yes. Wait here while I go inside."

The gloomy shop was lit by the dirty yellow haze of late afternoon. An accumulation of many smells, trapped by the oppressive July heat, pricked Jenny's nostrils: beeswax, the hot scent of cloves, the lingering aroma of food all mingled with the overpowering stench of London's gutters.

"Yes, mistress, how may I help you?"

Jenny swallowed as Pet spoke without looking around. Her aunt continued to roll ribbons in a battered oak box on the table. "It's Jenny."

"Jenny!" Pet cried in surprise as she spun about. One glance at her niece's woebegone countenance told her all she needed to know. "So they threw you out," she said, her small mouth tightening as she looked at the trunk.

Jenny nodded. ''I'm not seeking charity, merely a few nights' lodging until I find a place of my own. I'll work for you as before.''

''Not seeking charity!'' Pet marched from behind the pitted work table. ''What else can you call it, wench? You had all London at your feet but, being a simple fool, you allowed that man to come and go as he pleased, getting no binding . . .''

''I didn't come to listen to a lecture. If you'll not help me, I'll go elsewhere.''

''Nay, we'll not turn you out,'' Pet decided hastily, reaching for Jenny's arm as she turned to leave. ''Stay. You remembered us well when you had the money.''

Pet's compassion was unexpected. Jenny blinked in surprise as she beheld the sly smile on her aunt's plump face. ''My French maid's with me,'' she said. ''She's a fine seamstress. Can you take her on, for she knows no one in London?''

A frown of aggravation played across Pet's face, but she nodded in agreement. ''Aye, let the wench come inside. Likely your stay won't be for long.''

''No, for I'll set about finding lodgings tomorrow.''

''Fie, you always were an empty-headed little twit. 'Twas not quite what I meant.'' Pet winked, her smile growing knowledgeable. ''I hear the gossip bandied about the ale houses. Methinks a certain *person* won't let you stay impoverished for long.'' And Pet administered a playful pat to Jenny's shapely hips.

Gossip linking her name with the King's must have reached Swann Alley; news of her fall from favor would surely follow, but Jenny intended to use the situation to her advantage for as long as she was able. ''I beg not charity from either King, or commoner,'' she said haughtily, playing to her aunt's vivid imagination.

Pet slid her arm about Jenny's narrow waist, seductively tiny within soft folds of amber silk. ''With a lovely face and body like yours, you never need beg. He's made you not a titled lady, so perchance your fame will be on the stage. They say both Moll Davis and Nell Gwynne have him to thank for their current popularity—but, no matter, niece, you're welcome to stay with us as long as you wish.''

The smile Jenny gave her aunt was forced and taut. As long as Pet believed Jenny's royal lover would redeem her, she had a home at Dunn's Haberdashery.

* * *

Jenny had been back in Swann Alley three days, during which time Uncle Will avoided her. The neighbors, on the other hand, viewed her with undisguised interest. Supposedly they came to gossip with Pet or to examine goods, but in truth they came merely to gape at this notorious creature who had purportedly graced the royal bedchamber. In her element, Pet played up the gossip for all she was worth, basking in reflected glory. Details of the scandalous duel over Jenny's favors, coupled with many broad hints about her niece's foremost place in the royal affections, added greatly to Pet's esteem. And if she was not past telling outright lies to embellish the tale, who could blame her?

As the long, airless July days dragged by, Jenny decided Charles had no intention of sending for her. And the painful knowledge was a bitter truth to accept.

Plague was spreading rapidly through Cornhill, the constant stream of visitors to the haberdashery greatly increasing the risk of contagion. A proposed curfew to allow the infected a few hours of fresh air after healthy souls were safe indoors was but one of many ineffectual remedies employed by a city grown desperate in the face of calamity. Citizens shunned public places, staying off the streets until the teeming city appeared derelict. Grass sprouted between the cobblestones and thieves recklessly looted the homes of the sick. Men even grew afraid to purchase periwigs for fear the hair had come from plague victims. All the while the July heatwave dragged on unabated. Swarms of buzzing flies hovered over heaps of filth and lighted on corpses lying uncollected in the streets. At nightfall the rumbling death carts began their hideous mission, but the ever-increasing number of corpses made darkness too short to complete the loathsome task.

"La, this terrible heat, I declare, I'll melt away," Pet sang as she came inside Jenny's chamber, making a valiant effort to appear light-hearted and gay. She dabbed her perspiring face with a cambric square, then took a deep breath of a posy of sweet herbs dangling from a ribbon at her waist. "My plague remedy's selling wondrous fast," she said, glancing disapprovingly at Marie, who stitched beside the window. "There are new cases every morning. Crippled Sam and his wife lie near death. Will there be no end to it? That comet which blazed like a judgment in the heavens last winter foretold this terrible plague. I told Will at the time we were in for tragedy, but he just laughed at me, the old fool. We could have left the city then—there was money enough . . ."

"Is the plague remedy your own recipe?" Jenny asked sweetly, not anxious to endure another recital of her aunt's grievances.

"A family secret. 'Twas said to have been used to great avail in the Black Death. The ingredients are close guarded. A medley of herbs infused in malaga—no more can I say."

"Pet, come below." Doll appeared in the doorway, her lank blond hair no longer tortured into ringlets, but scraped back into a sweaty bun skewered atop her head. The prolonged heat had made her unduly short-tempered. "There's a whole shopful of people demanding your remedy. They say plague's spread to Swann Alley! God knows, we'll all get it with that lot clamoring below. Will ought to shut the shop. It's too hot to work anyway."

Pet stared in shock at her sister. Beneath her carefully tinted complexion, she blanched, throwing grains of rouge and powder into stark relief on her plump cheeks. "In the Alley," she repeated incredulously. "I don't believe a word of it! It's just not true, you stupid wench, you've likely garbled the tale as usual." Still muttering, Pet sped after Doll, who could be heard clumping noisily downstairs.

"Oh, madame, are we to die?" Marie whispered, tears flooding her round brown eyes. "Can we do nothing?"

Jenny had few words of reassurance. "Continue to pray, Marie, I know of little else."

The following morning, alarmed by the rapid spread of plague, Will Dunn shuttered his shop. The nearest plague house was ten doors from the haberdashery, but its inhabitants had been his regular customers.

"Let us flee. Surely we can find a country cottage," Pet pleaded, wringing her hands in agitation.

"It's too late now, dear heart, we must wait it out. Perchance we already sicken," Will said gloomily as he sniffled and wiped his hand across his sweating brow. The need to close his shop and the prospect of endless days of enforced idleness made him irritable. Suddenly he was seized by a sneezing fit and he buried his face in his large linen kerchief, shuddering anew with each explosion.

"Ring around a rosy, pocket full of posies. Achoo! Achoo! We all fall down," chanted Doll from the corner.

"Shut up, you wretch!" Pet screamed, swinging at her sister.

"Let her be, Pet, 'tis only a rhyme the children sing," Will soothed, preparing for another siege of sneezing.

"That's with getting overheated and refusing to change clothes," Pet snapped, placing her hand on her husband's brow. His skin was clammy, but not fevered. She visibly relaxed.

"Aye, mayhap you're right. I've taken a chill."

"Go to bed for a couple of hours."

"Nay, it's too hot to sleep with the windows shut, yet the stench is so bad when they're opened."

"Leave those windows alone," Pet shrieked as her sister made to open the casement. "No tainted air must enter."

"But it's so hot inside, I can barely breathe," Doll protested, sniffling and dabbing her running nose. "Mayhap I've caught Will's chill."

"You're always sneezing," Pet dismissed shortly. "Get down to the shop and set things to rights. Will must go to bed."

"Shall I help?" Jenny offered, not anxious to work with Doll, yet less anxious to endure the torment offered by Pet's curent mood.

"If you wish."

Pet led her husband to his room, still complaining.

A murky, sulfurous glow lit the morning sky. At either end of the alley bonfires burned in an effort to dispel the ill humors causing the plague; the twin blazes increased the already intolerable heat, robbing the narrow street of air and belching forth great black clouds of smoke.

With the door closed and the shutters up, the stifling shop was darker than ever. Garish orange light from the plague fires penetrated chinks in the shutters, wavering across the ceiling and dancing like demons over the paneling. Doll stacked bolts of fabric and cones of thread in the back room, much to the apprentices' displeasure, for now their meager sleeping quarters were reduced by half. Jenny sweated as she moved among the colorful fabrics, dulled now to somber hue in the airless murk.

"Help me carry this, or are you too ladylike?" Doll snapped, staggering beneath a bolt of mauve camblett. When their hands met, Doll swore beneath her breath and snatched back her hand.

"I'm sorry, I didn't mean to scratch you," Jenny apologized, thinking her nails had gouged Doll's hand.

"Scratch me . . . you're trying to steal my ring, that's what you're about! Didn't your fine lord give you nothing so valuable," Doll taunted, sticking out her tongue. "You might be pleased to know this was meant for you, you prize whore, but I got it instead. Naw, what do you think of that?"

"For me! I thought Lymon Perse gave it to you."

"Oo, 'im!" Doll's thin lips curled in derision. "The only thing he gives out's sides of meat, or braces of 'ens. Anyway, it's mine now. And don't think you can claim it, not after all this time."

Jenny leaned against the dark oak paneling, trying to stay calm as she cast back to the first time Doll had shown her the pearl ring: it had been on the morning of Kit's hasty departure.

"Who sent that ring?" she demanded, low and menacing.

"Dunno. Some fine lord I s'pects. What's it to you now?"

"It means a great deal to me. You'd better remember, or I'll rip your hair out!"

Doll took a defensive step backward. "Now don't you come over nasty wiv me! I might remember, and I might not."

Jenny's hand shot out to grip Doll's skinny arm in a vicelike grasp. "Who?" she demanded.

"Ow, you're hurtin,' " Doll squealed, appealing to the apprentices for aid, but the boys merely grinned and went about their tasks.

"Who?" Jenny twisted Doll's arm behind her, pressing her thin frame against the hard paneling. Anger colored her features as she stared into Doll's unlovely face. The truth made little difference now that Kit had forsaken her for another, yet she must know for her own satisfaction if he had sent her word of his departure for Ireland. "Who?" she repeated threateningly.

"A note came with it, but I can't read. The lad gave me a name—I don't remember. Ow, let go, Jenny, you're 'urtin,' " Doll wailed, struggling in her captor's grasp.

"Was the name Ashford?"

"Might've been."

"Remember, you cheating, lying . . ."

"All right! I thinks it was a Captain Ashford. But that don't mean nothing to me."

Jenny's breath shuddered painfully in her breast at Doll's squealed confession. Kit had not lied to her after all! This scrawny bag of bones who sniveled so piteously could have prevented all the pain, the heartache, the mistrust . . .

"What's going on here?" demanded Pet, suddenly flinging open the shop door. She went tight-lipped with anger to find Jenny and Doll quarreling instead of working. "You worthless sluts! Is this all you can do?"

"She's broke me arm. Look at them bruises," Doll wailed, holding up her skinny arm to show the discolored imprint of Jenny's fingers.

"And I'll break your head!" Pet screamed, cuffing her sister soundly about the ears before she spun about to face Jenny. "Your foreign wench is blabbering about a messenger. Perchance she sickens. Get you upstairs and see what the commotion's about."

Though Jenny wanted to stay and make Doll pay for her deception, she decided there would be time enough for punishment. Warily she skirted her aunt, expecting a blow to speed her on her way, but Pet had already turned her displeasure on the apprentices, who scuttled about like frightened mice when she bellowed at them.

Jenny found Marie crouched weeping before the window which stood open to admit swirls of choking smoke. "Oh, madame, they said I must be insane, but I did see him."

"Who, Marie? Who did you see?" Jenny asked, her alarm mounting as she beheld her maid's agitation. Could she be delirious?

"A messenger from the King. He stood below. I saw him in the firelight."

Though she doubted Marie's story, Jenny raced to the window and looked out; the street was deserted. "He's not there now," she said.

"You don't believe me either!" Marie cried in exasperation, burying her face in her hands. "You think I lie."

"Come, sit down. You're agitated and 'twill do you no good," Jenny said kindly, leading Marie to a padded bench against the wall. "What makes you sure it was a messenger from the King?"

"He wore the same livery as the man who brought the invitation to the Christmas Ball. Perchance it was he, for he's young and handsome and ever anxious to please his King.

Only someone so devoted would venture into this plague-ridden alley . . .''

That was not the argument of a déranged woman! Looking closely at Marie, and being assured she spoke the truth, Jenny ran to the window and leaned over the sill. A great gout of flame shot skyward and drove a black cloud of smoke against the windows.

"Charles Harris, are you there?" she shouted to the deserted street, her voice echoing eerily between the silent houses. "Charles Harris, for God's sweet sake, answer me if you're at hand." Jenny clasped her hands in agitation, a note of hysteria creeping into her voice.

After what seemed an eternity a man's voice, faint at first but growing stronger, called, "Mistress Dunn?"

"Aye, I'm Mistress Dunn. Up here, you good for nothing fool. Are you blind?"

A mauve plumed hat bobbed into sight below the smoky gable as the man stepped backward to the edge of the drainage kennel. "God be praised! My life would have been worth naught had I not found you."

"Your life may still be worth naught," Jenny replied grimly. "Have you not seen the marked doors?"

"Aye, but a knave such as I cannot be licked so easy. I'd all but given up my search. Make haste. Come below, mistress."

"Where am I to go?"

"That I cannot say. They told me you were forever asking questions. It's a damnable bad habit, you know." He smiled up at her, his fair mustache quirking in amusement. "Pack your furbelows, gather your belongings, and meet me in the street in less than five minutes. I'll tell the driver I've found you."

Frantically Jenny and Marie scrambled about the room, haphazardly thrusting garments into trunks, jamming in frilled yards of material when the lids refused to close. With a dozen streamers fluttering gaily from the bulging trunks, they staggered downstairs.

"Pet, where are you?" Jenny cried, feeling she at least owed her aunt an explanation.

"What do you want now, you troublesome baggage? I'm far too busy with Will, who's not feeling at all well."

"I'll write a note." Jenny motioned Marie to follow her down the stairs, where she hastily scrawled a message in

Will's opened account ledger. Instead of going through the shop, they went to the side entrance, where they were met by the King's messenger.

"What took you so long? I had to offer the scoundrel an extra twenty guineas to wait," Charles Harris complained, shouldering the trunk that Jenny set on the door step. "Hurry, before the bastard leaves with my gold."

Swirling smoke and bright flames danced garish shadows across the shuttered houses. As they passed the pyre, a feeble cry for help echoed from a nearby dwelling. The intense heat of the fire became almost unbearable as they pressed close to the buildings, skirting the blaze tended by an old crone glistening with sweat. In the adjoining street a coach waited, the driver hunched on the box, a cloth wound about his face to keep away plague germs.

Charles Harris opened the coach door and assisted the women inside. His blue and white garments flashed before the window like bird's wings as he lifted the trunks, for the driver refused to dismount to help him. A few minutes later he jumped inside the coach and slammed the door as the vehicle lurched forward.

"Did his Majesty send you?" Jenny asked, almost afraid of his answer, yet knowing she must ask.

Charles Harris winked. " 'Aye, you wicked wench, he sent me. You must have a pretty box of tricks to win his heart."

His suggestive wink made Jenny uncomfortable. "Where am I bound?"

"For the country, ungrateful one. For two days I've searched for you at his behest. 'Twas only on speculation I came to this hole, but they refused to open the door. Without your pretty maid, you'd still be rotting in that hellfire." Charles Harris reached out to tweak Marie's plump cheek.

Marie giggled at the unexpected attention. Her reaction irritated Jenny, who usually found little fault with the obliging girl. "We thank you for your kindness, Master Harris," she said sharply. "But before I follow blindly, you must tell me where we're bound."

"To Worcestershire. There his Majesty intends to revisit the places he knew during his flight. They tell me the countryside is most pleasant at this time of year. I'm sure you'll vastly enjoy your sojourn."

"Are you to come with us?"

"Only as far as the city gates—would you have me die of

boredom in that God-forsaken backwater?'' he asked, his pale brows raised in amazement. ''I follow the court, wench. 'Tis the only life I know.''

''Isn't the court to leave for the country?''

''Whenever his Majesty decrees, yet our sovereign seems in no undue haste to leave his capital. Tomorrow he takes the Duke of Monmouth with him to inspect the ships at Greenwich.'' Charles Harris broke off his conversation in order to rail at the driver for his slow pace.

Stranded vehicles blocked the streets; Jenny wondered uneasily if their drivers had succumbed to the lightning effects of the plague. People sometimes sickened for days until the dreaded buboes appeared in the groin and armpits; then again, so virulent was this plague that others, seemingly well at noon, were dead before dusk.

''Thank you for guiding us out of the city.'' Jenny clasped Charles Harris' hand in gratitude when he prepared to alight at the city gate.

''It was entirely my pleasure to have two such lovely companions,'' he replied gallantly, bowing over her hand. Then, with a wink, and a blown kiss for Marie, the handsome young courier disappeared in the warren of narrow streets.

Jenny lay back against the padded black leather seat and breathed a sigh of relief. How wonderful it would be to be rid of this teeming, plague-ridden city. She longed to live where seasons followed their appointed course, far from this airless, stench-filled city.

Beside her Marie dozed peacefully, a smile of satisfaction on her rosebud mouth. Jenny frowned as she reviewed Marie's susceptibility to male flattery, a trait she had not noticed before. She must take care that the French girl did not fall prey to the expert lies that formed the core of a court gallant's wooing. Just as I did, Jenny added mentally, her mouth setting in a bitter smile as she pictured Kit when last she had seen him, shirt sleeve crimson with blood, face drawn with fatigue. Her heart raced, skipping beats at the unexpected surge of emotion the picture generated. At least she now knew that Kit had not lied about sending her word of his impending journey. If only she had received that message, how different life might have been. But she had not known. And their ensuing estrangement had been founded on jealousy and wounded pride. Angrily she thrust the thought from her mind, seeing little point in dreaming about what might have been. Though she did not have the man she truly loved, she still had what most women would have considered a far superior prize—Charles Stuart, King of England.

For the next two days the road north wound through lush farmland splashed with pools of gold flowering mustard; rolling water meadows dotted with grazing black and white herds spread to the horizon. In the west loomed the Black Mountains, guardian of the Welsh border. The air was tainted not with excrement and rotting garbage, but was sweet scented by summer flowers and freshly mown hay. Past woods and streams they rattled, past orchards festooned with small hard apples, past ripening strawberry fields where the air was sticky with cloying perfume. Picturesque half-timbered villages dozed beside placid streams. The Worcestershire hedgerows bloomed pink with dogrose, while nodding foxgloves, rosebay willow, and scarlet poppies flamed among the roadside grass.

It was seven o'clock on a fine summer evening when they finally reached their destination.

Jenny alighted from the coach before a two-storied house of mellow Cotswold stone, golden in the evening sun. A hundred mullioned windows glowed red, winking in the fading light. The peaceful countryside echoed with the cries of homing swallows, swooping in graceful arcs, disturbed by the arrival of the coach.

"This be it, mistress," said the driver, clambering off his box. "I'll unload your bags, then I'll be on me way," he muttered, staying well back from his passengers. Despite the heat of the past few days the man still had a cloth wrapped about his face.

"Thank you, driver. What's the name of this place?"

"The young gentleman said it be Chaddsley Manor."

Without further ado, the driver deposited the two trunks at the foot of a shallow flight of steps. A few minutes later the lumbering coach disappeared in the fading twilight. The door to the house opened and a woman dressed in gray silk descended the shallow steps. "Welcome to Chaddsley Manor. I'm Lady Felicia Storey," she said with a charming smile. "I've been expecting you, Mistress Dunn."

Chapter 21

The September day lay hot and listless; beneath bright blue skies sun-loving grasshoppers chirped from the bramble-swathed hedgerows and honey bees droned lazily in the clover. Jenny picked up the shallow basket of purple plums she had gathered from the orchard. A carpet of overripe fruit lay at her feet, swarms of wasps attracted to the split plums, gaudy Red Admirals flitting about the fallen, fermenting pears.

Lady Storey had obligingly journeyed to Worcester to visit relatives, leaving Jenny in possession of Chaddsley Manor. Though her hostess treated her well enough, Jenny sensed disapproval behind her polished manner. A staunch royalist, Lady Storey had sheltered the young king after the battle of Worcester; but now Charles had strained old loyalties by asking her to house one of his mistresses for an extended holiday from plague-stricken London.

As Jenny entered the manor's shadowed, oak-paneled entrance hall, she was startled by an unexpected sound. So bright had it been outdoors that she was momentarily blinded. Then from the corner of the large square room came a familiar voice.

"So, little milkmaid, you come indoors at last. 'Odd's fish, I thought I'd have to spend all day hiding here."

"Charles!" Jenny shrieked as she fled to his outstretched arms. "Oh, Charles, when did you arrive?"

He smiled as he hugged her close, raining kisses on her smooth chestnut hair. "These two hours past. And for all that time you've been wandering willy nilly, gathering," he paused to lift the cover on the basket. "Plums," he continued, a twinkle in his black eyes. "Have you no heart?"

"I swear, Your Majesty, had I known you were expected I would never have left the house. Why did you not send word?"

"Because I wanted to surprise you, Jenny Wren."

Her heart pitched foolishly when he spoke his pet name for her in that low, husky tone. Oh, she loved him dearly, she did, she did. When she was with Charles she had no need of that other love whose shadowy presence invaded her solitude.

"You're not still angry with me?"

"Nay, should I be?"

"They whispered you were angry. That you . . ."

"They? And who are they? Foolish old wives in breeches. Don't tell me you believe all the claptrap you hear."

Eyes brimming with tears of relief and joy, Jenny raised her face to his. "When you did not send word I thought . . . oh, Charles, I thought . . ."

"That I no longer found favor with you?"

"Yes."

"You should be ashamed for having so little faith in me." He accompanied his chuckled reprimand with a sweeping caress of her shapely hips, accentuated by the soft clinging fabric of her old lavender gown. "Grant you, mistress, I was not pleased to hear the scandalous stories concerning your divided affection, nor was I pleased a man died as an outcome of the affair."

Jenny was too prudent to remind him that the duel had been fought on the strength of the lie he had so happily nurtured. "I had no hand in it," she pointed out, tentatively reaching for his face. The touch of his hot, suntanned skin beneath her fingertips made her shiver in anticipation.

Charles kissed her fingertips as she brushed his lips. "No, but 'tis your fatal beauty that drives men insane to possess you." The spark of laughter in his eyes warmed Jenny by degrees. "Have you forgotten that you confessed to me your mad passion for a certain gentleman? You also confided to me the more despicable antics of his rival, which pleased me not at all." He stopped speaking while he traced a lean, sun-bronzed finger across the swelling of her breasts. "Actually, I consider Sir Miles Russell no great loss."

"Then you'll not punish Lord Ross?" Jenny used Kit's new title with difficulty.

"I cannot, for he's been a good friend to me. And, though 'tis unjustly said I treat my enemies better than my friends, in this matter I'll withhold prosecution if he remains abroad for a respectable time. Why that woebegone expression? Does your heart beat faster at the mention of his name?"

Jenny swallowed uneasily as she noticed the tension in his jaw. "Nay, 'twas finished between us long ago," she assured him, fighting an absurd desire to weep against his fine blue velvet coat.

Charles gladly accepted her lie. Raising her face, his fingers were gentle on her fine-boned chin as he said, "Then come, Jenny Wren, let us speak no more of it. Will you not invite me to sup, for the hospitality's scant this side of Worcester."

They dined off succulent roasted pigeon with caper sauce, followed by a steaming blackberry fool swimming in fresh cream; sweet white wine complemented the meal. Beyond the mullioned windows sunset stained the evening sky with glorious color; turquoise, gold, and rose blended in fierce majesty above the windbreak of wych elms, while across the clipped lawns crept the purple shadows of approaching night.

Charles suggested they take advantage of the long twilight to ride about the manor. Though not as fond of riding as he, Jenny eagerly accepted his suggestion. Too impatient to wait while she changed into her habit, lest they miss the beauty of the sunset, he brusquely ordered her to ride astride in the manner of a country wench.

As they cantered down Chaddsley Manor's broad drive, Jenny was reminded of approaching autumn by a hitherto unnoticed gold tinge on the trees; the shortening days produced the dank evening chill that envelops autumn woods. They rapidly skirted the sprawling woodland, alive with chirping birds returning to their nests, to seek the sunken lane where afternoon heat lingered. On either side of the lane brambles hung heavy with ripe fruit; fragrant yellow honeysuckle and woody nightshade girded the hawthorn thickets.

"I'd never have forgiven myself if you'd sickened with the plague," Charles blurted unexpectedly as he reined in his horse, blocking her path.

They gazed at each other in the deepening twilight. Dark shadows underlined his eyes, his wide mouth forming a grim, narrow line.

"Thank God I was spared . . . and you as well, Your Majesty," she added hastily. A flicker of humor lit his dark eyes at her afterthought. He reached for her hand and, to Jenny's surprise, he almost swept her from the saddle in his ardor as he pressed his lips to hers.

"Oh, sweet, can you ever forgive me," he whispered, torn by remorse. "That I should ever have allowed others to dictate the workings of my heart . . ." he paused, wary of what he was revealing. "Do you love me still, Jenny Wren?"

"Yes."

"Then come, let us indoors to repledge that passion which damned near flickered to extinction because I was such a blind fool."

A fire had been lit in the green bedchamber. Though a grand royal suite had been prepared in honor of the King's visit, Jenny knew he would never crumple the sheets on that ornate four-poster with its gilded brocade hangings. Usually she was whisked away from his chamber long before daylight; tonight she would lie beside her lover until dawn.

Charles shut the casement, ridding the room of a smoke-tinged breeze that swept from the forest of twisted brick chimneys atop the roof of this Tudor manor house. "There, now we'll not catch our death of cold," he said with satisfaction. "I've always loved September. However hot the day, the nights are cool and the air's sweet as wine."

Jenny smiled at him, relaxing beneath his appraising gaze. No longer was she in awe of him; when they were alone she rarely reminded herself he was her King.

"I've missed you," she said sincerely, her red lips curved in an inviting smile.

Charles paused beside the bed, his white shirt gaping unbuttoned to reveal the matted dark hair on his chest. How exquisite she was; the most divine of creatures. Jenny was simple, honest, unspoiled—a good wench. And never once had she asked him for favors; it was a virtue he found especially pleasing.

"Would that I had a portrait of you thus," he breathed softly, his eyes skimming the firm mounds of her white breasts peeking invitingly through a shimmering curtain of silky chestnut hair.

"Nay, so many others have posed for your pleasure. I would not want it," she declined as a sudden twinge of sadness marred her mood.

Tenderly he swept her hair from her brow as he sat beside her on the edge of the bed. "Perhaps you're right. This way your beauty shall be mine alone. Our coming together is the dearest secret of my heart."

His ardent declaration speared her soul with unease. "Why must I remain a secret?"

His fingers still gentle against her cheek, Charles shook his dark head. "Merely because the time is not right for me to publicly acclaim you. Soon, my love. Have patience.''

"Is it because Lady Castlemaine hates me?"

"Barbara?" His surprise appeared genuine. "Why should she hate you?"

"Because she feels I insulted her at the ball. And she also resents my relationship with you, sire.''

He stretched beside her, chuckling as he took her hand and caressed her slender fingers. "Yes, I must confess, she's sought to enlighten me upon that score on several occasions. Be not offended by her words. Barbara has a tongue like a viper.''

"Sire." Jenny nestled closer to him, instinctively seeking comfort from his strong arms. "Will you answer a question?"

He had been wrapping her bright hair about his fingers like silky rings; he paused in his actions. "Must I?"

"Do you love Barbara Palmer?"

Charles laughed aloud at her candor. "What is love? Barbara's a bad habit of mine. And she still pleases my body.''

Jenny swallowed, finding her next question more difficult to voice. "Is that all *I* mean to you?" she whispered at last.

"Oh, sweet Jenny Wren, how could you ask that? You're young and fresh as country air. With you I can be myself. Or at least I can display the finer aspect of my soul, revealed only at special moments. If ever I've truly loved a woman, I've come closest to it with you.''

Absurdly, tears spilled from her eyes to splatter his hand.

"Do not weep. Did I not please you with my honesty?"

"You pleased me.''

Tears shimmered in Jenny's gray eyes. Leaping firelight played a golden symphony across her voluptuous body, dappling her breasts with shadows; so tempting was the picture that Charles slid the thin stuff of her shift aside, his hungry mouth following the passage of the muslin.

Jenny threaded her fingers in his thick black hair, holding his head, basking in the pleasure of his mouth. How close she had come to losing him. And yet he had come back to her of his own volition, not lured here by threats and screaming tantrums as was often the case in his relationship with the notorious Barbara. Tonight he loved her truly, if tomorrow he felt that selfsame way about another, that was his nature; these silent arguments were so often waged within her mind that Jenny had a ready defense for both sides. Surely if he loved her so well, he could remain faithful. Was it because he was King that Charles found such a demand impossible to fulfill? His passionate nature flared readily whenever, or wherever, he found arousal; to expect his fidelity would be like asking him to give up breathing. Someday she would seek that vow—not tonight, but soon . . .

"Love me back, you evil wench, don't just lie there taking," he hissed, tweaking her nipple to attract her attention. "What a selfish creature you've become. Seek me out. Caress me with your soft little hands. Make me leap afire," he urged, his eyes black as night in the fireglow.

"Yes, Your Majesty, I'll love you well in payment for . . ."

"No. Pay me for nothing, good wench, except the bestowing of passion."

Their hot mouths welded together in a breathtaking kiss. His limbs tremored against her while his hands pursued a course of their own, awakening every inch of her body beneath the muslin shift. Impatiently Charles cast aside the encumbrance. Sweeping his lean hands over the silky smoothness of her bare flesh, he moaned in ecstasy, his passion towering close to bursting at the fiery arousal.

It had been so long since he had made love to her that Jenny responded with ready fire to his caresses as the agonizing flame of desire mounted to an inferno between her legs. Tormented by his kisses, his hands, the pressure of his demanding manhood against her flesh, Jenny sobbed deep in her throat as she awaited fulfillment.

Charles responded to her fire, until his own passion was so intense that he doubted he could endure a moment longer without welding her to his molten flesh. Tonight there was no drawing back, no tantalizing withdrawal; grim-faced, he positioned her, the soft down pillow beneath her head, the coverlets kicked aside.

"I love you, Jenny Wren," he breathed sincerely as he speared her body with heat, driving home, desperate to unite them on the forge of passion.

"I love you too," she whispered, near delirious with the ache of her body. A passionate nature such as hers took not kindly to enforced celibacy, and so lonely, so deserted had she felt of late that her ragged emotions left her vulnerable to his expert touch.

There was no more speech. Together they raced onward,

upward, ascending to that other plane where passion held sway. Like showering, flaring fireworks her climax came, scorching and deep. Jenny plunged, swirling down into blackness with the hot strength of his arms wrapped about her, the comforting beat of his heart sweet music in her ears. Oh, yes, I truly love him, she cried fiercely to herself, trying to drown a small voice mocking from the shadows. Yet now, in the sweet vulnerability of spent passion, she hesitated to confess her undying devotion to this tall dark man who was born to wear the crown. An unnamed source held back such loving vows as Jenny closed her eyes tight, trying to dispel the image of a golden-haired man with blue eyes and a proud face.

It was almost a week before Jenny saw the King again. As Lady Storey had not yet returned, she felt free to indulge their love without any thought of reproach from her hostess. They breakfasted in bed, after which Charles made passionate love to her before falling into a deep, blissful sleep. Jenny dozed beside him for a few minutes. When she woke, he still slept, a faint smile of contentment turning his face boyishly vulnerable.

Jenny arose and dressed herself, not wishing to summon Marie and destroy this idyllic picture. Perhaps this would be the closest she would ever come to married bliss, she thought sadly, as she quietly closed the door so as not to wake him.

In the early morning hours the old house was quiet; during their mistress's absence the manor servants, while not growing dangerously lax in their duties, often failed to adhere to a strict timetable.

Jenny put on her cloak before stepping into the misty September morning. Yesterday, while they had strolled the grounds, she had noticed a cluster of crimson roses nestled in a sheltered corner of the walled garden. An unaccustomed crispness in the soft air foretold a sudden change in the weather; she intended to gather the roses before they were blackened by frost. Jenny stepped lightly along the flagged path to the garden. This past hour spent in her lover's arms had been sheer bliss. So devoted had Charles become of late that perchance he neared a decision over her future. Not that she demanded a public acknowledgment out of any desire for notoriety, but penniless as she was, without her royal lover's support she could find herself on the street. And there was little Marie's welfare to consider beside her own.

The roses' heady perfume was captured in a film of dew. Jenny buried her face in the perfumed blooms as she retraced her steps to the house.

The door to her chamber stood ajar. Thinking perhaps Charles had arisen in her absence, Jenny thrust open the door. She recoiled in shock as she beheld two figures reclining on the rumpled bed; so engrossed were they in each other that neither heard her entrance. A mounting wave of nausea gripped her as she watched Charles kiss the round fullness of Marie's exposed breasts. The maid giggled foolishly, stroking his neck as she squirmed in pleasure beneath his arousing hands. Prattling in French, Marie stroked the smooth dark expanse of his muscular back, admiring his body.

Jenny swallowed the bitter fluid that rose unbidden in her throat. The two people whom she had thought loved her well, whom she had trusted, sported shamelessly before her, their actions growing so intimate she could no longer keep her presence secret.

"Get out of here, you slut!"

In a flurry of startled movement, Charles raised his head, his lean dark hands dropping from the half-naked woman beside him. Marie squealed in alarm when she saw her angry mistress; lapsing into a hysterical gale of weeping, she scrambled from the bed, clutching the sides of her open bodice together in an effort to hide her nakedness.

"Get out! Never do I want to set eyes on you again!" Jenny screamed at the maid, clenching her fists to keep from striking the little fool as she sidled past, weeping piteously. Gradually Jenny became aware of the rose thorns tearing into her fingers, but the agony was bitter balm to her wounds.

"Jenny," Charles began good-naturedly as he moved to sit up. "Come, be not so harsh . . ."

"Harsh!" she cried, forgetting he was her King, remembering only that he was her lover who had betrayed her with another. "That slut could not wait until my back was turned . . . and you . . . you . . . how could you!"

A flicker of shame crossed his face. Then he shrugged, all remorse fled. "She's a delectable armful. There was nothing more to it than that."

"Is that all you have to say?" she yelled, her gray eyes

flashing as rage swept through her body in a tirade of heat.
"A delectable armful! Have you no limits? Did I not satisfy
you well within the hour? Did you not spout reams of untruths last night about your regard for me, as you have done
many nights before?"

"Not untruths."

"What then? I'm gone a half hour and you're already abed
with another!"

" 'Odd's fish, wench, you'd think I'd mounted the filly,"
he protested indignantly.

"No doubt you would, had I stayed gone long enough."

A cynical smile crossed his dark face. "And what if I had?
You do not own me. No woman owns me."

"No, of that I'm well aware. What a fool I was to think
perhaps you cared enough to . . ." Jenny bit back tears of
rage, hating her weakness, trying to master the trembling
underlip that betrayed her pain.

"I said I loved you and it was no lie," Charles said, lazily
reaching for his shirt draped over the chest at the foot of the
carved bed. "Nothing I've told you is a lie. You are beautiful. And my desire for you, my regard, is undiminished."

Aghast Jenny stared at him, so sure of himself, an air of
arrogant defiance about his saturnine face. "And think you
my regard is undiminished?" she demanded, growing aware
of the searing pain of rose thorns embedded in her hand.

"Come, dear wench, I've hardly remained faithful since
our meeting. What difference can one more chit make? She
was more than willing, I assure you. I had no need to seduce
the baggage, for she fell right eagerly into my bed."

"Of that I'm sure."

"Forget it ever happened. I'd have taken great pains not to
offend you. Had you not walked into the room unannounced . . ."

" 'Twas not merely the sight of your hands on her breasts
that offends me," Jenny spat, tears welling from her eyes.
"You've betrayed me within this house where I assumed you
would not seek another. You've betrayed me with my own
maid!"

"I love you still."

"But I cannot share you repeatedly with every wench from
here to Land's End! Is there no limit to your needs? Can you
not be faithful for two days?"

"I try never to be faithful longer than one night," he
quipped, sliding to the floor. Charles stood before her, casu-

ally stuffing his shirt inside his breeches as he spoke. "Faithfulness is a word that does not belong in our relationship. You knew, from the first, that you must share me with others. At the time, as I recall, you made little objection."

"But I thought . . . I thought," Jenny's voice died in a croak. He smiled at her sarcastically and in that instant she loathed him. With an explosion of anger, she pitched the crushed roses at his head.

Laughing at her futile action, Charles ducked and the blooms sailed to the far side of the bed. "This is the only part of me you can have, Jenny Wren," he reminded, stepping toward her. "Can you not be satisfied with being loved wholly one night at a time?"

"No. That satisfies me not at all," she ground out, her teeth aching under the tension of her jaw. "For some time I've battled my heart. Today you made that decision for me."

He glanced up sharply from adjusting his hose. "And that is?"

"I cannot continue to share you with a multitude of whores," she spat viciously, her face blanching with rage. "Barbara Palmer, Frances Stewart, Moll Davis, all the whores in Drury Lane have more of you than I ever had . . ."

"You're wrong," he interrupted, his face taut. "You've had a part of me they've never known. But, if you wish it, we'll end our arrangement. Never let it be said Charles Stuart pressed his suit on an unwilling female."

"Are you going to let it stand at that?" she whispered as sanity flooded back to remind her of what she had said, and to whom.

"If it is your wish. Since you cannot have my undying vow of fidelity, and, as you indicate, nothing less will suffice, we must say *adieu*."

"What of our love?"

"What of it? It is your wish, not mine," he reminded, reaching for his blue waistcoat. "I shall not hold this against you. You'll find, my sweet, I'm of a very even temperament. Someday you may even change your mind."

Through a wavering blur of tears she observed his cynical smile, his nonchalant, half-amused manner; she wanted to strike him for causing her pain. "Never!"

He inclined his head. "Very well, then I must betake myself of my travels. I trust you have no regrets?"

Jenny did not reply. Numb, she watched him gather the

remainder of his clothing as if nothing had happened. Pausing before the mirror, Charles carefully replaced his periwig, then he put on his black sugar loaf hat and adjusted it to his satisfaction. His dressing complete, he spun casually on his heel, a mocking smile playing about his dark face.

"What am I to do?" Jenny demanded, her limbs steel taut.

"You, my dear, can do whatever you wish."

"You do not care?"

"I care, but you are not my prisoner. You forget, Mistress Dunn, the current arrangements are fully to my liking, 'tis you who find fault with them." He strode across the room, careful to keep his distance as they passed in the doorway. "Do not be too harsh on the wench—a King can be a very persuasive lover."

"She'll never attend me again!"

He shook his head, a bemused expression on his face. "Such is the wrath of a wronged woman. And I thought you to be different. Perhaps I never really knew you at all, Jenny Wren."

His use of that pet name tore the very last of her composure to shreds. Rounding on him, Jenny reached for his blue sleeve, wrenching the material. "Never again will I . . ."

A bleak expression replaced his humor as he shook her hand from his sleeve. "You forget yourself," he rebuked sharply. "I am still your King."

"I'll be gone within the hour. Never again will we set eyes on each other."

"No!"

Jenny blinked as she heard the controlled anger in his voice. "Surely, after this, you can't expect me to stay . . . here . . . with her?"

"You may do whatever you wish with the foreign baggage— *you* will remain at Chaddsley Manor. It was my arrangement and you won't destroy it. That is a command it would behoove you not to break. When, or if, I wish your company, you'll be sent for. Now, madam, I bid you good day."

Without another word Charles spun on his heel. Every inch the King, he stalked down the narrow upstairs hallway and descended the oaken stair, leaving Jenny alone in the sun-splashed chamber, blood trickling down her wrist from the rose thorn wounds.

"My lady," Jenny began when she met her hostess on her

return from Worcester. "Though it's not my wish, I am ordered to remain beneath your roof. Therefore, instead of accepting charity, I demand to earn my keep."

Lady Storey blinked, amazed by this unexpected confrontation. "What do you intend to do for wages, my dear?" she asked at last, managing to gather her wits. In the brief time since she had crossed the threshold, she had already correctly assessed the situation: in her absence King Charles had quarreled with his mistress.

"I'm a seamstress by trade. I noticed your draperies and linens are in poor repair," Jenny said, plunging ahead, unaware of the embarrassment she was causing by her candid observations. "Will such repairs be sufficient to earn my keep?"

"There's no need . . ." Lady Storey began, but the steely determination in the younger woman's gray eyes halted her protests. "Yes, I'm sure it will be more than adequate."

In the space of one night autumn swept across the land; the air held the nip of frost and morning was heralded by chill mists that lingered in the valley. Jenny stared unseeing at the sweeping landscaped park, where tall golden elms tossed among copper beeches, driven by wind and light rain. Her idyllic interlude was over! Yesterday Charles had galloped away with nary a backward glance, discarding all those months of love and passion as easily as he discarded last season's coat. And she, poor fool that she was, had been so ill prepared for the change. Tears hovered about her curving black lashes as she reviewed, for the hundredth time, the hideous ending to a day that had begun so beautifully. How lonely, how bereft, she felt, her mood akin to the sad gray countryside beyond the window. As always, when her heart ached, despite the source of her grief, Jenny's thoughts turned to Kit, whom she had loved so well . . .

"Madame."

Jenny spun about to face Marie, who stood hesitantly in the doorway. "Come inside," she snapped, "and close the door."

Mistress and maid faced each other before the broad windows where the gray morning light cast unflattering shadows across their faces.

Marie's full lower lip thrust forward defiantly as she twisted her hands, rehearsing her speech. "Madame, I wish to speak to you about yesterday."

"There's nothing you can say. I am not blind."

"His Majesty . . . Charles . . ."

"Damn you, you have no right to call him that!" Jenny blazed, her hand raised to strike Marie's petulant countenance.

The maid retreated a pace. "His Majesty found me very desirable," she defended, her round brown eyes stony. "It was never my intention to . . ."

"Nay, but you went readily enough when he snapped his fingers."

"He is the King."

"And I am your mistress. I do not think I have used you ill."

"He is the King. And you cannot bind a man's fancy, madame."

"The King goes his own way. We owe each other nothing."

"I did not come to apologize," Marie threw out, tossing her head; twin spots of color burned on her full cheeks and her eyes shone with excitement.

"Good, for it would make no difference. I'm dismissing you. The only reason you're still here is because I allowed you a full night's rest."

"You've no need to dismiss me," Marie cried in anger. "I'm joining the King. With me he'll have no use for others because I'll satisfy him totally. He invited me to come to him. And I intend to do so."

So surprised was she by Marie's challenging statement that Jenny gripped the spool-backed chair before the window, her knuckles whitening on the wood. "You little fool," she managed at last, her voice thick with emotion. "Do you think for one minute he'll support you? Do you think he even gave another thought to your welfare after he left here?"

Marie tossed her head and refused to answer.

The stubborn set of the French girl's face told Jenny any advice she gave would be ignored. Today she no longer wanted to rip the hair from Marie's head, nor to pummel her soft flesh; her emotions lay like a leaden weight in the pit of her stomach.

"Go then. There are no further obligations between us."

With a defiant toss of her head, Marie met her mistress's eyes. "He loves me," she declared, as she backed through the door. "You are jealous!"

Jenny stiffened at Marie's hastily flung taunt. She could

hear the girl clattering down the corridor, expecting pursuit. The temptation to follow and offer chastisement came and went. Rain pattered softly against the diamond-paned window, drawing Jenny's attention to the watery landscape beyond; how heavenly this parkland had seemed in his company, how sweet the air, how magical the hours . . .

Jenny turned her back on the windows and took up a linen altar cloth to mend. The delicate cloth from the family chapel, worked by Belgian nuns over a hundred years ago, had a frayed lace border. Let foolish, empty-headed Marie pursue her royal lover in the rain. Perhaps, if Charles was in the mood, she would amuse him for a night; it was far more likely he had already forgotten her existence. Marie had chosen her future, basing it on an elusive, intangible quality as fragile as this Belgian lace: she would soon discover a man's interpretation of the word *love* bore little resemblance to a woman's!

Chapter 22

As the raw, icy wind stirred the bare branches of the plane trees surrounding The Close, Jenny pulled her red cloak tighter and increased her pace. Within her padded velvet muff she carried a letter summoning her to attend their Majesties' ball to be held this Christmas 1665 in the university town of Oxford, where the court had fled to escape the plague. At first she had thrown aside the summons, declaring she would never again be at Charles Stuart's beck and call. But later, after some discussion with Lady Storey, who had become her friend, Jenny decided the wisest course would be to obey.

While in Oxford the King and Queen occupied the Dean's lodgings at Christ Church. And Lady Castlemaine, who was awaiting the birth of her fifth child, was lodged opposite Merton College in the home of Antony Wood. The notorious Barbara had brought her other children with her, publicly flaunting her relationship with the King.

Jenny reached her lodgings off the Cornmarket. Tonight she was to be received by the King and Queen. A gown of sapphire-blue satin adorned with silver tissue spread across the tester bed, the silver glinting in the glow from the hearth; this beautiful gown had arrived by messenger two days before her departure from Chaddsley Manor. Why Charles had relented in his anger and invited her to join them for Christmas she did not know, but this expensive gown was his peace offering.

The minutes ticked by from the heavy grandfather clock outside her room as Jenny took great pains with her appearance. Her stomach pitched at the thought of being presented at court. Though she was sure Charles had not enlightened them, undoubtedly the avid gossips were privy to their recent disagreement. Not wishing to be the central topic of the courtiers' clacking tongues, Jenny had even toyed with the idea of packing her trunk and returning to the relative obscurity of her Worcestershire retreat; common sense, however, prevented her making so decisive a move—Charles' good humor was not infallible.

Later that evening, when Jenny entered the vast ballroom ablaze with crystal chandeliers, she felt highly conspicuous in her eye-catching gown. Her abundant chestnut hair was dressed simply, for she had no maid to create an elaborate coiffure. Charles' topaz pendant, nestling provocatively in the valley between her breasts, contrasted with her smooth white skin. Though Jenny had no official invitation to the gathering, the footman ushered her inside the ballroom, his actions suggesting that he had been alerted to watch for a lady so gowned. All around her people nodded and smiled in welcome, their unexpected friendliness baffling.

Fleeing plague-infested London, the lords and ladies of the King's profligate court, plus their servants, their dogs, and their horses, had reestablished themselves in this ancient town. And the King, once he had completed his nostalgic journey to the villages visited after his flight from Worcester, had repaired to Oxford to reign over them, transforming the quiet city into a miniature Whitehall.

"My dearest Mistress Dunn, you are an absolute vision."

"How we have missed you."

"Where have you been hiding all these months?"

"Will you honor me with this dance?"

Before the first hour was over, Jenny felt light-headed from the abundant compliments she had received from these splendidly dressed courtiers who had often ogled her but never before treated her with deference. She danced the bransle and the coranto with the most glittering wits of Charles' court, finding each man competing with his rivals to offer elaborate praises to her beauty.

The overheated ballroom grew stifling. It was not easy to give her admirers the slip, but eventually Jenny managed to escape to the wide terrace running the length of this lavishly appointed ballroom. The winter wind swirled icily against her bare flesh, but she welcomed its chilling breath of sanity. None of tonight's events made sense. Why, when Lady Castlemaine was here in Oxford—she who had frowned upon acceptance of impoverished Mistress Dunn—had the courtiers totally reversed their attitude toward her?

Jenny leaned against the icy stonework, shuddering involuntarily as the chill struck through her satin gown. Perhaps, when Charles arrived, he would help explain his courtiers' remarkable behavior.

"Oh, you are far too kind, my lord," squealed a woman's high-pitched voice.

Jenny turned in time to see a red silk gown slipping about the corner of the building. A burst of laughter and the low tones of a man's voice, followed by rapidly pattering steps as the woman hastened indoors, brought a smile to her lips. But as she dwelled on thoughts of lovers' meetings, her smile dissolved in pain. She had picked up her skirts, preparing to reenter the ballroom, when quick, heavy footsteps ascending the terrace took her attention. Something about the man's broad shoulders, the set of his head, the color of his hair, robbed her of breath. Simultaneously they glanced up and their gasps became a mutual expression of pained surprise.

"Jenny!"

Shock robbed her of speech as she stared into Kit's handsome face. There was no smile of welcome there; in fact, she could not perceive what emotion swirled through his mind, for his features remained stonily set.

They stood their ground, eyes locked intently as if they sought to probe the innermost aspect of each other's soul. A thousand unasked questions flashed through Jenny's brain. All these months she had longed for him, though Kit was no more faithful, no more truthful, than the King himself.

"Lord Ross," she managed in what she hoped was a gracious manner. "I trust you have recovered from your wound?"

"Thank you, yes. And, Mistress Dunn, I trust you have found yourself another lover?"

A word shot through her mind in answer to his taunt and her lips silently mouthed the epithet.

"What did you say?" he rapped sharply.

"I said you are a bastard," she repeated aloud.

The word hung in the frosty air, low and fraught with tension.

Kit smiled sarcastically and he inclined his head in a mocking bow. "Your servant, mistress. Do forgive me for robbing you of your previous lover."

"You robbed me of a lover, but he was not Sir Miles Russell," she hissed, as Kit took two steps forward.

"Who then? Don't tell me I killed the wrong man?"

"You robbed me of the ability to accept another man's love, of the ability to bestow . . ."

"What are you raving about?" he hissed, gripping her wrist. A shudder rocked his frame at the contact.

"Why are you forever appearing and disappearing in my life? Begone, for I want no more of you!" Jenny's eyes flashed angrily as Kit's fingers increased their pressure and she tried to shake him off without success.

"Do not flatter yourself. I came hither to beg his Majesty's forgiveness. I have spent these past months in self-imposed exile."

With Louise de Brand beside you, Jenny wanted to cry out, but she withheld her words. "Then go indoors and await him, for he has not yet arrived," she snapped, brittle, taut, her arm burning beneath his hand. For an instant a dream image flashed through her brain of a smiling Kit with outstretched arms enfolding her against the firm beating of his heart. With exquisite agony, she tasted the sweetness of his kiss . . .

"Thank you. I intend to do just that," he snapped. When she appeared not to hear, he shook her. "What ails you?" he demanded, drawing her closer with each movement as she remained stiffly unyielding to his words.

Jenny blinked as that beautiful dream dissolved in the mist of his breath swirling before her. "Nothing. Do not let me detain you, my lord."

But now it was he who appeared not to hear. An electrifying wave of emotion shot from his being to hers; Jenny was shocked by the impact. The noisy throng of courtiers dancing in the ballroom, the scrape of fiddles, the laughter, all dissolved within the cold dark night as they stood imprisoned by invisible bonds.

"Christ, you temptress," he snarled, seizing her and welding her body against his.

Jenny nearly swooned with delight, allowing herself to dissolve, growing softer, smaller, blending her soul with his. Kit's hot mouth engulfed hers and she shuddered with ecstasy, allowing him to take all her strength against him. He supported her, pulling her from the step, drawing her with him as he glanced about, seeking seclusion in the black December night . . .

"Mistress Jennet Dunn. Mistress Jennet Dunn."

Together they froze in the shadows of a clipped cypress as

the liveried footman walked the length of the terrace, a paper in his hand.

"Mistress Jennet Dunn is commanded to an immediate audience with their Majesties," he repeated in his sonorous voice as he paced along the terrace and disappeared indoors.

Brief though the interruption was, it served to restore their sanity. Kit thrust Jenny aside, then attempted to smooth her rumpled skirts until she angrily pushed his hands away.

"Thank you, my lord, I'm quite capable of restoring my own dignity," she announced coldly. "Goodnight and goodbye."

Tears pounded in a wave of pain as she turned her back on him and walked blindly up the terrace steps, not stopping until she was inside the brightly lit ballroom.

Queen Catherine, clad in leaf-green brocade, was seated on a gold chair beside the King. The merry dancers had deserted the center of the glittering room, making way for those who were to be received by their Majesties. Blindly Jenny followed the trailing orange silk skirts of the woman before her, keeping a discreet distance as the powdered dowager creakily made a curtsy to the royal pair. Now it was her turn.

"Welcome to our court, Mistress Dunn," said the Queen stiffly, extending her small hand to be kissed.

Jenny was shocked by the expression of cold detachment on Queen Catherine's sallow face.

"I'm most honored, Your Majesty," she mumbled dutifully.

"You are by far the fairest flower in Oxford."

The King's husky compliment brought a flush of color to Jenny's cheeks. It was painful to have to meet his gaze, for the memory of their last meeting was still fresh between them.

"Thank you, Your Majesty."

It was time to step aside. Jenny's knees knocked and her palms were clammy as she stiffly walked away to rejoin the watching throng.

Queen Catherine remained at the ball less than an hour. Her Majesty's departure signaled a riotous change among the guests as several lewd dances by a gaudily dressed party of entertainers set a licentious mood. Jenny's head pounded and her stomach churned as she feigned a shallow smile of amusement as a man, clad in a hair suit, cavorted about the room tapping the ladies' exposed bosoms with a baton strung with bells and scarlet ribbons. Now a fair-faced youth dressed in skin-tight flesh-colored satin sewn with holly leaves strummed a lute in accompaniment to bawdy versions of the most popular Christmas carols. All around her, the courtiers rocked with laughter. Jenny could not see whether Kit found the ditties amusing, for he was eclipsed by a man in a white plumed hat. Closing her eyes, she pictured him in his suit of black velvet decorated with silver braid, the shade contrasting starkly with his long golden hair. The memory of Kit's tight-lipped anger, his cutting scorn, burned painfully within her brain.

"Jenny Wren, how comest thou avoids me?" asked the King when the minstrel lad skipped from the room to uproarious applause. Charles stood beside her, his arm possessive about her slender waist.

"Nay, I do not avoid you, sire. 'Tis not for me to impose my presence upon my sovereign."

" 'Odd's blood, such formality! Can it still be my same 'good wench'?" he asked, his voice husky with laughter.

"I'm the same, perhaps a little more battle-scarred, but still the same."

"Am I not forgiven my indiscretion? I assure you, *I'm* in a forgiving mood this night," he whispered, his breath on Jenny's bare neck as he leaned close to her and kissed her earlobe.

"Did you find Marie satisfying?" Jenny asked, her voice brittle. She had fought the impulse to strike out at him, but had lost the battle.

"Marie?" Charles frowned, puzzled by her question. Then, as enlightenment dawned, he grinned, his hands hot on her shoulders. "Ah, methinks Marie must be the name of yon flirtatious wench who shared my indiscretion."

"You have not seen her since?"

"No. Did you really think I intended to?"

Jenny licked her lips, which were parched and hot. Could she believe him? Or was this just another smooth lie? "I did not know," she said.

"Come, hold yourself not aloof. Every inch of my body throbs to possess you," he confided, pulling her backwards until she was molded to his heated frame. Charles' hands slid about her waist, moving upwards, stopping just a fraction below the swellings of her breasts while the tantalizing heat of his lips slid down her neck and across her bare shoulders.

By now Jenny had become uncomfortably aware of the

other guests who stood watching this public love play with extreme interest. No one seemed in the least surprised by their monarch's open fondling of Mistress Dunn; in fact, they smiled indulgently, virtually applauding his dalliance. The more perceptive guests, however, glanced apprehensively toward Lord Ross, mindful of the duel he had fought over this woman's affections. No man dare challenge his King, yet the naval hero's fiery temper was legend. The observant were rewarded by the blaze of anger lighting his arrogant face, by the white clenched fists he took little pains to hide.

"Charles," Jenny began, attempting to turn within the circle of his arms, but the pressure of his body was too strong. "They're watching."

"Let them watch!" he dismissed with a chuckle. "Barbara too, if she's a mind."

That latter statement suggested that perhaps tonight he had indulged overmuch in the fine mulled wine.

Later, when the musicians paused between pieces, Charles led Jenny forth by the hand, drawing her toward the center of the floor. "My lords, my ladies," he announced, commanding the attention of all present. "Here is my dearest wench returned to the fold. She shall reign over you this night—the fairest mistress of them all. I dub thee Queen of our ball." So saying, Charles took a gold and diamond circlet from a waiting lackey and placed it atop Jenny's shining chestnut curls.

A round of laughter and applause greeted his actions. The guests parted to reveal the small golden chair upon which Queen Catherine had lately sat. Accompanied by much laughter and joking, Jenny was led to this makeshift throne where the King himself seated her. Then Charles lounged beside her and ordered the guests to dance an old English dance, Cuckolds Awry, for his pleasure.

Jenny knew the King had bestowed a great honor upon her by proclaiming her Queen of the ball, for without a doubt her place in his affections was secure after tonight's revelry. But she found no pleasure in the award. The reason behind the changing attitude of his hangers-on had become crystal clear: Charles must have announced beforehand that their questions concerning a certain lady would be answered tonight. To publicly settle her position must have seemed to him the perfect solution to their dispute. At any other time Jenny would have been pleased by Charles' open acknowledgment of his affection for her, but tonight she could think only of Kit. He had stared at her, stunned by the hidden meaning behind Charles' words, correctly interpreting the sly innuendo of the King's statement reflected on every flushed, laughing face. If only the King's public acknowledgment could have happened some other time, some other place, when Kit had not come to seek his King's forgiveness, but was a thousand safe miles away, close-locked in the arms of his foreign love . . .

The dance at an end, the laughing, colorful throng swept the King away from his makeshift throne and, amid much merriment, they proclaimed him Lord of Misrule. Jenny was left alone while they cavorted in the center of the room, most of the gentlemen very much the worse for drink.

"So now at last I have the truth!"

She had no need to look up: Jenny already knew who stood beside her. "Please, don't make a scene," she whispered anxiously, glancing to where the King and his friends donned garlands of greenery and joined hands in a Bacchanalian revel while their ladies clapped and sang a lusty peasant round.

"You belong to him! God in heaven, why did you not tell me? Why did you let me go on believing . . ."

"I tried to tell you Sir Miles meant nothing to me," she defended angrily, still keeping a weather eye on the revel unfolding in the center of the room. "You did not want me. You made that plain often enough. What would you have me do, walk the streets begging bread?"

"Walking the streets would be most appropriate," he hissed in anger, "though I doubt you would be offering bread for sale."

"How dare you!"

"I dare because of what we shared."

"And who was the first to destroy it?"

"You destroyed it by jealousy and . . ."

"I watched you leave the duel in *her* coach. Now tell me she means nothing to you," Jenny challenged, her anger scarcely contained.

"You would have none of me. And I'm no monk," was all he said.

"You have no right to condemn me. The King has been most kind . . ."

"Assuredly, for he has always been generous to his whores."

Like a slap in the face, Kit's words stung painfully. Jenny gasped and she stared at him, finding him livid with passion. "How dare you call me that?"

Kit did not touch her, though his hand snaked out, fingers flexed; then, thinking better of his action, he allowed it to drop lamely at his side. "Think you I have not cause to name you whore? You, who accuse me of infidelity. Not only did you betray me with Russell, but now you slide willingly inside his Majesty's bed. You are a whore and I am well shut of you!"

His final insult carried across the room. The revelers paused in their jollity, quailing somewhat as they beheld their sovereign's stormy face.

"Lord Ross," King Charles' voice rang out through the room, firm, clear, with no trace of intoxication. "Did I hear you insult a lady?"

Boiling with anger, his fists clenched into white balls, Kit spun about to face his King. Despite their past friendship he viewed his monarch as an adversary: a woman, desired by both, had successfully terminated their commitment.

"Forgive me, sire, I spoke naught but the truth."

Charles' dark eyes went black as coals in his swarthy face. "And that is, my dear Lord Ross?"

"I insulted no lady, Your Majesty, I merely gave Mistress Dunn her proper title. She is a whore! And whether you bed her, or I, it does not alter the fact."

A cry of anguish was torn from Jenny's lips. They had both drunk more than their share of wine, despite the fact that their sober anger belied intoxication. Charles had publicly forgiven Kit his past trespasses earlier in the evening, but this foolish, passionate defamation could erase all the captain had gained.

"Stay!" The command cut icily through the hushed room as Kit spun about, heading toward the door. "I will not upset Mistress Dunn further by demanding your apology. Your bad manners are unforgivable, Lord Ross, and though I will not relinquish the pardon I earlier granted you, get you out of my sight. Come not to court again, for you are no longer welcome here."

White-lipped, Kit bowed stiffly toward his angry King. "Thank you, sire, for your generosity. I will remove my offending presence this very night. As ever, Your Majesty retains my abiding loyalty. 'Tis a pity the owning of merchandise should have come between friends. I bid you enjoy what you have purchased in good health.''

The room was stilled with shock as Kit stalked away, his heels clattering on the polished floor. Then, as suddenly as the hush descended, it lifted: a wave of mad chattering erupted as everyone began to discuss the startling scene that had just taken place.

''Come, my sweet, let us retire,'' Charles said after the tumult had died down, his face lined with concern for Jenny's pain. He extended his hand to her. One glance at the stricken expression on her lovely face, at the tight line of white surrounding her pale lips, told him she had lied when she said Kit Ashford meant nothing to her. And though Charles was angered by the man's appalling display of bad manners, he bore him no permanent hard feelings. Ashford had fallen afoul of Jenny's affections; Charles questioned not the reason, he merely applauded the event that left her unspoken for, ready for the claiming.

''Thank you, Charles,'' Jenny whispered, fighting tears. She held her head high, trying not to appear as devastated as she felt. They walked sedately from the ballroom while all present dipped before their passage like rain-dashed flowers. As she left the room, Jenny caught sight of Kit's brother James watching their departure with interest; the expression on his young face sent a wave of fear through her heart. His recent amour with Barbara Palmer had perhaps completed his education in more than one field, for his features expressed great cunning and calculation. Uneasily Jenny looked away from his fixed gaze, focusing instead on the flaming torches at the entrance to the building, swirling like living beings in the icy December wind.

''My dearest love, be reasonable,'' Charles cried in exasperation as he battled with Jenny before the roaring hearth inside the Dean's lodging at Christ Church. It was almost a week since the grand ball where he had publicly acknowledged her as his own. ''A man provides for his mistress. And he provides for their children. It is accepted. There is no shame to it.''

Stubbornly Jenny listened to his speech. What once she would have been thrilled to hear—that he was giving her a modest London home in Chancery Lane—now filled her with distaste. Too often these past days had Kit's insult echoed through her head. A whore! And that is what Charles was making her. She was not his wife; they did not even live together in the commonly acknowledged manner. He serviced her when the whim took him, and for that he sought to provide her sustenance. "What other name can you give to my current profession? I'm purchasing your generosity with the only means available . . ."

"Enough!" Angrily Charles leaped from his chair to pace the room. "You cannot go on living above a haberdashery in Swann Alley. It is settled. You will take a house within the city and a country retreat—the manor of Hursthampton in Buckinghamshire lies vacant no longer."

"No, I can't. I won't be labeled whore!"

"Do you not love me? Has that changed?"

"No."

"Then why? Because of that churlish seaman, must you continually harp on the word *whore*? If you will, I've many whores, and so does every man at this court. I assure you, your former lover has certainly had his share of the aforementioned ladies."

Jenny found no humor in his speech. "Do you not reward loyal men who fought for your father's cause?"

"Yes, I've rewarded many. Why do you ask?"

"My father fought at Naseby. A pension for his service would be more acceptable to me."

Charles stooped to fondle the silky head of his spaniel bitch dozing before the hearth. What matter if the house was bequeathed in recompense for the long-ago loyalties of an unknown cavalier? If a remnant of Jenny's conscience was salved by providing a pension, she would be far more amenable to his demands. He would grant her request.

"A pension it shall be," he declared generously, his wide mouth lifting in a smile. "We must not quarrel. I abhor hysterical confrontations. Had I thought so simple a solution would be pleasing, I would not have waited for you to suggest it."

"Will the house be mine?"

"Of course. Most women demand grand titles to accompany their gifts." He smiled at her, pleased to find no guile upon her fair face. "Should our relationship bear fruit . . . but we shall see, we shall see."

Amiable once again, Charles sauntered to her side to plant

a kiss on her smooth brow. He stood before the hearth, warming his backside at the blaze.

"Will you visit me there?"

"When I have time," he agreed. "In the meantime you shall be free to do what you wish. If we should ever decide we do not care for each other in quite the same fashion, I promise that you will not find yourself without a roof."

A smile of pleasure lit Jenny's pale face. "Thank you, Your Majesty, you are most kind."

Charles put his hands on her shoulders and he drew her from her chair until her head rested against his chest. "Poor little Jenny Wren. Now that you have your nest, will you fly there today?"

"I should like to see Hursthampton as soon as possible." She closed her eyes, enjoying the warm security of his arms; security was often fleeting within the royal embrace. "But if you command, I shall stay in Oxford."

"Command?" He clucked in mock annoyance as he raised her pretty face. "I ask nothing you do not wish to give," he reminded sternly. "If you do not find pleasure in my court, you are free to travel to your manor. When winter's done and we return to London, you'll have another home to manage. Do you think you will be too busy to see me?"

"Never that," she assured, straining up to meet his lips. Today there was a new gentleness to their relationship, something they had not shared before.

"A coach is at your disposal." He paused, a gentle smile softening his face, "Remember, the courtiers mean you no lasting insult. You must not take their bawdy ways to heart."

Inwardly Jenny quailed at his reminder. The hurting scene, played like a theatrical tragedy before the entire court, would stay with her forever; the knowing smiles of courtiers passing on the street revived her humiliation. And this morning someone had boldly pinned a bawdy cartoon on her door. To Jenny's surprise, when she showed the coarse sketch to Charles, he had laughed heartily.

Now he retrieved the crumpled paper from the hearth and smoothed out the sketch of two donkeys gazing starry-eyed into each other's faces. The male, of startling anatomical proportions, wore a crown, the female, a pendant about her voluptuous bosom; there was little doubt who the figures were intended to represent. "The wit merely makes a play of your name, sweet," he assured, grinning at the short Latin verse accompanying the sketch. "Besides, the artist flatters me considerably." After a final glance at the crude sketch, he consigned the vulgarity to the flames.

"I find it insulting."

"In another mood, so might I," he agreed honestly. "Today it is amusing. Go then, Jenny Wren, and see how well you like your gift."

A glimmer of watery sunshine broke through the clouds as Jenny hastened along the damp Oxford street. Her heart soared at the thought of having a home of her own. And though perhaps the King's agreement to reward her for her father's loyalty was merely to humor her, the arrangement made her feel less ashamed.

When Jenny entered the dense purple shadows surrounding the cathedral, a young man, clad in a full brown cloak, emerged from a doorway on the opposite side of the street; he headed for the King's lodging, a crisp parchment cracking in his sleeve.

Charles glanced up from reading a dispatch when his unexpected visitor was announced. Young Ashford was not unknown to him, nor was the rumor suggesting he had been warming Barbara's bed of late. "I am told you have important information for me," Charles said, his dark brows quizzical.

James Ashford bowed, his smooth young face set in grim lines. "Yes, but Your Majesty may not be pleased to see what I carry," he began, withdrawing the letter from his cuff.

Charles took the proffered page and held it close to the candleflame, for on this overcast afternoon little light entered his study. He read and reread the message, hardly able to accept what he was reading. At last he looked up.

"Why are you anxious to expose your brother's part in a plot?"

James blinked at the King's unexpected question. "Merely out of loyalty to Your Majesty," he said hastily. "Loyalty to one's King and country supersedes all family loyalties."

"How did a letter implicating your brother and Captain Honoré de Brand come into your possession?"

"I cannot say, sire."

"A Popish plot to supplant my person with that of my brother—by curious coincidence, his name is also James." Charles stopped speaking and began to pace the paneled study, reviewing the alarming discovery. ''Are you sure this is not a forgery?'' he asked at length.

''I should know my own brother's hand.''

''Aye, that you should. But why? Kit was ever a true friend. Not a year ago he covered himself with glory in my name. I don't understand it.''

''Your Majesty, though perhaps I should not . . .'' James paused, allowing a few moments for his King's attention to rivet upon him, in the exact manner Barbara had suggested. ''There is the matter of Mistress Dunn's affections. I need not remind you my brother has killed one man because of her. None but a fool would dare openly challenge his King. Traitor he may be, but my brother is no fool.''

''Surely not that,'' Charles said softly, turning aside. He stared through the window at the bare trees edging the guadrangle. It was not possible Ashford sought to supplant him on the throne merely out of jealousy.

''You also dismissed him from court in disgrace,'' James reminded, warming to his task.

''Court never meant much to Kit.''

''People change, Your Majesty.''

Charles turned to survey the young man before him. ''And what do you stand to gain if your brother's convicted?''

James was prepared, the King's questions no longer disconcerting him. 'Naturally I would inherit the title and the estates.''

''Nay, lad, forfeited lands pass to the crown,'' Charles reminded him with a cynical smile.

''But, Your Majesty, surely the discloser of such a fiendish scheme to harm your royal person would be granted a boon,'' James ventured, in exactly the manner in which Barbara had schooled him this morning.

''This woman mentioned here, but not námed. Whom do you suppose she is?''

James looked down at the floor, studying the Turkey rug. ''Your Majesty, it pains me to suggest . . .''

The piercing look Charles shot him made James quail. ''Suggest not this unnamed female be Mistress Dunn,'' he warned sternly.

''The thought had crossed my mind, Your Majesty.''

''Then allow it to uncross it.''

''Yes, sire.'' James attempted to banish the growing unease he felt. There was a new mood of hostility radiating from his sovereign and he regretted ever mentioning that cursed woman's name. Lovely Barbara had guessed wrong when she suggested Mistress Dunn was in disfavor and the King would be only too glad of an excuse to put her away from him. Though James had a vested interest in disposing of his older brother, Mistress Dunn's downfall would have been merely to placate Barbara.

"Who else knows of this missive?"

He started to say no one, but James thought better of the lie. "My Lady Castlemaine's secretary showed it to his mistress."

"And where does that leave you? I was not aware you were so intimately acquainted with Lady Castlemaine's household." The flush burnishing James' smooth cheeks told Charles all he wanted to know about Barbara's relationship with him.

"I'll have this evidence studied by men far wiser than we. Do not leave Oxford without permission."

Charles watched his young visitor walking briskly across the quadrangle, his brown cloak flapping about his sturdy legs as he rounded the corner of the building. Could he take comfort from the fact that perhaps this was but another of Barbara's jealous schemes to defeat a rival, or had the contents of the letter a far more ominous meaning?

Chapter 23

The manor of Hursthampton was situated in a pleasant green valley at the foot of the beech-clad Chilterns. Nestled in a mossy hollow, surrounded by neglected lawns and flower borders, the manor house of honey-colored stone slumbered peacefully in the fading gold of a winter afternoon. Tangled woods spread in all directions, bare branches etched like black lace against the sunset sky.

The small Elizabethan manor house comprised four major bedrooms, three reception rooms opening off a square, oak-paneled hall, and the usual servants' quarters. Though blazing fires had been lit in an effort to dispel the damp, cold winter air seeped through every nook and cranny of the old house, great drafts billowing the heavy velvet curtains and puffing vast clouds of smoke down the cavernous chimneys.

Jenny inspected the supply cupboards by candlelight; she also directed the staff of three maids and two menservants to sweep down the cobwebs festooning every corner. So excited was she about her new acquisition that she could hardly wait for daylight, when she would be able to explore more fully. Despite the formidable task facing her, she was determined to turn Hursthampton Manor into the house of her dreams.

During the following two weeks the weather did its best to discourage her from taking up residence in her new home. Rain, sleet, and snow swept across the valley, blanketing the surrounding countryside in a permanent gray veil. A veritable gale blew through the ill-fitting casements and the constantly smoking hearths filled the air with motes of soot. Had she not been determined to mold this house to her liking, Jenny would have packed her trunks and returned to Oxford. Haughty Lady Castlemaine would not have endured a single night in this drafty old house; yet, inconvenient and shabby though Hursthampton was, Jenny had already fallen under its spell. Besides, she thought with a wry smile, when one has nowhere else to go, one is capable of enduring much torment.

The weather being inclement, it was unlikely Charles would

visit Hursthampton. Jenny missed his company, but she did not regret leaving Oxford. Here, in the heart of the country, she was untouched by the courtiers' offensive humor. Within the wild Buckinghamshire woodlands she had regained her peace of mind.

During a sunny respite in the bitter January weather, Jenny decided to inspect the boundaries of her estate. Two horses had been provided for her riding pleasure, an ill-tempered chestnut stallion, far too spirited for a novice, and a gentle bay mare. Jenny told the groom to saddle the mare, and while she waited the pretty, shy creature nuzzled her hand in greeting.

As Jenny careened over the spongy ground, the cold wind snatched her chestnut hair from its coils, flapping it in a cloud about her face. Invigorated by the rushing wind, she boldly urged her mare to greater speed, galloping toward the woodland.

It was deathly quiet inside the wood; the mare's hooves echoed in the silence. In the distance a woodpecker rapped crystal clear in the still winter air. On either side tall beeches glimmered silver gray in the weak sunlight as Jenny guided her mount along the unfamiliar path. A sudden flash of yellow, followed by a high, tinkling song, made her heart leap as she startled a pair of goldfinches perched on a nearby ash. The air was brackish, damp with the mild decay of winter woods.

Jenny dismounted. Here there were no raucous street vendors, no rattling coach wheels, no clatter of people walking along cobbled streets, naught but the peace of the January countryside.

"Don't be afraid mistress, I mean you no harm."

Shock stiffened every hair on Jenny's head as she spun about, aware of the suffocating pounding of her heart as a large, black-bearded man emerged from the brush.

"You're trespassing on my land."

The man touched his forehead. By his coarse clothing he appeared to be a servant; his gray woolen shirt, hanging loose on his broad frame, was ripped at the shoulder; his matching breeches, cut full like a seaman's slops, were begrimed with mire. On his large feet he wore down-at-the-heel leather shoes without buckles. Shabby and disheveled though he was, he did not appear to be dangerous.

"What be the name of this manor, mistress?" he asked, his

dark eyes scanning her rich clothing and the good lines of her mount—the mare seemed of particular interest to him.

"Hursthampton."

"And be it far from the river?"

"Less than five miles."

While he spoke, the man edged closer, until his rough hands were within inches of the horse's bridle. Jenny made a grab for the reins, but he was too fast for her; the stranger sent her sprawling into a stand of beech saplings.

"Nay, mistress, though 'tis not my intention to hurt ye, my master has sore need of your mount. His poor feet be walked raw."

Hot with anger, Jenny picked herself up. A branch had scratched her cheek and her dignity was sorely ruffled. "How dare you lay a hand on my horse? I'll have you arrested. My servants are but a few paces back." Even to her own ears the lie sounded lame.

The man smiled scornfully, cocking his shaggy head to listen for hoofbeats; only the unbroken silence of the wood swept about them. "Be they fairy folk, mistress? For they make no sound," he mocked.

Jenny's eyes glittered with tears of frustration. She was completely at this ruffian's mercy: had he a mind to ravish her, there would be little hindrance to the crime. "Who is your master that he directs you to steal a lady's horse?" she demanded angrily as she stepped toward him. Her bravado earned her a cuff across the shoulder.

"Stay back! I don't want to harm thee," the man warned menacingly. "The little mare will likely find her way home. We need her only till we reach the river."

"Don't you dare take my horse!"

Like a flash of lightning his fist snaked out and caught Jenny a glancing blow on the side of the head; she succumbed in a burst of flashing light, gasping as brackish earth filled her nose and mouth. From a muffled distance she heard the dull thump of hooves as the robber trotted away. The wretch! So sure was he of escape, he did not even gallop. Hot, angry tears filled her eyes while the throbbing pain in her head became unbearable. The last thing Jenny remembered was reaching for a branch to support herself when the wood tilted drunkenly; with a startled cry she fell sideways, the trampled bracken soft beneath her aching head.

Sleet was sifting through the foliage when Jenny regained

consciousness. The silent wood was cowled in shadow, heavy slate-gray clouds visible through a canopy of black skeletal branches. Her head ached and she had a lump on her temple where she had struck the tree. During the hour the temperature had dropped considerably as the winter wind moaned eerily among the trees, depositing flurries of seedlike particles on her head. Jenny shivered with cold. She had no idea how far she had ridden from the house, for here the woodland was so dense that Hursthampton was hidden from view.

Jenny retraced her steps along the narrow path, fighting recurring waves of giddiness. Suddenly, through the thinning trees, she saw Hursthampton's twisted brick chimneys, black against the leaden sky. And the welcome sight filled her with joy. Then the dull thud of approaching hoofbeats alerted her to danger. Giving no thought to thorn scratches, she took shelter in a tangled thicket of shrubs. When she tentatively stirred, trying to see who rode through the woods at such breakneck speed, she found the reckless horseman bearing down on her. And though she hastily drew back, her flame-bright riding habit made her an easily spotted quarry.

"Hold! Here she is!" The man yelled to a companion who rode some distance back on a bareboned carthorse.

Jenny was aware of a large figure enveloped in a dark cloak emerging through the sleet-filled gloom. Blindly pummeling her assailant, she fought hard against capture; the man's superior strength soon prevailed. Blurred vision and a blinding headache were her rewards for fighting so desperately.

"Christ, sweetheart, what ails you?" the man muttered, pulling her against him as she stumbled.

As if coming from a great distance, the question finally registered on her numb mind. Sweetheart! How so such intimate address from a desperate criminal? That this was the master of he who had stolen her horse she did not doubt, but why the concern in his gruff voice? Jenny focused her tear-glazed eyes on the man's broad, dark bulk.

"Who are you?" she demanded hoarsely, finding her throat gone dry.

"Has it been so long you don't remember me?" he demanded, tension in his voice.

Jenny found herself scooped up and deposited ungently in the saddle; the mare whickered with pleasure at the sight of her new mistress.

"A few minutes more and we'll be indoors. Be sure to tell your servants we're friends, won't you, Jenny."

Amid a swirl of sharp blown sleet a familiar face emerged; Jenny gasped in shock, her breath choking as she identified Kit Ashford as the desperate stranger. But this hard man was unlike the Kit she had known! Several days growth of gold-brown beard obscured his obstinate chin, while his golden hair was tangled beneath a misshapen hat that partially obscured his face. "You," she gasped, as a sickening bolt of emotion rocked her body.

"Aye, 'tis me. Pray treat me to no condemnation until we're warm and dry. And remember—order your servants to admit us."

Gone was the concern she had heard a few moments before, or perhaps those tender words had been part of an unreal world of pain. Kit had rescued her solely to obtain a night's lodging.

"And if I don't?" Jenny challenged angrily, attempting to sit upright in the saddle and avoid his supportive arm stretched across the mare's back.

"I warrant you'll regret it," he warned gruffly.

Jenny said no more: it was too hard to concentrate with her throbbing head, made worse by the jogging movement of the horse.

Though the maids were surprised by the unexpected appearance of these disheveled male guests, they accepted Jenny's assurances that the gentlemen were to be made welcome.

After a reviving cup of wine and a slice of buttered seed cake, Jenny felt more able to question Kit. Why was he stealing horses like a common thief? Why, indeed, was he wandering the Buckinghamshire countryside, unkempt, his fine clothing soiled and torn?

"Well, ask, I know you well enough to sense questions buzzing through your head like a hive of bees," Kit said after a long silence while he warmed himself before the hearth. His manservant had gone to assist the staff in preparing his master's bath.

"Your man hit me and he stole my horse," Jenny accused bitterly. "Why do you allow him to rampage through the countryside?"

"My dear Mistress Dunn, had I any idea the man would assault you. I'd never have allowed him out of my sight. He merely went in search of a horse, for no longer could I tramp the miles in these foolish court shoes. I apologize for Amyot's zeal. He's but a loyal West country man, devoted to his master.''

''I've a lump the size of a goose egg. I'm damp, cold, and likely I've caught my death . . .''

''Forgive me if I do not weep. I, on the other hand, am fresh bathed, well fed, and admirably attired,'' Kit mocked, indicating with a sweeping gesture his torn wine velvet coat and breeches.

Jenny swallowed and bit her lower lip. She had not been prepared for his mockery. ''What do you want?''

''A meal and a night's lodging.''

''You shall have it, providing you promise to be gone by daybreak. And you've still not explained yourself.''

''Before you stands a wanted felon with a price on his head.''

Jenny gasped, her hand going to her mouth in shock. ''How can that be?''

''I thought perhaps you might know. My dear brother James and delightful Barbara Palmer have produced damning evidence connecting me with a Popish plot to overthrow his Majesty. James was ever a sniveling, two-faced whelp!''

''It's not true! Oh, say it's not true!''

''Nay, you should know me better than that. Though I may quarrel with him, I'm ever loyal to Charles Stuart. I doubt even he believes the accusation wholeheartedly, yet 'tis said of late the King believes whatever Lady Castlemaine tells him. True or untrue, a warrant has been issued for my arrest. Mayhap I was a fool to run, but understanding the odds against receiving a fair hearing, I chose not to wait until the paper was served. My good friend Bab May warned me to leave at once. A troop of his Majesty's Horse pursues me. But, I trust, for your sweet sake, Mistress Dunn, I've managed to give them the slip.''

Fear for Kit's safety rocked her body. Jenny stared at him, overcome with an overwhelming wave of love. Shocked by her unexpected reaction, she straightened in her chair, strengthening her resolve to remain unmoved. ''I hope so too, my lord. My Lady Castlemaine has never been overfond of me. Should they find you beneath my roof, likely I too would be accused of treason.'' She paused, taking a deep breath before she asked, ''Besides, why should you think I'd be overjoyed to see you after your despicable conduct at their Majesties' ball?''

Her withering tone cut him to the quick. Kit turned abruptly on his heel and strode to the window. Beyond the pane the parkland whitened under the onslaught of sleet. ''Can you ever forgive me for so blackening your name?'' he asked at last, his voice gruff with emotion. '',Fool that I am as usual I allowed passion to overrule my head. The loss of the privilege to attend court, even earning the King's great displeasure, wounds me not as sore as the grief I've caused you.''

Tears welled in Jenny's eyes. She had not expected to hear him utter such words of remorse. Yet, sweet as it was to hear his apology, no words on earth could erase the humiliation she had suffered because of those few minutes of passionate anger, nor could words erase the knowing smiles and snickers of Charles' mocking courtiers. ''Your apology can not change what took place,'' she said coldly, longing to go to him, to accept his embrace, his kiss. But Kit offered neither.

''I understand how you feel.''

''How can you? No man can understand the humiliation a woman endures when she is publicly branded whore.''

Kit turned from the window, his face tense with pain; the candlelight cast slanting shadows over his head, plunging his eyes into darkness so that Jenny could not see their expression.

''I'm aware how greatly humiliated you were by my actions. My apologies, madam, for such churlish behavior. I entreat you to speak in my favor when next you . . . see . . . the King.''

A mocking tone had crept into Kit's voice and Jenny quailed beneath his scorn. She well knew what word he intended. Angrily she stood, clasping her temple as her head reeled with the sudden movement.

''As I promised, you shall have food, Lord Ross. And perchance one of my servants can replace your damaged shoes. Now, by your leave, I must retire to my chamber, for my head aches.''

''Nay, let it not be said I drove you from your fireside. So grand a manor this is for a seamstress late of Swann Alley. A reward, I trust, for your unstinting service to our King.''

''Damn you!'' Jenny cried, her face white. ''Came you here to beg charity, or to mock me?''

''Neither, sweet Jenny, for though I heard your reward

was the ancient manor of Hursthampton, I did not know in whose woods we rested. Granted, I came this way seeking you, for I owed you an apology before fleeing into permanent exile. The fact that you're not gracious enough to accept it detracts not at all from the spirit in which it is made.''

She glared at him, her fists clenched in anger. ''I hate you!''

Stiffly Kit inclined his head. ''Admittedly, I'm a poor substitute for the King.'' With this he turned on his heel and stalked toward the door.

Pain, passion, despair wrenched Jenny's body; mutely she opened her mouth to call him back; she reached out to him. God knows there was anger aplenty between them, pain and betrayal too. Kit had come to apologize, a deed a man of such inborn pride found difficult to perform, and, by delaying his flight long enough to see her, he had risked his life. After Kit left Hursthampton, she might never set eyes on him again! The chilling realization restored her sanity. Be he in France, or in the Tower, from this time forward Kit Ashford would be inaccessible to her. And though she had told King Charles she loved him, that emotion was nothing beside her passion for this hot-tempered sea captain.

''Stay,'' she croaked, finding her voice, choking on the growing lump in her throat.

Kit paused in the gloomy hall, gripping the lavishly carved newel posts of overflowing urns of fruit. When Jenny said no more, he took a decisive step on the stair.

''Please, stay,'' she repeated, tears streaming down her face.

He turned slowly, his face eclipsed by shadow. ''Stay, Mistress Dunn, I, who have insulted you beyond reason, who even now puts your life in gravest danger?''

''Oh, Kit, mock me not. I care not about the consequences.''

''Care not,'' he repeated infuriatingly as he turned on the bottom stair. ''What if your royal lover should ride forth tonight? You would care then, by God, you'd care . . .''

''He won't come.''

A cold dead silence enveloped the room. Like two marble statues they stood, frozen in separate attitudes of injured pride. Jenny decided to extend no further invitations to him; if Kit chose not to heed her plea that was his prerogative.

''You do not ask this out of pity for a fugitive?''

''Nay, the only pity I feel is for myself,'' she said huskily, trying to master her grief. "I want you to stay because, despite all that's gone between us, I love you still. Would you turn your back on me now that I'm humbled and disarmed?"

Kit strode into the room and swept her in his arms, pressing her against the torment of his prickly beard as he kissed her savagely. "Am I to interpret love for hate? Did you not so vow less than five minutes ago?" he whispered when their lips parted.

"I love you and I also hate you," she cried with maddening illogic. "Oh, damn you, must I beg you to stay?"

"Nay, Jenny, wild horses could not drag me from this house—nor even a troop of his Majesty's Horse. For all this time I've ached to hear you say those sweet words. All the anger, the misunderstanding between us, lies in the past. For this one final night let us come together absolved of everything."

Amyot poked his tousled head about the banister on the upper floor, reluctant to disturb his master at so intimate a moment. "Your bath's ready, master," he called gruffly.

"Come, then, my lord, allow me to be your handmaiden," Jenny said with quickened heartbeat.

Kit chuckled in delight as they ascended the stairs, arms entwined about each other's waists.

Amyot, surprised by the sight of his master and the fiery woman he had robbed embracing like lovers, stood uncertain on the upper landing.

"I will not need you tonight, Amyot. Go below and sup. You have well earned your meal."

Amyot bowed, humor tugging the corners of his mouth. "The bath, my lord?" he queried, not meeting his master's eyes, knowing full well who was to assist his lusty lord with his ablutions.

"My hostess will make the necessary arrangements," Kit said.

The oak-paneled rose bedchamber shone bright with leaping firelight. When Kit closed the heavy door behind him, he sealed them in their own private world, safe from the elements and from their own stormy past.

"First I insist my hostess avail herself of the bath water," Kit decided, moving the airer of warming towels from in front of the fire to allow the heat to spread throughout the room. "Come, no modesty, mistress, surely it is the least you can do to appease the starved lusts of a condemned man."

Jenny laughed at Kit's throaty invitation, a thrill of pleasure rippling the length of her body. "Because of you I am damp and cold and I ache like the devil. As a penance, my lord, you must soap my back."

"Agreed."

Jenny's hands trembled as she fumbled with the fastening of her habit. Kit lounged on the four-poster bed, making no offer to help her undress. When at last the garment was unfastened, she allowed it to fall on the rush matting; her undergarments followed. Jenny was revealed in her nakedness, her perfect body golden as a divine image in the fireglow. No longer could Kit keep his distance: she tormented, she tantalized—and he had waited so long.

The unexpected touch of his warm hands on her back made Jenny shudder, the reaction multiplying swiftly as his demanding lips swept a burning passage over her shoulders, her neck, and the soft white swelling of her breasts.

Abruptly Kit drew away, an apologetic smile on his face. "Forgive me, I'm too hasty. No woman relishes three days' growth of beard. Make haste with your bath."

Jenny tested the bath water with her toe: the copper tub kept the water at scalding temperatures, a fact she discovered last week, much to her own discomfort. How wonderful it was to lie back in the hot water, to feel her muscles relax, each bruise, each ache, dissolving in the soothing warmth. Yet with Kit's admiring gaze on her, Jenny was unable to relax totally, too disturbed was she by the excitement rippling along her spine . . .

"Now, madam, if I may." Kit leaned over her with a soaped sponge, gently laving her flesh, pinkened by the hot water. Great foamy white trickles of scented soap slid over her full breasts, crowning the rose-pink nipples with halos of white. He found the sight so arousing that it grew difficult to concentrate; soon, he even stopped trying.

His gentle touch was heaven. Jenny leaned back against the bath's high back with a sigh of contentment and closed her eyes. Tendrils of chestnut hair had escaped their pinnings and curled in a damp fringe across her brow while a glow of happiness brightened her cheeks where her thick dark lashes curved invitingly against the soft skin. Several times Kit drew back on his haunches to admire her. And though she pretended ignorance, Jenny observed his action through half-closed eyes. His tanned face, grizzled with new beard and scarred by wayward branches, was still so breathtakingly handsome that she trembled.

Now it was Kit's turn to bathe. Enveloped in a warm, voluminous towel, Jenny stood before the blazing hearth while he undressed. She shuddered with emotion when he cast aside his shirt and coat to reveal his heavily muscled torso. From the matted gold pelt on his chest Jenny's gaze followed the darkened line as it descended to his flat, taut belly and beyond. Unabashed, she gazed in rapture at his manhood, rousing beneath her scrutiny. So long had they been estranged that they had recklessly squandered the precious time they might have shared. Jenny blinked rapidly to clear the tears that hazed her vision. Fool, would she spoil this final night of bliss by melancholy thoughts?

Kit stepped into the bath. "Come, woman, soap me well," he commanded, lying back in the water.

Jenny did as she was bid, thrilling as her hands slid over his smooth muscular body, awakening a host of precious and arousing memories.

"I can manage that by myself."

Jenny laid aside the razor and bowls Amyot had set out to use upon his master. "Do you not trust me? Think you I might slit your throat?"

"Perhaps. Not on purpose, yet on that score you have not my complete faith."

When he was finished shaving, Jenny nestled against the smooth warmth of his face, so fragrantly arousing.

"Never did I dream we would share this night," he confided huskily as he stroked her cheek, his blue eyes dark with emotion.

"Nor I. Pray God it won't be the last."

"We must not dwell on the future. We'll live only for these stolen hours."

The bath pushed aside, they stood close wrapped in each other's arms, the tingling warmth of their flesh accelerated by their increasing passion. As if by mutual agreement, they moved to the bed, which beckoned invitingly beneath its gold-fringed canopy of rose brocade.

While sleet tinkled against the pane, Kit held Jenny in his arms, showering her responsive flesh with heated kisses. Passion swept them away in the winter night, suspending them in time and place. Kit traced his hot tongue over the silken length of her body. His hungering mouth was a living being as he sought the utmost response from her flesh, until she ached for assuasion. He buried his face in her chestnut hair, spread in shimmering waves over the goosedown pillows; he tangled his hands, his mouth, in the scented sweetness, breathing love words she had waited an eternity to hear. Ecstasy rapidly gave way to wild abandon as her own hands fired him to hitherto unknown limits, sending a tumult of blood roaring like an inferno through his veins. Her breasts, rising through the chestnut silk like rose-crowned mountains, made him moan to possess them. His imprisoning hands were not gentle, yet Jenny reveled in the delightful pain as the waves of tingling excitement mounted. Fire shot from her breasts to her loins, wounding like arrows as the frenzy of his expert caresses increased. Her own hands sought and captured the embodiment of his desire. In awe she beheld the tremoring strength of his manhood, more powerful than she remembered, full and thick, a blazing inferno of need.

At last, having reached the limits of their endurance and returned a dozen times, Kit spread her silken thighs, sweeping her smooth flesh with hot kisses as he positioned her on the bed. A sob was torn from Jenny's bruised mouth as the hot searing tip of his body met hers; she strained to absorb him, aching, yearning to feel him deep inside her. Kit thrust, slowly, the movement completed in a burst of heat that brought a scream of delight from her trembling lips. No longer did she have control over her body, as swiftly, completely, he satisfied the terrible longing that had wracked her soul this bitter time apart. Each thrust, each movement, swelled their desire, until they wept together in the intensity of passion. Kit swept Jenny to a place of fire-sparked ecstasy until she begged him to make that final shattering thrust and bring the sweet fulfillment she longed to know. Grim as death, a fierce and primeval passion possessed her as Kit thrust his magnificent body, pulsing as one with her own. Jenny was given no time to think, or breathe, as she was consumed by the fire of his passionate love.

Like battered warriors they gradually returned to their surroundings. Bruised, aching with terrible fulfillment, they clasped each other in the silent firelit room.

"And if it must be so, sweetheart, your love was well worth dying for," Kit whispered huskily, grief pounding behind his tender words.

"Nay, tempt not the fates," Jenny whispered brokenly,

holding him tight, desperate to keep him beside her.

"I love you. Whatever happens, always remember that."

"Oh, Kit, darling, why were we not more sensible? All this time we've been estranged . . . not loving . . . quarreling . . ."

He caught on his warm tongue the salt tears trickling down her cheeks.

"Don't weep. Love me, again. Oh, love me, Jenny, until it be morrow."

And smiling through her tears, she fastened her hands in his long golden hair and drew his beloved face to hers. With exquisite tenderness Jenny kissed his lean cheeks, his high-bridged nose, his hot lips that need only quirk in that distinctive grin to set her heart racing. She would remember him thus; whatever pain, or tragedy, lay before them, tonight would stay forever in her mind.

"Aye, we'll love the night away. And for this once dawn won't come until I will it. Together we . . . ."

But he silenced her passionate raving with a burning kiss, welding his freshly aroused body to hers. In the sweet taste of his mouth, as their breaths merged and his hunger robbed her of reason, Jenny forgot the rest of her impossible expectation.

The fire had dwindled to a bed of orange coals when next she woke. Again and again during that cold winter night they had repledged their love. Now Kit lay beside her, sleeping a sleep of exhaustion and content. She smiled tearfully as she saw a new vulnerability on his hard face, disarmed by sleep. How wonderful it would be if this magical night need never end. But she knew it must, and soon, by the gray light edging the windows. The January dawn came late to Buckingham-shire, but it always came. Alas, those foolish ravings she had mouthed last night could never come true. Jenny burrowed in the soft goosedown mattress, warm from the heat of their bodies, and she sighed with contentment as she stretched beside her lover. She would not sleep away the precious remainder of their time; instead she would gaze upon him, attempting to fix his image in her mind, for the treasured picture might need to last for eternity.

Jenny sank into a drowsy reverie, only to be roused a few minutes later by steps thundering up the stair. The servant, Amyot, raced toward their room, shouting to arouse his master as he ran.

"My lord! My lord! Be up. His Majesty's Horse are at the stables. Rouse ye before it's too late!"

Kit leaped to a sitting position, his blue eyes ice pale in the murky light.

"I'm coming, Amyot," he shouted in reply.

Leaping from the bed, he seized the heap of clothing Jenny had obtained from her manservant and frenziedly donned the coarse garments.

"What will you do?" Jenny cried, her eyes wide with fear. Much commotion sounded outside, jingling trappings, horses' hooves, and the excited shouts of many soldiers drifting to their room.

"Get out of here as fast as possible."

"You can't take a horse!" Jenny cried in alarm, as she lifted the heavy curtains to look into the stableyard. "The stables are alive with them! Quick, come this way."

Mystified, but trusting her completely, Kit grabbed a patched wool cloak and, still attempting to thrust his feet into the scuffed leather boots provided by his benefactor, he followed her.

Amyot was waiting nervously outside the door, eager for his master's command. "Will we fight for it?" he asked hopefully, his dark eyes gleaming with the thought of battle.

"No! Come quick. There's a secret way out," Jenny ordered tersely.

Her hasty command damped Amyot's spirit, but he followed obediently as she ran to the huge carved linen cupboard at the end of the corridor. Wrenching open the heavy door, Jenny pitched aside folded sheets and coverlets until the lower shelves of the massive oak chest were bare. Amyot carried a lantern, and Jenny seized the flickering light and shone it inside the chest to reveal a cut-out panel in the cupboard back. "At sometime in the past the owners kept a priest," she informed them as she desperately tried to work the mechanism that released this trapdoor. "The passage leads into the woods. From there you can make your way to the river."

"You're a blessed angel," Kit whispered in her ear, setting to with a will to help her release the door. Between them they levered aside the square to reveal a yawning black cavern from which exuded a blast of stale, icy air.

"Hurry," she hissed when he turned toward her.

"I cannot leave you to their mercy."

"You must. They know I'm here. If I disappear 'twill only make them more suspicious."

"By the Christ, you don't know what lecherous bastards they be," Kit growled, as he pushed Amyot ahead of him into the tunnel. He knew they were losing precious time, yet he could not leave Jenny unprotected to battle the collective desire of his Majesty's Horse.

Jenny thumped his chest, growing desperate as he stood unmoving, his face outlined by the garish lantern glow. "You've no choice! Would you condemn us all to the Tower? Get you gone, you great fool!" Urging him through the opening she pushed him again, fear making her voice taut. "Get you gone! What good are you to me dead?"

After a final, suffocating embrace, Kit reluctantly bid her goodbye. Then he was gone, his footsteps echoing along the stone-flagged tunnel as he ran in pursuit of Amyot, who had plunged ahead with the lantern.

Too desperate was Jenny to be fully aware of what she did; a few minutes later she was surprised to find she had returned the linens to their rightful place, successfully camouflaging the priest hole. She was securing the door latch when she heard the deafening pounding of fists on the outside door. Amid rough shouts of "Open in the name of the King!" Jenny raced back to the rose chamber, her way lighted by the feeble gray light of winter dawn.

As she lay shivering in bed, finding the mattress cold after their hasty departure, she heard the heavy tramp of many booted feet on the stair. Casting about the room one final time, she prayed no telltale item had been overlooked. The servant to whom Kit had given his torn finery in exchange for the man's second best suit had been cautioned to hide the garments if soldiers came; she could only hope the man had done as he was bid.

When the door burst open, Jenny leaped in surprise beneath the embroidered counterpane, feigning great bewilderment at the sight of a half dozen booted and spurred soldiers invading her bedroom.

"What's the meaning of this?" she demanded, her voice quavering with fright, not entirely feigned.

"My apologies, Mistress Dunn. We are seeking a dangerous fugitive."

"Here, in my chamber?"

The soldier's commanding officer had not even the decency

to appear flustered. "From the stories I've heard bandied
about, your chamber would be the perfect place to begin," he
said, a sneer on his arrogant features. He was young, hawk-
nosed and thin-faced, a dark mustache outlining his spare lips
in the fashion of his King.

"How dare you!"

Jenny's indignant explosion was lost on him as he ordered
his men to begin searching the cupboards, behind the curtains, and under the bed. Out of the corner of her eye Jenny
noticed Kit's shaving supplies, forgotten beside the hearth.
Her heart pitched. Desperate to distract the haughty captain
from pursuing his search, she swallowed her pride and allowed the bedcovers to slip down to reveal her breasts, barely
concealed by her flimsy silk night-rail.

"Captain, may I ask the meaning of this intrusion? It is
not usual for my sleep to be disturbed by a troop of soldiers."

His gaze roaming appreciatively over the provocative sight,
the young captain sauntered toward the bed. Clicking his heels,
the man bowed courteously as he reached for her hand. Jenny
allowed him to kiss her fingers, well aware of his devouring
gaze riveted on her rising bosom.

"Forgive me, mistress, my zeal overcame my manners. I
am Captain Lennet Keane of his Majesty's Horse. I have a
warrant for the arrest of a dangerous fugitive known to be
heading this way. I seek Christopher Ashford, Lord Ross, late
of his Majesty's fleet." Jenny gasped at the mention of that
name, and the young Captain smiled, his eyes moving briefly
to her pretty face. "You do know him then!"

Jenny coyly drew the bedcovers about her nakedness, while
still allowing her appreciative visitor an enticing glimpse of
flesh.

"Yes, he's known to me," she admitted quietly. "I've not
seen him for some time."

The captain smiled again but made no comment: there were
few who had not heard a recounting of the stormy scene that
took place at their Majesties' Christmas ball. "The blackguard plots to take his Majesty's life. We have orders to shoot
him on sight."

This time Jenny's sharp intake of breath was genuine. How
much head start had Kit gained on these soldiers? The path to
the woods was long, the river another few miles further;
without a horse, the journey would take several hours.

"You astound me, Captain. Why think you this man would seek me out?"

"I do not know, mistress. I know only that on several occasions he asked directions to Hursthampton. We have that information on good authority."

A plan to buy Kit enough time to reach the river was already surging through her brain. Jenny licked her lips invitingly and allowed another inch of bedcover to slip down. "Captain, I won't lie to you. I had a message from Lord Ross. Two days ago he wrote asking me to see him."

"Give it to me," the Captain ordered, outstretching his hand.

"Alas, I burned the offensive missive," she explained, eyes downcast. "I have no wish to reopen old wounds."

"When did he say he would arrive?"

"He did not."

Aggravation drew the man's thin black brows together. Still awaiting their captain's command, the troopers stood in awkward attitudes about the room, their search temporarily abandoned. "Very well, mistress, we shall await his arrival."

At the time no thought beyond the urgent need to delay Kit's pursuers crossed Jenny's mind. It was only later, when she was putting the finishing touches to her toilette while the captain and his hungry men supped below, that she wondered what to do next. Given too many days under her roof, Captain Lennet Keane might forget he was a gentleman; Jenny was the first to admit her background precluded noble treatment. And though the idea made her shudder with disgust, she knew what she must do to ensure Kit's safety: by encouraging the young captain's amorous attentions she could put precious hours of distance between her beloved and the pursuing troop of His Majesty's Horse.

By eleven the trees became visible as the morning mist lifted from the woods. Jenny voiced a silent prayer that Kit had reached the river and taken a boat under cover of the fog. So far she had entertained the King's captain with chitchat and an innocent game of backgammon; lately, however, he had begun to show signs of discontent.

Suddenly dashing the backgammon board to the floor, Captain Keane leaned toward her, his hot breath wafting against her cheek. "Madam, a man's yard is poorly satisfied by parlor games," he stated bluntly as he came directly to the point. "The games I seek with thee take place within the bedchamber."

"Captain!" Jenny's indignant protest was cut short as he grabbed her, welding his mouth to hers; at the same time he plunged his hand inside her bodice, greedily ravaging her breasts. Made furious by his boldness, Jenny delivered a resounding slap on his smooth cheek. "I'll decide when you may paw me, Captain."

His hazel eyes narrowed at her icy words. " 'Tis I who represent the law within this house," he reminded, his mouth an even line beneath the slim mustache. "An' it be my wish, I could claim you here on the floorboards."

At that point Jenny was saved from uttering a second retort by the sudden appearance of a soldier holding a bundle of wine-colored cloth. "Captain Keane," the man said, his face flushed, "the woman lied."

Jenny's hand flew to her mouth in alarm: the soldier was carrying Kit's suit.

Captain Keane bounded to his feet and seized the soiled garments; after a perfunctory inspection he flung the bundle aside. "You lying vixen! You seek to keep us here on our arses while yon blackguard flees." Jenny stared wide-eyed at his livid face, frightened by the cruelty in his narrow eyes.

"Perchance we can still catch him. He can't have gone far," the trooper tendered hopefully, not anxious to have his captain roused to a towering rage.

But Captain Keane was not open to helpful suggestions. Like a vise, his long fingers closed about Jenny's slender wrist. "So, your lover has not been here to service you in many a moon," he sneered, wrenching her toward him. "Do you think I'm fool enough to swallow your lies? You'll pay well for this, you slut. On your back. God knows how pretty you'll be when you've serviced all my men . . ."

He accompanied his explosive threat with a harsh slap.

"Captain." A second man came to the door, remembering to salute his angry commander only when he rounded his searing gaze on him. "We've word a boatman was hired a few miles downstream. Could it be the traitor?"

Giving a final shake that jarred gathering tears from her eyes, the captain released Jenny with an oath of rage. "A boat! By the Christ, how long has the bastard been flown?"

"The men could be saddled and on the road in five minutes, Captain."

"Aye, order it then." Spinning about, the young captain glared at Jenny, beside himself with thwarted passion. "As for you, you little whore, when I return you'll pay well for your deception—better than you've paid any other man you've bedded." Leaving this threat hanging in the silent room, Captain Keane seized his cloak and gauntlets from the side table and charged after his men, not sparing Jenny a backward glance.

Through the diamond-paned casement she watched them gallop forth in a shower of mud, thudding over the lawns, their jingling trappings echoing in the frosty air. She voiced a desperate prayer for Kit's safety. Pray God the little time she had bought him was enough, for she was going to have to pay right well for her purchase. A shudder passed through her body as she recalled the blazing anger in the young captain's face; when he returned her payment would begin!

Jenny paced the room, her trembling hands clasped tightly before her. Only a fool sat awaiting punishment! She would saddle her mare and ride away from Hursthampton. One glance at the stableyard changed her mind; anticipating her action, Captain Keane had left three troopers to guard the horses. A foray to the several entrances of the manor revealed a similar guard. There was still the priest's hole, yet Jenny did not credit that plan with much success: by the time she emerged in the woodland, the winter day would have waned; her chances of finding her way to safety with approaching night were considerably slim.

An hour later clattering hooves sounded outside. In a few minutes either a disappointed or triumphant Captain Keane would swagger through the doorway. Was it a self-destructive urge that had made her wait, declining all reckless plans of escape? She should be apprehensive as she awaited the soldiers' arrival, yet Jenny's strong intuition prepared her not for fear.

One of the maids knocked timidly on the open door. "Mistress," the woman began, her eyes round with surprise, her lips trembling with the portent of her message.

"Yes, what is it?" Tense, Jenny awaited the woman's news, praying her worst fears were not founded.

"There's . . . oh, mistress!" The woman's face broke into a tearful smile of delight. "His Majesty the King waits below."

Reeling as if from a hammer blow, Jenny's heart leaped

high before resuming its frantic pounding. "Thank you, Abby, I'll come downstairs," she said, trying to erase the quaver from her voice. Once again Charles Stuart had saved her from disaster. And the tears stinging her eyes came from many emotions as she smoothed her hair in place and followed the maid downstairs to the oak-paneled hall.

Chapter 24

Pale sunlight broke through the heavy clouds, momentarily sparking the windows with diamond flashes before disappearing as the lowering sky closed in on Chancery Lane. Jenny moved from the drawing room window and picked up her cloak.

In February, as fear of the plague abated, the court had returned to the city. Charles, growing more possessive since his public acknowledgment of her new status in life, had insisted Jenny travel with the others: a modest house in Chancery Lane, close by St. John's Head tavern, had been her reward. Though pleased with her London home, Jenny longed to return to peaceful Hursthampton. It had been nearly seven months since Kit had fled the King's soldiers in that gray winter dawn. To her knowledge he had not been arrested, so she assumed he had gone into exile. The Papist plot, in which he had been named a conspirator, had come to naught.

James Ashford strove to become a member of the glittering circle of courtiers who shared the King's confidence. Forever striving toward this goal, he boldly confiscated the thoroughbreds from his brother's stable, presenting the very finest horseflesh to the Crown. Yet to James' immense disappointment, his sovereign did not reciprocate by awarding him either the title he coveted or the vast family estate in Ireland. Jenny hoped Charles' lack of generosity revealed his doubts about Kit's treachery, perhaps suggesting he awaited his subject's own explanation of the condemning evidence before passing final judgment.

Since her return to London, Jenny's social activities had been few, for she declined those invitations the King did not specifically order her to keep. Her lack of enthusiasm for court life annoyed him, but so far Charles had kept his ill humor to himself. Lately she was unable to respond to her royal lover, since memories of Kit robbed her of passion. Good-natured, and patient as usual, Charles bore with her, suspecting the ill news of Lord Ross's part in the Papist plot

359

and his subsequent flight abroad as the reason for her sudden coldness.

Jenny went to the kitchen and asked the cook for a basket of provisions to take to Swann Alley; Pet would likely be in need of cheer on this gray day. Soon after her return to London Jenny had visited her aunt, not knowing what to expect from a district so heavily devastated by plague.

The Alley had become a sad, forlorn place where blades of grass sprouted between the cobbles. Many businesses were empty, their owners dead. The houses stood dismal and neglected, with great slivers of paint peeling from their woodwork; broken windows had not been replaced and sagging shutters swung crazily on broken hinges, creaking in the wind. The breath of life had departed Swann Alley.

To her shock, Jenny found that only her aunt and the youngest apprentice had survived, and Pet so changed she would have passed her on the street without recognizing her: haggard, her flesh sagging in great folds, Pet looked twenty years older, while constant depression stole her pride until she scuffed about, ill kept and slovenly. The thriving haberdashery was no longer open for business. Pet supported herself by taking in sewing, eking out a meager existence as best she could, virtually destitute without her indulgent husband. Each time Jenny visited the shop, she hoped for a miraculous reversal in Pet's outlook, but she realized her expectations were highly improbable.

Thunder boomed in the distance, echoing through the streets like cannon fire; the first drops of rain splashed cool against her face as Jenny rounded the corner of Swann Alley. In the wicker basket beneath her cloak she carried butter, eggs, a haunch of pork, and a loaf of bread. The King provided her with a modest pension in reward for her unknown father's loyal service to his crown, and though he considered the allowance a joke, in an effort to salvage her trampled pride Jenny forced him to stick by his promise. She had even returned Charles' gifts of clothing and jewelry until he informed her that he was vastly displeased by her actions. Jenny suspected her lack of passion toward him had dampened Charles' ardor for, of late, these lavish gifts had stopped coming; given time, his visits to Chancery Lane might stop altogether. As the warm summer days advanced, their meetings became fewer and fewer.

"Pet, are you home?" Jenny called with forced cheerfulness, pushing open the creaking front door to the now deserted shop. Dust lay thick on everything.

"Is that you, Jenny?"

Pet emerged from the inner room, her once fashionable gown hanging like a shapeless sack on her gaunt frame; blue circles shadowed her eyes, her small mouth assuming a perpetual droop; wildly disarrayed, Pet's blond hair sprouted about her head like a gorse bush. "You didn't come last week," she accused, taking the wicker basket and lifting the cover. Pet sniffed the basket's contents and whined in disappointment. "There are no sweetmeats. You know how I crave them. And me too poor to even put bread on the table."

Jenny swallowed her rising anger. Ever was Pet an ungrateful soul. Even now, in these dire straits, her complaints were readily forthcoming. "I'd no sweetmeats on hand. Maybe next time," Jenny said, fighting to keep her temper.

Pet sniffed and dabbed her eyes, the mannerism a jarring reminder of her dead sister's perpetual sniffles. "Don't forget."

"I won't."

Jenny moved after Pet's shuffling figure, unlooping the fastening of her cloak as she went. Strewn everywhere were half-sewn garments, trimmings, and tall cones of thread. Little Fred squatted cross-legged in the middle of the room stitching an emerald-green skirt with silver braid; though the youngest and seemingly the frailest of Will Dunn's apprentices, he alone had survived the plague.

"How are you feeling today?" Jenny asked, knowing before she asked that Pet would not feel well.

"My head aches more each day. I tell you, I'm in dire need of a potticary. And me so poor I've barely enough money for food."

Jenny allowed her aunt's whine to go unremarked upon. By the look of the cluttered workroom, since her last visit Pet had completed few orders. "When you finish these garments you'll have money enough for food," she assured, brushing aside a clutter of fabric remnants to make room to perch on the low worktable. Her remark was met with a vicious glare.

"It's all very well for you to talk, my fine lady, you who bed with the King himself, but what about poor me? Enough money for food indeed!" Pet flounced about, viciously kicking at the heaped fabric on the floor. "I could use more nimble fingers to help sew these orders to get that money, but there's no help forthcoming there. Oh, no, now you're too grand by far to lift a needle to help me.''

Begrudgingly Pet offered Jenny a cup of flat ale. Far from being able to cheer her aunt, Jenny found herself becoming depressed by Pet's complaints. She had already asked herself a dozen times why she had been foolish enough to come here today. Only twice before had her aunt's mood even approached pleasantness. Yet, unlovely as Pet was, Jenny felt deeply sorry for her; formerly so recklessly extravagant, she had been dealt a crushing blow by poverty; alone, unloved, she had lost her looks, until she had become merely pitiful.

''When you're feeling better, I'd love to have you dine with me,'' Jenny suggested with a supreme effort at cheeriness. For once her words elicited a spark of pleasure.

''Would you really invite me to your grand house?'' Pet's raddled face was a study of surprise as a dawning smile lifted the corners of her bitter mouth and brought life to her dull eyes. ''Me, so poor, so shabby . . . oh, niece, you're uncommon kind!''

Jenny gripped Pet's hand warmly, pleased to have penetrated the mask of self-pity that had become Pet's daily mien. ''It would please me greatly to have you as my guest. We'll celebrate with a fresh baked cake decorated with marchpane. You can wear your best gown.''

''Aye, I've many a good gown put aside.'' The pleasure dimmed in Pet's face, eagerness dying like a flickering flame. ''What think you I'll look like now in my finery?'' she asked sourly, glancing down at her gaunt hips. '' 'Twill look no better than a winding sheet.''

''Nay, we'll alter the gown to fit,'' Jenny offered with a sigh.

''Mayhap, if I've a moment's time to call my own. All this work still to be sewn. If I live to be a hundred, I'll never be done. And that Fred, the lazy little sod, sews only when I'm breathing down his neck.''

At the mention of his name, Fred's eyes flickered upward; then he bent to his task with renewed effort, made nervous by Pet's angry glare.

''I'll see if I can find an extra seamstress to aid you,'' Jenny offered, slithering from the cutting table. She had already overstayed her welcome.

''What, one of those lazy sluts! I'm lucky if I get an hour's work from them and then they demand to sup at my expense.''

Pet's irate voice drifted after her as Jenny walked through the dusty shop. "I'll find a good honest wench,'' she offered. "Now I must be on my way, 'tis growing late.''

"Oh, yes, be on your way, leave your poor aunt to cope by herself. I suppose his Majesty's coming for a grand dinner party.''

Jenny allowed the spiteful remark to pass. She gave Pet an affectionate parting hug. Steeling herself against the tirade of complaints she knew from experience to expect, Jenny opened the door and a puff of rain-washed air swept inside. The streets gleamed with moisture after the evening shower.

"Mind you, there's only one extra mouth to feed now,'' Pet said, glancing at the sky. "We had a half dozen lads at one time. Tim's dead, you know . . . all his family died. Young Lenny ran away . . . gone back to Islington so I've heard . . .''

Jenny left her aunt muttering to herself on the doorstep. As she rounded the corner, leaving the gloomy, lifeless alley behind, a shudder of relief passed through her body. Each time she arrived at her aunt's house, Jenny hoped Pet would have managed to gather the scattered threads of her life; each time she departed, it was with the reinforced knowledge that such a reversal was becoming very remote.

The rain brought premature twilight to the summer's day; brilliant silver bordered the heavy black clouds building above St. Paul's, stark and ominous against a saffron sky. Refreshed by the brief shower, the air, which had been an oppressive haze, blew cool against Jenny's hot face. She quickened her steps, anxious to be back in Chancery Lane.

At the corner of St. Michael's Alley Jenny paused, awaiting the slow passage of a beer wagon. As she stepped into the street, she discovered her cloak was snagged. Spinning about, Jenny beheld a man standing in the shadows, his foot planted firmly on the hem of her cloak. By his shabby clothing and furtive actions she suspected he was a thief. Quickly she wrenched on the fabric, letting out an exclamation of anger when the man refused to budge. "Get off my garment,'' she snapped. "If you think to rob me, you've chosen ill, for I carry naught but an empty basket.''

To her horror, while she spoke several accomplices emerged

from shadowed doorways along the alley. Jenny ripped open her cloak, dropping it to the cobbles. She dashed into the street, but a dozen rough hands stopped her flight. Her shrill screams for help were swiftly silenced by a dirty hand that clamped like a vise about her mouth. There was something vaguely familiar about this band of thieves; then, as the first man emerged from the shadows, Jenny understood why. A numb chill stilled her heart as his cloak slid aside to reveal a swarthy gypsy face scarred across the cheek by a two-inch weal.

"You've become quite the lady, *gorgio*," Manuel sneered, his thick lips curled in scorn as he looked her up and down. "But I find no fault with it—I've always enjoyed the finer things in life."

His ragged companions chuckled at his statement as they pulled Jenny deep into the murky cobbled alley. She struggled desperately, kicking out at her captors in a vain effort to be free. When the confining hand moved slightly, she sank her teeth into filthy flesh. The man yelped in pained surprise before he cuffed her soundly about the head. Her senses reeled and a strange taste filled her mouth and nose as Jenny sagged to the cobbles. From a great distance issued a string of vile curses before Manuel's voice dissolved into a world of black unconsciousness.

When Jenny opened her eyes, she was being half-carried, half-dragged along a narrow, fetid street. She struggled to right herself, demanding of her dim-faced captor, "Where am I? Where are you taking me?"

"You're in Alsatia. Here all are friends," Manuel replied gruffly. He retrieved Jenny from his companion and took her weight against his body.

Mounting fear dulled all hope of rescue. Alsatia was known throughout the city as a refuge of thieves and cutthroats; the law did not enter here unless accompanied by a company of musketeers, for every fetid tenement, every squalid alley, presented a refuge for the lawless. Whole mobs of irate slum dwellers, brandishing whatever weapons came to hand, would run down the alleys in armed support of one of their own.

Scam . . . Gyves . . . the names of Manuel's hideous companions in crime throbbed through Jenny's dazed brain as they headed toward a den of squalor amid the crumbling despair of the Alsatia tenements.

Darkness masked the squalid building the men entered.

Imprisoned in their midst, Jenny stumbled up a flight of rickety stairs, fouled by excrement and ascutter with rats; she gagged as a warm furry body rushed across her foot. Seemingly oblivious to their horrid surroundings, the men climbed ever higher, until they reached the attic of this decaying structure. Manuel thrust open the door and two gypsy guards leaped to their feet, alert to danger.

Manuel spoke to the men in Romany before turning to Jenny. "You're home, *gorgio*. This is my house."

So deep in shock was she over Manuel's unexpected appearance, over her abduction to this stinking hovel, that Jenny's voice was stilled. Soon perhaps, she would wake from this nightmare to discover she lay in her own bed between clean linen sheets, but, try as she might, when she closed her eyes, Jenny failed to awaken in her bedchamber in Chancery Lane.

"What do you intend to do with me?" she demanded, after a few minutes, her faculties gradually returning.

Manuel shrugged and he handed her a cup of hot soup. "I shall do much as I did with you before, *gorgio*," he said, a wide grin lifting his thick lips to reveal even white teeth.

"Things are different now."

"How so? My feelings are unchanged. Are you saying you care naught for me?" he asked in a menacing tone, his dark face within inches of her own.

Turned coward by his nearness, Jenny was unable to meet his eyes. "Now I'm no longer a penniless wench in need of a shelter," she explained lamely.

A harsh sigh of relief rasped in his throat. "You had me worried, *gorgio*. I've only to look at you to know that. Because you ran off with some rich bastard who decked you fine as a duchess for the privilege of dipping in the well doesn't alter things. Since the plague, I've learned to endure much torment."

While he ate his soup by the flickering light of three candle stubs, Manuel explained how he had accumulated sufficient wealth to purchase this ancient dwelling. The ghoulish light of dancing flames was a suitable accompaniment to the horrendous story he revealed.

"While you lay abed between clean sheets, I wrestled the dying for their dearest possessions."

Jenny expressed no outward shock at his revelation. She kept telling herself none of this was real: the smell, the filth, the scuttering rat sounds behind the wainscot, all belonged to a hideous nightmare.

"Gold rings, watches, money. Dame Plague proved an able accomplice by felling them in the streets. Sometimes I must needs crack a few heads to be first on the scene," he paused, intent on her pale, expressionless face. "There were whole houses of them. Doors standing open, not one soul left to defend their goods." Manuel leaned forward, his dark-skinned hand capturing hers. "And through all that hell, I dreamed of finding you, *gorgio*. At first I thought you'd joined the angels. Then Scam saw you in Cornhill. Each day I've waited. I'd nearly given up hope until today, and there you stood, lovely as I remembered . . . even lovelier." His hand encircled hers in a crushing grip.

"Why did you seek me?" Jenny asked, freezing at his touch. She could virtually read his mind, for his eyes gleamed hot with desire.

"We're bound to each other for all time. Our destinies follow the same path," he explained gruffly. "Just as the prophecy foretold, disaster befell my people. All but this handful of scum are dead. Within a week of our wedding, Marta was gone. Rosa too. Plague struck the camp like a lightning bolt. But because my mission was not yet fulfilled, I was spared . . . you too, *gorgio*. As Rosa prophesied, I shall lead my people west."

"How?"

"Always I've craved to be a gentleman, and at last that dream is reality. When I've sold my goods, we'll take to the road. Do you remember Cornwall with its wild coast? 'Tis where we're headed."

"No!"

Horrified by his statement, Jenny snatched her hand from his. Near insanity gleamed in Manuel's green eyes, replacing even the heat of desire as, like one possessed, he breathed life into his cherished dream.

"Yes!"

"You cannot take me to Cornwall against my will. I'll be missed," she protested, trying to pull free as the waiting gypsy guard came forward and pinioned her in the chair. Impatiently Manuel motioned for the man to release her.

"Not today, *gorgio*—soon. Here, have some more soup. We've plenty of time to reacquaint ourselves. Listen, and pass not judgment until you've heard it all."

Warily Jenny eyed the burly gypsy guard who still watched her like a hawk, prepared for her to make a bid for freedom; at his waist hung a gleaming dagger; a pistol butt poked menacingly from the top of his belt.

"I won't go with you, but if it pleases you, you can tell me your plan."

Manuel's face was grim as he looked at her bleak face, but the cherished dream fermenting within his brain soon dispelled his ill humor. "Listen, and listen well. Not only did I wrestle black, putrid corpses, foul with their own juices, not only did I enter poor homes to relieve the dying of their worries, but many of valuable possessions as well. Furniture, paintings, gold, wine, jewelry—this house is crammed with my reward for those months of hell. Better than that, in this drawer is my entry into the society that spat on me."

Manuel unlocked a drawer in the scarred oaken table and withdrew a sheaf of papers; he spread them before her in the dim candlelight.

"What are they?"

"These, my feeble-minded *gorgio* bitch, are the keys to the world of respectability. Never again will people curse me as a thieving gypsy dog. I'm Samuel Fowler, brother of Squire Richard Fowler . . . see this." Manuel pointed to a faded name in careful script. "Two good Cornishmen were gasping their last when I helped them home. One died on me—the other, well, he had no earthly use for these."

Jenny swallowed. To further Manuel's dream the unknown Cornishman had probably been hastened on his way. "But how can you pretend to be he?" she demanded scornfully, thinking his fantasies had finally overcome his reason.

"Because, you fool *gorgio*, brother Samuel was gone from Cornwall for most of his adult days. I helped them write a will of sorts. These papers identify me as Squire Fowler's London brother; his rings, his watch, his clothes, all are carefully stored. Once I've disposed of the rest of my goods, we'll journey to Fowler's Cove to occupy his fine house. 'Tis as I've always dreamed."

Jenny picked up the Last Will and Testament of Richard Fowler, Esq. in which he bequeathed all his wordly possessions to his beloved brother, Samuel.

"Where's the real Samuel Fowler?"

Manuel shrugged. "Who knows? I tossed him on a death cart. Since then I've been he."

"You're mad!"

Eyes narrowed in anger, he scooped up the documents and replaced them in the drawer. As his dark hands moved among the papers, Jenny noticed two rings on his right hand—an unconscious bequest from the dead.

"Be that as it may, pretty one, but you're going to share my insanity," he growled, turning the key in the drawer.

"You must release me at once. If it's money you want . . ."

"Money!" The word was an explosion. "Money!" Leaning over her, Manuel gripped her forearms until the flesh ached. "Nay, 'tis *you* I want. Forever your body torments me. No other woman will do. But that's the price one pays when fate has ordained the future. I'm Squire Fowler and you're my lady wife!"

A commotion at the door averted his burning gaze from her face as Jenny squirmed beneath his punishing grip, trying to pry his fingers apart. "You're hurting me!"

Abruptly he released her. "I intend to hurt you later, but in a far more pleasant place," he promised with a dawning grin. While he spoke Manuel slid his hands down her neck, his fingers rough and hot against her flesh.

"There's a man below, Manuel; he says he's come for the cherrywood furniture," announced a wiry young gypsy with a patch over his left eye.

"All right, I'm coming." Manuel turned to Jenny, who had risen from the table, preparing to follow him. "You stay here. Much as I enjoy your company, I don't want anyone to see you. Forgiving I may be, but your fat bastard protector still lives and breathes within this city and the loss of a prize like you will cause him more than a few sleepless nights."

Two gypsy bodyguards stepped forward to obey Manuel's sharp Romany command. Unused as she was to hearing the language, at first Jenny did not recognize the order to bind her; while Manuel ran downstairs she was tied to a chair and a gag stuffed in her mouth.

The squalor of Alsatia's tenements was revealed in hideous detail during the following weeks. The gypsy band fenced stolen merchandise, dealt in smuggled cargoes, and murdered to order. And all the while, Manuel's hoard of silver mounted as he methodically liquidated his ill-gotten gains. Like ghouls, he and his friends had stripped corpses and forced entry into undefended homes, all the while boldly defying the killer stalking London's streets. Jenny had no idea how Manuel had avoided the plague; perhaps there was much truth in his belief that destiny shaped his future. Daily he regaled her with stories about their dream existence near the crashing seas of remotest Cornwall. The house to which he lay claim stood atop a headland overlooking the sea; the dying squire had even provided a vivid description of the vicinity, unwittingly helping his dishonest friend to claim his fortune.

July and August crawled by, the days and nights interminable in the close attic prison. Only by dark and in his company did Manuel allow Jenny to leave the garret. Often she spent the day planning her escape, only to find no opportunity to enact the plan as he walked beside her, his strong arms clasped about her body.

But though Manuel controlled her physical being, and though he frequently availed himself of her body, he was unable to recapture the pleasure they had known.

"Why are you so damnably cold to me?" he demanded in a menacing growl. Moonlight flooding through the window outlined his broad frame as he stood, his shirt in his hands.

Jenny turned her face to the peeling plaster wall. "Things between us are different now."

"That's no answer," he raged, leaping toward her.

Roughly Jenny was dragged to a sitting position, then shaken until her teeth rattled and her hair spilled in a tangled mane about her shoulders.

"Manuel, stop! Will you shake me senseless?" she cried, her head buzzing with the constant movement.

"Why won't you love me? Tell me? Why?"

An answer came to her dazed mind, but Jenny was too prudent to utter it: Manuel would not understand that she loved another; nor would he understand that after months of being a favorite of the King of England his rough and ready ways left much to be desired. And most of all, he would not understand how she cringed at the thought of joining her body with his.

"Struck dumb are you?" he cried, cuffing her about the head. "Well, dumb or not, cold or not, you're still mine!" He backed away and reached for the leather bottle of cheap wine that always stood on the table. "Does your heart beat fast for your fine lover? I could easily learn his name and club him one dark night when he's mincing home from his lady-love. I could—but I won't. And don't tell me who he is. I've come too far now to spoil things by being caught slitting some rich bastard's throat. Though, by God, sometimes the ache is on me, my hands long to feel his throat . . .''

Jenny stared dully at him, realizing he was no longer speaking; Manuel had tilted the leather bottle and drained it. Nowadays the bottle was his constant companion. Once, in a rare moment of vulnerability, he had confided he needed the soothing forgetfulness induced by wine to dull the hideous images of those plague-infested nights when he had followed the heaped death carts. Wine also dulled the loathsome cry of ''Bring out your dead'' that echoed through his brain when he lay down to sleep.

''Don't worry. I don't intend to reveal his name.''

Manuel wiped his mouth. ''Do you love him still? Are you seeking to protect him from me?''

''Nay, even you're not fool enough to . . .'' Jenny swallowed down the scornful words, aware she was revealing too much. Luckily Manuel had turned his attention to a second bottle and was not heeding her speech.

''When we leave London you'll love me then,'' he said before he tilted the full bottle to his lips. ''There are too many memories here. Once summer's past we'll leave.''

Summer was almost past. Jenny leaned on the broken window ledge and stared disconsolately through the begrimed pane into the narrow street below. A brisk wind, suggestive of autumn, fluttered debris against the buildings. Oh, Charles, why did you not care enough to seek me out? she thought unfairly, watching the limping beggars stealing from their lairs to take up positions about the city's streets. There was little chance of even the King finding her here.

''Can you see the flames?'' asked Gimpy, the guard of the day, as he limped to the window.

''What flames?''

''The fire blazing yonder. It be St. Magnus church,'' Gimpy informed her importantly, pushing her aside as he took up his position at the grimy window. ''Are you blind? Look, the flames are going higher.''

Jenny opened the window and stuck her head outside; in the distance great belching orange flames and clouds of black smoke puffed heavenward. The church of St. Magnus the Martyr stood at the bottom of Fish Street Hill leading to London Bridge; it was the route she had taken on her flight from Annie Strength-in-the-Lord Wooten's bawdy house. The revived memory sent a cold shudder through her body.

"Naw, don't be afraid, we's miles away," Gimpy assured her with a rare flash of kindness. "Didn't want you to miss it, that's all. Everyone's talking about the fire. Biggest we've had lately. What with this wind blowing, 'twill be lucky if it don't burn down a few more of them churches before it's over." Gimpy chuckled in high delight at the thought of churches blazing on the Lord's Day, for he was ever an irreverent soul. "Manuel says to tell yer he'll be back tomorrer. Got 'im some important business afoot." Gimpy limped from the room, leaving Jenny by herself. The smell of smoke blew in the strong east wind that was creaking shutters and signs as it buffeted along the narrow street. The threat of fire was ever-present in this predominantly timber-built city, whose old, medieval dwellings were well seasoned; after the second dry summer in succession, the buildings would burn like tinder.

Amid the warning peals of St. Paul's bell, frightened citizens piled their goods into carts and fled to the river. The fire was already blazing an inferno along the Thameside wharves and warehouses, where tallow and other combustibles were stored; it soon advanced to the surrounding rookeries, leaving thousands homeless. Throughout Monday and Tuesday, the great fire raged on. Cornhill eventually succumbed to the flames, which burned the Exchange. Jenny wondered if Pet was safe, but from her prison room she could offer her aunt no more than prayers. The holocaust spread to great St. Paul's itself, and a molten stream of lead from the melting roof poured down Ludgate Hill, while huge blocks of Caen stone were hurled through the air like cannonballs in the intense heat. By night the lurid sky gleamed bright as day, the strong wind blowing heat from the inferno through the city streets already gray with lung-choking smoke as the fire raged unchecked.

On Wednesday, Manuel left about his nefarious business before dawn; Jenny assumed he was looting houses in the path of the fire. Afraid she would attempt escape because of the general confusion in the city streets, he ordered Jenny bound until he returned.

Before noon Gimpy brought her the startling news that the fire had leaped the Fleet River after consuming Baynard's Castle, a sister fortress to the great tower and guardian of the western approach to the city. Whitefriar's, the correct name

for this teeming slum popularly known as Alsatia, lay directly
in the flames' path! Anxious to learn if they were in immediate danger, Gimpy ran into the street, leaving Jenny alone.

The morning sky was dark with smoke, and an acrid stench
filtered through the ill-fitting window as Jenny waited for his
return, uneasy in her bonds.

''Gimpy!'' she screamed in alarm as wide tongues of flame
appeared above the tiled roof of the house at the corner of the
street. No answering steps came. With great effort, she rocked
her chair, inch by inch, toward the windows, sure the thumping noise would bring Gimpy to investigate; to her surprise
Jenny completed her journey unhindered. Hysterical people
were pouring from their homes, milling below. A chain of
firefighters hauled buckets of water to quench the flames, but
after such an extended drought, the water level in the cisterns
was low. Gangs of men fought to create fire breaks by pulling
down dwellings, their efforts defeated by the fierce wind,
which had shifted direction in the night. Great sheets of
windborne flame effortlessly leaped the space, rapidly ignit-
ing neighboring dwellings and consuming them like a raven-
ing beast.

For what seemed like hours Jenny waited for Gimpy's
return. Gradually the horrible truth dawned on her: Gimpy
was not coming back. She was bound inside this house in the
path of the flames. Most of the goods sold, Manuel had rented
the filthy lower stories to tenants who paid by the night;
surely someone would hear her cries for help. But whether
they heard or not, nobody came to investigate Jenny's screams.

Sweat beaded clammy on her brow as she tried to loosen
the bonds on her hands. Frantically working to the accompaniment of the sounds of rising panic in the street, Jenny
sawed the rope across a jagged splinter on the chair seat,
working it back and forth, slowly fraying the hemp. At last
the remaining thread broke.

Tears of relief filled her eyes as she freed her hands and
smashed open the window. While she had been sawing her
bonds, the room had grown hot and stifling as if the air was
being sucked from the building. Jenny levered herself up, the
chair a confining prison as she leaned over the sill, screaming
for help from the milling crowd below. Roaring flames licked
the house across the street. The firefighters flung buckets of
water on the blaze, but their efforts were in vain as, with a
great roar, the building became a glowing pillar of flame.

Jenny yelled as hard as she could, coughing and choking on the lung-filling smoke. Desperation made her suddenly strong as she smashed the chair against the walls until its rickety legs collapsed. Sobbing from her exertions, she slithered out of the rope-tressed seat; fortunately, Gimpy had not tied her securely, being anxious to investigate the spread of the Great Fire. Belching smoke and flame shot skywards, and Jenny went rigid with fear as she realized the house was alight. The crowd of sweating firefighters turned their attentions to this side of the street, recklessly smashing door lintels and hacking timbers in a desperate effort to create a fire break.

"Help me! Help me!" Jenny screamed, her lungs bursting.

A young man glanced up; at first, through the belching smoke, he could not see her; then, with an excited gesture, he waved toward the garret window where she hung, coughing and gasping for air. For a few inactive minutes the crowd shouted excitedly, pondering the best method to rescue the trapped woman, while the roaring flames swept upward, consuming the rickety stairs. At last, deciding on a course of action, someone yelled for Jenny to climb to the roof and cross the leads to the neighboring building. The prospect was terrifying, yet as she glanced toward the door and saw an orange glow advancing up the stairwell, she knew it was her only hope.

The window was so small that she had to struggle to squeeze through it; several times intense heat and choking smoke drove her back. Yelling encouragement, Jenny's rescuer waved a shovel, indicating an area between the adjoining roofs sheltered from the flames by the overhanging eaves. Jenny pulled her skirts high and knotted them about her waist, uncaring about the revealing display provided for the onlookers. The leads were hot against her bare feet. So terrifying was the view below that she steeled herself not to look down into the milling, noisy crowd. At last she reached safety, where she crouched trembling under the eaves; sweat ran in rivers down her face and trickled down her sides; her legs were weak and shaking.

"Come down, wench, have a care," bellowed the young Atlas. "Tarry not, the fire be gaining on you."

A rusting drainpipe lay within reach. Jenny gripped the warm metal and swung herself down to a projecting roof several feet below. Her heart hammering as if it would leap from her body, she slid another few feet, her palms speared by shards of peeling paint.

"Jump! I'll catch you!"

Like a voice from heaven, the young man still directed her. Blinking to clear her burning eyes, Jenny gritted her teeth and grasped hold of the descending drain; on this final descent she ripped her palms and cried out in agonizing pain. She landed on an overhang above a door, trying to see her rescuer through the billowing smoke. Flame exploded to her right. Blurred, inhuman voices roared through her ears, the words drowned by the roar of the encroaching fire. Suddenly, through the blackness, a pair of massive hands reached up; blindly Jenny gripped them, sobs of relief torn from her burning throat as she swung to safety and tumbled in a heap on the cobbles.

"Be ye burned, mistress?" asked a concerned voice. The crowd pressed close as she struggled to her feet, shaking her head, tears streaking her begrimed cheeks.

"No, not burned," she croaked, barely able to talk. Someone thrust a flask of ale into her hands and she gulped the soothing beverage, hardly able to swallow for the ache in her throat.

"Get you away, the timbers be going!"

The crowd scattered.

Jenny grabbed hold of the young man's hand as he swept her to safety. Looking like a blackamore, he grinned down at her, his teeth white in his soot-darkened face, his lips unnaturally red. "Were you alone?" he asked, supporting her against his body, which reeked of burn and sweat.

"Yes."

The man led her to a group of women who stood weeping at the far end of the street, clutching their children and bewailing the spreading devastation, before he returned to fight the fire. Jenny leaned against a wall and tried to catch her breath; her chest and lungs felt as if they were seared. All around her buzzed disjointed snatches of conversation: "The King hisself be fighting the fire . . . Duke of York in the saddle all day . . . two thirds of London burned . . . people camping at Moorfields . . . prisoners and loonies rampaging the streets . . .

Jenny covered her ears, shutting out the sound, listening only to the throbbing, joyful message racing through her brain: she was alive. And, most important, she was free!

"Where be your man?" called one of the women as Jenny

limped away, picking her way over the slimed cobbles. Not answering the woman's question, she walked on.

The adjoining street was blocked by several loaded carts as cursing, whip-flailing men argued over their right of way against a garish backdrop of leaping flame. After retreating down a nearby entry, Jenny stopped to rest, finding the exertion of her flight tiring after such long confinement. She was massaging the sole of her right foot when she heard a man's rough voice bellowing a string of curses. A rattling cart hurtled into view, plowing indiscriminately into the crowd gathered outside a blazing tavern. The vehicle's driver ignored the debris raining down from blazing timbers shooting skyward, as, like a frenzied charioteer, he careened over the cobbles, bearing to safety court cupboards and tarnished virginals. Too late, Jenny realized who drove like a madman through the blazing streets: Manuel stood at the reins, a long whip cracking about his head. She turned to flee, praying he had not seen her. Jenny knew that hope was futile when the goods-laden cart clattered alongside her and Manuel leaned down, sweeping her aboard without slowing his frantic pace; the feat was so neatly done that it would have elicited loud cheers from an admiring Southwark crowd.

"By all that's holy, I thought I'd lost you this time!" he cried in relief, his voice harsh from the smoke.

At first Jenny fought him, denying the rescue, but Manuel lost little time in subduing her protests as he slammed her painfully against the low-backed seat. With a sharp crack of the whip, he urged the carthorse to a faster pace. Jenny nearly fell to the cobbles as the conveyance lurched drunkenly around the corner into Fleet Street, as yet unscathed by flame. Despite the cart's breakneck speed, so desperate was she to regain her freedom that Jenny edged to the side, intending to jump to safety.

"Do you want a taste of the whip yourself? Be still, woman!" Manuel ordered tersely, yanking her back by the hair. "I swear, you're crazed by the fire."

They changed direction, heading toward the river, forced to slow down because of the press of refugees. Here men blasted houses to create fire breaks. Smoke-blackened citizens formed a bucket chain, working feverishly in an effort to douse the flames licking about an ancient church whose roof was already afire. Two authoritative figures on horseback rode amid the charred debris, tirelessly directing and encouraging the workers. One of the men finally dismounted to lend ready assistance on the bucket chain, loudly exhorting his fellows to work faster to earn the guineas he offered in reward. When the choking smoke haze lifted temporarily, Jenny recognized that tall, black-haired man, who set to with a will to heft buckets of water in this desperate fight to halt the Great Fire . . .

"Charles!" she screamed, hardly able to credit what she saw. "Charles . . . over here! Oh, Charles, please help me, help me!" The words, which sounded clear as a bell to her own ears, came out muffled and indistinct through the blanket of smoke.

The King turned in her direction to call for more buckets; the Duke of York glanced at the cart, maneuvering his horse sideways to allow it passage. Desperate to be heard, Jenny renewed her cries for help, but the shouts of the firefighters and the roaring flames drowned her feeble voice.

"Stop your blathering!" Angrily Manuel grabbed her with his free hand, ramming her painfully against the seat.

"Charles! Oh, please, Charles . . ." Jenny screamed before Manuel hit her, sending her sprawling backward across a rolled Turkey rug.

"That'll keep you quiet," he growled in satisfaction.

Whipping the horse unmercifully, Manuel chose an alternate route, lowering his head to avoid the blazing spars of timber crashing around them. A burning brand fell on the rug, and with a curse he kicked it away. Crouching, he drew a blanket over Jenny to protect her clothes and hair. At Temple Bar he rested the horse. The fire had not spread this far, though all around him panicking citizens tried to salvage their belongings, casting terrified glances toward the east where great St. Paul's, etched against a lurid, flame-red sky, smoldered to its death atop Ludgate Hill.

Raindrops splashed against her face. Jenny opened her burning eyes, blinking in bewilderment as she saw trees and hedgerows and green open fields.

"Oh, so you're up and about at last, are ye?"

Her heart hammered in fear as she recognized that voice. Manuel reached for her and hoisted her onto the seat, grazing her back against the woodwork in the process.

"Sorry to have to put you to sleep, me darlin', but addled as you were, they'd have thought you'd escaped from Bedlam."

"Where are we?" Jenny asked dully, a growing weight of apprehension settling in her soul.

Manuel shrugged, slowing the pace. "Somewhere outside the city. The others are joining us near Chelsea. You acted so crazed, almost as if you didn't want to come."

Jenny stared at her bleeding palms, wincing as pain throbbed in waves through the swollen wounds. If only he knew how little she wanted to come! Jenny glanced at the unfamiliar countryside, chilled by the drizzling rain. Everything was beginning again! Her finery, her better life, all hope for the future had been left behind in Chancery Lane; by now her home was probably little more than a heap of charred timbers. If only Charles had heard her, if only he had turned in time to see who called out to him so desperately; yet, in all probability, had he looked, he would not have recognized the barefoot, smoke-blackened waif in the ragged dress, her singed hair straggling about her shoulders in a matted cloak.

When they pitched camp in open country she would escape Manuel's guards, Jenny vowed, defiantly lifting her chin. But almost as the resolve was made, chilling reason stole her slim hope of deliverance: if her house had burned, she had nowhere left to go. Dressed like a beggar maid, she would not be admitted to the Palace grounds. Besides, given Charles' declining interest, she doubted he would be overly concerned with her future. He never treated a woman cruelly, but he usually demanded mutual passion in payment for his attentions.

"Don't think to flee back to your rich bastard," Manuel growled suddenly, his dark face brooding and sinister. "Never will I let you go. You've got secrets aplenty to delight the heart of the Marshalsea constables, *gorgio*, don't forget that. And I'm privy to them all," he added, glancing at her smoke-grimed face for a betraying flash of emotion. "I'd see you rot in Marshalsea before I'd put you back in *his* bed. You belong to me for as long as we live."

Manuel's gruff threat rattled through her brain in time to the clopping hoofbeats as Jenny slumped against the hard wooden seat, picking pieces of rusted paint from her bleeding palms as the summer raindrops mingled with the tears on her face.

Chapter 25

Manuel led his small band of followers through the west country's vastly changing scenery. They skirted the edge of brooding Dartmoor, where rain descended in an enveloping gray curtain: so lonely were the moors that Jenny thought she'd never see another living soul; even the shaggy-coated wild ponies grazing the tangled grasses shied away at their approach.

Across Devon's verdant pastureland, over desolate upland moors and rolling hills, they traveled. Jenny lost count of the weeks they had been on the road. Autumn mist and rain swept the land, yet with the exception of the barren moors, the season was warmer here than in Sussex. Vegetation unknown to the travelers sprouted along the lanes, and an abundance of rose hips, elderberries, and blackberries festooned the hedgerows. At dawn Jenny gathered mushrooms and edible toadstools from the meadows while the men trapped rabbits to roast over the open fire.

At last, one clear, crisp morning, they reached the rocky Cornish coast. Swooping cormorants, razorbills, and screeching gulls circled overhead, their cries mingling in an eerie chorus.

Jenny stood on the headland in the buffeting wind, a blanket wrapped around her body to keep out the cold, and she stared in wonder at the frothing whitecaps dashing against rugged cliffs fifty feet below. Here the searing wind had turned stands of gnarled blackthorn to starkly pointing fingers. Noisy herring gulls swooped unceasing in their search for food.

"At last," Manuel breathed. "Isn't it a grand sight?" He slid his arm about her shoulders and for once Jenny did not resist his embrace.

"Never did I think to see the sea, so long have we been on the road."

"Where's your faith? Didn't I promise you a hearthstone

come winter?'' he asked, hugging her against his side, good-natured on this, the threshold of a new life.

Jenny smiled. Without Manuel to lead them the gypsy band would have perished: his unfailing sense of direction and his knowledge about wild foods and medicinal cures had stood them in good stead on the trek west. Her injured hands had festered, and Manuel mixed herbal potions to cure the fever and infection. Long weeks of travel with the gypsies had reduced her to a half-wild creature living from hand to mouth; no longer did she feel like Mistress Dunn, late of the King's affections. Long ago Jenny had discarded plans for escape: alone in this wild land without any means of support, she would be at the mercy of the first man she met.

Devon's lush scenery had reawakened Jenny's yearning for Kit, as she eagerly absorbed each aspect of the land where he was born. Since he had fled into exile he had never contacted her, and she had grown to accept the painful fact that she had become a memory in his past. The stark admission brought tears to her eyes and Jenny could not stop them trickling down her cheeks.

Ever observant of her changing moods, and still hopeful of rekindling her passion, Manuel caught the droplets on his finger. ''Are they tears of happiness?'' he asked softly.

Jenny turned away without answering, fighting to master her composure as she set her face toward the pounding sea and stared far into the dark horizon. Cornwall began a new chapter in her life; she must live it as best as she could.

Manuel bid goodbye to his followers at a crossroads five miles from Fowler's Cove. Without sunshine the majestic scenery turned bleak and desolate, the only sounds the mournful cries of gulls and the sea hammering relentlessly against the steep cliffs. The sharp sea wind penetrated even the thickest clothing, and Jenny huddled miserably in the cart, wishing Manuel would hurry with his farewells. As befitted a monarch, he graciously received each man's tearful homage. Jenny momentarily compared him to King Charles and her stomach lurched sickeningly. Separated by time and space, she was able to review more objectively the King's tenderness toward her; he had often wounded her by his infidelities, yet she knew Charles had loved her in his fashion. Never would he believe she waited at the ends of the earth at the command of yet another king.

They arrived in Fowler's Cove by late afternoon. The small

fishing village nestling at the foot of steep cliffs was little
more than a cluster of whitewashed fishermans' cottages ringing the harbor wall. A narrow, tortuous path climbed the
granite cliffs to a square, white-painted house set on a rugged
promontory jutting out over the ocean.

"There 'tis," Manuel breathed, tears misting his vision,
"just the way he described it."

Jenny quailed in surprise. Far from the splendid manor
Manuel had led her to expect, the squire's house appeared
small and isolated perched on its barren crag. A flood of
longing for gentle Hursthampton possessed her.

"How can you be sure that's it?" Jenny asked, shifting on
the hard seat.

"He said the house overlooked the village like a castle on a
hill," Manuel replied, his green eyes agleam with joy over
his discovery. "There's a smut on your cheek, Mistress
Fowler. You must be presentable when we meet our new
tenants."

Jenny rubbed her cheek and smoothed her chestnut hair,
braided into a demure coronet on top of her head. Absently
she plucked grass stalks from her buckled shoes, which Manuel
had miraculously produced yesterday; a pair of stockings, a
lace-trimmed petticoat, and a serviceable gray woolen dress
completed her transformation into the squire's dutiful wife.
From another source Manuel had obtained a thick red cloak
that helped cut the bitter sea wind. And though she knew he
had silver aplenty, not for one moment did Jenny suppose he
had purchased the goods; most likely he had stolen the garments from unsuspecting women. But she pressed him not for
details. If Manuel bedded a dozen others she could not blame
him, for of late her passion for him was nonexistent.

They clopped sedately down the narrow cliff path, wending
their way into the small village.

Jenny waited beside the tarpaulin-covered wagon while
Manuel walked inside the village inn to introduce himself. A
semicircle of wide-eyed children stared at her, but when she
spoke to them, holding out her hand in friendship, they ran
away, gabbling an unintelligible dialect. Fowler's Cove was
such a bare, impoverished place Jenny was surprised to see
that the fishermen lounging against the net-strewn harbor wall
were smoking clay pipes, while their women, who came
outdoors to stare curiously at the laden cart, were dressed in
thick woolen clothes and stout leather shoes.

Manuel soon reappeared, a fixed beam on his dark face as he labored to appear as a benevolent member of the gentry. They left the narrow cobbled village street, crawling at a snail's pace up the nearly perpendicular road to Squire Fowler's house.

"I'm Samuel Fowler, your late master's brother." Manuel smiled as he introduced himself to the maid who opened the front door of the low, whitewashed house. Jenny hovered in the background, her stomach churning as she wondered if Manuel's deception would be discovered. Her continued well-being depended on his proficient acting. The heavy Irish brogue of his genteel tones would have revealed him as an imposter to a more well-traveled wench, but the rosy-cheeked country girl stared in wide-eyed curiosity at this arresting man with the scarred face.

"May we come inside?" Manuel asked, his toe in the door. "The wind's brisk." Without waiting for the girl's consent, he held open the door, ushering Jenny before him. "My wife, Jenny," he introduced, with a gleaming smile. He hoped the maid did not know the wife of her late master's brother; if she did, however, he would bewail the fact that his poor, dear spouse had succumbed to the plague and pass Jenny off as his new wife.

The square stone dwelling was warm and cozily furnished; polished brass gleamed on the dark-paneled walls, and though old-fashioned, the carved oak furniture had an air of solid permanence. Jenny hastened to the blazing hearth, shivering with pleasure as a welcome blast of heat penetrated her damp skirts. The punishing sea wind turned everything damp.

"You'll be Master Sam'l," the girl said, her apple cheeks dimpling as she dipped a curtsy. "Welcome to Fowler's Cove. We heard tell the master died in that dreadful plague in London town. We thought likely you too . . ."

"Fortunately, I was spared. Have no fear, I'm prepared to identify myself. It wouldn't do for just anyone to be able to lay claim to such a fine property, now would it?"

The young maid blushed as Manuel stroked her dimpled cheek. Jenny flashed him a warning glance, not feeling it appropriate for a staid merchant like Samuel Fowler to be ogling the maid within the first few minutes of their arrival.

Within the hour most of the inhabitants of Fowler's Cove had climbed the steep cliff path, anxious to meet their new squire. To Manuel's credit, he passed their scrutiny with

flying colors. Jenny could hardly believe his gentlemanly
demeanor and careful speech until she recalled their first
meeting, when he had frightened her out of her wits by
pretending to be a gentleman. Manuel ought to have starred at
His Majesty's Playhouse.

"Yes, poor Richard, such a sad loss," he was saying
gravely, while he paced before the hearth, hands joined behind his back, Samuel Fowler's gold watch chain winking on
his dark waistcoat. "I could not abide the city a minute
longer. As soon as we could, my wife and I sold our business
and set out for Cornwall. Pray God, we need never leave."

His speech was greeted by a murmur of good-humored
agreement: Manuel's deception was working exactly as he
had intended.

But delighted though he was for the first few weeks to be
able to play the country squire, the inactivity of Fowler's
Cove began to tell on Manuel's nerves. The late squire had
owned a well-stocked cellar brimful of French brandies and
Portuguese and Spanish wines; it was to this comfort Manuel
turned to ease his boredom.

Jenny found the cliff-top house well appointed. The furniture Manuel had brought from London was in place in the
dark-paneled rooms to add an air of elegance to the solid
country house. The tarnished virginals had been an item of
great interest to the villagers, and Jenny had to pretend the
instrument had belonged to her late sister to explain her
inability to play a tune.

After the first few weeks, life at Fowler's Cove never
approached happiness. As Manuel's consumption of the contents of the squire's wine cellar increased, his mood darkened
accordingly. Terrified at the thought of being isolated with
him during a winter of violent moods, Jenny sought to ration
his liquor consumption, but Manuel flew into a towering rage
at the mere suggestion.

The tearing winter wind battered the shutters and howled
down the chimney like a lost soul; in the distance could be
heard the angry breakers crashing against the jagged cliffs.

"Get me another bottle," Manuel demanded, lurching against
the table, where he upset a bowl of quince preserves.

"You've already had more than enough."

He glared at her, his green eyes hard as stones in his sallow
face. "Who asked you to lay down the law? Get another

bottle, and be quick about it. Or mayhap I'll send little Bessie, she's an obliging wench.''

Jenny's mouth tightened. She no longer experienced jealousy when Manuel distributed his sexual favors among others, but the prospect of him defiling the childlike maid set her blood aboil.

''Leave her alone! She has a sweetheart in the village.''

''We've done little . . . yet.'' He winked suggestively and pitched his empty bottle on the floor. ''Surely you couldn't blame me if I did take her,'' he snarled, his thick brows drawn together. ''The cold sea's chilled your blood, *gorgio*. Or mebbe your rich bastard protector stole your last drop of heat.'' Manuel stumbled toward the tall oak settle where Jenny sat knitting before the hearth. ''Come here, mayhap I can content myself with you tonight.''

Jenny's first impulse was to strike him out of loathing for his drunken lechery, but when she thought about soft-cheeked Bessie, humming as she cleared away the supper dishes, she decided against retaliation. ''What do you want?''

''Want! That's obvious, *gorgio*. I want what I used to get from you.'' His eyes narrowed menacingly as he ruminated over her coldness; then, grasping Jenny by the arm, Manuel dragged her toward him as he sprawled on the settle. The exploring hand he slid over her breasts was not gentle; when he pinched her nipple, she gasped with pain. Manuel blindly ignored her resistance as he pulled open the bodice of her gray worsted gown.

''Stop it! What if she comes back?'' Jenny protested, trying to stay his hand.

''What if she does? It's high time the wench got an education. All the better for her man if she knows what life's about. Come, be not a shrew. Though I take a hundred others, you know none satisfies body and soul as well as you can.''

Jenny stiffened as Manuel pulled her into his arms. Tonight his kisses were not cruelly demanding; he nuzzled her neck, whispering unintelligible endearments. His attention soon shifted to her full breasts, hanging like ripe fruit from her unfastened gown. What once had filled her with fire, Jenny now endured without protestation, praying Manuel would be unable to pursue his desires; his increasing taste for liquor frequently robbed him of his virility.

"Why don't you love me any more?" he asked at last, his voice quavering with hurt. All the anger, the temper, died as he gazed soulfully at her in reproach.

Jenny swallowed, a tugging reminder of her former affection bringing a lump to her throat. "We are different people now, Manuel. The other men who took me spoiled what we knew . . ."

"No one could spoil that! We were so good together—so good." His hand was gentle against her cheek, her neck. "Don't I arouse you any more? My body's not changed."

"Mine has."

Manuel drew back, hurt by her honesty. For a few minutes longer he slumped before the hearth, brooding in silence. His cherished dream of becoming a gentleman had turned bitter as gall. He could beat Jenny, he could rage at her, yet even he knew he could not make her love him. And without her love, this dream he had nurtured all his days was worthless. Within sight of fulfillment those rich bastards had robbed him again by stealing his woman's passion, by changing a hot-blooded angel into a cold shrew! Damn those titled protectors who had stolen her from him, who had decked her body in perfumed silk and lace! Damn them all to hell! Accusingly Manuel glared at Jenny's beautiful face, now little more than a mask, at her lovely bursting breasts, the very sight of which could turn his limbs to water. She had cheated him. He imprisoned her body, but her treacherous soul floated far out of reach. Only the comfort of the bottle remained constant.

Jenny did not stop Manuel when he plucked a fine French brandy from the dresser.

They were startled some time later by rapping on the paneling beside the hearth. They stared at each other, afraid and defensive at the same time.

"Squire, be that you?" asked a muffled voice from inside the wall. The tapping grew louder and more urgent. "Squire! Jem Carter's hurt bad. Let us in."

Manuel cautioned Jenny to silence as he stepped toward the paneling, his drunkenness sliding from him like a cloak. "Who seeks Squire Fowler?" he asked, the only betrayal of intoxication the hoarse thickening of his words.

"Skeet and Worrit," the voice replied.

Meanwhile Manuel had been skimming his hands over the carved paneling, searching for some secret mechanism to open a door and admit whoever waited without. At last he touched a carved boss in the center of the design, and a panel slid aside to reveal two surprised, water-soaked seamen.

"You're not the squire! Where be Squire Fowler?" one of the men demanded, glancing about the room, further surprised to see Jenny standing beside the door, prepared for flight. "Who's she?" he asked, jerking his stubby thumb toward her.

"My wife. Are you in trouble?"

The seaman stared in amazement. "Trouble?" he repeated, before joining his red-bearded companion in laughter. "Trouble, is it? Don't tell me you don't know?"

"You'll have to forgive me my ignorance, but I'm a relative stranger from London. My poor brother Richard succumbed to the plague. This house now belongs to me."

"Naw, Squire can't be dead! We got word but a few months back . . . orders like." The man paused, nervously licking his lips.

"We never seed you afore," growled the red-bearded man. He shouldered his way past his more timid companion and stood straddle-legged, his boots puddling salt water on the rug. "You don't look like the Squire."

"My brother and I were unalike in appearance. But I assure you, I am who I say I am. I've papers to prove it in my strong box if you care to examine them," Manuel said smoothly, stepping back to allow both men access to the room. "Come, you're soaked to the skin. Perhaps you can better explain your situation over a cup of brandy."

"Jem Carter's leg's hurt bad. After we sees to 'im, we'll take that brandy, Squire," the bearded man said after a few minutes' deliberation.

From the aperture they pulled an unconscious, blanket-swathed form. Manuel crouched beside the injured man, and lifting aside the blanket, he expertly ran his hands over his limbs.

"His hip and leg are broken," Manuel said, his face grave. "How did it happen?"

" 'E slipped on deck," said the bearded Worrit. While he spoke he wiped his hands across his mouth, longingly eyeing the brandy, gleaming tawny in the firelight.

"Surely you men weren't fishing in weather like this!"

The two seamen stared at him in disbelief before they simultaneously broke into rough laughter. "Squire kept things to hisself, for sure," said Skeet, shaking his head in amaze-

ment. "We're not *fishermen*, your honor, we be smugglers
from Coverack. *The Guelder Rose* lies at anchor past the
point. 'Twas not our choice to unload on a bad night, but this
cargo be needed desperate down London way. Besides . . ."
Skeet winked, nudging his companion, "the ship's cap'n's
got an itch like a bonfire. Pretty Tamar Carter be just the
piece to quench it."

Manuel nodded in understanding as he knelt beside the
injured seaman. "So brother Richard was your lander," he
said, his green eyes glittering with excitement.

The smugglers glanced warily at each other. "Thought you
didn't know nothin'."

"Nor do I, but my life's not been spent in a cocoon. If it
suits you, I'll take over where he left off."

A wave of nausea swam hotly to Jenny's throat at Manuel's
eager offer. Far from turning down his suggestion, as she
hoped they would do, the smugglers seemed only too pleased
to accept.

"Be all right with us, Squire. You know cartmen to carry
the stuff?"

"I know a gypsy leader who'll spirit the cargo away qui-
eter than the fairies. You'll not be disappointed."

"Well, this be a good night's work, after all," said Worrit,
stroking his beard as his lecherous gaze lighted on Jenny.
"What about her?" he demanded, jerking his stubby thumb
in her direction.

"She's safe," Manuel assured them and he flashed his old
confident grin, his teeth gleaming in stark contrast to his
wine-dark lips.

Jenny's stomach lurched sickeningly as unwanted memories
invaded her mind. It was not Manuel's nature to be content
smoking a pipe before the hearth; the promise of excitement
on the wrong side of the law while still appearing respectable
thrilled him beyond belief.

"Dearest wife, pour brandy for my friends. And send
Bessie to me—I need to get a message to Lizard Point."

Christmas came and went, unmarked by celebration. With
Bessie's help, Jenny baked a rich fruit-filled cake and made
brandy mincemeat, but Manuel barely tasted her efforts, too
occupied was he with his exciting new occupation.

One gray January afternoon, when the sea was churning
like a whirlpool, there came an unexpected knock on the

kitchen door. Jenny was surprised to find a strange woman on her doorstep, a red wool cloak flapping about her shapely body, her black hair tossing in the wind.

"I be Jem's sister Tamar, mistress. I come to see how he be," Tamar Carter announced, tossing the hair from her eyes as she spoke, the better to see the squire's wife. To her surprise she found Mistress Fowler quite beautiful. Tamar's eyes narrowed to unlovely slits at the unpleasant discovery. All her life she had been the district's reigning beauty; it angered her to think another might steal that title from her.

"Oh, Tamar, do come in, Jem's feeling much better."

Jenny reached out to draw the other woman over the threshold, entranced by her dark beauty. It was not difficult to see why a lonely sea captain braved stormy seas to visit this black-haired beauty, whose full red lips and sky-blue eyes promised untold delight. Yet though she greeted the girl in genuine friendship, Jenny sensed hostility sizzling behind Tamar's black-fringed eyes.

"I brought him some fancies. Mother baked them," Tamar said, slipping off her cloak to reveal a voluptuous body clad in blue homespun. "I'd've been here sooner but . . . I . . ."

"Wanted to be with the captain of *The Guelder Rose*. I understand," Jenny said with a smile, thinking to ease the tension between them. "I loved a sea captain once," she said and stopped, unprepared for the stabbing pain caused by that simple statement.

Tamar immediately warmed to the squire's wife. "Ah, then you know the spirit of a seafaring man, mistress?"

"Yes, I know it well."

Long after Tamar had gone upstairs to visit her injured brother, Jenny stared through the window at the churning gray sea, fighting the crippling pain that circled through her stomach to pierce her heart. What a simple statement to cause such discomfort! She must bite her lips to still their trembling as she was engulfed by a hot wave of envy for beautiful Tamar and her lusty captain.

Since Jenny hadn't lived by the sea before, she was surprised to find that the warm spring days altered the color of the water. She smiled in delight when she first beheld the broad expanse of lazy blue water lapping the foot of the cliffs. Puffs of white cloud trailed across sunny skies, the reflection of the sea lending unusual clarity to the air. When

the sun shone and the warm breeze blew, Cornwall became
an enchanted land; gone were the tearing icy winds, the
destructive tides. Large clusters of delicate sea pinks clung to
the rock at her feet. And even the sea birds' cries no
longer sounded like the tormented shrieks of abandoned souls.

Manuel was so deeply involved in the local smuggling that
Jenny had gained precious freedom, previously denied. Now
she was allowed to walk on the headland, or into the village,
without his watchful presence; for this reason, and because
the extra earnings from the contraband had allowed them to
engage Dorrit, Bessie's sister, and her brother Isaac to help in
the house, Jenny no longer begrudged him his unlawful excitement.

Jenny shielded her eyes from the glaring sun as she tried to
identify the dark vessel bobbing at anchor beyond the point.
The ship would come no closer to the shore. By night the
smugglers rowed out to the cargo ship and brought back the
goods in their own crafts. The large vessel must belong to
Tamar's captain, for she had not been up the cliff path to visit
for over a week. As Jenny watched the distant ship, her
imagination supplying a ready picture of the lovers, a wave of
loneliness speared her heart. Abruptly she turned her back on
the sparkling sea and walked home.

When she entered the gleaming, stone-floored kitchen, Jem
Carter, hobbling about on a crudely fashioned crutch, was
awaiting her arrival.

"Squire's been taken bad, mistress," he mumbled, his
blue eyes downcast.

Jenny's mouth tightened. She need not inquire what "taken
bad" meant: Manuel had been sampling the fine French
brandy presented to him by the captain of the cargo ship lying
at anchor off the point. Tonight was a big job, and she
wondered at his foolhardiness in risking the other men's lives.

"Thank you, Jem. Are you going home today?"

"The dark-haired boy nodded, his face flushed with pride.
"Going to try, mistress, but on a cart, not walking the road
yonder. And I thank ye and the squire for the doctoring."

Jenny walked inside the gloomy oak-paneled parlor to find
Manuel slumped across the table, a half-filled glass in his
hand.

"I thought the brandy was to be for a special occasion,"
she snapped accusingly.

"It's Wednesday, isn't that special enough?" he growled,

rousing himself. His sallow face was already growing bloated from drink. "Who appointed you guardian of the bottle?"

"You know there's a job tonight."

"They can manage without me. I've made all the arrangements."

"Manuel." Jenny came to stand beside him, carefully weighing her words. "I can't call the house my own with foreign seamen popping into the parlor at all hours of the night. Without your protection I'm afraid."

"Well, you needn't be: once they learn how cold you are, they'll lose interest soon enough."

Jenny turned away, realizing she would get no sense from him in his current mood.

By nightfall, Manuel was hopelessly drunk: he slumped in the parlor chair, unshaven, his shirt unbuttoned. Months of inactivity were turning his immense arms and shoulders soft, while his former pride in his body had succumbed to the lure of the brandy keg. While he snored and mumbled in his stupor, Jenny nervously awaited the warning tap on the paneling. Everything depended on her. She did not relish the idea of dealing with the ruffian crew of a foreign ship: the fact that Worrit, Skeet, and a handful of local men led the operation brought little comfort. The seamen eyed her hungrily, but always before Manuel had been well in control. Perhaps the local men's loyalty was such they would not touch the lander's wife, but Jenny had not as much faith in the crew of a foreign merchantman.

As usual, Bessie, Dorrit, and Isaac had been given the evening off. This precaution was taken in case the customs officers questioned Squire Fowler's servants, who would be unable to betray what had taken place inside the house.

The night was deathly quiet. A pale crescent moon tossed fitfully amid banks of cloud that shifted to suddenly plunge the headland into inky darkness. After the long trek up the stone passage to the house, the smugglers were always thirsty: Jenny set out several bottles of wine for them. When the tap came on the paneling, she leaped in alarm: twice more the signal was given and on the fourth tap Jenny rapped an answer.

A party of bearded seamen spilled inside the parlor. One glance at the sleeping squire told them he would be of no use tonight.

"Squire be sleeping sound, mistress," Worrit remarked, a knowing twinkle in his eye.

Tight-lipped, Jenny nodded. "He's already made all the arrangements. Here's your money." She took bags of silver to pay them from a locked chest in the corner. Still the men made no move to leave; it was as if they were awaiting something. From below echoed dull thumps as boxes and brandy ankers were placed in the storage cavern beneath the house. Worrit and Skeet stood slightly to one side, while the others came forth to claim the wine bottles.

"Dutch, some of 'em—froggies too," Skeet confided to Jenny in a hoarse whisper. "They's off *The Guelder Rose*. Their captain having gone callin', they wanted to come ashore."

The men chuckled as they passed around the bottles. But when Jenny stepped toward the door, thinking to leave them to their refreshment, she found a burly seaman barring her way.

"Be kind to poor, lonely sailor," he said, reaching for her soft cheek.

Fear blanched Jenny's face as they slowly surrounded her, lechery unmistakable in their eyes. "Don't you dare lay a finger on me," she threatened, her eyes blazing with anger. "You will respect this house!"

The men winked at each other and stepped closer.

"Aye, mistress," Worrit said, his lip curled to reveal gaps in his teeth, "they respect this house. But since their captain gived Squire a present, they want to take a present back for the captain."

Jenny relaxed a notch. A present! She cast about the room wondering what she could give them to satisfy the request. "Let me see . . ."

"You present. He like you. An eye for women, the captain has." So saying, the burliest of the seamen grasped Jenny's waist, while another took her feet, another her arms. Worrit and Skeet stood aside, chuckling in delight at the game.

"How dare you! Put me down!" Jenny screamed, kicking at the men, her arms flailing ineffectually within their strong grasp. "Manuel! Manuel! For the love of God, wake up!" Her shriek was muffled by a salty hand as the men hastened inside the passage, effectively subduing her resistance.

Manuel turned in his chair, mumbling in his stupor, but he did not hear Jenny's cries for help.

Her strength was soon spent. Jenny sobbed over the helplessness of her plight as she was borne through the long dank tunnel to the shore. The sheer strength and number of her captors precluded further resistance. The sailors wrapped her in a blanket and then in an oilskin before they carried her aboard the smugglers' twelve-oared craft. Laughing about the grand trick they had played on the drunken squire, the crew rowed steadily out to sea, heading for *The Guelder Rose*, where a single lantern winked amidships as she creaked and swayed on the swelling tide.

The immense bulk of the cargo ship loomed ahead. Like the head of a great sea monster, *The Guelder Rose*'s high poop deck reared above her as Jenny, still bound hand and foot, was delivered into a host of strong arms reaching from above.

''The cap'n'll likely be too tired to appreciate this present,'' joked an English sailor. The other crew members' bawdy remarks were delivered in a mixture of tongues as they eagerly surrounded the prize. Jenny's favorable appearance merited appreciative comments before the sailors reluctantly returned to their task of hefting the remaining ankers of brandy and boxes of lace goods aboard the smugglers' twelve-oared craft.

''Get your hands off me!'' Jenny cried as a red-haired giant seized her about the waist. She uttered no further protests, for the man hastily tied a cloth about her mouth.

Bound and gagged, Jenny was carried down a narrow flight of stairs to a dimly lit cabin, where she was dumped unceremoniously on the bunk.

The key grating in the lock told her the red-haired crewman had gone back to work. Jumping, hopping, ungainly in her bonds, Jenny reached the door, where she beat against the wooden panels until her fists hurt. Despite her efforts to arouse them, no one came to investigate. A wave of helplessness washed over her and she fell across the bunk, where she sobbed herself to sleep

Chapter 26

Jenny woke to the creak and sway of the vessel riding the swelling tide. Daylight danced a reflection of waves across the pale ash paneling in the captain's cabin; screeching gulls swooped over the decks, circling and diving as the sails were furled. A key grated in the lock and she crouched against the wall, prepared to defend herself.

"Good morrow, mistress," greeted the brawny sailor who came inside the cabin bearing bread and a pitcher of ale. "Get you ready for a voyage. We've weighed anchor."

Jenny's mumbled curses were unintelligible because of her gag. She glared at the sailor with renewed hatred as he put down her breakfast and came to unfasten her bonds. She intended to bite his hand, but suspecting her intention, the sailor kept her well restrained until the last, when he threw her back on the bed and backed away.

When he had gone Jenny gazed hopelessly at the square bowed windows adazzle with silver. Now that the vessel had weighed anchor, she was bound wherever *The Guelder Rose* was bound! And the vessel's captain had complete dominion over her! In the bleak white house crowning the Cornish headland, she supposed Manuel slept on, blissfully unaware of her plight.

A few minutes later she heard brisk steps beyond the cabin door and men's gruff voices speaking French. The frightened beat in Jenny's throat matched the fluttering of her heart as she realized the foreign captain was coming to claim his prize.

The cabin door opened and someone came inside; a companion's heavy tread could be heard clattering up the narrow wooden stair to the deck. Perhaps, after his night with Tamar Carter, the captain would be too well surfeited to pledge his claim; but she took small comfort from the thought. Jenny hid her face in the pillow, refusing to look at him, though she felt his hot-eyed gaze upon her, piercing as knives. No doubt the

392

lecherous bastard was waiting for her to turn and greet him. He would have a long wait!

Jenny's heart thumped like a drum as she heard him walk across the cabin floor, his boots thumping on the bare boards.

"Why so dejected?" he asked.

His muffled question filtered through the pillow. Whatever his nationality, this captain spoke English.

"Don't you dare touch me! Take me ashore this instant!" Jenny demanded, coming out of her hiding place, her gray eyes ablaze with anger.

The captain spoke not, though he gave a sharp intake of breath.

"Don't pretend you don't understand, you foreign bastard!" she cried, her eyes traveling up past his muscular legs encased in fawn breeches, past the broad leather belt spanning his narrow waist . . .

"By all that's holy! Jenny!"

Her gaze snapped upward. A gold-bearded mirage appeared and she blinked to clear her vision. There stood Kit, deeply bronzed, his lower face obscured by a full, curling beard.

"You! Oh, God, how can it be?"

Abruptly he came to life. He knelt on the bunk, his eager arms reaching for her. "Oh, Jenny, sweetheart, never did I dream it was you. They said they'd delivered a gift from the local squire."

Jenny almost succumbed to the power of her emotions: she almost allowed herself to be swept into his strong arms, her body aching to feel him against her, her mouth burning to taste his . . .

"You're Tamar Carter's lover!" she spat, suddenly remembering that painful truth. Her face went white with rage. " 'Tis you she pines for. You who satisfies her beyond belief. You . . ."

Kit blanched. "Jenny!"

The word was a menacing command but she heeded it not. Pain-filled anger roared through her body like wildfire. "Don't lay a hand on me! How so the vows, the tender promises, you made? Not once have I heard from you since the day I saved your skin. Not one word did you send to tell me whether you were alive or dead."

"How was I to know you were in Cornwall?"

"You knew I was at Hursthampton, yet you sought me not!" she challenged, her gray eyes blazing.

"I did not know who would intercept the message. Would you like to have been taken to the Tower in my stead?" he demanded angrily, withdrawing his embrace.

"Oh, 'tis a likely lie. But you cannot weasel your way out of being Tamar's lover, so don't even attempt it," she snapped, as his mouth opened and closed soundlessly. "I'm well acquainted with your method of pining away out of sweetest love."

.Anger over her sarcasm smudged a banner across his cheeks. "You've scant cause to reproach me, for I heard on good authority you went right willingly to his Majesty's bed. And he presented you with a town house in Chancery Lane out of gratitude for your sweet passion."

Panting, they faced each other, robbed of further speech. The creak and groan of the timbers, the flap of the sails as the vessel got under way filled the small cabin. Kit marched to the window and flung open the diamond-paned casement to admit a sharp, salt-tanged breeze.

Jenny crouched on the bed, watching him. At this instant. she both loved and hated him. The rising sea breeze ruffled his golden hair as he gazed out to sea, watching the white streamers frothing in the wake of their passage.

"There's no turning back now. I cannot risk capture."

"You weren't so eager to turn back before, or do you not fancy your old love, Captain Ashford?"

"I didn't know it was you."

"Nay, or a surety you did not. Mayhap you fancied some further bed sport, Tamar's charms not being sufficient to satisfy your lusty appetite."

Kit spun about, his fists clenched in anger at her taunts. "You know I'm no monk. Though I couldn't have you, it didn't mean I stopped loving you."

"Love, Captain?" Jenny's laugh was a brittle, high-pitched sound. "What a strange way you've always had of showing your love for me. Tell me, did it increase in fervor when you lay between her thighs?"

Kit did not answer. Anger surged through him, throbbing intolerably as he stared at her, disheveled, tear-stained, but still so achingly beautiful it brought a lump to his throat. Never again had he expected to see her: for as long as he lived he was denied his homeland under penalty of death. Many long nights he had been tormented by pictures of her lying in Charles Stuart's arms, responding to that master of seduction with the easy liquid fire he remembered so well.

"Should I ask you the same question?" he growled, suddenly finding his voice. "Did you think of me when you sighed in ecstasy over the King's lovemaking?"

"Ask whatever you wish!" Jenny cried, sitting up and drawing her arms protectively about her knees. Tears spilled from her eyes as he glowered at her in anger, his strong legs planted firmly apart on the rolling floor. "Never did I forget you, much to my own sorrow. For love of you I displeased him greatly—your memory robbed me of passion until I could no longer respond. It seems that your memory has walked beside me all my days, but it has rarely brought me joy!"

"Then, Mistress Dunn, I give you leave to discard those joyless souvenirs of an ill-starred emotion. I'm not a man to beg for crumbs of affection, nor to force myself upon a woman once the passion's flown."

His harsh reply made Jenny shudder. Numb with misery, she blinked away her tears, longing to reach out to him and offer her arms, longing to beseech him to forgive her, but her pride would not allow such treachery.

"If that's how you feel, you can return me ashore."

"No. I cannot risk it in daylight. You must wait." Kit slowly unclenched his locked fists, his gaze never leaving her face.

"Until when?"

"Until I next bring a cargo of goods to Coverack. We're bound for Brittany. I won't change course to satisfy your whims."

"My whims!" Jenny's eyes flashed in anger at his statement. "Whims! Nay, Captain, surely it's you who are moved by whims. I'm told you come ashore, despite all risks, when you're eager for Tamar's arms. Must I await the next surging of your desire?"

Driven beyond endurance by her taunts, Kit caught her a glancing blow. "Despite what you may believe, my desires will never be satisfied by the Tamar Carters of this world. Fool that I am, I withhold part of myself for someone who cares for me no longer. Do you know, you shrewish bitch, how many long nights I've ached for you? The loss of you wounded me more severe than exile from my country."

The stark emotion in his voice touched a responsive chord in Jenny's heart. Oh, how much she longed to believe him! All her well-nurtured dreams had come to fruition in this passionate, unfaithful man who had nonchalantly cast aside her devotion in favor of the easy charms of more accessible loves.

"Surely you don't expect me to believe that."

"Believe what you wish," he growled, reaching for her and subduing her resistance.

While he gazed down at her the anger in his eyes softened and changed, until Jenny saw desire flaming there. In anguish she warred with her own easily ignited passion. Never again! Though she had cherished sweet hopes of reunion, not once during those foolish dreams had she suspected the handsome, lusty captain Tamar claimed as her own had once belonged to her!

"No!" she cried in warning.

Deaf to her refusal, Kit cruelly bent her to his will. In one swift movement he pinned her against the groaning bunk, stifling her feeble resistance. "You are my prize. 'Twould be lacking of me not to enjoy what the thoughtful squire provided for my pleasure. You were not bought cheap, Mistress Dunn, for that anker of fine French spirits cost a pretty penny."

Jenny fought desperately to regain her freedom. "Would you rape me, you heartless bastard?"

Kit grinned at her exclamation, but the expression was without humor. "Ah, so you learned some pretty words to match your pretty clothes. Charles' courtiers were ever obliging."

His taunts only increased her rage. "Don't touch me! Everything is over between us. Tamar is welcome to your lusts."

"Is that so?" Naked passion burned in his blue eyes, where there was no remembered tenderness or soft lovelight. " 'Tis most gratifying to learn at last how you really feel about me. Heartless bastard that I am, I promise not to disappoint you."

Jenny punched him as he forced her deeper into the bed. The heated frenzy in her veins sprang from several sources: anger, disillusion, and raw emotion all warred for possession of her being. And though she ranted at him, though she insisted she hated him, Kit had never ceased to arouse her to deepest passion. As they battled on the bunk their striving, straining bodies mirrored so well their former lovemaking that she sobbed aloud in frustration. "Rape me then, for 'tis the only way you'll have me."

"Raping you will give me the greatest of pleasure," he assured her grimly.

When Kit grasped her wrists and pulled her arms above her head, Jenny thrashed helplessly, pinioned like a wild creature, tears of pain and rage spilling down her cheeks. Because he lay across her legs, imprisoning her, Jenny was unable to draw up her knees in defense, nor could she kick him when he pressed his burning face into her bosom, kissing her breasts through the thin fabric of her gown. Flashes of heat pierced her flesh at his every touch. Desperately Jenny attempted to deny the softening emotion of awakened passion, tried to ignore the tingling sensation that shot from her breasts to lodge between her thighs as he took her erect nipple in his teeth, nibbling the sensitive flesh until she sobbed aloud for the pain of her arousal.

"Have done!" she cried, thrashing from side to side on the crumpled pillow as tears rained into her hair.

"This is the sweetest rape I ever imagined."

Still holding her arms high, Kit took his free hand and ripped open her bodice, revealing the stirring pleasure of her breasts to his hungry gaze. No other woman had ever aroused him like this. God, she was the sweetest contraband he had ever laid eyes on! The sheer throb of passion was apparent in his limbs as he fought to discard the tenderness that prevented him treating her as his prize. Kit shuddered with emotion as he swept his hand over the silken arousal of her breasts, a dozen searing memories rekindled at the touch.

Jenny's efforts to remain aloof were failing miserably as she tried to steel herself not to respond to his lovemaking. The torture of his hot, sensitive hands on her flesh stung like a dozen scorpions. And though she denied her love for him, she could no longer deny her passion as his hungering mouth swept over her body. He had pulled her skirts aside to bury his burning mouth in the most secret part of her body. Oh, the devil! The devil! He knew well enough what he was doing. Burning tears welled to her eyes and the lump in her throat swelled near to bursting as she throbbed beneath the agonizingly sweet torment. Kit kissed her neck, her throat, forcing her deeper into the bed, positioning her so that the penetrating strength of his arousal drove into her through his clothing, tormenting beyond endurance. Suddenly, when she was at her most disarmed, he pulled from her.

Jenny blinked. Bereft of the heat of his fine body, she ached with the pain of unfulfilled passion. "Kit," she managed through the sobs shuddering her chest.

"What, have you developed a taste for rape, my love?" he questioned sarcastically. His hands shaking, he maintained a short distance between them. "Well, I have not. You're free to return ashore when next we sail the Cornish coast. Forcing you to take me is not near the delight I imagined."

A terrible wave of loss washed through her veins as Kit walked slowly from the bunk, his face purposely averted. For an instant Jenny questioned the sanity of her actions, but the wild coursing of her blood drowned out all pleas for caution echoing in her brain. "Oh, Kit, love, please . . . don't leave me . . . not now."

He stopped a few feet from the bunk, still refusing to turn about.

The unyielding set of his broad shoulders struck fear in Jenny's heart. With an anguished cry she seized his hand, urging him back. She slid her arm about his compact waist; she hugged his narrow hips, his lean flanks, steel taut beneath her grasp, but still he did not yield. The final capitulation of her pride cost her small sacrifice as she cupped his strong, sun-bronzed fingers about the globe of her breast, urging him to resume the caresses she craved.

"Have you developed a taste for rape, mistress?" he repeated hoarsely, desire screaming through his veins as he tried not to respond to the temptation of her flesh.

"Nay, merely a deep hunger for your lovemaking," she whispered, drawing him to her. Jenny rose from the bed to lock her arms about his neck. In a frenzy she rained kisses on his face. Then they fell together, their breaths merging, their limbs close-locked as all antagonism evaporated in the heat of their arousal.

"And what of those accusations you fling at my head whenever we meet? What of the hatred you persistently express for me?"

"Oh, damn it, be quiet—all the Tamars in the world wouldn't keep me from wanting you. You're a devil! And well you knew I could not resist."

Kit chuckled, his face warm against her soft neck, his golden beard tickling her skin. "For a while I thought this time you finally meant what you said, you lying little wretch. Never would I have raped you.''

''Oh!'' Jenny slapped him in indignation but he seized her wrists and pressed her back into the bunk. She smiled, her mouth curving beneath the heat of his lips. It did not matter that he had tricked her; it did not matter that he had set Tamar Carter afire with his splendid lovemaking—all that mattered was that they were reunited again.

''Never leave me, Jenny, stay with me forever,'' he breathed, all humor flown. His blue eyes gleamed bright with the sheer intensity of his emotion as he slid his arms about her back, crushing her against his muscular body as he matched the fiery core of their passion.

''If you'll have me, I'll sail to the ends of the earth with you, Captain Ashford.''

''Even if it means forsaking England?''

Without hesitation she nodded, tears spilling from her eyes, but they were tears of joy. ''England is meaningless without you. My home is here, in your arms.''

''Oh, Jenny.'' For some unaccountable reason, Kit found the cabin walls blurring. Tense with emotion, he held her close, rejoicing in the soft swell of her voluptuous body against his. A lifetime of searching was over; this was the woman for whom he had been created.

''Love me, Kit, as if we've never been apart, as if there'd been no others,'' she whispered, tracing her tongue along his hot neck, shivering at the sweet, well-remembered taste of his flesh.

Kit rejoiced in the heated throb of passion that shot between them.

''I've never truly loved another,'' Jenny whispered hoarsely.

''Nor I.''

Impatient to claim her, Kit covered her mouth with his own, drawing forth all the life, the warmth of her being. As Jenny's ecstasy mounted, she grew more abandoned, until her limbs became liquid fire striving, straining against his as she hungered desperately for his love. Her gown soon lay discarded on the cabin floor; Kit's clothing followed. In the first golden flush of morning sunlight they admired the perfection of each other's bodies, aching to possess that beauty for all time.

Jenny smiled as she stroked his broad shoulders, his deep

chest, moving over his taut muscular belly to the burning heat of his swollen manhood: so full, so thick was the velvet-sheathed fire throbbing in her hand that Jenny's desire became unbearable. Urgently she directed him, desperate to feel the longed for thrust deep within her belly. *The Guelder Rose*, riding the swelling waves as the course was set for Brittany, disappeared—Jenny remembered only the delight of joining with him in the most intimate expression of their love.

Kit moved purposely inside her, his strong thrusts of passion sweeping her to that soft black world she had thought never to know again. As his movements increased to a frenzied pitch, Jenny screamed aloud, her cries echoing through the cabin as she was swept on a tide of passion to that land where she died and was born again.

Screeching gulls swooped over the headland in ceaseless flight as Tamar Carter half-ran, half-walked, up the steep cliff path to the squire's house. Rage and jealousy ignited an inferno within her breast as she reviewed the deed about which that sniveling Worrit had boasted, his tongue loosened by too many cups of brandy. To think the simpering woman who had professed such loyal friendship had secretly coveted her lover! Tamar clenched her fists as she pictured her handsome captain close locked in passionate embrace with that jade.

But as she walked the rocky path, seething afresh at every step, her emotions shifted course. No longer was she convinced her lover was blameless in the affair: a man did not become so expert at pleasing a woman without vast experience. Perhaps he had seen the squire's lovely wife on one of his visits ashore and had schemed to have her brought aboard his vessel. And though Worrit said they took her against her will, Tamar realized such a story was necessary to soothe the squire's temper when he learned of his wife's infidelity.

By the time she had reached the white house hugging the windswept headland, Tamar was convinced both the squire's wife and the captain of *The Guelder Rose* had enacted a prearranged plan.

The door opened slowly in answer to her thunderous knock.

"What is it?" Manuel demanded, his eyes unfocused. A woman's shapely body swam before his vision, then retreated. With a grunt, he rubbed his eyes and shook his head in an effort to rouse himself to full attention. "Tamar! What do you want with me?" he asked, his voice slurred.

"Let me in, Squire, for I've news you wouldn't want others to hear."

Manuel stepped back, steadying his faltering balance against the oaken chest beside the door. Never before had he been this close to the local beauty and, though he was in no state to make use of her, he could still appreciate Tamar's finer points. Manuel attempted a welcoming smile, but his face throbbed in unison with his head. "What news?" he growled, slamming the door behind her.

"Where's your wife?"

"In bed. Why?"

"Have you looked?"

"No . . . but then I've no need."

"Summon her," Tamar demanded, her face contorted with jealousy.

Manuel bellowed for Jenny until his ears rang; beside himself with anger when she made no reply, he thumped up the stairs, cursing beneath his breath as he stumbled on the worn treads. His ensuing bellow of rage when he found the bed had not been slept in confirmed Tamar's suspicion.

Manuel appeared at the head of the stairs, wavering on the top step, his head buzzing with rage and pain. "Where is she?" he demanded.

"Your wife has fled aboard my lover's ship," Tamar cried, her anger so intense she could scarcely get out the words.

"Your lover?" Manuel repeated, puzzled by the woman's statement. "What do you mean?"

"She's with the captain of *The Guelder Rose.*"

"I don't believe it! How could Jenny leave me for some foreign bastard?"

"He's no more foreign than you or I—he's an English fugitive from the King's justice. Beyond that I know little, except he's born a gentleman," Tamar revealed, drawing a shuddering breath through painful lungs. "She's your wife! Go after them and bring her back. Will you stand there like a coward? Make haste, you fool!"

Manuel gave Tamar a stinging slap across the face. "That's enough! God, my head rings like a belfry. Be done with your screaming, you stupid bitch." Attempting to sort out his muddled thoughts, Manuel stumbled through the room, his dark face livid with anger. If what this local wench said was true, Jenny had successfully given him the slip.

"Go after her! Stop them! She shan't have him—he's mine."

Manuel responded to her orders with a bellow of rage as he shoved Tamar aside and raced from the house. Stumbling, sliding on the rocky ascent, he ran blindly, barely conscious of the woman behind him, her voice still shrilly accusing. He rounded the point and Manuel bellowed an anguished curse when he saw the dipping white sails of *The Guelder Rose* on the far horizon.

"Go after them! Go after them!" Tamar cried, unable to accept defeat.

But Manuel no longer heard her. Staring unseeing at the expanse of shimmering water where the ship's white sails skimmed the waves like mighty bird's wings heading west, he uttered a black curse with all the vehemence of his Romany ancestry: Wherever *The Guelder Rose* was bound, he would follow. Whether it took a month, a year, or an entire lifetime, he would catch that treacherous captain. Jenny was his and no other man should have her. Impotent rage thundered like a living being through his veins, possessing him completely as he made his vow. If needs be he would follow Jenny and her new lover to the ends of the earth! Twice before had he hated a man as fiercely as he now hated the unknown captain of *The Guelder Rose*: only Lord Ross's arrogant nephew and the rich, laced bastard who had disfigured his face had been worthy of such deep emotion.

As Manuel reeled drunkenly from the taunting vision of those sun-dipped sails, it never occured to him that the objects of his bitterest hatred were one and the same.

Chapter 27

Jenny breathed a sigh of happiness as she stood beside Kit at the rail of *The Guelder Rose*. On this golden June day the sea sparkled diamond bright, rippling to the far horizon like a silken banner. With the coast of Brittany at their backs, they headed northwest, white sails flapping in the wind speeding them toward the Cornish coast. Once the contraband cargo of Flemish lace was landed, they were bound for Ireland, where Kit intended to visit his County Wicklow estate while the vessel was overhauled at Dublin dock.

"Will you be glad to be back on dry land?" he asked, slipping his arm about her waist.

"Ashore or afloat, as long as I'm with you, it matters not."

Kit smiled tenderly, tightening his grasp about Jenny's small waist. "You're the perfect woman, 'tis what I most wanted you to say," he whispered, kissing the top of her head.

The mate came to speak to him and Jenny reluctantly stood aside to allow them privacy. Leaning against the rail, the salt spray peppering her face, she watched her lover, head bent in concentration as the Dutchman explained his point. The breeze tore at Kit's golden hair, tossing it in waving abandon about his wide, square shoulders. His handsome face was turned from her, but her imagination readily supplied the image of sun-bronzed skin in startling contrast to his pale blue eyes. Kit's face had grown leaner since his wanderings began and at her request he had reluctantly parted with his luxuriant beard. With pleasure she admired his compact waist and narrow hips, his strong legs accentuated as he stood firm, feet slightly apart, maintaining his balance on the rolling deck. The full sleeves of his snow-white cambric shirt flapped in the breeze; the soft fabric molded lovingly to his muscular back. Jenny shuddered with well-remembered delight as she relived the blissful hours she had spent in his arms, lulled by the sound of waves breaking against the timbers. Each day of sadness, each hour of pain had been worth enduring because it had brought her to this time, this place, reuniting her with the man she loved.

The silver moon tossed in a cloud-banked sky as they lay at anchor beyond Mount's Bay, stealthily delivering their contraband cargo. The lace would be sold in the London markets as Point d'Angleterre: since the law of 1662 forbidding the import of Flemish lace, it had become a valuable commodity. *The Guelder Rose*'s hold was crammed with four hundred thousand ells of luxury for the King's court. Calm as a millpond, the vast black sea shimmered about them, the midnight silence broken only by water lapping against the vessel, and the steady pull of oars as the smuggler's boat drew away.

Their cargo safely deposited, *The Guelder Rose* slipped out to sea, forsaking Mount's Bay with its formidable island fortress, her course set for Ireland. Inexplicably Jenny was filled with foreboding as she stood on deck, watching the castle diminish to toy size in the distance. Even this hauntingly lovely moonlit night tugged at her memory as if she sought to recall some terrible, half-forgotten event; or perhaps her premonition of doom was for a tragedy yet to come.

"We've four hours till dawn; let's go below," Kit suggested huskily. He pressed warm against her back, his strong hands imprisoning her hips against the arousing hardness of his body.

Discarding her morbid thoughts, Jenny turned in his arms, hungrily offering her mouth for his kiss. It was so foolish to be afraid. Nothing could ever part them again.

The ancient demesne of Rosshythe, County Wicklow, overlooked the picturesque vale of Clara. Behind the estate swept the green-clad Wicklow mountains, where waterfalls thundered great crystal showers and spring flowers rioted among the grass. From the upper story of Kit's grand house Jenny could see the sparkling River Liffey as it twisted sinuously between marshy banks abloom with pink ragged Robin, royal fern, and tall yellow flags.

"Oh, Kit, it's so beautiful," she gasped, turning from the broad window, her face alight with pleasure.

"And better yet, it still belongs to me," he reminded her,

transient bitterness clouding his face. "Or at least, it belonged to me before I took my last voyage."

The heavy thud of apprehension began afresh in Jenny's bosom. "Why do you say that? Surely the King's men will not pursue you here. How can they even know you're in Ireland?"

"They know, else this property would have been seized long months ago and awarded to some dissolute character who heartily amused Charles when his spirits ran low . . ."

"You don't hold his friendship in much esteem."

"The man I knew was a loyal friend—I'm not as sure of Lady Castlemaine's lap dog."

"But he has never insisted on your capture," Jenny reminded.

"That's right, and his omission puzzles me. But come, we've far more pleasant things to do on a warm summer's day," Kit said, dismissing the subject. He took Jenny by the hand and led her toward the wide marble staircase descending into the grand crimson walled entrance hall.

They made a leisurely tour of Rosshythe's many rooms, all splendidly appointed with high molded ceilings and large windows framed by heavy silken draperies; the walls were covered in embossed brocade, which, though worn, added an air of opulence to the vast chambers. The furniture was a mixture of ages and styles: solid Tudor oak settles stood beside modern gilded chairs, while the huge dining room wall cabinets of burl walnut decorated in arabesque marquetry held valuable plate used at the wedding of the King's grandmother. Several lifetimes of treasures were held in trust within the echoing galleries of Rosshythe Manor.

Jenny's favorite room was a small drawing room at the rear of the house that overlooked a broad expanse of smooth, flower-edged lawns. Thick purple velvet curtains framed the tall windows, which afforded a perfect view of the formal gardens backed by a dark topiary hedge and crisscrossed with Italianate borders. Even Whitehall Palace gardens were not as lovely as these, nor did they sweep over so many acres of unblemished countryside before reaching the silver river flowing beneath a low arched stone bridge.

"Never once have you asked me how I came to be aboard the Dutch *Guelder Rose*," said Kit as he sprawled in a red velvet chair before the hearth, his long booted legs stretched before him.

"Perhaps I was afraid to ask."

He grinned. "When I was chafing in France, near dead from boredom, I signed on with a French galleon. We were set upon by Dutch pirates and the galleon went down, but we managed to seize the enemy vessel for our own. My crew are a mixture of those Dutch desperados, my own French seamen, and a sprinkling of stout English lads for good measure."

"Do you suppose the King knows you're captain of *The Guelder Rose*?"

"Knows?" Kit's eyebrows shot up. "Dearest Jenny, my brother's probably drawn him a map to assist in locating me. Of a certainty he knows, yet he prefers to let me stew in my own juice. Why else has he not sent his soldiers to take this land forfeit? Or, if not that, then at least to present the house and title to my dear brother James in reward for his loyalty."

"Perhaps he has little love for your brother and does not wish to reward him," Jenny suggested quietly, recalling the rumors about James Ashford and Lady Castlemaine.

Reading her mind, Kit laughed. "Because they share Barbara Palmer's bed? No, vengeance is not Charles' way."

"He could have forgiven you."

"After the scene I created at their Majesties' ball!" Kit shook his head, surprised to see a tinge of color pinking Jenny's soft cheeks. "Does the memory still cause you pain?"

Eyes downcast, she nodded, unable to face him with the reminder of her shame alive in her face. For the thousandth time he wished he might relive that hour of bitterest anger, might take back the wounding name he had flung so carelessly out of pain and spurned passion. He paused, clearing his throat before he continued. "We exist on borrowed time until his Majesty deigns to either condemn or forgive me. On those terms alone have I lived these months past. If you stay with me, Jenny, you too must accept the rules."

Her head came up, crystal tears gleaming in her eyes. "When I said I'd stay with you forever, I understood the danger involved," she reminded him gravely. "If the King is as privy to your movements as you believe, then he must surely know it is I who accompany you."

Kit smiled tenderly, taking her small hand in his and raising it to his lips. "Yes, and that too causes me pain. Never would I intentionally put you in danger, sweet."

Safe within the warm room, lulled by the rhythmic tick of the gilded French clock on the mantel, Jenny nestled in his arms, shutting out the danger of the King's warrant issued on flimsy evidence concocted by Kit's ambitious brother James. A sudden chill seized her heart as the unpleasant reminder of yet another danger came to mind: there was still Manuel to contend with! King Charles may not have chosen to take action; James Ashford may have retreated to cool his heels; but Manuel's blind gypsy vengeance was a powerful force of evil still to be reckoned with.

Early one June morning, when the dew lay crystalline on the scarlet petals of the roses beneath the low dining room window, Jenny was startled to see a lone rider galloping up the broad drive, his cloak streaming a dark banner behind him. Her stomach pitched at the sight.

"Christ! What now?" was all Kit said as he swung from his chair and strode into the red-walled entrance hall to receive his unexpected visitor.

When he returned, Jenny knew the news had been bad. And that overwhelming feeling of dread she had experienced that moonlit night off Mount's Bay settled like lead in the pit of her stomach.

"We tempted the fates by our discussion," Kit said, his face grim.

"What is it?" she asked, her voice breaking as she saw his stricken expression.

Soundlessly Kit extended a folded parchment from which the torn seal of England dangled like a clot of blood at the end of a scarlet ribbon.

The hand that accepted the summons went numb as Jenny slowly read the command instructing Christopher Ashford, Lord Ross, to return to London to answer the charge of treason. The document was signed by the King's own hand. "And if you don't go?" she whispered fearfully.

"Then it will give him the needed goad to seize this land."

"What will you do?"

"There's only one thing I can do. I must answer the summons. I doubt Brother James will expect such prompt action."

"Oh please, Kit, take me with you," Jenny pleaded, her eyes filling with tears. She had been tempted to beg him to flee, yet one glance at the grim determination on his face made her discard that thought.

For a long time Kit paced silently before the window, where the rising wind tossed leafy branches over the clipped yew hedge, dappling the green lawns with rippling shadows. At last, his decision made, he turned to her where she perched nervously on the edge of a blue brocade chair.

"Because I've no desire to be parted from you again, you can accompany me to court." Kit raised his sun-bronzed hand, silencing the excited cry his joyful news evoked. "But only if you're prepared to throw yourself on the mercy of your . . . of his Majesty," he said with difficulty, swallowing several times over the bitter thoughts that filled his mind. "I might be clapped in the Tower the minute I step ashore. Neither of us knows what prompted the King to make his move."

"You're asking me to use my former . . . relationship . . . with him?" Jenny asked incredulously.

"If I'm in the Tower, 'tis the only choice you have. He's ever generous to his . . ." Kit turned aside, the word sticking in his throat.

"Whores," Jenny supplied sharply.

"That's not the word I intended."

"But 'twill do, failing another."

"Don't antagonize me today! My nerves are far too raw to treat you patiently," he growled, swinging from the window to face her. "Given the distance, no doubt you can spend many months in Ireland before my beloved brother seeks to have you evicted."

The anger in his words was like a slap in the face. Jenny stared at him, all color draining from her cheeks; despite their deep love, their repledged vows, an undercurrent of the old antagonism still flowed between them. "What if I refuse?"

"Then, my dear, you must take steps to save yourself—there's nothing else I can offer." Kit strode toward the door, crumpling the royal summons in his hand. "I must ride to Dublin to arrange the voyage. Though Charles is ever a patient man, it would seem his patience has run out."

"Kit!"

Jenny raced after him, holding her heavy blue skirts above her slim ankles. She caught him at the front door, where sunlight pierced the stained glass coat of arms, spilling a rainbow over the dark polished floor. "Don't you even care that I resume my . . . relationship . . . with him?"

Kit turned to face her, his jaw tense, his blue eyes paled to the tint of winter sky. "Care," he repeated, his voice hard. "Dear God, what sort of man do you take me for? I seek to save your neck, you foolish wench. Abed *in* lousy straw, I doubt I'll be much match for Charles Stuart. Don't you know every minute you spend in his company will be torture?''

Tears flooded her gray eyes at the raw emotion in his voice. ''Oh, Kit, I'm sorry,'' she managed to whisper through her tears, ''but you seemed so . . .''

''We are not wed. And Charles has a better claim on you than I. After all, he is King of England,'' Kit growled as he stepped outside. ''As soon as *The Guelder Rose* is provisioned and I can dredge the crew from the Dublin brothels, we'll sail.''

''Please, Kit, don't make it so hard for me. You know I want to come with you, but to return to the King . . .''

He was already sprinting down the oval steps to the gravel drive. ''Whatever your decision, I'll still love you,'' he said. ''We'll discuss it further on my return—if you're still here.''

''I'll be here.'' Jenny leaned against the cold door, overcome with grief at Kit's parting words. His attitude had been a shock. Miserably she watched him seize the courier's horse by its bridle and lead it out of sight around the west side of the house.

Kit summoned a groom, telling him to attend to the courier's mount. While he saddled his chestnut stallion he fought to master the pain that surged in his stomach like bile. Fool that he was, he had just ordered the woman he loved back into the arms of her royal lover in a desperate attempt to save her skin. The agony of knowing she was destitute would be alleviated by that calculated move, yet the pain of his decision would haunt him all his days.

Face set in a grim mask, Kit swung into the saddle, setting his horse's head toward the Dublin road. This might be the last journey he made as a free man, for he had no way of knowing whether a party of his Majesty's Horse awaited his arrival at the Dublin dock.

The warm summer days were pleasant, yet Jenny found little beauty in the tranquil Irish countryside, her peace of mind shattered by tormenting thoughts of Kit. Why had he been so callous, so unconcerned about her future? Nay, not merely unconcerned; he had virtually insisted she reopen her love affair with Charles. Any woman who threw herself on Charles Stuart's mercy offered her body to him—there was no other method of securing his compassion. All her old doubts, her old fears, about the sincerity of Kit's love returned to haunt her. Surely a man who loved her as deeply as he professed to do would not seek to thrust her in another's bed! Whatever the reason behind Kit's unreasonable demand, Jenny knew that if she traveled with him to London, she had to at least pretend to abide by his wishes.

Rosshythe's beautiful gardens were bathed in bright moonlight. Jenny tossed and turned in the large bed in Kit's bedchamber, tortured by the bittersweet memories of their shared nights in this huge four-poster with its blue damask hangings. How she longed for his return! It was taking far longer to assemble the crew and provision the ship than she had expected; the nagging fear that perhaps Kit had been apprehended on his arrival in Dublin was too terrible to contemplate.

After much futile tossing and turning, Jenny finally arose. She slipped her green silk bedrobe over her shift, knotting the gold-fringed sash about her slender waist as she descended the marble stair. At best, since Kit's departure, the atmosphere within this palatial house was strained. The unfriendly Irish servants spoke hardly any English. And though Kit conversed fluently with them in Gaelic, adding the outlandish tongue to the list of foreign languages he had mastered, Jenny understood not one word of their speech. She did not relish the idea of trying to get the surly foreigners to prepare a midnight meal.

The large stone kitchen lay in darkness, a dying fire smoldering red in the hearth. At Jenny's approach, Bridget, the kitchen maid, leaped from her chair, alarmed to have the mistress find her asleep.

"What is it?" the girl mumbled, sleepily rubbing her eyes as she spoke.

"I'd like a cup of milk and a pasty. But I can get it myself."

"No, your ladyship, sit you down. The master'd skin me alive if he found out, and him likely to walk through the door at any time. Just yesterday Niall said he'd a feeling the master would be home before the moon wanes."

Bridget traipsed across the kitchen to light a candle.

Jenny stirred the fire's dying embers to faltering flame and she crouched before its meager heat while the Irish girl noisily prepared her meal. Bridget was the only servant to

ashore in the bay, for Rosshythe Manor lay but a few miles from the sea.

In vain Jenny drummed her heels against his legs; she thumped him viciously, but Manuel only laughed at her feeble strength. When her actions became too distracting, he cuffed her about the head, successfully quieting her resistance.

The sound of waves breaking against shingle made Jenny think she was aboard *The Guelder Rose* until her awareness of the jogging horse and cruel clasp about her waist dispelled the illusion. Horror-stricken, she recalled the terrifying events of the last couple of hours and fear silenced her protests as she realized she was completely at Manuel's mercy.

"Only a few minutes more, me darlin'," he grunted as he turned the horse's head toward the shingled beach, moonlit beside the silver sea.

A few feet from shore a moored rowboat bobbed in the shallows, awaiting Manuel's return; farther out to sea, shadowed against the gleaming water, rode a vessel at anchor. All Jenny's hope of rescue dwindled and died at the sight of Manuel's companions waiting to take them aboard.

"Where's your handsome captain now?" Manuel sneered, his mouth lifting in the well-remembered grin that chilled her blood. "No doubt he's sporting between the ample thighs of his whore. Such a disappointment it'll be when he returns to find you gone."

"He'll kill you."

"If he can find me."

"He'll find you."

Manuel's eyes narrowed as he tried to control his rage at the mere mention of the hated captain. "Such a dance the bastard led me, but never did I think 'twould lead me here. Perhaps you can give me his real name, for it seems he has a multitude of identities."

"Why should I?"

"Shouldn't I know the name of the man I'm going to kill for daring to touch you?"

Jenny was chilled by the determination in his voice.

"Never," she vowed, her gray eyes glittering with fierce emotion in the moonlight.

Manuel shrugged. "No matter. Wherever *The Guelder Rose* goes, he goes too. 'Twill be a simple task to lie in wait for him some dark night and slit his throat."

"Take care! He's a lord. You'd best sheathe your knife if you don't want to hang." Jenny cried. trying to wrench free, but he held her fast.

"What?" Manuel snarled, his face tightening.

"He's not just a poor ship's captain. you fool! He isn't just a guest here—this land is his. He owns it—your land!" Jenny laughed in derision. She had little hope of outrunning him on foot. but astride the horse she could gallop to freedom. if only he would slacken his hold long enough for her to break free.

Though Manuel reeled in shock. Jenny's unexpected revelation increased rather than decreased his strength. "By God, they did not tell me that! You mean the captain of *The Guelder Rose* is Lord Ross!"

"Not the Lord Ross you knew. for he's long dead. but his nephew . . ." Jenny stopped abruptly. Too late she recalled Manuel's long-standing hatred of Lord Ross's nephew, who had him thrown off this land. Kit was that despised person! Her eyes dilated in fear as she saw the black hatred mounting in Manuel's swarthy face.

"By the Christ! I've a mind to return and challenge the bastard!"

"He'll kill you."

Manuel smiled cruelly as he reminded her, "No, *gorgio*, have you forgotten . . . destiny is on my side. It's stood me in good stead these years past. And though the search was hard, never for a minute did I despair of finding you. My destiny is not complete without you."

When Jenny tried to run. Manuel kicked her legs from under her so that she fell to the wet sand with a shriek of pain.

While Jenny lay sobbing at his feet. Manuel stared at the single light of the dark vessel bobbing on the water. They would not wait much longer. If he did not signal the *Lapwing*'s lookout soon, they'd weigh anchor and be gone. Yet hatred, so long fermented, rapidly stole his reason. The man he had loathed all these years had taken Jenny from him. Perhaps it was he who had kept her in London—the same bastard who'd stripped her of passion. Too many alcohol-sodden years combined with rage to destroy his remaining sanity. Manuel lost the fight against the temptation to return to Rosshythe to await his bitterest enemy. He turned his back on all hope of rescue, his decision made. The *Lapwing* bobbed at anchor beneath the silver moon awaiting a signal he would not make, for he cast his lot with destiny.

Thundering hooves on the sea road snapped him back to the present. No sooner had Manuel spun about to identify the rider than a great chestnut stallion pounded along the beach, flailing showers of wet sand in his wake, his rider crouched low in the saddle, stirrups shortened to increase his speed.

A cry escaped Jenny's lips at the sight of the horse bearing down on them. No two riders rode like that! A vision of the Newmarket racetrack flashed before her eyes as she recalled the race ridden between King Charles and the unknown Irish lord . . .

"Kit! Oh, Kit! Have a care. He'll kill you!" she screamed in warning.

Kit brought his horse to a spraying halt and leaped from the saddle. He ploughed over the shifting sand in his heavy jack boots, a drawn sword in his hand, the deadly blade flashing white fire in the moonlight.

"By the Christ, you gypsy thief, how dare you lay hands on her?" Kit yelled, his face thunderous.

Manuel grabbed the broad-bladed knife from his waist. "Come closer, you bastard. For all my life I've longed to slit your throat."

Jenny scrambled to her feet, removing herself from the arena as the two men faced each other. The gleam of insanity flickering over Manuel's coarse features frightened her.

"Kit, take care!" she cried in alarm as Manuel leaped forward, already crouched in fighting position.

"Aye, take care, my fine lord," Manuel mocked as Kit pitched his hat aside. Bright moonlight flooded over Kit's grim face and Manuel stopped, an oath on his lips. "You!" he bellowed in frenzy, blood mounting in his cheeks as he stared in hatred at his opponent.

"Aye, Brandon, you scum, it's me. I warned you never to set foot on this land again," Kit growled, desperate to reclaim his love unharmed from this peasant upstart. When the servants had told him who held her captive he could scarce believe it. Damn them all for the ignorance that hobbled their wits while Brandon made off with Jenny! On his return the cowards would pay well for their superstition—*if* he returned. One glance at that practiced crouch told him the gypsy was no novice with a knife.

"Nay, my grand lord, I've far more than that old score to

settle. Remember a fine June night three years ago when you sliced a gypsy's face with your sword? You disfigured me for life for daring to seize your horse.''

Kit scowled, searching his memory for the incident. ''Aye, I remember—so you're the thieving wretch who tried to steal my horse?''

''Ever since that day I've vowed to take your life. Tonight you'll oblige me, for you're thrice cursed,'' Manuel raged as he leaped forward, casting all caution to the winds. ''Ever were you a coward hiding behind your sword. Meet me fairly with a knife. We'll fight to the death like men of old. And this pretty whore shall be our prize.'' As he spoke Manuel reached inside his boot and withdrew a second knife, which he aimed at his enemy's heart.

Had he not leaped aside, Kit would have been skewered by the whistling blade. Ramming his sword in the soft sand, he faced his challenger, armed only with a broad-bladed knife. Though he was no expert, Kit was not unfamiliar with the weapon: many a time had he seen the decks run red as men fought to the death, waterfronts of foreign ports being skilled teachers of the deadly craft.

Jenny was appalled at Kit's foolhardiness in choosing to fight Manuel on his own terms. Fear dried her throat as she watched them maneuver into position, bitter hatred from the past possessing both men as they took their stance on a strip of shingle.

Kit lunged first and Manuel twisted away. They circled each other, moving round and round, performing an age-old ritual beneath the searching moon. In the background waves lapped against the beach, sifting through beds of shingle before gurgling out to sea. No longer could Kit understand the insults Brandon flung at him, for the gypsy had reverted to his own tongue. Manuel lunged unexpectedly, but Kit deftly turned aside. Once more they circled each other; this time it was Kit who cut at thin air, his target flown. Time and again they repeated their movements, panting with tension and exertion. Neither man spared a thought for the woman over whom they fought, crouched sobbing on the sand, powerless to prevent the fatal outcome of this moonlit duel.

''Come, you coward, will we take all night?'' Manuel bellowed, suddenly mindful of the *Lapwing* impatiently awaiting his return. ''Take me! Take me!'' he taunted, deliberately laying himself bare in an attempt to lure his opponent close enough to deliver the death thrust.

Uttering a growl of rage, Kit leaped forward, careful not to get too close as he drew first blood with a well-placed slash on his opponent's upper arm. The unexpected wound drove Manuel into a frenzy. He leaped forward recklessly and toppled Kit on the sand. Grappling, they rolled over and over, coming dangerously close to the lapping waves. After a final, punishing barrage, Manuel broke Kit's grip and leaped to his feet.

When Kit attempted to stand, the wet shingle shifted beneath his weight, bringing him to his knees. Uttering a cry of triumph, Manuel leaped forward, anxious to end the fight.

"Kit, for the love of God, take care!" Jenny shrieked, racing toward them, not knowing what to do to save him, knowing only that she must make an attempt.

Her cries momentarily distracted Manuel, who snarled at her to stay back. He jumped forward to deliver the death blow, for his man had not yet risen on the quaking shingle, but growing too anxious, Manuel placed his foot on the same shifting patch. With a cry of surprise, he fell on Kit's upraised knife, the cry becoming an anguished wail as the twelve-inch blade pierced his heart.

Jenny stood back, afraid to advance on that thrashing figure who scrabbled his booted feet in the shingle, writhing in agony until the shore beneath him grew dark with blood. At last, with a final curse that gurgled in his throat as blood frothed over his lips, Manuel lay still.

Kit scrambled to his feet, clumsy on the shingle. He leaned over the fallen man, expecting trickery, but even this wily gypsy could no longer defy death: here, on a moonlit Irish shore, Manuel's destiny had been fulfilled!

"Oh, Kit, are you hurt?" Jenny gasped, racing to his side. Beneath her hands his muscles felt iron hard as she clutched him, trembling with shock, fear, and relief as he took her in his arms.

"Dearest Jenny, I must needs ask you the same question," he whispered hoarsely, cradling her against his chest, where she gave vent to a gale of weeping. Kit smoothed her tangled hair, damp and unruly beneath his hands, soothing her until the storm was past.

When her tears were spent, Jenny raised her face to his,

straining upward to receive his tender kiss as he enfolded her even closer in his strong arms. "Oh, Kit, you love me still," she whispered after their lips parted, resting her head against his broad shoulder.

"I should be angry that you ever doubted me."

"But those things you said . . . when you wanted me to . . ."

"You were ever a ninny! Don't you know I hated every word of that idiotic speech? I was trying to save your pretty hide. Charles Stuart's too kind a man to let you walk the streets. If, by answering his summons, I'm arrested, I cannot protect you. So, though it be against your nature, love, you must play on his weakness for a pretty face."

Jenny blinked away the tears poised on her dark lashes as she pressed against him, thrilling to the steady beating of his heart. "We'll worry about that when we reach London."

Kit smiled, resting his burning cheek against her sleek hair. "Come, sweetheart, let's go home."

Kit stopped beside Manuel's still form, rolling him over for a final look at his enemy's face. Here lay the second man he had fought and killed because of that lovely woman who had ensnared his soul at first meeting. A final contest for possession of her love lay ahead—but the contest waged with Charles Stuart would be heavily weighted against him.

Jenny watched Kit standing beside his fallen foe and fear licked through her stomach as she anticipated his ensuing questions about Manuel's crime. When none came, she rejoiced in the knowledge that Kit assumed Manuel's attack was to avenge the past. Those shameful half-truths she had told him to explain her presence in Cornwall had been so convincing that Kit was not even aware Manuel was the generous squire of Fowler's Cove.

Chapter 28

On the late July day, the ancient port of London was a seething mass of masts, noise, and color: vessels flying the flags of many nations thronged the river in convoys to and from the city. *The Guelder Rose* had appeared an insignificant old tub beside the grander vessels of his Majesty's fleet, though the recently refurbished gilding on her high, carved poopdeck outshone the weather-beaten merchantmen incoming with cargo from the four corners of the earth.

The day before, as they glided between sunny meadows on their journey upriver, past the mammoth mast-choked navy yards of Deptford and Woolwich, Jenny's apprehension had mounted. So great was her unease this morning as they made the final leg of their journey to the Palace that she barely looked at the devastated, smoke-blackened heart of the ancient city, visible from the river. A wide swath, from the Tower in the east to Fetter Lane in the west, lay in ruins from the Great Fire. Kit repeatedly assured her she must not be afraid, but his grave countenance revealed he was not nearly as confident as he pretended. Because the soldiers had not seized him in Dublin, and because they had been allowed to sail into port unmolested, Jenny's hope for his safety had been strengthened. Perhaps the King had decided to forgive him. Surely her presence would not condemn him to life imprisonment—she could not even bear to think that their liaison might cost him his life. It was repeatedly said that the King's was a forgiving nature, yet so often had she seen hot anger barely contained beneath his laughing exterior that Jenny took small comfort from his nickname, the "Merry Monarch."

Kit had purchased for her a fine India silk gown of deepest rose, lavishly trimmed in gold lace. Jenny carried a carved ivory fan adorned with lilac and gold ribbons to match the confection entwined in her smooth chestnut curls. Though her outward appearance remained composed, beneath her sumptuous gown Jenny's knees knocked and her heart raced sick-

eningly as they drew ever closer to Whitehall Stairs. Kit was
seated beside her in the boat, his lean face set, lines she had
never noticed before etched deep on either side of his mouth.
He clasped her hand and spoke reassuring words despite his
great apprehension.

"We'll be there soon," Kit said gruffly. Familiar buildings
slipped past as the boatmen rowed steadily toward the looming
collection of buildings called Whitehall. "Remember what
you're to do, if . . ." he paused, swallowing the lump that
rose in his throat as he gazed lovingly at her.

"I know what to do," Jenny said gravely, pressing his
strong hand in reassurance.

Kit was resplendent in ice-blue satin laced with silver, the
coat cut expertly to emphasize his broad shoulders and narrow
waist. A wide-brimmed black hat, piled high with silver
plumes, sat rakishly on his perfumed hair, glittering like
beaten gold beneath the summer sun. His appearance was
magnificent, as befitted a private audience with his King; his
only lack being proof of his innocence of treason.

They put in at Whitehall Stairs and Kit handed Jenny
ashore, slipping his arm about her waist as they ascended the
steps after paying the waterman. He had chosen to petition for
clemency alone, though his loyal crewmen wanted to stand
beside him to vouch for his integrity by telling the King of his
worthiness as captain of *The Guelder Rose*. The men's
unswerving loyalty was touching, yet Kit had to remind them
that King Charles knew right well what a good captain he
was, having but recently saved the royal flagship from enemy
hands; his Majesty's doubts concerned his fidelity as a subject.

The lofty Whitehall corridors aroused a wave of mixed
emotion as Jenny walked sedately beside Kit. How often had
she come here, hastily smuggled inside the King's bedchamber by the dutiful Chaffinch. Charles had delighted in showing her his retreat, wherein he conducted scientific and
anatomical experiments, such diversion necessary to satisfy
his brilliant, inquiring mind. Jenny had also been privileged
to inspect his private closet, where he posed for portraits and
discussed grand plans for the rebuilding of Windsor and
Greenwich. Admission to these secret abodes was granted
only to those whom Charles considered trustworthy enough to
be allowed a glimpse of his more serious side, carefully

hidden from the multitude behind a frivolous, pleasure-loving mask.

There were few courtiers to be seen today, for during midsummer most disported themselves on the river or at Hampton Court, where the lush greenery provided a pleasanter setting than the crowded London streets, abuzz with flies and stinking to high heaven beneath the brazen sun. In fact, when they had to wait so long to be admitted to the audience chamber, Jenny began to wonder if his Majesty himself had not taken leave of the rambling Palace in search of pleasanter vistas.

Eventually a gentleman of the bedchamber appeared in the doorway and motioned for Kit to follow him. Jenny was left standing at the windows overlooking the Privy Garden, where she gazed at the sundial, watching a couple of sparrows squabbling over a crust of bread. As she pondered the outcome of this audience, the consequences irreversible once Kit stepped through those double doors to the audience chamber, she became freshly aware of the reckless beating of her heart. The bright flowerbeds and neatly clipped lawns blurred into a kaleidoscopic haze as she reviewed the probable ending to this summer's day. If Kit was arrested, she would flee the Palace, defying him in his final request: the need to throw herself into the King's bed would make her a whore indeed.

Several passing courtiers had acknowledged Kit's presence, yet none of the greetings could have been termed friendly. She supposed that the courtiers, being such a wily, self-seeking race, had not yet chosen sides, preferring instead to wait until they learned which way the wind blew, not anxious to befriend a condemned traitor. Yet surely, had it been the King's intention to have Kit imprisoned, he would have been arrested when they entered the Palace.

"Will you come with me, Mistress Dunn."

Jenny spun about to see the dark-suited servant who had formerly taken her back and forth to the King's chamber. The color fled from her cheeks as she stared at him, putting her own interpretation on this summons: Kit had been arrested and Chaffinch had come to take her to the King!

Thomas Chaffinch smiled in sympathy at her distress, noting the trembling white hand that clutched convulsively at her throat as she backed away. "Nay, Mistress, have no fear. Come, we must hasten."

Jenny wanted to flee this sprawling palace wherein lay memories both pleasant and ensnaring. Sensing her inner doubts, Tom Chaffinch took her hand and urged her toward the door.

The winding journey to the King's privy chamber was a nightmare. Jenny longed to ask the servant if Kit had been arrested and was at this moment bound for the Tower, but pride stilled her tongue. A mere servant had scant influence, despite his deep involvement in the King's private affairs. She was being taken to the one man with the power to set Kit free. In the past Charles had avidly craved her attentions; for that reason alone, she hoped he would now be merciful.

When Jenny stepped inside the King's room, the black-suited servant backed away, quietly closing the door. On this hot July afternoon the gloomy bedchamber was uncomfortably close; by the tainted atmosphere, she guessed correctly that one of the King's many spaniels had disgraced himself in his master's absence. The rustling of material, followed by a man's brisk step, alerted her to the small dressing room off this grand bedchamber with its red velvet-draped four-poster hung with gold tassels.

"Jenny!"

Steeling herself for the sight of the man who had been both her lover and her King, Jenny looked full upon him. Charles wore a black and silver dressing gown, his head appearing small and somewhat bare without his flowing black periwig. He outstretched a slender, sun-tanned hand to raise her from the floor where she had dipped a deep curtsy in obeisance to her sovereign. Their eyes met, and Jenny was shocked by the change in his swarthy face, where age lines grooved deep to create the cynical mask he would wear for the rest of his days.

"Your Majesty," she said.

Charles clucked his tongue impatiently. "How formal we've become, Jenny Wren."

Blood mounted in her cheeks at his rebuke, but she could find no light-hearted words to answer his charge. Charles must have recently returned from the tennis courts, for his sweat-soaked costume lay on a chair where he had flung it, his tennis racket propped against the rosewood cabinet where the wines and brandy were kept. If he had been out on the tennis courts indulging his passion for one of his favorite sports, he could not yet have seen and condemned Kit!

"Your Majesty . . ."

"Charles."

"Charles . . . I . . ."

"Do not petition me to save your lover," he said, his dark face somber.

Jenny's startled gasp was audible in the quiet room, where the silence was broken only by the steady tick of the clocks Charles kept on the mantel. Their communication was interrupted by a servant coming inside the chamber to remove the offending evidence of the spaniel's residency. While the man wiped and washed, neither Jenny nor Charles spoke; at last, bowing as he walked backward, a covered chamberpot in one hand, a broom and a rag in the other, the servant took his leave.

Charles grinned, his wide mouth assuming that familiar expression Jenny had known so well. A memory tugged at her heart and she hastily squashed the weakening reminder of what they had once shared and could never share again.

"Where were we?" he asked, reaching for her bright hair and smiling in pleasure at its beauty.

"You know about Kit . . . and me?" she faltered, her gray eyes huge in her pale face. Charles stood so close that she was enveloped in the wave of heavy perfume he used to mask the rankling reminder of the tennis courts. When he looked full on her, she saw herself mirrored in the black depths of his laughing eyes; and though she knew him well, today Jenny could not decipher the emotion behind those dark eyes.

"You yourself told me about him at our first meeting. Do you not remember?"

"Yes, I remember."

"He's still unworthy of your love," Charles reminded her, his slender, olive-skinned hand moving over the curve of her cheek in a tender caress. "A man who would desert a woman like you does not deserve such loyalty."

Jenny smiled at his compliment, growing uncomfortable beneath his caresses. "We have resolved our differences, Your Maj . . . Charles, as I hope we both might resolve ours."

"There's nothing to be resolved. Though your house in Chancery Lane was torn down to prevent the spread of the fire, Hursthampton still awaits you. During your absence I had the gardens relaid. I think you'll be well pleased with the results.''

"But I cannot . . .''

The King placed his strong hands on her shoulders, pulling her toward him, his dark gaze fastened on her pale face. "You would give up your rewards for the love of a randy sea captain?'' he asked, his mouth quirking in amusement.

Hope leaped within her breast at his amused tone. "Have I the choice, sire?''

"Forever have you been free to choose.''

"I did not absent myself from your presence out of disregard. During the fire I was taken against my will to the West country . . .''

Charles placed a silencing forefinger on her soft mouth. "Hush, there's no need to explain. Nor is there need to return gifts lovingly bestowed. Never was it my wish to ensnare a reluctant wench. If you have chosen yon sea captain over me, so be it. Regardless of your choice, we share memories that are ours alone. In happier days, thoughts of him didn't rob you of passion—but 'twas the reason you did not warm to me of late, was it not?''

Jenny nodded, unable to meet his knowledgeable dark eyes.

"I suspected as much.'' Charles sighed, gazing sadly at her lovely face and recalling the delight they had shared. "Because we loved, you expect me to forgive his treachery, don't you?''

Her eyes filling with tears, Jenny looked up at him, finding his face blurring to a dark oblong. "If you have compassion for my feelings, you'll not comdemn him.''

"But he has stolen you from me. That in itself is a serious crime,'' he reminded her as he slipped his hand gently over the prominence of her breast, the familiar gesture performed absently, as if, for the moment, he had forgotten they were no longer lovers. Catching himself, Charles smiled lazily at her and dropped a soft kiss on her brow. "Are you convinced Lord Ross is my loyal subject?''

"Yes. He would never ally himself with your enemies,'' Jenny defended hastily, wondering if this was but a game in which the King delighted.

"Evidence of his treachery was presented to me.''

"By his jealous brother and others who meant him harm!''

"Jealousy does not always render accusations untrue.''

Charles reminded her gravely. Her emotional outburst had surprised him. Jenny had not named the others, but he surmised that she was well aware of Barbara's involvement in the incident, whereby she had sought to dispose of a rival and reward an eager young lover at the same time.

"In this case it does."

The hot flush mounting in her cheeks made him smile. Stooping, Charles kissed her soft mouth, his lips hot against hers. "What a lucky man he is to have such a loyal woman." A flicker of sadness dimmed his smile as he sighed and set her aside. "I've not condemned your reckless lover to the gallows—nor even to the Tower," he added, as she opened her mouth to ask. "There is much owed to Kit Ashford both by me and my father—'tis not my nature to repay loyalty with treachery. I'm not quite the fool certain people assume me to be. Dark conspiracies occur with such frequency that there must be no loyal Englishmen left in the realm."

Charles was smiling again and Jenny smiled back, her heart fluttering with excitement as she awaited the end of this taunting, flirtatious game at which he excelled. She could have demanded his answer in the beginning, but perhaps he would not have been so generous had she turned shrew.

"Please, dear Charles, for all the love we shared, tell me I'm free to go . . . and that *he* is free to accompany me. He loves you well. Despite his raging temper, he is a loyal friend."

"How can I dispute so pretty a defense? 'Odd's blood, but you're a winning wench. It does me sore to have to hand you over so easily." Charles reached for a bell pull to summon his servant.

"You will not arrest him."

"I will not arrest him."

"And he's free to return home?"

"If that is his wish."

Jenny's face was suffused with joy, and she came gladly to Charles' outstretched arms, allowing herself to be enfolded against the comfort of his chest while she cried. "Thank you, dearest Charles," she whispered brokenly, "forever will I love you for it." She pressed her tear-washed face against his brocade dressing gown, feeling momentarily safe and cherished against the steady rhythm of his heart.

Charles rested his dark head against her bright one, his wide mouth curving with pleasure at the feel of this soft,

delectable creature in his arms. Though Jenny preferred another man, he did not fault her for it, despite the dying of
their passion he still felt great affection for her.

''Forever will I be your friend,'' he vowed, his low voice
filled with emotion. ''You have but one promise to make
before you leave.''

''And what is that?''

''You must allow me to be godfather to your first-born son.
And if you name him Charles it would not come amiss,'' he
suggested, his mouth twitching.

''You have my word.''

She stepped away from him as the door clicked open and
Thomas Chaffinch stood framed in the opening. Backing
away, Jenny dropped a curtsy. ''Thank you, your Majesty,
for your kindness.''

''And thank you, Jenny Wren, for yours,'' he said.

Kit paced impatiently along the Stone Gallery, his fists
clenched in impotent rage: he knew no more than he had
known when he alighted from the boat at Whitehall Stairs.
Today the King had been far too occupied with his tennis
game to keep his appointment with him, which suggested no
deep anger on his part, but with Charles Stuart one could
never tell. The King's ministers had not even given him the
time of day when he petitioned them for their attention to the
matter. He had complied with this dangerous summons because he wished to reinstate himself in his sovereign's favor,
and it infuriated him to think the King found a game of tennis
more important than the discussion of his future. When he
returned to the Stone Gallery, his anger had mounted when he
discovered Jenny was gone. Chaffinch assured him she would
soon be returned to this spot. And for that event he had
waited for some time. Mayhap the game of tennis was but an
excuse to cover Charles' dalliance in bed! Tension bound his
jaw as he pictured the probable scene within his Majesty's
bedchamber. Yet how could he blame Jenny? Had he not
urged her to accept whatever favor Charles Stuart chose to
bestow?

Kit paced the corridor, his high-heeled black court shoes
clacking rhythmically as he marched up and down. Only a
few petitioners lingered within the gallery; most had already
retired, giving up hope of having an audience before morning.

From the direction of the Royal apartments came the echo of footsteps. Alerted, Kit spun about as the door opened at the end of the long corridor and a woman dressed in rose pink emerged.

"Kit!" With a cry of joy, Jenny picked up her voluminous petal bright skirts and sped toward him in her soft kid shoes.

Stiffly Kit waited, unable to greet her with the warmth he wished because of the hot tide of jealousy swirling through his brain. Had she given herself to the King to save his neck? Such costly freedom he could not turn aside, yet it would walk beside him all his days.

"Oh, Kit, Kit, sweetheart, you're free!" she gasped breathlessly as she flew into his arms, clutching his strong body, faint with delight at finding him unharmed.

"Free?" he echoed, his voice tight. "At what cost?"

Jenny smiled as she hid her flushed face in his magnificent coat, hearing the jealous tension throbbing in his voice. Oh, men were such fools! To think how long she had loved this hot-tempered captain, even risking her life to ensure his freedom, yet now he stood unyielding, his immense masculine pride wounded at the thought she had bartered her body in exchange for his life.

"You great fool! Did you not beseech me to fling myself on his mercy? Did you not order me to resume . . ."

Kit gripped her tight, his hands biting painfully into her upper arms. "At what cost?" he repeated grimly.

Jenny's joyful laughter pealed through the vast reaches of the Stone Gallery. "I've bought your life merely with the promise to name our first-born son after his godfather. Now, are you satisfied, you jealous man?"

Kit smiled, the tension slowly erasing from his handsome face. "You're both the cross and delight of my heart," he whispered, dropping a kiss on her chestnut hair. "I can hardly believe I'm free. And it's all thanks to you, sweetheart. But, come, let us leave this tomb while we're still able."

"Gladly, my lord, but we'll not return to your floating home."

Kit paused, his hand tightening about her waist. "Where shall we go?"

"To Buckinghamshire, for I've a great desire to see my gardens."

He smiled as he swept her in his arms, his hot mouth

fusing with hers in an ardent kiss. "At once, for the loveliest flower of all wilts in the London heat."

Smiling at his poetic extravagance, Jenny slipped her arms about his compact waist, pressing against him, uncaring that their passionate embrace might be observed. "Dearest Kit, to know that at last we can be together is all the happiness I need."

Ever discreet, Thomas Chaffinch, discovering the attractive couple locked in each other's arms, backed away, quietly closing the door leading off Whitehall's shadowed Stone Gallery.